NO MAN CAN TAME

THE DARK-ELVES OF NIGHTBLOOM BOOK 1

MIRANDA HONFLEUR

Paperback ISBN: 978-1-949932-03-4

Cover art by Mirela Barbu

Map by Rela "Kellerica" Similä

Editing by Laura Kingsley & Deborah Nemeth

Proofreading by Patrycja Pakula for Holabird Editing & by Charity Chimni

AUTHOR'S MAILING LIST

Visit www.mirandahonfleur.com to sign up for Miranda's mailing list! You'll get "Winter Wren" for free.

ALSO BY MIRANDA HONFLEUR

Blade and Rose Series

"Winter Wren" (available on www.mirandahonfleur.com)

Blade & Rose (Book 1)

By Dark Deeds (Book 2)

Court of Shadows (Book 3)

Blade and Rose: Books 1-3 Digital Boxed Set

Queen of the Shining Sea (Book 4)

The Dragon King (Book 5)

Immortelle (Book 6) Available 2021*

The Dark-Elves of Nightbloom Series

No Man Can Tame

Bright of the Moon

An Ember in the Dark

Crown To Ashes

The Curse of the Fae Lord Series

Dark Lich Prince (Book 1)

The Court of Wolves Series

Blooded (Book 1)

The Witch of the Lake Series with Nicolette Andrews

This book is for...

Shelby Palmer, Mary Nguyen, Erin Montgomery Miller, Lela Grayce, Emily Allen West, Katherine Bennet, Ryan Muree, Emerald Dodge, Shannon Childress, Susanne Huxhorn, Jennifer An, Anthony S. Holabird, Wanda Wozniczka, Nicole Page, Spring Runyon, Judith Cohen, Eugenia Kollia, Judy Harding, Lisa Woo, Sarah Keffer, Dana Jackson Lange, Jennifer Moriarity, Tricia Wright, Scarolet Ellis, Alicia Moten, Jackie Tansky, Tanya Wheeler, Roger Fauble, Shauna Joesten, Maggie Borges, Donna Swenson, Seraphia Sparks, Marilyn Smith, Pamela Kitson, Mary Maceluch, Fiona Andrew, Lindsay McKenna, Chao Mwachofi, Belinda Hoy, Karen Borges, Kathy Brown...

...and everyone else who's supported me and spread the word about my books from the start. I couldn't do this without you, and you being in my corner has meant the world to me.

CONTENTS

For my mom,
For being my biggest fan.

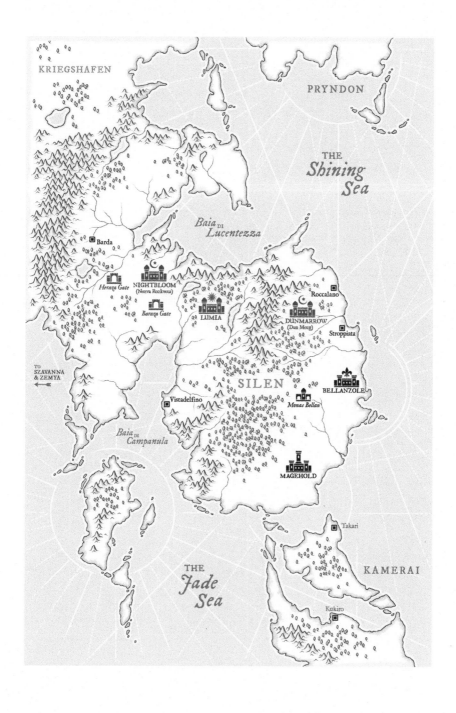

CHAPTER 1

The raven leered down his long black beak at Aless as she twirled, his gaze so intense it burned.

A blur of bodies in jewel-toned silks and brocades circled her and her sister, Bianca, in three-quarter time. Ravens, cats, bears, peacocks, wolves... The animal kingdom had come to their king's call beneath arched ceilings and canopied swaths...

Or maybe to catch a glimpse of his infamous daughter back from her worldwide hunt.

She was pleased to be home again. It would give her another opportunity to tackle Papà about finally building the public library Mamma had always wanted. He'd barely spoken to her since she'd arrived.

Tonight she'd donned a lion mask with a full, voluminous mane and a grotesquely painted facade. If she was to be gawked at anyway, the least she could do was make it count. Besides, if she could catch Papà's attention—good or bad—perhaps he'd have her dragged to see him and she'd finally get a word in about the library.

Signore Raven leaned against a pillar and raised his chin, peering at her through his mask. Oh, he'd been looking at her all evening with those hungry, dark eyes. And not in the aghast gawking of most of the nobiltà. He wanted something—and considering he definitely wasn't royal, he wasn't a man Papà would approve of.

All the more tempting to give Signore Raven what he seemed to want so badly.

Signore Cat next to him was the same, ogling Bianca as if she were a plump, unwitting canary. Bianca hadn't been sent around the world by Papà in offering, so she would no doubt know who these courtiers were.

"Don't look now," Aless whispered from behind her lion mask, "but the cat and the raven have been struck dumb."

Bianca giggled and spun, her slippered feet clicking on the parquet floor to the music of the harp, the flute, the drums, and rebecs, amid a chorus of practiced laughter and effusive tones of conversation. All of the palazzo's ballrooms dazzled, but this place, the Sala di Forza, was a tribute to one of the Terran faith's greatest heroes, Forza, son of Nox and a mortal woman, a demigod of great strength. Painted with his exploits, great hunts and battles celebrating strength, war, and masculinity, it was Papà's favorite.

It was suffocating.

With Papà, it was *always* strength, war, and masculinity. Lorenzo was a master swordsman and could hit a target with his throwing knives from thirty yards—so no matter his shortcomings, Papà favored him. And since Papà didn't allow her to learn any of the martial arts—and she loved books as Mamma had—there was just no way to win with him.

Her only option was to lose. And to lose so boldly and so notoriously that Papà couldn't ignore her. But no matter the spectacle and gossip, Bianca could always be counted on to stay by her side. A loyal sister, and a trusted friend.

Bianca adjusted her elaborate tabby-cat mask and tucked a lock of shining onyx-colored hair behind her ear. "The Belmonte brothers."

Ah, so the raven and the cat were none other than Luciano and Tarquin Belmonte. Their reputations preceded them. Especially Luciano's—Bianca hadn't stopped talking about him for months. But that was her way—no, the family's way. Once an Ermacora made up her mind, there was no dissuading her, and pity for anyone foolish enough to stand in her way.

And Bianca had certainly made up her mind about Luciano.

The taller of the two, Signore Raven, had to be Tarquin, the younger brother and general of the Belmonte Company of mercenaries; the older of the two, Signore Cat, was Luciano, and after their father's passing, now visconte of Roccalano.

Morally fluid, physically fit men, who were good dancers and—if rumor held true—skillful lovers, but lacked the blood and moral obligation of royalty.

Aless guided Bianca off the dance floor to the nearest trestle table heaped with marzipan torte, custard tarts, and colorful berries. She popped a grape in her mouth and held out a goblet until the telltale splashing of poured wine ceased. After a sip of the bubbly white, she handed the goblet to Bianca, all the while keeping her gaze locked on the Belmonte brothers.

"Maybe Luciano will finally become your latest entertainment?" she asked Bianca, who hid her face in a goblet of wine. "Not that I'm complaining," she whispered, giving Tarquin a slow —*very* slow—once-over, "but what are they doing in Bellanzole?"

Bianca leaned in. "The Belmonte Company has been handling our... issues with the Immortali. The army didn't have the expertise to clear the harpy nest in the cliffs, but ever since Arabella Belmonte, their sister, disappeared a couple months ago, Luciano has been studying them and Tarquin has been handling them. They've become experts on the Immortali, so Papà hired their company."

The Rift had torn the Veil a few months ago, and the Immortali had re-entered the world as if stepping from the pages of myth and legend. Some were peaceful here in Silen, like the light-elves, the dark-elves, and the fae, and others were monsters who killed with impunity—harpies, wyverns, basilisks, and more. Papà had deployed many of his forces to combat the piracy ravaging the coasts and his trade routes, and so the reserves had to be stretched thin fighting enemies no one understood—no one except the Belmonte brothers, apparently.

"Say a prayer for me, Aless." Bianca gripped the goblet tightly. "I think I love him. I think I want to... marry him."

Marry? With talk like that, Bianca would be the one directing Papà's attention, whether she wanted to or not. To any woman of the Ermacora royal line, Luciano was forbidden fruit when it came to marriage. Still, in her wistfully recounted daydreams, Bianca always seemed to find herself in an orchard of forbidden fruit anyway, with a ladder just tall enough to reach anything she wanted.

"I know you have your heart set on him," she replied, "but maybe you could... adjust your expectations a little."

Bianca gulped the wine, then upturned the goblet and drained it entirely. Liquid courage? She glanced over her shoulder at the Belmonte brothers.

"I'm already twenty-three," Bianca insisted, "with no other prospects, so perhaps Luciano could be more? Papà may be keen on sending you to every eligible royal bachelor in the region, but not me."

"Three. Three royal bachelors in this past year—"

"In this past year alone." Bianca raised her chin. "And those three *are* all the eligible royal bachelors. All the others are already married or betrothed." She frowned, her eyes meandering up and off to the side. "Or little children."

"Papà is only keen on sending me around because he wants to get rid of me. Unlike his favorite daughter." Since Aless had reached marriageable age, Papà had sent her to maybe... a dozen or two royal bachelors. Although this year, he'd only sent her to two princes and one king. Maybe it was a sign that he was giving up and would finally leave her in peace with her books.

Bianca set down the goblet. "It's only because he finds you so meddlesome. Once you decide something must be, you don't let up. It can make you... difficult. This public library thing of yours has been a thorn in his side."

She straightened. Mamma had spent her life teaching the paesani to read, and when she'd died, all that had stopped. For nearly a decade, Papà hadn't just stalled Mamma's plans to build a public library—a center of learning for all—he'd actively avoided it. It was *meddlesome* to want to dedicate her life to seeing the library built, to want to teach any and all who wanted to learn, just as Mamma had wanted? She huffed.

"I want to do more than just be foisted onto royal bachelors," she declared. "Is it so wrong to have dreams of something more?"

Sighing, Bianca shook her head. "Difficult. Your spine may be healed now, but you're still the Beast Princess." With a final shrug, she sashayed back onto the dance floor.

Heat spread across Aless's skin, climbing over every inch until she burned. Beast Princess? It had been some time since someone had called her that, at least to her face.

Trying to ignore the rapid pulse in her ear, Aless popped another grape into her mouth and stormed toward the door. Whispers followed her, but she didn't care. This was only a stupid party, and her time would be better spent studying the Immortali in her books.

Her chest collided with someone—a woman in a rabbit mask, who curtsied quickly.

"Pardon me," Aless blurted, inclining her head. A circle had formed around them, no doubt waiting for yet more gossip fodder. But she hadn't been the Beast Princess all her life without learning to tame her temper... at least a little. But perhaps this would be enough to earn a meeting with Papà.

The rabbit woman didn't reply, but looked on toward the food.

Odd. But Aless cleared her throat and gestured in the direction of the trestle table. "Please, help yourself. I promise I don't bite," Aless joked with a toothy grin, tapping her lion mask. At least not anyone who didn't bite first.

The woman curtsied again. A man in a fox mask approached, curling an arm around the rabbit woman's waist.

"Ah, forgive my darling fiancée, Saverina, Your Highness. She's taken the Vow of Silence."

A vow not to speak until her wedding. Many parents in

Silen demanded it of their daughters for arranged marriages among the nobiltà—both a show of piety and a way to ensure loose lips didn't beget unfortunate slips. "How ruinously traditional."

The fox man tittered. "One can only hope the tradition continues after the wedding!"

Aless forced a laugh. "How utterly draconian of you," she said as sweetly as she could while the man nodded along effusively.

"Indeed! Very kind. By your leave, Princess," he said, taking a bow before leading his avowed speechless fiancée away.

Most of the paesani couldn't read, but the nobiltà's only excuse was willful ignorance. But knowledge wasn't as prized here as it once was. Papà—and everything he stood for—was evidence of that. Sighing, she looked out at his opulent domain.

Masked guests dressed in the height of Bellanzole couture mingled and danced. The nobiltà and the nuovi ricchi devised this adventure, preened for one another as usual, their eclectic fashion diverse—within an allowable variation, of course.

Except for Signore Raven—Tarquin Belmonte. No, he'd thrown the *allowable variation* to the winds and had come here to shock. To arrive cloaked in death was to object. In his raven mask, black brocade doublet and trousers, and a feathered mourning cloak, he filled out couture well, and he had a lot of nerve showing up to a masquerade at the Palazzo dell'Ermacora dressed in funereal garb. As much nerve as a princess in a grotesque lion mask.

She grinned. A man with a spine. Good. At least one courtier who didn't fall all over himself bowing and scraping before Papà.

Bianca had found something to *do* instead of squabbling. There was wisdom in that. She'd do her all to get that meeting.

Eyes locked with his through her lion mask, she turned, rearranging her ample costume mane behind her, and glided through the crowd with ease, mingling, brushing off eager courtiers as she stalked from the Sala di Forza and out onto the balcony.

He'd follow, of course. The perfect moment to come. She traded brightly colored silks and paintings of Forza's many mythical victories for the faraway diamonds dusting the black velvet sky.

Gripping the stone balustrade, she closed her eyes and took three deep breaths. The soft, fresh scent of roses embraced her, surrounded her, as it had countless times in her dreams and fantasies. The same dense, overgrown courtyard of vining roses in full bloom sprawled before her, mysterious and lovely, exhaling the most spellbinding perfume in the clearest, purest air. She reached out a fingertip and could almost feel the velvety soft, shimmering petals—

"The lion's den is the balcony, is it?"

Next to her stood a vision in black feathers, nearly six feet tall and built like a gladiator. Tarquin Belmonte. She blinked, and that spellbinding perfume faded. She gave him a coy once-over. "Don't you have a carcass somewhere to peck at?"

A half-laugh. "I have sight of better game."

Suppressing a grin, she shook her head. "Bold as a raven."

He rested his hand on the stone balustrade, too, his warm skin just barely touching hers. "Nothing less than bold can be expected to win a princess."

"Is that what you came here for?" Nobody dealt in boldness like the Beast Princess. She turned to him, covered his hand with hers, and reached for his raven mask. "To 'win' me?" When he didn't move, she took it off.

Carnelian-brown eyes gleamed in the starlight beneath black lashes and matching close-cropped hair; the lines of his coarse jaw were strong, and the corners of his mouth turned up mischievously, as if he knew something she didn't.

She hadn't expected a handsome face to match the tall, well-muscled physique. But then, she hadn't seen Tarquin Belmonte in years, since before he'd taken over his father's mercenary company and grown into that role. And my, had he *grown*.

"Princess Alessandra," he said sotto voce, his Roccalano accent melodious, "I have come here for anything you wish of me."

She should have laughed, but no part of her could muster anything like it. Not at him. Not at those bold words.

His gaze stroked over her once and again. "I know it is a masquerade, but why a lion? And a grotesque *male* lion, at that?"

She smiled, reaching for borrowed words. "Telling you would reveal the answer in the most unexciting way."

He quirked a brow. Let him sweat a little.

Lively notes plucked on the harp inside—a quessanade corrente.

"Then shall we begin the revelation with a dance?" He offered her his hand. She took it and replaced his mask upon his head, then he tucked her arm around his and led her back into the grandeur of Sala di Forza.

Across the room, Bianca danced with Luciano, two matching masked cats, but Papà's willowy page, Alvaro, approached them. He bowed and spoke to Bianca, who smiled, nodded, then promptly bid Luciano goodbye before gliding to the hallway.

Only one thing could drag Bianca away from her forbidden fruit.

And now Alvaro, his young face lined grimly, made his way to her. He bowed. "Your Highness, Princess Alessandra, His Majesty requires your presence."

"Does he?" She held back a grin. Success—finally. She spared Tarquin a disappointed shrug. Their *revelation* would have to wait.

"It must be the Immortali again," Tarquin said darkly. "A corruption that must be eradicated from the kingdom."

A corruption? He had to mean the monsters *among* the Immortali? The harpies, the basilisks, the wyverns—not the peaceful Immortali people?

She frowned, but such fire smoldered in Tarquin's eyes that it burned the question from her lips.

"Your Highness," Alvaro prompted.

As if she would pass up her long-awaited meeting with Papà. She hmphed.

With perfect form, Tarquin inclined his head to her, and she acknowledged him before turning to leave. What Tarquin didn't know was that Papà would never desire her presence for input regarding an *important* matter—such as conflicts with the Immortali. No, when it came to what really mattered, Papà preferred she be like a rabbit-masked courtier under a Vow of Silence.

This would be a scolding, nothing more, but she'd use it to her advantage.

As she followed Alvaro through the dimly lit hallway, Bianca offered her a thin smile. A pitying smile.

So she assumed... Bianca had assumed what everyone would assume.

Papà had only one use for his Beast Princess.

Aless shook her head and swallowed. She'd barely set foot at home—Papà wouldn't send her away for yet another courtship. Not so soon.

Would he?

ALESS GLARED UP AT PAPÀ, seated up on his throne beneath the high vaulted ceiling. He'd left the masquerade right after she'd arrived—because he'd been *so* pleased, no doubt. But he looked the epitome of regal, dressed in expensive violet silk brocade and wearing the jeweled crown on his coal-black hair streaked with ash. Royal guards in purple cloaks lined the room, standing in perfect formation, immovable, intimidating.

Here in the throne room, he could remind them exactly where they stood—far, far below—and who *he* was. King.

But for once, he actually detailed the kingdom's dire need to her and Bianca.

Papà stroked his close-cropped beard. "That scoundrel Sincuore and his pirate rats have all but devastated our navy. Our resources must be diverted to replenishing it, meaning we need protection *and* peace in the heartland."

While the coast needed defending, the heartland was rife with immortal beasts attacking the paesani, as well as unrest between humans and the Immortali.

"The Belmonte brothers have both come here expecting marriages in exchange for their mercenary services," Papà continued, "but I have only one daughter to give to the Belmonte family, and she is going to Luciano."

Bianca smiled at her. So she was getting her Signore Cat. The orchard of her daydreams was coming true, and it had never been so wonderful to have been so wrong. Aless held back an inward grin.

But why had Papà called them both here?

"We are making peace with Nightbloom." He leaned back in his throne.

The dark-elves? Papà was going to stop the hatred after all—

He'd said he had only *one* daughter to give to the Belmonte family. That meant...

Peace by marriage.

To the dark-elves.

Her blood ran cold.

He's offering me up to Nightbloom?

Holy Mother's mercy, he wanted her to marry one of *them*? They had claws and fangs, lived in underground caves where not a single rose would grow. No hint of Mamma's gorgeous gardens there. They ate lizards and lichen, had creepy yellow irises, ghostly white hair, and blue skin like a snake's. Her skin crawled.

She cast her gaze aside, at the massive tapestry of Forza slaying the hydra. That mythical monster was about as attractive to her as a dark-elf male. She didn't hate them, but she definitely didn't want to marry one of them, kiss one of them, sh-share a marriage bed—

She fought back a gag. Those clawed hands on her body, fanged teeth in a mouth kissing hers—

A shudder rattled her bones. Peace was a worthy end, but Papà couldn't expect her to—to *wed* one of *them*.

She didn't want to. She would never. There had to be some way to fix this.

"Bianca, you will be wedded to Prince Veron of Nightbloom," Papà declared, and her gaze snapped back to him. "And Alessandra, you will be married to Luciano. We're fighting wyverns, harpies, basilisks, and all manner of beasts—we can't afford to fight the dark-elves, too. Their numbers could help us quell the Immortali beasts in the heartland, help relieve the burden on our military. There will be a wedding ceremony here for Bianca and Prince Veron, then another in Nightbloom, and the peace will be sealed. In between, you will wed Luciano, Alessandra."

Aless blinked over her wide eyes and swallowed over a lump in her throat.

Bianca's smile faded like a pappose dandelion in the wind. Her olive skin paled, and the sheen of her agate eyes dulled.

No, it was all wrong. Everything.

"Papà." Aless shook her head. There had to be another way. There *had* to be. "Might there be a different way to secure the alliance than with a marriage? Is there any other possible way?"

Papà's eyes narrowed, and he interlaced his fingers. "Blood is the only way an alliance like this could be upheld. The bond of shared blood."

Shared blood? He had to mean children.

She frowned. "How can a marriage between a mortal and an immortal work? Can the species even breed? Are children possible?" She'd never read of such a thing.

"Quite possible, I'm assured," Papà replied matter-of-factly, his face a dour mask. "And elders are treated with respect in their society. The gap in aging would be handled appropriately."

The gap in aging. What a quaint way of phrasing the rapidity of Bianca's old age while her so-called husband would remain young, watching her wither. Probably eager to remarry to one of his own kind, counting down the days.

Was that the manifestation of Papà's love for his favorite daughter? Sending Bianca to someone who'd eagerly await her death, a place where she'd waste away without love or anything that brought her joy, just to serve as a broodmare for his precious alliance?

A soreness formed behind her eyes, and she rubbed her sweaty palms into her tulle gown. "How can you do this, Papà? Surely you know how Bianca feels about Luciano?" She wrapped an arm around Bianca's trembling shoulders.

He breathed deeply. "This is what's best for you."

"*I* know what's best for me." She glared at him. "I refuse to marry Luciano. You must release Bianca from this... this night-mare of a betrothal."

Papà dropped his forehead into his hand. "Alessandra, this wedding will happen with or without you. You can either appear in person or be married in absentia, but you *will* be married, and Luciano *will* take you to Roccalano, with or without your assent. You will do this, or you will be useless to this kingdom."

Useless. He'd called her that before, a long time ago, although she was certain he hadn't known she'd been listening. When she'd been eight years old, Mamma had been lamenting the latest physician's torture devices.

Must we put her through so much suffering? This treatment must be agony, Mamma had said. And yes, that back brace had been extreme, too rigid, too tight, painful to tears.

We must, Papà had answered sternly. *Unless her spine is healed, she'll be useless in this world.*

In the hallway outside the solar, she had covered her mouth, hidden her tears, smothered her sobs. Even at eight years old, she had resolved to learn everything she could about running a kingdom, even if she had to do it alone. And to never be *useless*, no matter what Papà thought of her.

And here she was. Boxed into the only purpose he had for her.

Or so he *thought*. She refused to look away from him. He wouldn't ruin Bianca's life, not as long as she had a sister talented at stirring up oceans of trouble.

Bianca sobbed into her shoulder, and Aless rubbed her back gently.

"And Bianca?" she asked. "She clearly doesn't want to marry that dark-elf male. Will you see her dragged away to their... their cave?"

"If that is what is required." He regarded Bianca, her down-turned mouth, and his gaze softened. "But Bianca has always understood the burden of royalty. I have faith she will not disappoint."

What a man of honor, this prince! He'd drag Bianca kicking and screaming to his hole in the ground? "Such a *moral* and *kind* man you've chosen for her."

"He is," Papà answered, unperturbed. "He's mending the rift between our people. He's a paragon among his kind."

"Maybe *you* should marry him, then."

"He and his people have been mercilessly attacked by humans for months, and he's followed orders not to engage, not to fight back at all. He has an iron will and a disposition toward diplomacy."

Humans had been attacking him and his people for months, and he'd been under orders not to fight back? "So before he's even met Bianca, he'll already hate her because she's human."

Brilliant. Even better.

Bianca swept her forearm across her eyes and rested a hand on her arm. "Aless... It's all right. I'll... I'll do what Papà says." She sniffled. "And haven't you been saying how much you've wanted to do something important for our kingdom? Luciano is... an influential man, and I'm... I'm sure you'll find a way to work together. This is your chance."

Bianca was in love with Luciano, and Papà had just announced her betrothal to a dark-elf! How could she stand there and say this was all right? Bianca had been waiting for a marriage since her sixteenth year; she was twenty-three now, had finally fallen in love with a man, and was to be married off to some... dark-elf? How could she just accept this?

If it were me, I'd fight tooth and nail. I'd find a way to make the dark-elf release me, even if no one helped me. I'd do it on my own.

If it were her...

If.

Bianca offered her a sad smile and a nod as she turned toward Papà, but Aless grabbed her arm.

Her heart thudding in her ears, she met Bianca's gaze. She wasn't going to marry her sister's love. She wasn't going to let Bianca live a bleak life. She could make it right. She—

Bianca drew in a sharp breath and shook her head. It didn't matter. She didn't need Bianca's permission.

"Papà," Aless said, sweeping up her tulle skirts as her heels clicked up to the first step of the dais. "Offer me instead. I'll wed Prince Veron."

Behind her, Bianca gasped. "Aless, you can't! You don't know what you're—"

"No. I do know what I'm doing." She watched Papà's face for any sign he agreed, but it betrayed nothing. "Please, let Bianca marry Luciano, and I promise I will marry Prince Veron."

Papà heaved a long-suffering sigh. "Bianca can be trusted to do her duty. *You* cannot. Luciano will know this by now"—her reputation, of course, preceded her, too—"but Prince Veron is not a Sileni. He won't understand your... *spirit*, and this kingdom needs a peace with Nightbloom to succeed."

Papà was right; Bianca would do her duty. But in doing so, she'd utterly destroy her life.

"There's no sense in both Bianca and me being unhappy," she replied, shaking her head vehemently. "Let me take her place. I will marry Prince Veron."

Papà rested his chin on his fist. "Alessandra, you know I love you. But if we are being honest, you are willful, short tempered, sharp mouthed, and presumptuous. You are every-thing a man *does not* want in a wife. You try to hire street urchins for your household, donate your coin to peasant rebel-lions, find every opportunity to show the nobiltà you 'disagree'—"

It was on the tip of her tongue to object, but he did say *sharp mouthed*.

She sighed. Yes, she'd done all those things. He had no reason to expect anything like silent obedience from her.

Silent...

Maybe there *was* a way to persuade him, an old tradition among the most devout of Terrans—something the priests and paladins of the Order of Terra still did, designed to create circumstances for introspection and self-reflection. Even if in name only... "I won't say a word to him. I will swear a Vow of Silence and say nothing to him until the wedding."

A vow. And she'd say nothing to him. It wasn't quite the old tradition, but hopefully Papà wouldn't ask too many questions.

A GRIN TUGGED at the corners of Papà's mouth. What amused him more? Her keeping her peace now, being married off to one of the Immortali, or promising to keep her mouth shut?

Maybe all of it. "This is an easy choice. Make Bianca happy," she said, squeezing Bianca's hand, "and get rid of me. All in one sweep."

Papà sighed again with heavy shoulders, no doubt weighed down by two decades of her disappointing him. "I'm not trying to 'get rid' of you."

She shrugged. He could couch it in whatever words he chose. He'd decided he'd had enough of her, and that he'd needed to sacrifice Bianca. Each of them knew this truth, hard as it was, no matter what else he said.

But his silence persisted, and Bianca's hand went limp in hers.

"With this marriage"—Papà stood—"you will be making peace between two nations. There is no greater thing anyone can do for our kingdom, Alessandra."

He'd agreed to it!

She wanted to grin, but... she'd just won a wedding to one of the dark-elves. Maybe there was something more she could add to the bargain. "And the library? I want to teach in Bellanzole like Mamma did."

He looked away. "I gave your mother too much freedom, and that is what killed her," he said softly. "If she'd only stayed in the palazzo instead of venturing among the rabble, she would still be alive."

And that was it? Because Mamma had been killed, no one could ever do anything again?

After years of research, she'd worked tirelessly on the proposal, but he and Lorenzo hadn't replied. He could at least give it serious consideration. "I handed you plans for the library, and lists of all the masters to build it, and suggestions to finance—"

"That was what your mother wanted, and look what happened to her!" Papà shouted.

She shuddered. Mamma had died, but she'd devoted her *life* to sharing knowledge with others, teaching everyone willing how to read, gathering wisdom about the natural world and all things that grew. She'd always been known as the wild heart no man could tame, but Papà had loved what she had loved and had done the impossible—or at least he'd pretended to support her. After her death, everyone had forgotten her wish. Just as they had forgotten her.

But I haven't. "Papà, please—"

"Libraries mean paesani who can read, write, and think, who can write pamphlets and treatises, and protest instead of working. Find new ways to destroy us." He heaved a sigh. "This is a volatile time. The kingdom cannot take such a risk."

"Papà, that's—"

"The truth. And Alessandra, do you have any notion of what it costs to build a library and keep it maintained?"

"Yes. It was all there in the—"

"Not monetary cost. You laid out a tax plan to see it done. But the non-monetary costs of taxing our signori, especially *now*, when many of them are stretched thin or deep in debt to finance defenses against the Immortali? There's another *harpy* nest just outside of Stroppiata! We have bigger concerns right now. By enacting your plan, I'd be sowing the seeds of rebellion myself.

"Our survival has not come without sacrifice. Your sister, Giuliana, she married Emaurria's Prince Robert to become queen, to help protect our kingdom and forge favorable trade terms when her time came. And she was killed. We lost not only our precious Giuliana, but the boons she would have granted our kingdom. And you failed to captivate the new king."

Captivate? The king was in love with another woman; there had been little else to do but leave gracefully. "He was already—"

"Whatever the reasons, you failed. This is a responsibility you must accept and now account for. The terms are set, and fulfilling your duty now will mean no more paesani lives lost to battles with the dark-elves, no more money spent on it by signori for defenses against them, and it will mean a military ally against the other Immortali, knowledge of this new world, and valuable trade."

Bianca approached and bowed her head. "Papà, please. Aless is taking my place, and the least that—"

Papà held up a hand.

There was no use trying to convince him. He'd already made up his mind; she and Bianca were no more than pawns.

Her library, a place where she could help anyone who wanted to learn and grow, nobiltà or paesani, human or Immortali—had it only ever been a dream, just like the courtyard of overgrown roses and its spellbinding perfume?

But she—she would do what was required to make peace

between her people and the dark-elves. It didn't necessarily have to be *marriage*.

I'm not useless. But I won't let you define my purpose.

She'd agree to this arrangement, but as soon as Bianca and Luciano were married, she'd find a way to persuade this dark-elf prince to release her, to let their *friendship* show the peace between their nations. Marriages had solidified peace for millennia, but these were modern times. Surely consensual, honest friendship could demonstrate a partnership without resorting to a marriage neither party desired?

In fact, the entire kingdom could stand to see the point: it was time for a change.

She crossed her arms and lowered her gaze. "Fine."

"Good." He descended the steps and placed a hand on Bianca's shoulder. "Your wedding will be three days after Alessandra's. Congratulations, *luce dei miei occhi*." He cupped her face in one hand. "You will make a beautiful bride."

Bianca smiled as he dabbed at her tear-streaked cheeks. Her large, agate eyes were soft. "Thank you, Papà."

He grinned back at her, then raised Aless's chin with an abrupt finger. "Alessandra. Try not to destroy the peace. I know it is difficult. But try."

She scrunched her face, and his eyes gleaming, he walked away, his guards trailing him.

Her life could be over, and he jested? Holy Mother's mercy.

She'd agreed to wed the dark-elf prince, and to say nothing until their marriage vows, and so she would. No words to *him*, anyway. She would complete the wedding in Bellanzole and say no words until after that.

No *words*. She smiled. But there were other ways to get a point across.

CHAPTER 2

*A*s the tree he perched in swayed in the raging storm, Veron held his bow at full draw, tracking the hind through the wind-battered foliage. He'd been here for hours and was not going home empty handed. Not today.

His people had been starving for several months, scraping by on small game and what sustenance they could find in the Deep before the crops could stabilize in a couple months.

He couldn't afford to miss, but if he couldn't get a good shot, he wasn't about to let the animal flee and suffer until she died. A waste of a life.

There would be a good shot. Deep, Darkness, and Holy Ulsinael, there would have to be.

As the hind picked her way through groaning trees and fluttering shrubs, she paused every so often, swished her tail, swiveled her ears irritably. *Not yet.* So agitated, she'd jump at the snap of the bowstring. *Not yet.*

His arms ached as he held the excruciating full draw weight, twisting his position to keep her in his sights, and she emerged past the enormous trunk of an old oak, halting in the howling wind, and as his tree swayed, he timed the shot—

The distant, roaring call of his fellow *volodari* hunting team. Short, sharp—a warning.

He loosed.

She balked.

More calls from his team answered, their longer, acknowledging roars closer—Vlasta's, Dhuro's, Rút's, and Gavri's—

His arrow lay in the undergrowth battered by the storm. The hind was gone. He'd shot too late. Just a second too late.

And for that, his people would continue to starve.

The acknowledging growls repeated, and he roared back, listening to the calls return all the way to Vlasta's distant one.

He stashed his bow, dug his claws into the bark, and rappelled down the trunk. His boots slopped into the mud—they still didn't fit right, and now they'd slosh the length of the way home.

Other than the storm, all was quiet, with not a single person in sight, much less an enemy. But still, he drew his *vjernost* blade. Made from the magic-nullifying metal *arcanir*, it could also kill most Immortals, on the chance a basilisk or a wyvern had attacked.

But it wasn't basilisks or wyverns that had been the most pressing threat recently. No, it was the *human* Brotherhood that had been hunting him and his people for months. Entire parties of volodari from other dark-elf queendoms had disappeared while hunting or foraging. A few from his home, Nozva Rozkveta, had evaded them with only injuries, but if nothing changed, it would soon come to deaths on one side or the other.

The echoing roars led south, and staying low in the concealment of the shrubs, he made his way through the stormy forest. A crack ahead, high in the canopy, and a long scratch—Gavri, his *kuvara* royal guard.

Like a living and breathing shadow, she splashed into the mud in her black leather kuvari armor, her long white braid sopping wet, and she shook out her hands, throwing scraps of bark off her claws. Her deep-amber eyes fixed on him, and she cocked her head south.

He nodded. Given her call, Vlasta must have sighted an enemy. If she was in trouble, they had to get to her.

They retraced their steps toward the tunnel gate they'd emerged from—Baraza Gate, where Vlasta had taken the first hunting stand. They passed the second stand—where his brother Dhuro should have been—but it was already empty.

By Deep and Darkness—

Voices rang out, human voices calling out in Sileni—near Baraza. Gavri tugged his sleeve southeast, toward another gate.

Wordlessly, he followed her lead, and as the shouts neared, he and Gavri quickened their pace to a run, leaping over deadfall. If they didn't make it to a gate before the humans caught up to them, there would be no re-entering Nozva Rozkveta at all. They'd be stranded.... and likely killed.

Gavri's heel hit a pile of soaked leaves, and she slipped into the mud—he caught her arm and yanked her up. The humans' shouts increased in urgency. They were gaining.

Ahead, a dark-elf bore another over his shoulder—Dhuro carrying Vlasta, a broken arrow shaft protruding from her side, buried in her gut.

No. *Not* one of his people. *No.*

She was still breathing, whimpering. Alive. A shot like that wouldn't have killed her—at least not quickly. It was meant to end her slowly, *painfully*.

Goose-feather fletching. A human's arrow. The Brotherhood.

He and Gavri caught up to Dhuro, who heaved a breath of relief as they continued to the nearest gate—Heraza.

"The others?" he hissed to Dhuro as they ran.

"Already home," Dhuro bit out from beneath low, drawn eyebrows, and bared his fangs.

Dhuro hadn't agreed with Mati's orders not to engage the Brotherhood, but he'd obeyed as a proper subject to the queen first and as a son second. A rage, however, had simmered in Dhuro from the first attack—a narrowing of his eyes, a clenching of his jaw—and now, while holding a bleeding huntress in his arms, that rage bubbled far too close to the surface.

It was a rage he knew as keenly as Dhuro did.

Just get home. Holy Ulsinael, just let us get home. Because if we meet the Brotherhood, orders or no orders, I can't promise not to kill them. Just let us get home...

The Bloom thicket tangled ahead before Heraza Gate. He took Vlasta from Dhuro carefully, whispering to her as she groaned, as her face creased. The Bloom parted, letting them through to the locked stone door, then wove back together behind them.

Smearing wet hair from her face, Gavri frantically tapped the Nozva Rozkvetan knock on the stone door.

Nothing.

As she did it again, Dhuro stepped up next to her and joined her, both of their hands beating the rhythm.

No answer.

The human shouts closed in.

In his hold, Vlasta whimpered as her blood ran down his leathers, mingling with the mud while Gavri and Dhuro continued.

"We're almost home, volodara," he murmured to her, and she nodded weakly, raindrops rolling down her face, or tears.

The door creaked open.

They scrambled inside, and the two kuvari guarding Heraza barred the stone door after them. Danika and Kinga.

"*Where were you?*" Dhuro shouted as he cornered them.

Both Danika and Kinga immediately bowed. "Your Highness."

"Dhuro," Veron said, prodding him with an elbow, still holding Vlasta. "We need to get her to the mystics. Come on." He headed down the tunnel toward Central Cavern with Gavri as she shook her head.

"*Where* were you?" Dhuro repeated, snarling the words at the kuvari. "The Brotherhood nearly *caught* us."

Danika stayed bowed. "Captain Riza recalled the kuvari to reinforce Baraza, but when Your Highness and Prince Veron didn't show up there, the Stone Singers sang it shut and we were ordered back to posts."

"Dhuro," Veron called over his shoulder, and Gavri took a deep breath next to him as they headed to the mystics' life-spring with Vlasta.

Dhuro could hardly shout at Mati about his frustrations over the Brotherhood; as their queen, her word was law. But taking it out on two kuvari, especially when Riza had given the order—that wasn't helping either. Dhuro could take it up with

Riza later, who'd lay him out on the stone—with Mati's implicit approval—if he so much as barked at her.

As they made their way, the lavender glow of the bioluminescent mushrooms high above on the stalactites lit the enormity of Central Cavern, tempered by the soft white light of the glowworms and the sprawl of flora that had always bloomed here, even without the sky realm's sun.

Below, the blackstone dwellings spread among the interwoven pathways and shining streams high above the Darkness's embrace. Stone Singers crowded smaller walkways, singing stalagmites into dwellings in their deepest and darkest bass tones, beseeching stone to meld together and form to their collective will.

Nozva Rozkveta was serene, even as the Brotherhood thirsted for dark-elf blood just outside the gates.

He and Gavri had almost reached the mystics' lifespring with Vlasta when Rút caught up to them, breathing hard, her face lined as her wide eyes fixed on Vlasta.

"*No*," she breathed, reaching out to touch Vlasta's hand, one of her claws broken. "When I heard the call, I-I tried to lead them away, so she could escape. But even then, I could feel her weakening, and—" She covered her mouth, running alongside them.

"Your claws," Gavri said with a gasp, and Rút curled her fingers.

Damaged claws meant weakness, and the weak were seen as a disgrace to their families. But to mention that now? Really? He scowled at her.

Gavri cleared her throat. "She'll be all right," she offered to Rút. "And Queen Zara won't let this go. You'll see."

Rút and Vlasta had made the Offering to each other and had been lifebonded for eight years; they shared anima. If one weakened, the other would strengthen her, and if one died, so would the other…

"We're almost there." He plunged through the dark entryway and into the mystics' lifespring, where Xira—the oldest dark-elf among them at nearly four thousand years—ran to meet them, her dark-purple robe trailing, and apprentices huddling around her.

"Take her to the waters, Highness." Her long white hair shimmering beneath the lavender glow, Xira led them to a brightly lit pool, and he climbed the shallow stairs to gently lay Vlasta inside while Xira checked her and removed the arrow, eliciting a pained cry from Vlasta. "She's still breathing. Good." Xira cocked her head to Rút. "You, too. In with her. You'll both need the strength of the lifespring to fortify you."

Because if Rút's anima wouldn't be enough, Vlasta would die. And if Vlasta died, so would Rút. Such was the danger of the lifebond.

Chewing her lip, Rút nodded several times as she held Vlasta close in the lifespring waters, stroking her short, wet hair and whispering words of comfort. Here, seated on a large Vein of anima, Nozva Rozkveta's life was stronger than any other queendom's, and the lifesprings were concentrated with anima, places they'd used for recovery since before recorded history.

This would work. It had to.

He braced on the warm, smooth stone while Gavri patted his back. Vlasta and Rút would survive—both of them. A lifebond was an act of absolute love, rare in its complete and utter devotion because with one death, it could claim two lives instead of one. Queens and their most valued kuvari among the Quorum elite royal guards rarely lifebonded, as their loss would leave a queendom weakened.

It was, in a way, fortunate that his own father, Ata, hadn't been lifebonded to Mati when he'd betrayed his family and gone to his death. Gone with a kind, placating grin that haunted Veron's memories as Ata had secretly left them for the last time, given his life away.

Veron lowered his gaze to the stone. He'd never weaken Nozva Rozkveta that way. Ever. At twenty-seven, he hadn't even contemplated making the Offering to anyone, let alone the death sentence that was lifebonding.

Heavy footsteps echoed into the lifespring's cave.

"Will she be all right?" Dhuro asked, half growl and half whine. "I swear by Deep and Darkness, if—"

"She will recover, Your Highness," Xira said, meeting Dhuro face to face as he dripped rainwater and mud onto the gleaming blackstone. "But"—she turned back to Veron and Gavri—"they'll need to have something substantial to eat to recover their strength."

Something more than the individual rations of small game, cave fish, shellfish, and wild bits of edible flora.

The humans had the entire bounty of the sky realm while *his* people had to scrape and scrounge for the smallest of meals to share—and they couldn't even hunt in peace.

"They can have my rations," he said.

"Your Highness," Rút breathed, sitting up, but he held up a hand.

"It's done, Rút." He'd just redouble his efforts hunting in the coming days.

"Mine, too," Dhuro said, thumping a fist to his chest. "The Brotherhood will pay for this. They have to."

Xira rested a gentle hand on Veron's shoulder and directed a fleeting glance in Dhuro's direction. "I'm certain Her Majesty will be relieved to know Vlasta and Rút are safe."

In other words, *Get this raging prince out of my lifespring.*

He nodded. "Come, Brother. Mati will want to know what happened."

"I'll report to Captain Riza," Gavri said, her eyes soft as she parted ways. After having loved his oldest brother Zoran for eight years before he'd left, she knew *exactly* how Dhuro could get.

Heaving a sigh, Dhuro left the lifespring with him, and they headed toward the black crystal spires of the palace in the heart of Central Cavern.

"The volodari of other queendoms are dropping like flies to the Brotherhood." Dhuro forced a breath out of his nose and shook his head. "It won't be long before they focus more of their attention on us."

"Mati said she's handling it. It is not our place to question." A queen spoke and her subjects obeyed. Every last one. And Mati had said she would resolve the crisis, and to trust her.

"I know. I know." Dhuro ran a palm over his damp mass of shoulder-length hair. "I just wish she'd trust us enough to tell us what's going on."

They passed the kuvari at the entrance and headed down the main corridor, their boots sloshing.

I just wish. That was Dhuro. Always Dhuro. Pushing for more, for privilege, instead of obedience. He'd spent some time among the humans before the Sundering, and had returned with *I just wish* and *Why can't she just* and *I think that* instead of the stoneclad obedience he'd been born to.

More like Ata. Their father had thought he'd known better than Mati, and had betrayed her and given up his life for that rebellion.

He shook his head. Unthinkable. Unacceptable.

Dhuro strode toward the glaive-bearing kuvari guarding the doors to Mati's quarters, but they barred his path.

"Prince Veron *only*," one of them—Lira—said to Dhuro. "By Her Majesty's order."

Crossing his arms, Dhuro stood his ground, staring down at her a moment before grunting and stepping aside. "Figures. Share the knowledge, will you, Brother?"

He eyed Dhuro. Of the many things that could happen, sharing anything a queen said in private wasn't likely. "How about a sparring session later instead?"

A corner of Dhuro's mouth turned up. "That'll do." With that, he took off.

Lira and her partner opened the doors and stood aside. "Your Highness."

Captain Riza emerged first, fixing him with sharp eyes that soon gentled. Resting a palm on his shoulder, she breathed deeply and gave him an encouraging nod. If Riza of all people was trying to encourage him, then whatever Mati had to say to him wasn't going to be good.

"Gavri is looking for you," he said, breaking the silence.

She gave his shoulder a final pat before donning her usual stone-faced expression anew and passing him by.

As soon as he stepped inside, Lira and her partner closed the doors behind him.

Within, bioluminescent *roza* vines twined around pillars, climbing and sprawling across the ceiling, casting a soft white glow inside. Roza had always been plentiful in Nozva Rozkveta, and some had already begun to bloom.

Mati strolled back and forth across the roza-vine rug, bobbing baby Dita in her arms while his sister Vadiha slept on Mati's bed. When everyone had awoken after the Rift, Vadiha had still been with child, thank the Darkness, and she had given birth to Dita not five weeks ago. After Mati, Vadiha was Nozva Rozkveta's strongest warrior, and she'd scarcely had the energy to stay awake to feed Dita, let alone train. The food shortage had been especially hard on her, and even with increased rations, and the volodari—her husband and their sisters among them—hunting at all hours, she still wasn't getting enough nourishment.

His hands clasped behind his back, he waited while Mati lulled Dita into a shallow sleep, then glanced at him and toward a bench, where he sat down.

"Anything today?" she asked quietly, her voice low and even as she kept her gaze on Dita's little slumbering face.

He shook his head. Coming home empty handed was always difficult, but all the more when he looked at Vadiha and Dita, who relied so desperately on the volodari teams' success.

"You didn't engage the Brotherhood."

"On your orders, we did not," he answered. "Vlasta took an arrow to the gut, but Xira said she and Rút would recover."

Mati nodded softly, brushing a wisp of fine baby hair off Dita's brow. "The conflict with the humans—and this famine—will soon be ended."

She had said it would. And it *would*. Of that he had no doubt.

"I have been in negotiations with the king of Silen via correspondence," she said, rocking Dita gently.

Negotiations? So that had been why she'd ordered them not to engage the Brotherhood. All this time, she'd been negotiating with the humans. And the other dark-elf queens must have known as well—there had been no word of dark-elves fighting back.

All for this.

If there was a bloodless way to end the conflict with the Brotherhood, then it was worth pursuing.

"Until our crops are stabilized, the Sileni are going to deliver food, both to Queen Nendra and to us, which we will distribute among the allied queendoms by way of the tunnels. This will begin as soon as the agreement is finalized in Bellanzole. And we have devised a diplomatic means of handling the Brotherhood."

Good. As keen as he was to end the persecution, as good as it would feel to spill the Brotherhood's blood... Blood would only beget blood. This was the whole of dark-elf history. Spilling blood only to spill more. It had to end somewhere, and if they could make peace with the humans—and survive—then he would do everything in his power to make that happen.

And if they couldn't make peace with the humans... then he'd make certain *his* people would be the ones to survive. The humans were numerous, but his people had trained for battle from the moment each of them could walk on toddling legs—if it came to war, the humans would fall.

"In return, they want our assistance in keeping the Immortal beasts at bay."

That was simple enough. All the volodari were trained in combat against all beasts—Immortal or otherwise. "Is that all?"

She met his gaze and held it. "I've agreed to give them one more thing."

If it meant food for Vadiha and an end to the conflict with the Brotherhood, then that was worth almost anything.

"You."

CHAPTER 3

*V*eron swept out an arm and caught the stone before it could hit his fey horse, Noc.

Good catch, wasn't it? he thought to Noc, who only snorted. *Come on. It was good.*

Good, Noc thought back. *Yes.*

"Get out of our kingdom!" an elderly human woman wailed at him from the small crowd, spittle flying from her mouth.

"Divine take you!" another cried. "And all the rest of the monsters!"

Monsters.

"Silence!" Riza spat from beside him. "You human filth dare attack Prince Veron? Danika, Gavri"—she cocked her hooded head toward two of the kuvari guarding him—"cut out their tongues. Now."

Danika and Gavri dismounted, boots thudding on the summer grass, and drew their vjernost blades. The small crowd shrank away.

"Captain," Veron warned, muffled through his face mask. Danika and Gavri halted, although they stood ready to attack.

Riza turned to him and inclined her head the merest fraction. "Your Highness."

One of the human children ogled them wide eyed. Veron chuffed softly and tossed the stone to him. The Brotherhood merited all of Riza's anger, but these humans? They were peasants—agitated, but not murderous. Even now, they shrank away, some looking to him with big eyes.

He pulled aside his leathers at his chest to expose the royal black sun tattoo over his heart to the humans. "No harm was done, Captain. They did not know me."

Her eyes narrowed. "Highness—"

"No harm was done." Firmer this time.

Mati's orders to them all had been clear: *Keep your peace, but do not allow any harm to come to the prince. Harm none unless he is harmed.* And even Riza wouldn't dare to disobey the queen of Nozva Rozkveta.

"Highness." Riza nodded coolly. "Mount up!" she bellowed to Danika and Gavri, then turned on the humans, scowling. "Remember this day, humans. You keep your tongues at the mercy of Prince Veron u Zara u Avrora u Roza, Valaz u Nozva Rozkveta, Zpevan Kamena, Volodar T'my. But disrespect His Highness again, and I won't be able to hear his mercy over the sound of your blood spraying."

Subtle, Riza. Very subtle.

The crowd scattered, some humans sprinting away, others running with occasional glances over their shoulders. The human child stood frozen, grass-green eyes wide as moons, clutching the stone to his chest. The boy could only be a few years older than Dita. He'd always liked children, and human ones were no different, even if they didn't recognize royalty.

"Hyah!" Riza urged her horse forward.

He smiled behind his face mask at the human child as the cavalcade moved once more, continuing down the cypress-lined road to Bellanzole and the soaring Palazzo dell'Ermacora.

Most humans probably hadn't seen one of his kind in millennia; their ignorance was understandable, if inconvenient. Dark-elf royals did not adorn themselves in the golden crowns and circlets to which the human peasantry was accustomed to seeing on theirs; dark-elves knew their royalty by their bearing, their demeanor, their faces, and as a last resort, by their black sun hearts, tattooed by royal czerni ink at birth.

Nozva Rozkveta's scribes had been working tirelessly to bridge the gap between Old Sileni and the modern tongue, and although he, his party, and many of the other dark-elves spoke the modern tongue now, that didn't cure the ignorance.

Mati had sent him—and the entire host of dark-elves—on a diplomatic mission, leaving camps of dark-elf troops in his wake to help keep the peace for themselves and the humans against the beasts, all part of the bargain struck between Nozva Rozkveta and the kingdom of Silen.

He rode up to Gavri, who eyed him peripherally and hissed.

"I don't question my queen's wishes," she said, shaking her head vehemently and sending her braid swinging from side to side, "but you, one of our most valued princes, are doomed to make the Offering to one of *them*? It's a sad fate."

"Do not question Queen Zara," Riza snarled at her, and Gavri inhaled sharply but nodded.

He'd known both of them his entire life; they were as much

his friends as they were kuvari. They could always be trusted to tell him the truth.

He gazed out ahead, at the humans' world of lush green, so different than home. Human mages shaped this sky realm with magic like the Stone Singers shaped the Deep with song, spelling buildings and roads like the Stone Singers sang stalagmites, stalactites, columns, and pillars. He still had memories of sketching sky-realm flora and fauna with Ata as a boy, when he'd been training to become one of the volodari. But after Ata's death, he hadn't sketched much of anything.

The humans and their sky realm were different, but difference was not inherently bad. He'd brought a myriad of roza blooms grown from the Vein of Nozva Rozkveta's power, a gesture he hoped would demonstrate the bridge that could exist between their realms.

"It's what I was born to do, Gavri," he replied, and her head perked up. "I've been raised knowing my life is not my own, but to be bargained away by my mother, to strengthen Nozva Rozkveta and our people."

Riza nodded. "And you perform your duty with honor and valor."

Gavri bit her lip. "But they... they are just so *ugly*."

He laughed under his breath while Riza snarled at her again.

Oh yes, humans were ugly. Their women weren't taut and toned like dark-elf women; human women were soft like the very livestock they raised for slaughter. They had no fangs or claws, which even dark-elf children had. And their skin—thin, delicate, so easily broken.

By Deep and Darkness, what he'd give to be in a hunting stand now, in a raging storm, instead of on his way to make the

Offering to one of *them*. It was enough to make him shift in his new boots, which fit even worse than the old ones. Ata had been a skilled hand with leatherworking, and no pair of boots had fit right since his... death.

Too picky, Noc chimed in.

You don't wear boots. If you did, you'd be picky, too. Trust me.

The human, Noc clarified. *You both live, both walk on two legs. Man. Woman.*

As if that were the whole of it.

But he didn't have to desire the human. He just had to make the Offering to her. With this agreement, Vadiha, Dita, and all his people would no longer starve—that alone gave it merit. And there was far more to Offering than mere desire. There was trust, partnership, encouragement, companionship. And any human woman who'd agreed to make the Offering to him had to be open minded; that alone gave her potential as a partner. In any case, there was nothing more important than doing Mati's will, for the peace of Nozva Rozkveta.

He drew in a deep breath. He was only twenty-seven—unless he counted the 2,372 or so years all the Immortals had been petrified since the Sundering... which he didn't—and by the end of the week, he'd be making the Offering. To a human.

By her agreement to it, she welcomed him into her life. That much was certain. And it meant this peace between them would succeed; and once it did, the peace between their people would, too.

As long as she was honest, he could trust her, and as long as they could trust each other, they had a chance.

"We will do what's right. This Offering will go smoothly," he assured them both. Besides, Riza had helped him choose an impeccable Offering gift for the princess. "And once it does, all of this unrest will dissipate."

Riza scoffed, then shrugged. "I pray to the Deep for it, Your Highness." Hesitating, she lowered her gaze for a moment, her brow furrowed. "But... Gavri's objections aren't entirely without merit. If there's one thing I've learned about the humans, it is that they can never be trusted, especially when it comes to doing what's right."

♆

BENEATH THE LATE-AFTERNOON SUN, Aless held still in the court-yard, her spine straight, her shoulders back, her chin high. The summer breeze riffled the rosy-pink silk brocade of her gown and the carefully styled curls cascading down her back. The jeweled circlet was warm against her forehead, but Papà had left specific instructions with her ladies-in-waiting and maids. They had decorated her like a horse for dressage.

"You really won't speak to him, my lady?" Gabriella, her friend and lady-in-waiting, whispered, tucking a lock of hair behind her ear.

She'd already promised Papà she wouldn't. And it really didn't matter, did it? Her choice didn't matter, so why would her words? This prince would probably arrive on his mother's orders just to look her in the mouth and check her gait. A chattel didn't need to say a word to be *useful*.

He'd simply place her in his cart, take her to the dark-elf cave, and shelve her like some trophy to present whenever the need arose to prove peace with the humans. They'd say, *We have no quarrel with the humans! Look, one of our princes has a human wife.*

And because the dark-elf women ruled Nightbloom, she would never have a say in anything, never make herself useful there, just remain a pawn as she had here, except in an alien culture that spoke an alien tongue, and surrounded by strangers who had no reason to be friendly with one of her kind.

Mamma's library would never be built, she'd never help anyone learn to read, nor Immortali and humans learn about one another in a place of peace and knowledge.

Surely this dark-elf prince didn't wish for this fate any more than she did, and yet they both had to do this dance at the behest of their parents and rulers.

Which didn't make it any better.

A bee lazily flew by. *Sting me. Please, please, please sting me. Anything to avoid this meeting.*

Hooves clopped beyond the iron gates, and a cavalcade of riders trotted into the courtyard, ringed by the Sileni Royal Guard. The strangers were cloaked and hooded in black, shadows but for their unsettling yellow irises and ghostly white hair. The occasional glimpse of slate-blue skin peeked over the face masks covering their mouths and noses.

The dark-elves.

As they began to dismount, they revealed leather-armor-clad muscle on lean, athletic frames. Each of them had to be at least six feet tall. The tallest of them—on a massive, mesmerizing destrier, its ebony coat gleaming in the sun—was bulkier, with broad shoulders, thick biceps and thighs, a muscular chest. A male.

He hitched the blade at his side and dismounted nimbly, rubbed his hand and wrist, and took in the courtyard with narrowed, searching eyes. They settled on her. Intense. Eerie.

Different from the rest. The only male among them. It had to be *him*.

But neither he, nor any of his party, were dressed in a manner befitting royalty. They all wore mere black leathers and plain cloth, like any common soldier. Maybe a sign of how *special* he considered this meeting.

He would have already met with Papà at Bellanzole's walls for escort into the city. Papà had met this Immortali male and, despite his obvious insult, had allowed him entry to this courtyard.

But would anything have deterred Papà from this bargain? He'd sold Bianca's hand in marriage, sight unseen, to this Immortali male. He could be ugly, disfigured, beastly, utterly disgusting—even beyond being a dark-elf—and would that have changed Papà's decision at all?

Of course not. He'd bought his peace already. Cheaply. And hadn't even tried anything else.

She stiffened as the male approached her, escorted by one of his own and a Sileni royal guard. Maybe her Vow of Silence was for the best, as her words would have been just as frozen as the rest of her.

He inclined his head. "It is my honor to meet you, Princess Alessandra," he said, his low voice like velvet over honed steel, muffled through the black cloth face mask. "I am Veron."

That voice—deep and flowing like the mirror-black rivers of the Lone.

Holding her breath, she looked at his hand—gloved—his fingers pointed, but he didn't offer to take hers.

"It is your custom to take hands," he said, matter of fact. He removed the gloves and passed them to his companion, a sharp-eyed female standing at attention, a soldier by the look of her. He extended his hand, slate blue, with long fingers capped in points.

Claws.

The moment had almost passed when she shakily offered hers in return.

Callused skin closed around her fingers as he raised her hand gently, pulled down his face mask, and lightly pressed his lips to her knuckles.

The barest touch, and a shiver tingled down her spine before she could stop it. He could kill her. With little more than a sweep of his hand.

As he straightened, she covered her reaction with a smile, which he returned.

Fangs. Sharp, pointed fangs, like a lion's. She held her smile, kept it plastered on her face. Hopefully it would keep any other reaction from showing.

"It is the first time you have seen one of my kind in person." His eerie eyes stayed fixed on hers, unwavering, his callused hand still wrapped around hers.

Nothing moved in the courtyard. Holy Mother's mercy, even the breeze didn't dare blow.

She nodded. That smile was still plastered on her face—she returned her expression to some semblance of normalcy.

Like the rest of him, his face was hard, all brutal planes and angles, with even harder eyes. As a statue, he might have been terrifyingly beautiful, but living, breathing, he was simply terrifying. Like a nightmare from a children's fairytale.

At any moment, he could lunge at her, pin her to the ground, sink his fangs into her flesh and tear it open. Drive his clawed hands through her body. Rip her apart. He could do all that and seem completely natural.

"It is my hope that, in time, you will find us familiar despite our differences."

Familiar? Maybe. Any less terrifying? Likely not. But she nodded again.

"Would you care for a walk around the courtyard? I will answer all your questions to the best of my ability. Perhaps we might become better acquainted before the ceremony tomorrow."

She turned to Gabriella and pointed to her own mouth.

Gabriella's hazel eyes flickered between her and the prince. "Princess Alessandra wishes me to tell you that she has sworn the Vow of Silence and cannot speak to you before the wedding, Your Highness."

Aless faced him once more. Or rather, his scowl.

"A vow of silence?" His face tight, he clasped his hands behind his back, and his companion narrowed her smoldering yellow eyes. Like glowing embers. "Your people expect such things from their women?"

Did Papà neglect to mention that he hadn't agreed to the marriage until she'd offered the Vow?

She nodded.

His hiss punctuated the quiet, and his companion hissed, too. Their eyes turned hard, fierce, like those of lions ready to pounce. He'd hidden his hands—his claws—and who knew what they would do?

Shivering, she took a step back. But if he disliked the Vow of Silence, then he wasn't as bad as Papà. Maybe even reasonable.

He looked her over and relaxed his posture, revealed his hands from behind his back and let them fall to his sides.

Her gaze fixed on them, on their sharp claws, until he inclined his head.

"There are preparations before the ceremony tomorrow," he said, his voice wooden. "I take my leave, Your Highness. Good day to you."

She matched his gesture, and with that, the Royal Guard escorted him and his companion toward the palazzo.

Still as stone, she stood, watching until they disappeared inside and the doors closed.

"My lady?" Gabriella rested gentle fingers on her forearm.

Another shiver wove through her. Her heart pounded, so hard and so fast that surely Gabriella heard.

"Come, my lady. Let's get you inside." Gabriella took her arm and led her in the opposite direction, toward another entrance into the palazzo.

She walked alongside her lady-in-waiting, but the surroundings were a blur. Those eerie eyes. Sharp claws. Pointed fangs. Slate skin. Steely velvet voice. Ghostly hair. The way he hissed, the lithe way he moved—

Trembling, she shook her head, shook out her hands. There was no choice. Unless she married him tomorrow, Papà would not keep his end of the agreement either. She had to, or else Bianca would.

Finally, Gabriella helped her into a suede armchair next to a large, mysterious box, and within moments, Bianca sprang away from where she'd been looking out the window, with a swath of sapphire brocade skirts trailing as she ran and laid her head in Aless's lap.

"I'm so sorry!" Bianca cried, taking her hand.

Aless stroked her hair softly and dismissed Gabriella with a wave of her hand.

"You're really going through with it?" Bianca's voice broke.

She had to. Kind-hearted, daydreaming Bianca could never

handle a marriage to a dark-elf, but *she* could, for her sister's sake.

"Come on, Aless," Bianca urged, nudging her. "Never mind the Vow. Speak to me. *Please.*"

After Bianca's wedding, they'd be parted; Bianca would go to Roccalano, and she would go to Nightbloom. The idea of spending most of their remaining time in silence was... painful.

She sighed. Well, she had only promised Papà she wouldn't speak to her... fiancé. "I... will go through with the *wedding.*"

Bianca raised her head, frowned, and sat back on her haunches. "What do you mean? Is there another way?"

There might be. She'd go through with the wedding in Bellanzole as promised, because it was required for Bianca's sake. For her sister, she would marry him. For three days, she would endure—whatever she would have to endure—and then she would witness Bianca's wedding to her beloved Luciano. Bianca and Luciano were both human, and once they consummated their human marriage, their bond would be unbreakable. But after that?

She would do more good for peace bridging the cultural divide and teaching than being kept as some trophy in a cave. Even if Veron didn't approve of the Vow of Silence, she could never be one of the dark-elf women, those who truly held power in Nightbloom. She'd just be... a token.

"After this wedding, there's still the second ceremony in Nightbloom before this agreement is sealed. I'm going to use the time in between to try to convince him we don't need to be married for there to be peace between our nations. I'm sure he doesn't want to marry a human any more than I want to marry a dark-elf."

Meeting the prince today... Yes, he'd been intimidating, but he'd also been well spoken, polite—considerate, even. "Maybe he'll listen."

In fact, she had the perfect wedding gift for him: her new copy of *A Modern History of Silen*. She still had Mamma's copy, and the parallel gift would have meaning. It would show her willingness to share this new world with him and his people, and to welcome them as a part of it as he filled the remaining pages with the peace she hoped their people would forge together.

With him on her side, they might convince Papà and the Queen of Nightbloom to reconsider. She and Veron could still act as ambassadors of peace, as friends, demonstrating that relations between their people could be good. Maybe she could suggest the library as a joint venture, earning goodwill for the dark-elves from the paesani.

Bianca sniffed, blinking away tears. She swabbed her face with the sleeve of her sapphire frock. "And if he doesn't listen?"

After their wedding here, Papà had said they were set to go on a Royal Progress throughout Silen to Nightbloom to present their harmonious union and inspire peace among the paesani, the nobiltà, and the dark-elves. There would be plenty of time to develop a contingency plan.

She shrugged. "I'll find a way."

Bianca looked away, her eyebrows drawn, and bit her lip. "Luciano told me that Tarquin is an influential member of the Brotherhood, hoping to find justice for Arabella. With their help, and the Belmonte Company, your freedom can be assured."

The Brotherhood? Tarquin was involved with that hateful group? What he had said about the Immortali... *A corruption that must be eradicated from the kingdom.*

No, he wasn't like her at all. He was one of *them*. The Brotherhood.

Shortly after the Rift, the Brotherhood had come together to "advance human interests." Somehow "advancing human interests" always seemed to involve violence against the Immortali. For every perceived injury to humans, the Brotherhood retaliated twofold. Thankfully the Immortali seemed less prone to such violence, as no such faction had emerged on their side—that she knew of. "But Luciano isn't a member?"

Bianca shook her head.

"Good. Anyone involved with the Brotherhood has sunk too deeply into hatred." As much as she didn't want to go through with this marriage, she didn't bear the prince, or the other dark-elves, any ill will. There was no way she'd work with the Brotherhood. Ever.

"But they'd liberate you in a heartbeat—"

"No." She took Bianca's hand. "I appreciate your care, but I'll think of something." She smiled. "Don't worry about me. Let your only concern be your wedding, your honeymoon, your happiness."

"How can I think about that?" Bianca's smooth brow creased.

"That's why I've done all this. So you must be happy. Promise me." With any luck, she and the dark-elf prince would achieve peace through alternate means, both be free of each other and this arrangement, and Bianca would get to stay with the man she loved.

Bianca's lovely agate eyes hardened, and she gave a determined nod. "I promise." Her gaze lowered. "But what about your library? Maybe Papà will still help?"

There had been no hope of that earlier either; she knew that now.

But she wouldn't give up. She'd never give up. Books had been Mamma's life and had changed her own, given her companionship and escape when the Sileni court and even Papà himself had been ruthless in their treatment of her, of a useless pawn. Books had power, the power to defeat hopelessness with escape, ignorance with enlightenment, fear with knowledge. And she wanted every person to have access to that power, to harness it, for peace, understanding, and better lives.

And they would have it, just as Mamma had wished before she'd died.

Maybe a Terran shrine would take her in. A High Priest or Silen's Paladin Grand Cordon himself—Sir Massimo de' Nunzio—could hear her out about wanting to build a library, to care for their paesani. The Order of Terra was known in Silen for its dedication to charity and peace; Nunzio would hear her out. He would. And the Order, so instrumental in forging peace, would no doubt be open to letting the dark-elves take part in the venture.

Veron seemed like a reasonable man. Maybe he'd support the idea to his mother.

"I'll find another way," she said to Bianca. "I have all the plans finished. It's only a matter of finding the right investor." And the Order would have the funds. Maybe she could send the library plans ahead to Nunzio and meet with him in Stroppiata during the Royal Progress to discuss it. But Papà would have her correspondence watched.

"Luciano and I could help." Bianca perked up. "We could write to wealthy potential investors, find someone who's interested."

Her mail would be watched... but Bianca's? Luciano's?

"I'd love your help. I'd like you to send something for me, if you could."

Bianca nodded. "Of course."

Later tonight, she'd have Gabriella deliver the plans to Bianca with instructions.

"Oh! Your gown arrived." Bianca darted toward the large, mysterious box and opened a flap. "It's bittersweet, Aless, but the gown is at least beautiful."

Papà had been planning to marry her off for years, and no doubt the gown had taken almost as long to make. "I won't be needing it."

Bianca's mouth fell open. "But... Then what will you wear?"

Oh, she'd given plenty of thought to that over the past few days. When Mamma had given her *A Modern History of Silen*, she'd written inside, *Be brave, my rose, and fill the remaining pages with your deeds.*

I will, Mamma.

Fortunately, her bellani d'oro were still good with some of her dressmakers. The ones who didn't fear Papà. "I will wear my thoughts, Bianca."

Papà had bargained them away like chattels—in this day and age. *Let the signori know exactly what I think about that.*

❧

AFTER PULLING OFF HIS BOOTS—THESE new ones still didn't fit right—Veron paced the dim bedchamber barefoot. Silence. They'd *silenced* her. He rubbed his chin. "Why? Why would she be expected to swear such a vow?"

Gavri shrugged at her post in the doorway next to Riza.

"Perhaps her voice is like claws on limestone. Or perhaps she's a twit, and her father doesn't want you to find out."

He snarled. "That is my soon-to-be *bride* you are insulting." His gaze locked with hers in the lengthy silence before she looked away.

He drew aside the heavy window drapes and peered into the courtyard. A storm. Dark clouds had shrouded the heavens, and the world below darkened with them; heavy drops pelted the lush green leaves, the grass, the stone walkways and benches. Umbrella pines swayed in the unrelenting wind. The sky realm changed with the hour.

It was hard to get a fix on Princess Alessandra's personality. What mattered to her? What did she enjoy doing? What did she think? Her wide eyes had answered none of those questions. Their meeting had only revealed her fear and the troubling notion of her silence.

"You suspect she is unwilling," Riza said quietly.

He did more than suspect.

"What?" Gavri snapped. "Prince Veron is an exemplary—"

"She's a human, Gavri," Riza shot back, earning a groan from Gavri. "They see things differently."

Princess Alessandra was unwilling. What else could possibly be so damaging that would require a vow of silence? "I came here believing that my bride had agreed to this."

Gavri grunted. "This human king substituted one daughter for the other. Perhaps there is some defect she would otherwise confess to you, if not for this vow."

King Macario had explained that, much to his embarrassment, Princess Bianca was in love with another man and making the Offering to—marrying—him, but that Princess Alessandra was equally beautiful, willing, and younger.

Humans prized the youth of their brides—more childbearing years.

"No, the king swore Princess Alessandra was healthy, fertile, not with child, and willing." Before the meeting, it truly hadn't mattered to him which human bride he had to—as they called it—"marry," as long as she had agreed and was honest. There had been no reason for him to interfere with a love match.

Riza stood taller, raising her chin slightly. "With all due respect, Your Highness, even if she *is* unwilling, does it matter? Queen Zara gave you her orders."

Thunder rolled, then lightning flashed white into the room.

"Does it really matter *what* the human wants?" Gavri added.

He stiffened and glared at them. By Deep and Darkness, of course it mattered. He was bound to obey Mati's orders, but not without care.

And yet both Riza and Gavri seemed to be in agreement. He forced himself to relax.

"Duty must supersede honor, Your Highness." Riza clenched her vjernost blade's pommel. "Sometimes, to save thousands, one must be sacrificed."

Gavri nodded, her brows drawn.

The peace. How many dark-elves and humans had died to this conflict? And how many more would?

Their parents had already sacrificed him and Alessandra for the sake of those lives. Could he do the same? The Brotherhood's attacks had to end. The famine had to end. If he wavered now, how could he return and look Vadiha—and Dita—in the eye?

His duty was to Nozva Rozkveta, its queen, and its people. All else came after. Riza and Gavri were right. Even if Princess Alessandra was unwilling, his hands were tied. As were hers.

But there would be *two* ceremonies. If he was right about everything, then there would be the entirety of the Royal Progress back to Nozva Rozkveta for him to elicit her assent. They *had* to marry, but whatever her fears were, he could allay them. If she could never see him as a lover, Princess Alessandra could live her life as she wished, to the best standard he could deliver, and he could live his. A practical arrangement.

He could never defy Mati's orders, so he would find a way to persuade Princess Alessandra on the way to Nozva Rozkveta.

He heaved a sigh. The hunting stand in a storm only seemed more and more appealing as the days went by. "I'm going to bed."

"Sweet dreams, Your Highness." The corner of Riza's mouth twitched—a grin, for her at least.

Gavri eyed her with an impish grin and puffed a breath, blowing a wisp of hair off her face.

They both well knew he'd barely get in a wink. At least with this on his conscience.

But he rounded the canopied bed, out of their line of sight, and undressed, then parted the bed curtains and settled in. The soft mattress yielded under his weight, and he stretched out, curling an arm behind his head. It had been a long time since he'd slept in a human bed. They were far more luxurious and intricate than the practical dark-elf beds, but he missed the pleasing give of moss filling and the coolness of plant-fiber bedding. No doubt Princess Alessandra would prefer something like this instead—he'd have to arrange one for her.

Everything in Nozva Rozkveta was prized for its practical value. He'd have to explain that to her. An Offering—a wedding—celebrated not just a union, but what each partner could offer the other. And he'd been raised his entire life to become a person of worth: a capable hunter, swordsman, archer, and rider; well educated; strong, honorable, and valorous. A prince Mati could trade confidently when the time came.

And the time had come.

Tomorrow, he would make his Offering to Princess Alessandra of Silen. He'd never been to a human wedding, but they wore armor, carried weapons, and rode horses everywhere else, so weddings were no exception, right?

CHAPTER 4

*A*less dismissed all her servants from the private chambers outside the nave of L'Abbazia Reale. She smoothed the wrinkles from her wedding gown, yards of Pryndonian white lace and intricate pearl beading. It was a gorgeous gown, one any happy bride would eagerly wear down the aisle.

Any *happy* bride.

She paced the gray rug, whipping the gown's train about her. No matter what happened afterward, today she would be officially *married*. Even if she could persuade Veron not to complete the second ceremony in Nightbloom, they would always be married by Sileni law.

But if they didn't live as husband and wife, that wouldn't matter, would it? And it wasn't as though she'd need to remarry for love. As long as the Paladin Grand Cordon could help her see the library built, as long as she could teach there, she didn't need a thing more.

This would all work out. Terra willing, everything would go as planned.

Tradition had ruled over so many lives, including her own, for long enough, and other voices had chosen for her. Maybe standing up to that today, even a little, would make a difference.

Yes, she would marry Prince Veron and she wouldn't destroy the peace, but she would speak her mind on it, in the only way left to her. Papà may have given her no other meaningful choice, but she still had this.

A soft rap came to the door, then one more. She opened it. "Bianca."

Bianca gave her a wide-eyed look, her mouth falling open, then cleared her throat and hastily waved in two servants with a trunk.

"Were you seen?" After they entered, Aless glanced out into the hall, left and right, but no one else was about other than the Royal Guard. Good. No one to tell Papà.

"No." Bianca nodded to the servants, who set down the trunk and left. "Are you sure you want to do this?"

"Of course. We have the dress ready and everything." Aless pulled aside her hair and bared the lacing down her back. Bianca's quick fingers began undoing all of Gabriella's hard work.

"I didn't mean the wardrobe change." Bianca pulled the last of the laces, and Aless slid the gown off her shoulders, stepped out of it, and threw open the trunk.

Blood red.

Smiling, she took out the gown and handed it to Bianca, who helped her pull it over her head without disheveling her hair.

"I told you I'm doing this for you." Aless slipped her arms over the bust line, and Bianca began lacing the back and then rearranged the tulle netting carefully. The bodice fit like a glove, and the skirts flared out in dramatic fashion, with a ten-foot train worthy of a princess.

"But this statement of yours," Bianca said carefully, "won't this sabotage your marriage?"

Being thrown together like two horses in a pen would have already sabotaged this marriage. She sighed. "Yesterday, when Gabriella told him about the Vow of Silence, he seemed... enraged."

Bianca's hands paused in their work, and her footsteps retreated. "Enraged? As if he would get violent?"

"Not exactly." She held up her hair again. His reaction had seemed almost—almost protective of her. "At least not toward me."

Bianca settled the black raven-feather funereal cloak about her shoulders and arranged the twelve-foot train over the gown while Aless let her hair fall free, and clasped the front of the cloak.

"He had this expression of fury, and he hissed... It was as if the very notion of me being sworn to silence offended him." A good sign. She turned to Bianca, who settled the white-lace wedding gown into the trunk.

"The dark-elves' royal line is matriarchal, right?" Bianca closed the trunk. "It is their women who hold power. Maybe he agrees that others shouldn't dictate the course of your life—nor silence your voice when it comes to your future."

Yes, dark-elf women didn't "meddle" in politics—they ruled. "Maybe."

"Well, the entire nobiltà will hear your voice today."

Be brave, Mamma had said. She would. And ensure her voice was heard.

The familiar, overbearing notes of the pipe organ invaded through the walls and door; she stepped into her black jeweled slippers, checked her diamond earrings, then gathered her pearly-white wedding cloak.

"It's time." Bianca hitched up her periwinkle silk-taffeta gown, then opened the door.

Veron would be waiting beyond the corridor and outside the entrance to the nave of L'Abbazia Reale.

The pipe organ summoned her there, and she went as bid. The way from the side chamber to the entrance was quiet, only her heeled steps and Bianca's fighting the silence as they passed the purple-clad Royal Guard at their posts.

No one waited outside the massive entry doors.

Was he coming? No doubt he was as *eager* for this marriage as she was.

But she took up her position, and Bianca fanned out her train behind her.

A rhythmic clopping on marble echoed from the opposite corridor.

Her head swiveled to face the sound.

The massive ebony destrier filled the corridor, muscles rippling, copious mane and tail flowing as it trotted closer.

Inside the abbazia.

Royal guards circled the enormous horse, hissing clipped words to one another, while a stoic Veron sat astride the beast, all six and a half feet of him clad in fine black-leather armor.

A bow hung across his chest.

A saddle quiver full of arrows.

A long sword and a scroll strapped at his side.

A round shield on his black-cloaked back.

Knives sheathed in his knee-high riding boots, in a baldric, and on his gauntleted wrists.

Her mouth fell open. He looked armed for war.

"Your Highness"—a royal guard stammered— "horses... are not allowed inside L'Abbazia Reale."

His gaze locked on hers, Veron dismounted nimbly and handed the reins to the guard, then gave the beast a pat before approaching her.

No part of her would move. Not her gaping mouth, not her feet, not her hands. To stare was her only ability.

He wore no face mask nor hood today, his blue skin bared for all to see. His ghostly white hair was adorned with braids that met, intertwined, and hit to mid-back. With the Rift so recent, most of the people here today would have never seen a dark-elf, much less an unmasked one.

Was he... was he making a statement, too? Going through with this, just as she was, but not silently either?

With a confident, regal gait, he strode to her, then lowered to a knee, bowed his head, and looked up into her eyes.

"Alessandra Ermacora, princess of Silen, I, Veron of Nozva Rozkveta, offer you power"—he rested a hand on his sword pommel—"survival, skill, defense, wisdom, and partnership"— then on his bow, his knives, his shield, the scroll strapped to his belt, and he took her hand—"to harness for your ends or ours, as we walk our lives together from this day forward for as long as the Deep allows."

His yellow irises stayed locked with hers, making her heart pound, and a breath escaped her open mouth as she remembered to breathe.

"This is my people's tradition," he said quietly and stood.

"We call being wed 'making the Offering.' We give ourselves to one another, offering all we can do and all that we are."

Did... did he expect her to respond in kind?

She swallowed, her gaze wandering the many offerings he'd brought. "Veron, prince of Nightbloom, I..."

She blinked. What was she offering him? Could she truly offer anything, when her heart hadn't even been in this? When, more than anything, she wanted to follow in Mamma's footsteps? "I..."

A huff came from behind him; his companion from the day before. The sharp-eyed female guard. She wore fine leathers today, too, and no face mask nor hood to cover her midnight-blue skin and short, spiky white hair.

The footmen opened the doors, and the pipe organ's volume was almost deafening as it blasted forth.

Veron offered her his arm, and remembering to close her mouth, she took it. They entered L'Abbazia Reale's nave on the long, crimson runner leading to the front, compressed into its lengthy, narrow path. A susurrus mounted as they entered, wide-eyed guests eyeing Veron as if he were Nox himself, come to claim their souls and drag them to the Lone.

Light poured in from the unattainably high windows, crowning the massive statue of Terra that held court at the front, overwhelming and breathtaking. Imposing. Demanding quiet obedience.

Not today. From *either* of them. With her dressed in a blood-red gown and a funereal cloak and Veron in black leather armor and weapons, all of Silen would believe that while they swore vows, neither of them did so without objection.

But Veron, by his words, had done this from a cultural

perspective. Had Papà not mentioned human wedding customs? Assumed that the dark-elves did the same?

Despite his sincerity, Silen would see a different symbolism in his attire today. Unintended, certainly, but the people wouldn't know that.

As they proceeded to the time of the pipe organ, she pulled the clasp on her wedding cloak and let it fall from her shoulders, revealing her raven-feathered statement.

Gasps rippled from the nobiltà crammed into the pews. Veron's arm contracted slightly, just a soft creak from the leather armoring his bicep. But no more. They did not stop.

No reaction from the royal box up in the right balcony, removed from the abbazia proper and separate. No shouted orders. No Royal Guard closing in.

Success.

The music continued, and so did they.

Padre Graziano, the former High Priest of Monas Bellan, awaited at the front, towering on a dais just below the massive statue of Terra looking down at them all. His wide eyes speared her blood-red gown, the shock wrinkling his lined face even more than old age already had.

Good. This was a royal wedding. News would spread far and wide, the nobiltà and the paesani would talk, object, and this would have to stop. At least for the *next* generation.

When she reached the front, she knelt, as did Veron. While Padre Graziano shook his face to alertness, Veron's gaze meandered toward her.

"Willing?" he whispered, so low she wondered if he'd spoken at all.

It was a simple question, but the answer wasn't so simple. To spare her sister a walk through fire, she would walk it herself. But was that willing? Veron seemed kind, reasonable, and if she had to marry a strange dark-elf, there could have been far worse men. But if she *had* to, was that "willing"?

Padre Graziano cleared his throat. "Please join hands."

Veron held out his palm, and she placed her hand on his.

Padre Graziano wound a golden ribbon about their hands. "As your hands are joined, so are your lives, as you support one another, protect one another, strengthen one another."

He then offered the vow to Veron and bid him repeat.

Veron turned to her, his pale eyebrows drawn as he assessed her. "I, Veron of Nightbloom," he said hesitantly, "promise you, Alessandra of Silen, that from this day forward, I will be your husband, your ally, and your friend." His uncertain look lingered as Padre Graziano offered her vows.

"I, Alessandra of Silen, promise you, Veron of Nightbloom, that from this day forward, I will be your wife, your ally, and your friend."

She met his gaze. No, she hadn't desired this marriage, but she did participate in this ceremony willingly. For Bianca's sake, and for the sake of future Ermacora women. Hopefully Veron would be open minded about finding another way to forge the peace between their peoples instead of the second ceremony at Nightbloom. She nodded to him.

The tension in his bearing visibly lessened, and his expression softened.

"Veron of Nightbloom and Alessandra of Silen are now bound to one another. What Holy Terra has bound, let no man sever," Padre Graziano announced as he removed the ribbon.

Veron helped her up, and holding hands, they faced the nobiltà, who clapped softly and stared—at Veron, at her gown, some craning their necks to look into the royal box.

She followed those looks to Papà's seat. The white of his teeth didn't show, nor even a smile that she could discern. Just a hard, expressionless mask.

He wasn't happy. Good. Then he was beginning to understand how she felt, how Bianca would have felt, probably how Veron felt. Even if Papà hadn't wanted to see her as more than a chattel, he'd have to now.

Down the aisle, they passed Luciano and Tarquin Belmonte, and Tarquin—rigid as that statue of Terra herself— stared a hole through her, his carnelian gaze fixed upon her with such intensity that it felt like he looked *through* her. What was he seeing?

She shivered as they walked past him.

Veron walked her out of the abbazia and out to the cobblestone drive, where a grand white coach-and-six awaited.

He stepped in front of her, barring her path with his arm.

The sky darkened, enormous shadows cast upon the cobblestone streets, and a wave of gasps and withered cries rolled through the crowd outside.

Veron reached for the shield at his back as two winged creatures soared overhead, bright sunlight glittering on iridescent violet and tan scales.

"Don't move," he ordered, and Holy Mother's mercy, she couldn't even if she tried. Every part of him was rigid, focused, honed to the point of a blade as he kept his eyes fixed on the creatures.

"Th-those a-are..."

"Lesser dragons," he answered quietly. "En route toward the sea. Uninterested in us, by the looks of it," he whispered, "so perhaps on some Dragon Lord's order."

Lesser dragons... Dragon Lord...

Her entire body trembled, like a mouse under a broom, and there was no stopping it.

The shadows passed, and Veron's bearing relaxed, his arms slowly falling to his sides as he stepped away from her.

"M-maybe it's g-good you wore armor," she offered, trying to swallow past the lump in her throat.

"I'd love to think so." His mouth curved as the footmen opened the doors to the carriage. "But if they'd wanted us dead, armor or no armor, we would be."

A nervous laugh escaped her as Veron helped her into the carriage and then sat across from her. Bianca and the sharp-eyed dark-elf guard entered after them, eyeing each other silently.

Dragons. They'd just seen *dragons.* Beings she'd only ever known from books.

But the door closed, the driver called, and just like that, they were on their way to the feast and their wedding night.

As THE COACH jostled over cobblestone, Aless stole a glance at Veron sitting across from her. His keen eyes scanned their surroundings beyond the window, and with his many weapons, he was as intimidating as any guard. More so, even.

While the entire crowd had gasped and trembled, he'd stood firm in the face of dragons. The next time those dragons appeared, they might not ignore the city, and if her people were fortunate, the dark-elves would help them.

Veron didn't need weapons to be intimidating... That imposing physique made him strong, as strong as any guard— no, stronger. He rested a clawed hand over a knife sheathed at his wrist. Those claws—and those fangs, although she dared not look at them—meant he never needed a weapon.

He'd come to the wedding ceremony armed like a warrior. He'd said it was a dark-elf tradition, but... had he known how it would appear to humans? The dark-elves seemed to know vastly more about human society than humans knew about theirs.

But then, she hadn't considered how her own statement would appear to the dark-elves. At all.

She'd made her point to Papà, and to everyone, about choice. But... she clenched the tulle fabric of her blood-red gown in fists. It hadn't been her intention to oppose Veron, but that was how it might've looked.

No doubt the whole of the nobiltà already gossiped about her unwilling bridegroom armored from head to toe. Rumors would be spreading far and wide about how even a dark-elf only reluctantly wed the Beast Princess.

Considering the rumors about her, too, it would serve her right. She bit her lip.

The sharp-eyed guard next to Veron was glaring at her, and mustering the confidence to say anything to him beneath that glare was a losing battle. Maybe her statement had gone over even worse with the dark-elves than she'd thought. Later on, once she and Veron were alone, she would have to apologize to him.

Maybe he'd be relieved once she told him they didn't have to wed. She'd lied in her promise, but maybe he'd overlook the lie in favor of freedom for them both.

A squeeze of her hand—Bianca intertwined their fingers and didn't let go until the coach pulled up to the palazzo's main gate. A crowd had already assembled, clapping and cheering to the bright fanfare of brass horns and rain of colorful confetti. Footmen opened the carriage door, and the sharp-eyed guard exited first, then Bianca, and then Veron, who held out his hand to her.

Those exotic eyes met hers, yellow like a lion's, and she shivered, but he didn't waver. Her heart pounding, she extended a hand to his, and he helped her exit, a sharp claw just barely grazing her wrist with a scratch. She suppressed a wince and schooled her face, willing no reaction to show.

The crowd pushed in, even against the line of Royal Guard, cheering and shouting and staring wide eyed, but Veron's form was regal, and he held her hand as they ascended the crimson carpet into the palazzo.

Inside, shimmery bright-red roses gladdened the cavernous foyer, the loveliness of the blooms too beautiful for reality; she had seen their like only in dreams, and even then, they hadn't reached out with color so vivid it could touch her, a scent so embracing it wrapped her in familiarity and comfort. Where had they come from?

Next to her, Veron seemed unaffected, looking only ahead toward the distant figures of Bianca and his sharp-eyed guard, but his hold on her hand wasn't cold—it was warm, gentle.

Even if neither of them had wanted this, he'd given her no reason to deserve the rumors she'd caused.

"I wanted you to know," she whispered, and he eyed her peripherally, "that I was trying to make a point to my father about choice. With the red dress and raven feathers. I wasn't trying to offend you, although it occurred to me that that's exactly what might've happened. I'm sorry."

"What point was that?" he answered, just as quiet, looking ahead.

She exhaled lengthily. "That we should have a say in our own futures."

He stiffened. "You didn't have a say." That steely velvet voice was low, icy.

A dreaded conclusion?

Willing? he'd asked during the ceremony.

He had cared. Maybe more than she'd assumed.

Her face turned abruptly toward his, then she looked away again, wiping a damp palm on her gown. "I... I did. Although not in the way you might expect. My father betrothed me to my sister's love. I offered to trade places with her."

Those vivid yellow eyes widened, infinitesimally, for just a moment.

She could imagine him summoned to a throne room much like Papà's, his towering figure lowered, kneeling before a dais where his mother held court, surrounded by dour, silent subjects bearing witness from the shadows. His head kept bowed as she decreed her orders that he marry a woman so different from him, so undesirable. Orders he refused to disobey, no matter his feelings on the matter.

"Did your mother ask you whether you wanted this?" she thought aloud.

"No." The answer was matter of fact, as if there could only ever be one answer. "The queen does not *ask*. She expects. And we rise to those expectations. Such is the life of a prince, and of any dark-elf. Ready to sacrifice for the good of the Deep, for the good of all dark-elves."

"Sacrifice," she whispered, repeating the word, and her voice trembled a little.

He would never have been eager for this marriage, and that suited her plans—her plans to convince him that they didn't need to complete the second ceremony in Nightbloom—but there was something so very sad about him having no say in his happiness, something that squeezed at her heart. He was bound up, wrapped in duty like a curse, one he couldn't break.

In this, they were the same.

His hand tightened around hers, just a little. "Forgive me," he said deeply, quietly. He leaned in, toward her, his nearness making her quiver as those vivid eyes met hers and softened. "I spoke without thought."

So near, so close, that terrifying, if alien, beauty was hard to ignore. The slate blue of his skin was the color of distant mountains, blue-gray behind a veil of mist. The color of ancient rock formed in the earth before she had been born, before humans had.

Before she could reply, the doors to the great hall opened, and both Bianca and the sharp-eyed guard stood aside as she and Veron entered. The guests had not yet arrived, but the hall certainly wasn't empty. Servants bustled back and forth, carrying all manner of platters, bottles, glassware, and viands. The musicians were already setting up in the corner, and massive floral arrangements adorned the outskirts of the hall, matching ostentatious centerpieces on tables.

Veron took in everything with a narrow gaze, as if such preparations were foreign to him. Maybe they were. What, exactly, was a dark-elf wedding feast like? She turned to him, but Bianca's soft grip closed around her arm.

"Come," Bianca said with a subtle smile. "Let's get ready for the feast."

The sharp-eyed guard murmured something to Veron, inclining her head.

"See you at dinner, Alessandra," Veron said.

She offered him a smile. With the briefest of looks exchanged, she and Veron parted ways. It wouldn't be long before the guests would start arriving, and she would have to return to the great hall long before Papà could arrive—at least if she wanted to avoid his further ire.

And then... the consummation.

CHAPTER 5

*I*n her dressing chamber, Aless stroked a finger over the swath of crimson chiffon spread out on her chaise longue, ethereal and romantic. A nightgown for later tonight. Bianca had selected it, along with a dazzling array of rubies and gold.

"You make it look like I'm trying to seduce him," Aless muttered.

Behind her, Bianca pinned the train of the red gown. "Maybe that'll make things easier tonight?"

Tonight.

She shivered.

After the feast, she and Veron—along with a host of lords and councilors—would depart to her bedchamber. For the *consummation.* The bed curtains would be drawn, and in the presence of these officials, she and her new dark-elf husband would have to—to—

"Are you scared?" Bianca asked softly.

Scared. Oh yes, she was *scared.*

That is, she had been with many a lover, many a *human* lover. All men she'd chosen herself, strong and handsome, well bred, alluring. With those men, she had been bold, fierce, confident. She had pursued them and seduced them and played with them as she'd pleased. There hadn't been a single worry in her mind, no more than the pulse-pounding mystery of whether each would prove capable and worth her time.

But Veron...

Veron. She ran a fingertip over the scratch on her wrist.

She hadn't even become accustomed to just *looking* at him without holding her breath or shaking. Even his voice rippled shivers down her spine. They'd only just met, were so different from each other—*too* different. Maybe two dark-elves weren't concerned with claws and fangs, as their skin seemed firmer, too.

But one of his claws had only *grazed* her wrist as they'd exited the carriage, and it had left a scratch. Stroking a finger over it, she knitted her eyebrows together. So commonplace a thing, helping a lady out of a carriage, and he had left a mark.

Even if they... overcame their differences, how careful could he be? How much control could he have? Being raised a dark-elf, how much could he know about the limits of a human? In the throes of pleasure, even humans forgot themselves, gave themselves over in mind and body to sensation, and what would happen to her if he did?

The scratch was shallow, almost beneath notice, but if he forgot himself for just a moment—

"Aless?" Bianca stood before her, face pale and creased with worry, and took her hand. "I'm touched that you want to do this for me. I am... and thank you for stepping in. But you don't need to do this. The marriage hasn't been consummated yet, and we could still—"

"I'm—I'm just nervous." Holding a smile in place, she embraced Bianca. There was no way she could even consider sabotaging her sister's happiness. Not when Bianca actually loved Luciano. "Don't worry about me. I'll be fine."

Bianca struggled in her hold. "You're just saying that, and —"

"No," she said, tightening her embrace. Her heart fluttered in her chest, but she had to make Bianca believe everything would be all right. "The witnesses will be there tonight, remember? And after that, I have my plan, right?" Her voice broke, and along with it, her composure. No matter how hard she tried to hold everything in, a couple of lone tears escaped.

She closed her eyes and took three deep breaths.

Never had she wanted to fade away into that sprawling courtyard of overgrown roses more than she did now, surrounded by them and their tangible air of magic, in that place of dreams where she knew she belonged. A thicket of tangling vines, wild and winding, reigning there and yet making a place for her, clearing a corridor through the green and letting her inside.

"I don't want you to do it," Bianca whispered. "I know I said—"

"It's done." Pulling her shoulders back, she moved away and smiled at Bianca, who sniffled softly. "It'll be fine. You'll see. You'll get to marry Luciano, and Veron and I will come to an agreement. Neither of us wants this, so I think he will be motivated to work with me. And then..."

She would still technically be married in the human realm, and Papà would never let her return if she reneged. She would find herself as the Order's ward, at best, and she'd ply every ear among them until the public library was built. A place where she could make a difference.

Her eyes overbright, Bianca gave a small nod. And there it was—an understanding. She had resolved to do this, and Bianca wouldn't fight her.

Good. At least one of them could be happy.

In the mirror, her cloak of raven feathers was gone, and the dramatic wedding gown was pinned up, perfect for dancing. Did the dark-elves dance? Did Veron dance?

"Did you see Papà's face in the abbazia?" Bianca asked with a half-laugh. "I've never seen his eyes so wide. And Lorenzo, his eyebrows shot up so high, but his eyes were half-moons, as if he'd been smiling." Bianca tried to hide a smile herself, but she failed.

Lorenzo was Papà's firstborn son and heir, but for years he had bucked that yoke, struggling in vain for a simple life that he could never have. Oh, if only they could have traded places— she would have gladly accepted the responsibilities he wished to shirk, and he could have as simple a life as he wanted being traded away like a pawn.

"Maybe he'll put in a good word for you with Papà," Bianca added. "Help you get back into Papà's good graces."

"I think he has no more good graces to spare for me." She narrowed her eyes at her own reflection before turning toward the door. There was nothing left for her here. Ahead of her, she had only negotiations with Veron, and a life outside the palazzo, whatever she could make of it. "Come. I think my wedding feast is about to begin."

Bianca joined her as she exited the dressing chamber and headed for the great hall. Tonight, she and Veron would find a way to survive the consummation, but before that, there was an entire hall filled with courtiers, some of whom belonged to the Brotherhood, who were here for a human–dark-elf wedding feast. No doubt Papà had already prepared the Royal Guard, and she would have to prepare herself. As much as she wanted out of this marriage, nothing about her exit strategy could ruin the peace. She wouldn't allow it.

The herald announced her and Bianca, and as they entered, all of the guests seated at the many tables stood, including Veron at the head table, wearing a finely tailored black jacket with silver rose buttons—one of Lorenzo's—form-fitting trousers, and his own boots. Lorenzo must have spoken to him —helped him.

A kindness. *Fine of you, Brother.*

Veron's gaze rested on her, even but purposeful as he clasped his hands behind his back, cutting a strong figure. He didn't look at her with the intensity of the men who had desired her—it didn't take a lot of thinking to realize *why*—but even a serene look like this was unsettling in how perfectly controlled it was. As a child, he must've feared to even have a hair out of place and risk his mother's disapproval. Even now, the shadow of that risk had followed him here.

She and Bianca moved to the viand-laden head table, where a sweetly smiling Luciano pulled out a chair for Bianca as Veron did for her. Those two. They probably already had adorable pet names for each other like *kitten* and *tomcat*.

As she inclined her head to Veron and took a seat, a chill slithered down her spine, and her eyes meandered toward the direction of Papà's gaze.

He was *smiling.*

He raised a goblet to her, glanced past her toward Bianca and Luciano, then leaned back.

Her heart pounding, she stared at the spot he'd leaned into before, at *nothing* now. The low hum of the hall faded in favor of the pulsing thud in her ears, loudening and loudening.

Holy Mother's mercy, he'd—he'd *played* her.

The way he had called both her *and* Bianca into the throne room to announce the marriage arrangements—

He had—he had *manipulated her* into this.

She had never been able to ignore an injustice, not when she could do something to fix it. And Bianca...

Bianca had pined after Luciano for *months*, and Papà was a lot of things, but not ignorant, especially where his *favorite child* was concerned. He could've predicted her exact reaction and planned for it, expecting her to submit for Bianca's sake.

And she *had* submitted.

But not completely, not while she still had moves to make that wouldn't jeopardize Bianca's happiness. Papà wouldn't get away with this. He *couldn't*.

Her hands had gone numb, and there they were in her lap, fisted so tightly her blood wouldn't flow.

Her gaze tracked Papà again. If he'd thought he could play her, *deceive* her, and think her so *stupid*, then he should've thought of the consequences.

These consequences.

Of being outed publicly for his treatment of her, as he'd be right now.

She scraped the chair back, but a hand closed around one of her fists. A slate-blue, clawed hand.

Glaring at Veron, she was about to demand he release her,

when she met that even gaze. That even, tightly controlled gaze, which panned toward the dance floor, and back to her.

He raised his white eyebrows once, as if to encourage an answer.

An answer to what? Had he spoken?

She swallowed, and music filtered in, a prelude—an *extended* prelude. Her clenched hands slowly relaxed.

"Alessandra?" that steely velvet voice asked, but there was a softness there, a gentleness.

"Hmm?"

"The dance." He blinked. "Do you—"

"Oh, yes," she said quickly. The first dance.

Surrounding the dance floor, myriad faces followed her every movement, the collective whole of the nobiltà watching her carefully, watching the *peace* carefully. She'd seemed to oppose Veron during their wedding, and he her, and she still needed to show the semblance of acceptance, if only a little longer. And then hope to transition to genuine, clear friendship.

If she didn't play her part well, the symbolic peace between her and Veron would fail, and along with it... the peace between their peoples.

I won't let that happen.

No matter what Papà had done.

Forcing a smile, she rose with Veron, allowing him to guide her as the musicians yet again extended the prelude, wary of those sharp claws. It would begin with a quessanade.

The quessanade... A human dance. She drew in a sharp breath, and Veron's eyes swept toward her briefly.

"Do you know how to dance the quessanade?" she whispered.

His pale eyebrows drew together, his lips pressed into a thin line. "I know the human dances well—"

Thank the Mother.

"—but I haven't danced in over two thousand years," he answered, not a muscle moving out of turn.

Two thousand—

"Do you trust me?" he whispered, as they approached the center and assumed the position.

Two-thousand-year-old human dances? "You haven't—"

"Do you trust me, Alessandra?" His voice was soft but firm as his hand clasped around her waist, just the barest scrape of claws against tulle.

Either she would have to lead, or... or she would have to trust him.

No, this could go completely—

But as the first movement of the dance suite began, he drew her in close, just barely apart from his chest, and led her in a gliding step, in a whirling rotation that flowed from one turn to another and another. A dazzling array of colors spun around them, but those shimmering golden eyes stayed locked with hers in unbreakable focus, intense, determined, and he kept perfect form, his hold strong but guiding.

This had to be how her ancestors had danced thousands of years ago, face to face, eye to eye, close enough to breathe in that blend of fresh earth and the scent of the purest water, like a forest stream so clear that the smooth stones at the bottom were perfectly visible, their surfaces honed by hundreds of years or more to the sleekness of glass. Her fingers brushed their hardness—but no, it was his shoulder through black brocade. *Holy Mother's mercy, so awkward—*

Those eyebrows pulled inward, and those pale eyelashes

shuttered, his unbreakable focus glimmering a moment as he glanced down at her mouth and back to her eyes.

"Good dance," she breathed.

A corner of his mouth turned up. "They called it the rotante. The young adored it, and the old—"

"Were appalled by it?" she offered, as he led her into a turn.

An amused inclination of his chin as other couples took to the floor, following his lead to attempt this *rotante* themselves. Excited voices and giggles surrounded them.

The closeness of this dance would have been scandalous, no doubt, but by today's standards, it was quite tame compared to the sarabande or the volta. "Unafraid of scandal, Your Highness?"

"Veron," he corrected, searching her eyes. "I... chose the most modern dance I knew."

A two-thousand-year-old dance? She held back a laugh, but when a smile played on his pinched lips, she allowed a grin. If she had succeeded in leading, this would have been a disaster. "How do your people dance at weddings?"

A glimmer. "We don't. We do dance for a few occasions, but for most, we have games."

Games?

Lorenzo cut in, beaming like a debutante newly revealed, and Veron joined their hands with a smile, the point of one of his fangs peaking. *Fangs.*

"Spare your worry, Sister," Lorenzo remarked with a broad grin. "I won't keep you long tonight."

Tonight. She breathed deeply as Lorenzo led her, and Veron took Bianca's hand. The dancing had gone well, but tonight —*that* was an entirely different matter.

"This will be the newest trend at court," Lorenzo drawled. "What is it called?"

"The rotante," she answered.

Tonight, she and Veron would be in a bedchamber, surrounded by officials. She'd be wearing that... *nightdress*—no, that flimsy swath of chiffon that could barely be called a *garment*—and would he ask her to trust him then, too?

"Once you look past all the"—Lorenzo frowned—"*differences*, you might like him, Aless."

Like had nothing to do with it. She *liked* plenty of people well enough, or at least didn't hate them, but that didn't mean she chose to *share a bed* with them. And what about Veron? No doubt he wasn't interested in her either. Did anyone care what he chose? What either of them chose? Or did tradition stand in for choice when Papà or the queen of Nightbloom deemed it so?

Bianca laughed nearby as Veron turned her, his movement controlled, smooth. How much time had he spent learning this dance, and all the others? He had put in more thought and effort as one person learning human culture than the whole of this room had probably spent on his.

And that dark jacket, those tailored trousers—they fit him well, if a bit tight. His build was a bit larger than Lorenzo's, who had a big frame but spent less time training it. He worked enough to hone his skills with the dueling sword and throwing knives, but he'd always preferred beds over training yards.

"Thank you," she said to him, "for the wardrobe change."

With a crooked smile, Lorenzo tilted his head. "Careful, Aless. A kind word or two like that, and rumor may spread that you're going soft."

"Holy Mother forfend," she deadpanned as Lorenzo looked away.

Tarquin cut in before she could object, dark-brown eyes gleaming in that too-handsome face. After what he'd said the night of the masquerade and his rumored membership in the Brotherhood, she wasn't interested in learning any more of him and his hatred. She followed his lead, but her entire body had gone rigid.

"Even a lion can be afraid sometimes," he said carefully as he glided into step.

"That is when they are most dangerous." She didn't meet his eyes. Wouldn't. He didn't merit the respect.

"A sole lion may be defeated with ease," he replied, not missing a beat, "but only if it forgets its true strength. The pride."

The Brotherhood? "This lion has no need of a pride," she bit out.

"You don't need to wear a mask, princess," Tarquin whispered. "Not with me. The pride is watching. Only say the word, anytime, anywhere, that you protest, and our strength will... relieve your solitude."

She shivered. Anytime? Anywhere? How could—

He was already gone, and Luciano was in his place, smiling. "Well, Your Highness, what do you make of this dance?" He led her into it.

This dance was becoming dangerous. And now, more than ever, with the *pride's* eyes on her, she'd have to watch her step.

CHAPTER 6

*V*eron paced the length of the bathing chamber, disrobed down to his shirt and braies. Pausing, he yanked off his boots—well made, but too tight—and resumed his circuit.

They waited in there—the human councilors and lords, their holy men—to know this marriage would be completed.

That was a problem.

To the humans, a marriage was incomplete without what they called the *consummation*. The first act of lovemaking between a bride and her groom. For royals, especially, as often-times such massive consequences relied on marriages, it was imperative that the consummation be viewed by credible witnesses and its performance marked in documents. He well knew this, as it had been so even two thousand years into the past.

Alessandra's attire had been a statement, she'd said, and it had had an effect, based on the humans' gasps in their shrine.

Or perhaps arriving in full armor on horseback with all one's weapons was not the marriage custom here.

But she hadn't stopped. Her arm had remained wrapped around his, and she had proceeded down the aisle. Whatever statement she'd been making, it hadn't been a refusal. Nothing good, but... not a refusal.

They hadn't spoken the entire ride to the palace, and hardly at all during the feast. Instead, they had just danced, then eaten the humans' food silently while the guests had drunk themselves into a stupor.

And then... this.

Riza had been right; even if both he and Alessandra had been unwilling, this ceremony had needed to happen. As right as she was, everything inside him right now didn't care.

There would be a woman in the next room, his new bride, with whom he would have to consummate this marriage. His likely *unwilling* bride.

To do so would be—

Dishonorable. Unconscionable. Vile.

An answer. He needed to find an answer.

A door clicked shut in the other room. Alessandra.

He stared at his own door. How long had it been? He shouldn't have left her to be the first one out. *He* should have awaited *her*.

First, they'd exchange gifts, and then—

He eyed the long, flat wooden box on the nearby table. There had been no way to know whether she was a skilled archer or not; if she was, she'd appreciate the Nozva Rozkvetan rosewood bow, and if she wasn't, he'd teach her everything she needed to know. But would she like it?

With a deep breath, he rolled up his sleeves, tucked the box under one arm, then opened the door.

In the scant candlelight, she stood on the other side of the room, wearing a long, flowing red sheer nightgown that pooled on the floor, with a wrapped parcel in her delicate hands. She wore jewels on her fingers, wrist, ears, and around her neck in a ruby-encrusted golden necklace. Her hair was loose and voluminous, a warm brown like rain-dampened cypress bark, a shade lighter than her dark eyes. The nightgown hung by thin, delicate straps, leaving her long, elegant arms bare.

He suppressed a shiver. Every part of her looked so *soft*. There was no hardiness to her, just give... Give that would have never survived the difficult conditions in Nozva Rozkveta, nor any queendom in the Deep for that matter, if she were on her own.

But now she had *him*. Together, they'd survive anything.

She moved to the window, as far away from the hovering group of humans as possible, and he joined her. Nearly shoulder to shoulder, he looked out at the dark city with her, glittering with lights as far as the eye could see, beneath a starry sky.

What could he say to her?

Mati had ordered this. He trusted her completely, had pledged his allegiance to her. Whatever she ordered, he would do.

And Alessandra, she had orders from her father, too, didn't she? Neither of them wanted this, but for the sake of the peace, they had to show a united front.

Just before the dance tonight, the way she'd gone rigid in her chair—something had angered her. Made her livid. She'd had that wild look about her, like a volodara about to go berserk, and he hadn't been certain whether his touch would quell that wildness or unleash it.

One of the humans in the group cleared his throat impatiently.

"Alessandra," he whispered, placing the box on the ample windowsill, and she peered down at it, eyebrows raised, then eyed him. "Accept this gift as a token of my commitment."

With a soft smile, she grazed the length of the box with a fingertip before gently flicking open the brass closure. She lifted the lid, revealing the deep reddish-brown Nozva Rozkvetan rosewood short bow. Her eyes flashed bright as reverent fingertips smoothed over the wood. "It's beautiful," she breathed.

"Only the royalty and kuvari of Nozva Rozkveta are permitted bows of our rosewood. Its perfect balance of density and strength make it the most sought-after bow wood in the land." Or at least it *had* been two thousand years ago. "Do you know how to use a bow?"

A light blush. "Papà forbade it. I've only attempted it once, and I can't say I was very good."

"If you wish to learn, I will teach you," he said, brushing the rosewood. "I will always do my all for you, and that includes helping you hone skills to hunt for and defend yourself, should you ever need to."

For a moment, she didn't move, didn't speak, just watched the bow with a dreamlike intensity, and then finally she nodded, breathing in lengthily as if awaking. "Thank you. I'd love to learn, Veron."

It would be something they could do together while they got to know one another. Perhaps, in time, they'd be friends.

She extended her own wrapped parcel to him brightly. "This is for you."

By its shape, it was clearly a book. About what? He accepted it and cut through the twine with a claw, eliciting a gasp. Her hand covered her wrist, but not before he glimpsed a hair-thin scratch. Fresh, recent—

No. Had he—?

He hadn't meant to, but at the feast, or—

When I helped her out of the carriage.

"Alessandra, did I—"

"It's fine." She grinned, *beamed*. Forced it.

By Deep and Darkness, he'd *hurt* her. He hadn't even known, and he'd caused her injury. "Forgive me, I—"

Only her eyes indicated the direction of the human officials, and she gave the slightest shake of her head.

So she didn't want them to know about this. If the humans found out, they might call him—and all dark-elves—dangerous. Violent. Incompatible with human society.

All dark-elves had claws, their look and sharpness a point of strength. A clawless dark-elf would be like a toothless lion, weakened, devalued, seen as lesser—something any child of Mati's could not do, so as not to reflect poorly on her or Nozva Rozkveta.

But Alessandra—

Smiling, she nodded toward the parcel. "I hope you like it, but if—"

He drew away the paper wrapping with a rustle, revealing a thick tome. *A Modern History of Silen.* Well, he could certainly stand to learn what had transpired in two thousand years of stone slumber.

On the title page, in elegant calligraphic script it said, *To*

Veron: Silen would be honored to create history with Nightbloom as these final pages are filled with the peace we will forge together. Aless

These final pages? A thrill wove through him as he glanced up at her sparkling eyes and turned to the back of the tome. Of its thousand pages, perhaps two to three hundred were blank at the end.

He huffed his amusement softly. A thoughtful gift. She intended for him to write in their peoples' shared history into this Sileni tome, a symbolic gesture. The last time he'd written in a book, it had been sketching with Ata, as he'd taught him about the sky realm and its exotic flora and fauna, before Ata had—

"It was newly transcribed," she said, eagerly thumbing the gilded pages, "and the bookmaker left space to continue recording, just like in the copy my mother gave me." Her eyes brightened. "Actually, the latest Magister Trials from a few weeks ago were just added, and only this edition—maybe only *this* first new transcription—has it. The Emaurrian candidate, in the second trial, she looked the Grand Divinus in the eye, and, well, you'll see, but—"

He grinned at her over the tome, and she bit her lip. So books excited her. A *lot*. Something they could share. "Thank you. I look forward to filling up these remaining pages."

As she reddened, another throat-clearing came from the councilors. They were beginning to grate on his nerves.

Alessandra glanced over her shoulder, then back at him. "It's time," she said quietly. Gravely. They left the bow and the book together on the windowsill.

Steeling himself, he offered her his hand, and with a swallow, she took it. He ignored the crowd as he escorted her to the curtained bed, pulled aside the ethereal fabric, and helped her up. She sat stiffly, her olive skin pebbled against a chill, and fidgeted with the sheer red fabric of her nightgown. He didn't look at it too closely, didn't dare, especially when she seemed so nervous.

But that wasn't what tonight was about, for either of them. It was about trust. They had both been ordered into roles they'd never desired, and for the sake of the peace, for the sake of their peoples, they wouldn't buck these roles, even if they were neither attracted to one another nor in love. So they had to build trust, a friendship, a partnership. If any of this was to succeed, those bonds would be crucial between them. And at least a foundation.

She would have every honor, and more. She would have everything she needed, everything she wanted, anything on this earth that he could provide.

There was a washbasin nearby, and he took it—and a towel —to the edge of the bed, placed it on the floor by her feet. She eyed the basin curiously, and another human in the group cleared his throat again.

Alessandra lowered her gaze.

By Deep and Darkness, not only were these humans to *witness* this "consummation" they demanded, but they intended to hurry it along, too? And to interfere? Such blatant disrespect, for him, and worse, for *her*. The night of the Offering, the acceptance, was *private*. A time when a couple calmed after feasting and games, comforted one another, affirmed their vows in private—and, if they so chose, made love. It was a sacred moment for two, and two only.

Another throat clearing. "Your Highness, if we could—"

"No." He speared the elderly little human with a glare and strode to the exit doors. Enough was enough.

He pulled them open, then gestured to the humans. "Out. Now."

They all stared at him, then exchanged glances with one another.

"Your Highness," the same human objected, "it is this kingdom's custom that—"

"It is not my custom, nor that of my people, nor was it part of the marriage agreement that this 'consummation' be witnessed. Leave. Now." He stood firm, his glare at them unwavering, steeling through his uncertainty.

Mati knew the full details of the agreement; he didn't. She had told him what he'd needed to know, and she hadn't mentioned this specifically. It was possible he was wrong.

But he had to try.

One by one, the group of humans trickled out into the hall, until only the one who had spoken remained. The little man stared back at him defiantly.

Whispers came from the hall. "What will he do to her?" one asked. "Perhaps we should call a healer," another suggested.

Veron didn't break eye contact with the little man. This was the sort of idiotic ignorance they aimed to defeat. And as much as he wanted to *defeat* it right in its bulbous nose, *defeat* it until it shrieked in fear and then fled, instead he took a breath.

Finally, he closed the distance between them—the man cowered—and baring his teeth, Veron shoved him out into the hall, where Riza and Gavri were posted. He shut the doors on the whispering gossip and wide eyes, and turned the lock.

A cough came from the bed.

He turned, and Alessandra was observing him over the rim of a wine goblet as she drank.

"What will you do to me, dark-elf prince?" she mocked with

a nervous laugh, then took another sip before setting the goblet down. "Will you chop me up into little pieces and eat me? Will you skin me alive and wear my hide?"

He shook his head, and a grin rent free. "I don't know. Perhaps we should call a healer."

Another nervous laugh. Hopefully he could put her mind at ease.

He moved back to the bed, back to the basin. Her curious gaze followed him, the mirth still glimmering there as he lowered to a knee and rolled up his other sleeve. He gestured to her foot. "May I?"

She frowned, a small, puzzled one, but nodded.

Silky fabric brushed against his fingertips as he lifted the hem of her nightgown, baring her feet. They were narrow, small, unblemished, as if she hadn't ever walked barefoot on the stone. Perhaps she hadn't.

He gently bathed one in the warm water, smoothing his hands against her too-soft skin.

She shivered, then smiled. "Is this a dark-elf custom?"

"It is." He patted her first foot dry, then grasped the other delicately and repeated the process. "On the night of the Offering, it says to a bride, 'I am not too proud to serve you. I will never be too proud to serve you. It is my honor and pleasure.'"

She held her breath as he poured water onto her skin from his cupped hand. Slowly, sluggishly, she blinked. "Things are quite different where you're from."

He laughed. He could say the same to her. The outlandish things that had happened today alone could fill an entire tome. "Different... in a bad way?"

She shook her head. "Just... different."

After toweling her other foot dry, he set the basin and towel aside. She moved over in the bed, and he went to the hearth and put another log on the fire.

His heart pounded as it never had. It wasn't fear, exactly, as he'd had lovers before this and knew what happened between a man and a woman. This was required for her human kingdom to acknowledge the marriage.

But no part of her was anything like a dark-elf woman, not ferocious, nor intimidating, nor dangerous. No claws, no fangs, no muscle nor combat prowess to speak of. Was human love-making anything like the fierce, raging, unrestrained madness that was a night with a dark-elf woman?

There had been a gleam in her eye, when she'd taken off the white cloak in the abbazia, that could have rivaled that of any queen of the Deep. Heat flushed in his chest. That look had been ferocious, yes, but fleeting. Then the wildness smoldering in her at the feast... as her fists had clenched tightly enough to break.

But to her, he was little better than a beast, wasn't he? Nothing like a human man. Not someone she desired nor envisioned herself with.

There were no witnesses here. Not anymore. Would it really *matter* if this consummation happened?

With a silent exhalation, he turned back to the bed, offered her what he hoped was a consoling smile, and joined her, careful to keep his distance.

He sat next to her as she lay deathly still, barely moving but to breathe. Staring up at the bed's canopy with intense focus, she looked as though she were preparing herself mentally for an amputation.

He suppressed a laugh. No, he really oughtn't laugh at her when she was making such an effort to bear this indignity.

"Alessandra, I do not share *their*"—he nodded to the door—"expectations for this night. You need not fear me."

Only her eyes moved in his direction, wide and a chatoyant tiger's-eye brown. "But the consummation—"

"Is not a custom required by my people." He kept his bearing loose, open, unthreatening.

She blinked, her breath coming faster, harder, shifting that sheer red fabric of her nightgown in folds. "Then you don't wish to"—she closed her eyes—"to..."

"No." He watched the tension melt from her body. "This arrangement is new to both of us."

She sat up, leaned her back against the pillows, and nodded, bunching up the covers at her chest.

"Neither of us wants that tonight, but I don't mean to close the door on this, either. I want you to know that I'm open to your wishes, and that you shouldn't fear rejection should you express them to me." Now that they'd made the Offering to each other, she would never be heartsore with him, ever, not if he could help it.

She reddened. "But you don't find me desirable?"

Raising his eyebrows, he looked away. She'd asked that directly? Admirable, and... difficult. "You're intelligent and bold, but we only just met yesterday. I am yours and yours alone, but this... will take some time."

She laughed. "So then you don't."

"I don't need to ask you the same." He hid a smile.

She slapped the duvet. "You're the first dark-elf I've ever seen face to face!"

"So then... you don't." It was his turn to laugh.

She waved him off and sighed. "Good. I'm glad we cleared the air."

"So am I. Trust is the one expectation I have," he answered.

A long silence. "Veron, I... There are many things I want to discuss with you, but I don't wish to offend you. Well, to offend you more than I already have."

He huffed. It would take more than a style of clothing to offend him. "You haven't. And you can discuss anything with me."

She bit her lip, stroking the duvet. "Maybe after Bianca's wedding?"

That was in three days. It seemed as though she planned to attend.

There was only one problem: he was under strict orders from Mati to leave with her tomorrow. "Alessandra, we... we can't stay."

Her eyebrows drawn together, she stared at him. "What?"

"We're scheduled to leave tomorrow." Had her father not told her about the schedule for the Royal Progress? The famine in the queendoms?

She threw off the covers and knelt on the bed, angling to face him. "Veron, my sister is marrying in three days. My *sister*."

"I know," he said gently, but even so, her eyes were widening, glistening. "I'm sorry, but—"

"It's my sister's wedding. I can't—won't—miss it," she said with a vehement shake of her head.

"I cannot disobey a direct order, Alessandra." No matter how much he wished she could stay. "Not even for this. And we have a strict schedule—"

"Please," she said, her voice breaking. "I'm begging you. I can't miss her wedding—I can't. She and I, we've always been the closest of all my brothers and sisters, and she's in love with him, Veron. This will be the happiest day of her life, and you and I are moving away. I have to be there, please, just for her wedding, so could we just delay our departure, just a little, shift the Royal Progress arrangements, only until after Bianca's wedding, and—"

Tears rolled down her cheeks as he shook his head.

Her father really hadn't told her anything. Had let her hold out hope.

Holy Ulsinael, he wanted to take her in his embrace, comfort her, but what could he say? He had orders from Mati. Vadiha and Dita were *starving*, as were the rest of his people, who awaited them and *food* on specific days. Nothing would change that they had to leave tomorrow. "People are expecting us, expecting we'll bring—"

With a sob, she covered her mouth and scrambled from the bed.

"Alessandra, let me just—"

She stormed out to her dressing chamber, then slammed the door behind her.

CHAPTER 7

*I*n the palazzo's courtyard, Aless stood before Papà in the weak morning sunlight. Even after manipulating her into a marriage, he still hadn't been done trying to break her. He and the queen of Nightbloom had set the Royal Progress schedule, and everyone involved had known about it but *her*.

Papà had *known* she'd miss Bianca's wedding, and he'd said nothing. He'd even left Veron to break that bitter news.

Ever since Mamma's death, Papà had looked at her differently, and a distance had grown between them, and grown and grown. Everything she cared about was wrong, and anything she did was punished, and it seemed he was never done punishing her. She hadn't fit in here, not in a long while, and now she was leaving, for maybe the last time.

Bianca had finally gotten what she'd so long carried a ladder for in that orchard of daydreams.

And Papà couldn't have even given *her* the sweet farewell of witnessing Bianca's wedding. Not even that.

"You are so much like her," Papà said, his dark-brown eyes dull. "This will be best for you."

So like *Mamma*. Mamma, whose entire palazzo library and every book he'd had destroyed.

No, this was best for *him*. Getting rid of her, like he'd gotten rid of Mamma's memory.

"Remember your promise," he whispered.

"Goodbye, Papà," she replied, before moving to Lorenzo, who wrapped her in his arms.

"I sent some things along with you for Veron," he said, "so you two can match in equally... haute couture. Despite the piety of Stroppiata, Duchessa Claudia is a fashion snob."

"Thank you." With a half-laugh under her breath, she pulled away from Lorenzo as he gave her a soft smile.

"You're getting away from the palazzo," he whispered with a twinkle in his eye. "Make the most of it."

Unlike him, she'd never wanted to escape the palazzo, but rather to become a more useful part of it. Maybe that was what she had carried a ladder for, only for her, it would ever remain a daydream.

"Make the most of being here, too, Brother," she whispered back, giving his stubbled cheek a goodbye kiss as she at last turned to Bianca.

Veron clasped arms with Lorenzo as she took Bianca's hand and met her eyes, red and welling with glistening tears. With a lace-trimmed white handkerchief, Bianca dabbed at her face, her lower lip trembling, then shook her head sadly.

Aless pulled Bianca into her arms, holding her tight. Next to her, Veron said his goodbyes to Lorenzo.

At their wedding, Veron had said, *I, Veron of Nozva Rozkveta, offer you power, survival, support, defense, wisdom, and partnership, to harness for your ends or ours, as we walk our lives together from this day forward for as long as the Deep allows.*

Papà had kept this from her, yes, and he bore the brunt of the blame. But she'd begged Veron, *begged* him to delay their departure, shift the Royal Progress arrangements, just until after Bianca's wedding.

But his *mother* had given him a direct order, and that had been that.

What was important to her was supposed to be important to him, too, wasn't it? What would life be like if even this hadn't merited some compromise?

Bianca wept softly into her shoulder. "We've sent the package to Nunzio."

Good. Then she could discuss the plans with him when she arrived in Stroppiata, where the Order of Terra was head-quartered.

All the more reason to persuade Veron against the second ceremony, if he'd listen. If he'd even be *open* to viewpoints other than that of his mother and queen, that is.

Honesty is the one expectation I have, he'd said. Fine words. But what good had her honesty done her about Bianca's wedding? She'd tell him her plan once they were on better terms, once she'd proven she could deliver a peace before the second ceremony.

Bianca sniffled. "I just wish—"

"I know. I'm so sorry, Bianca," she whispered, stroking Bianca's hair softly. "I wish I could stay."

"I'll visit you," Bianca cried. "I promise."

A lovely thought. She pulled away and smiled softly. "You'd

better. I'll want to hear every detail."

Bianca beamed through her tears and nodded, swiping a muslin-clad arm across her face, a smiling, weeping, loving face against the backdrop of lush green and the white stone of the palazzo.

This was it. Goodbye, as no matter what happened from here on, she'd never live under Papà's roof again.

Papà, standing first in line, raised his chin and met her eyes. He'd been the first to bid her goodbye, reminding her of her promise. She remembered all right. She'd promised to *wed* Veron, which she had done, and the rest was up to her and Veron.

Papà tipped his head toward the waiting cavalcade just as Gabriella took her arm, leading her away. With food, coin, her belongings, and picture books for the children along the Royal Progress, the number of carts had grown.

"Come, Your Highness," Gabriella said. "We've a long road ahead of us."

A long road indeed.

She fisted her gray skirts. Just as she was about to turn away, Veron approached Bianca—and bowed. Low.

In the ensuing silence, he remained utterly still, his powerful form as if sculpted from stone, ready to endure for centuries, millennia.

He'd bowed. Apologized to Bianca.

Bianca's perfectly sculpted eyebrows shot up.

So did hers.

ALESS PULLED ASIDE the curtain in her carriage. All was verdant and beautiful outside—the cypress trees lining the road, the

fields of grass, the umbrella pines in the distance, and the occasional fields of artichokes or orchards of lemon trees. So bright
and cheerful. Maybe Bianca was airing out her wedding dress
right now, smiling and laughing with her ladies-in-waiting,
preparing for the big day.

Veron had apologized to Bianca, but he'd still gotten his
way, hadn't he? Could he be trusted, or did he only wear a
mantle of earnestness, beneath which only his mother's will
lived and breathed? Begging him had been awkward, but being
rejected had been even more awkward.

He rode just ahead, his hooded figure nevertheless identifi-
able by his broad shoulders and bearing, atop that massive
beast he called a horse. She narrowed her eyes.

He glanced over his shoulder in her direction.

With a huff, she yanked the curtains shut and crossed her
arms.

"I'd hoped he'd find a way for you two to remain for Her
Highness's wedding," Gabriella whispered from the seat next
to her.

At least Papà had sent *one* familiar face with her.

"Will his mother always have the final say over everything?"
Gabriella asked under her breath.

"Too early to tell." Aless exhaled slowly, stroking the cotton
batiste of her gray skirts. But it seemed Veron didn't have a
disobedient bone in his body. He'd been reasonable and kind,
and because of that, she'd hoped he might soon hear her out
about a friendship instead of a marriage.

But now she wasn't so certain.

If his mother had ordered this union, then to alter that, it
would take more than simply *asking* in order to convince him.
She'd need to sort out the library plans with Nunzio and

present Veron with an idea for a joint venture, something to symbolize their peoples' new peace and ongoing friendship. A place where humans and dark-elves could unite.

It would start with this one place, the library, and then grow. Maybe someday, Silen would be a land where humans, dark-elves, light-elves, and other peaceful Immortali all lived together in harmony.

Once she and Nunzio spoke and planned in concrete terms, she could bring their ideas to Veron and hope for the best.

Gabriella patted her hand, imparting warmth with a gentle hazel-eyed look. "I wish they weren't so cold to you, Your Highness," she said. "Perhaps it would be better if the Brotherhood helped you escape? Would they do that, or would it have to be violent?"

The Brotherhood—no. She did not want any part of that. As much as she wanted freedom from this marriage, she didn't wish for the Brotherhood's plan of fire and death to succeed.

"Before we left," Gabriella continued, "there was word that they sacked a light-elf settlement near the coast. People were saying the Brotherhood put all of them on a ship to Sonbahar in the dead of night."

Sonbahar? For what? The slave markets? Unthinkable. "Are you certain?"

"That's what they're saying, and that now the surrounding villages will be 'safe.' They seemed just fine before."

Safe? Safe from what?

There had been rumors that sick or misbehaving children were light-elf changelings, that any maiden or child that disappeared was abducted by the light-elves or the other Immortali. That light-elves cursed crops, stole random trinkets from people's homes, poisoned livestock...

But surely no one had believed such farfetched tales? Light-elves had no magic and rarely if ever ventured out of their forests. They placed no value on jewels or precious metals, let alone worthless trinkets.

Human women fled their husbands, children got lost, crops failed, livestock died. It was easier to blame the Immortali than to accept the cruelty of everyday life. And the Brotherhood encouraged it.

"Where was this?" she whispered back to Gabriella.

"Near Portopersico, I think."

A small village on the coast just east of Bellanzole—there had been a light-elf settlement nearby?

Tarquin and the Belmonte Company had been clearing out harpy nests near Bellanzole. Had he led this attack? He and his watchful "pride"? Where would they strike next?

It would be days before she and Veron would arrive at Stroppiata, their first stop, where they'd be presented to the duchessa, to earn a promise of her friendship. Too long of a time to go without news. She'd have to tell Veron about the Brotherhood and—

"Just how many trunks of silks and baubles do humans need to cart around?" the dark-elf guard with the braid asked outside the carriage, in *Sileni*, no less. Clearly wanting to be overheard.

The sharp-eyed guard shushed her, but Veron grunted in reply. It was about as much as he'd said all day since their argument last night.

The dark-elves had gaped at her luggage—really, it was only ten large trunks or so; she'd packed light for *moving her entire life*. What did they expect, for her to bring just one change of clothes and nothing else?

Besides, the cavalcade had left Bellanzole with dozens of carts bearing food and coins, all to distribute to humans and dark-elves alike along the Royal Progress. No complaints about *those*, it seemed.

"They have no respect," Gabriella muttered. "You are a princess of Silen. You travel and dress in the style befitting your station."

Nothing she was and nothing she had was acceptable to the dark-elves. Everything she owned was extravagant, unnecessary, indulgent. They wouldn't be pleased until she wore a burlap sack and tied her hair with a daisy chain. "Fortunately, I don't care what they think."

Gabriella smiled and gave her a nod of encouragement. "Besides, all that leather can't possibly be comfortable. Their fashions don't have to be ours, do they?"

She smiled back. Her dresses won over leathers any day, but especially Sileni summer days.

"And what an insult," Gabriella added, pursing her lips, "to provide you with no household."

That had been the least of her concerns. Even if Veron agreed to her plan, she'd never have any wealth to speak of ever again. All of her wealth had come from Papà, and by his choice. He'd never welcome her back after this, so... so she'd have to learn to do things for herself.

She had what she needed for camp. Papà's household had packed an elaborate silk tent, and naturally, he had sent no one to pitch it.

No one but her.

"We'll make do," she answered. Compared to dealing with Papà, it wouldn't be hard at all. Not like telling Veron about the Brotherhood—and Tarquin—would be.

CHAPTER 8

*V*eron pounded his tent's first stake into the ground while Alessandra and Gabriella rifled through the countless packs and chests from Bellanzole. "Has the princess been given one of our tents?"

Gavri huffed under her breath. "Yes, she has. I saw to it myself. No doubt she's turning her nose up at it. Typical human."

Stubborn, spoiled human princess. Dark-elves *and* humans were dying daily, fighting over senseless reasons, and Vadiha and Dita were *starving* waiting for this food from Bellanzole. He and Alessandra were tasked with sowing peace, ending the famine, and she'd wanted to let them keep suffering longer for a wedding? Of course she'd wanted to be there for such an important day in her sister's life, but delaying the Royal Progress for that would have had negative consequences for so many more people—starving people—that Alessandra either didn't seem to notice or didn't concern herself with. He set another stake and hammered it.

"How dare she treat you with such disrespect," Gavri added, but Riza glared at her. "You don't need to appease her, Your Highness." When Riza snarled at her, Gavri held up her hands and backed away before taking her leave.

It didn't matter. Disrespect? He didn't care about that. There was far more at stake. Their union and this Royal Progress through the realm was their one chance to stop the flow of blood before all-out war, and Alessandra couldn't see past her own immediate family. Even beyond Mati's orders, there was sound reason she ignored because it suited her.

She paid lip service to peace, but did she even understand what war truly was? The stench of blood and entrails after combat, the screaming widows and crying orphans? The disease that came after, and the famine resulting from the loss of able-bodied people and the bankruptcy of the powers financing it all?

Had she ever looked any of them in the eye, or had she only heard news from her lady-in-waiting and seen paintings of battles in the grand human ballroom, while faceless servants filled her goblet and brought platters of cakes and fruits?

He moved along the tent's round edge, and Riza handed him another stake.

"Give her time, Your Highness," she said nonchalantly as he hammered.

He speared Riza with a peripheral glare as he moved along. Could time fix this?

"She is young. Very young. And has been kept sheltered," Riza said, handing him the stakes as he needed them. "Now that she is touring her own land, her eyes will open to many things. Be patient." Riza stepped back and admired his work, then hmphed under her breath. She nodded toward the carts, where Alessandra and Gabriella were removing a large, bundled tent.

A *yurta*, or at least similar to what his people used for more permanent camps. What about the smaller tent Gavri had given her?

"Perhaps you may need to be a little *more* patient."

Alessandra's *yurta* was about six times the size of this tent, twice as tall, and made of purple-and-white-striped canvas. That monstrosity would take at least three people and two hours to assemble.

"Humans are drawn to ostentation like harpies to anything shiny." Riza tsked and brushed a hand through her short hair. "That thing, for one night's camp? At this rate, she'll be sleeping outside."

He rubbed his chin, then sighed. "No matter how we disagree, my bride will always have a place to sleep." He'd suggest the tent Gavri had given her; hopefully Alessandra would see reason.

Riza nodded, a faint smile on her lips. "You treat her like a dark-elf bride, Your Highness—albeit a very inadequate one."

"She *is* a dark-elf bride, Riza."

She raised an eyebrow, then her mouth curved wider. "Her Majesty would be proud of you."

Deep, Darkness, and Holy Ulsinael willing. But this wasn't just for Mati's praise; he and Alessandra would now be living a life together. He needed to make amends, and she... well, *she* needed a tent pitched.

Rubbing his face, he headed toward the heap Alessandra was now digging through. Her skirts in the dirt, she burrowed under the purple-and-white stripes, muttering while Gabriella held the canvas. As soon as he took hold of it, Gabriella released it, inclined her head, and excused herself.

"Raise it higher, Gabriella. It's suffocating in here," Alessandra said. Except Gabriella was making her way across the camp.

Suppressing a grin, he did as she bade.

Wood thudded against wood and ropes hissed while she shuffled around inside. "Yours looked so simple, but this one is —not. I'm definitely not going to ask *him* for help. Are you certain there are no instructions?"

He schooled his face. "None that I saw," he answered, unable to hold back the amused lilt.

No answer came as she froze beneath the canvas, then scooted completely under it.

"Alessandra..."

A heavy sigh. "I suppose you're here to tell me you have *orders* that we must share your tent."

He took a slow, deep breath. A *very* slow, deep breath. "I'm here to ask you whether I can pitch the tent Gavri gave you."

"Who?" she shot back. "No one gave me anything."

He rested a hand on his hip. "One of our tents. She gave you one."

"No, she didn't, whoever *she* is. I think I'd remember that."

Then what? Gavri had made it all up? Why? She wouldn't betray him. *Ever.* As one of his best friends, Gavri *knew* his father had lied to him once, just *once*, and had never returned to Nozva Rozkveta. Gavri would never—

"Besides, I have my own, thank you."

He scoffed. "Even for three experienced people, this tent would take at least two hours to put together."

She hmphed. "Oh, *now* you want to help me?"

This again. "I already told you—there are greater concerns than—"

"No, there aren't. That's what you led me to believe. That when it came to making an Offering, it meant there were no greater concerns." A tremor shook her words. "But I suppose my understanding doesn't matter, only your mother's commands."

He shook his head. "Our first stop is the city of Stroppiata in two days," he said gently. "Did you know they've planned our reception for weeks now?"

"A reception can be postponed," she shot back.

"How about a parade route, a banquet, and the feast the duchess promised her people? Those people are waiting for us to arrive in exactly two days." When she didn't reply, he added, "And then three days after that, we're going to Dun Mozg—you may know it as Dunmarrow—a small dark-elf queendom farther inland. Queen Nendra's people are starving, and they're expecting us that day, will be celebrating us that day. My own sister barely has the energy to feed her newborn daughter, and we are bringing her food in Nozva Rozkveta. How long should she wait while we postpone for a wedding?"

A barely audible throat clearing came from the tent. "Why didn't you tell me that sooner? That the people were expecting us on specific days?"

"I told you we had a strict schedule, that people were expecting us." But even as he'd spoken the words then, she'd stormed out in tears and hadn't wanted to listen to another word.

And he shouldn't blame her for it. At least she seemed of a mind to listen now.

"I didn't know about your sister. I didn't think the people were looking forward to the specific day. I thought..." A deep breath. "I don't know what I thought."

To people who barely survived on rations, the distribution of plentiful food was everything. She had to know that. Didn't she notice the suffering of people now living in her own land?

The canvas shifted as she slowly wriggled out from under it, her brown eyes big as she eyed him, dusting off her dirt-marred hands. When there had been no servants to pitch her tent, she'd gotten her own hands dirty. She'd tried to do it herself. Perhaps she wasn't as spoiled as he'd thought, just... hadn't been allowed beyond the walls of the world she knew.

"You were thinking about your sister," he said softly and crouched to meet her at eye level. "When my mother told me the schedule, I didn't realize my bride's sister's wedding would be a few days later. If I'd known..." He would have wanted to speak up, to ask Mati whether he and his bride would be allowed to stay, perhaps send some food on ahead. "I'm sorry."

Kneeling in the grass, she rested her smudged hands in her lap, centered on the gray fabric. Errant dark curls had escaped her elaborate coiled hairstyle, framing her face, spilling over slender shoulders. She bit her lip. "I should have heard you out. I'm sorry, too."

There was so much more to discuss. The night of their wedding, she'd also mentioned wanting to talk to him about something. But this... unfortunate situation with Bianca had thwarted everything.

He rested a hand on hers. "Come with me. I'll find you another tent."

As he began to rise, she took his hand. "Wait. Can I sleep with you tonight?"

The question stopped him—stopped him completely—but he swallowed and helped her up as he stood.

"I mean—" she whispered. "Won't it look bad if we sleep apart? As if we don't agree, as if there's disharmony between us."

She was right, but there *had been* disharmony between them.

He'd assumed separate tents, but... "As long as it doesn't make you uncomfortable."

"It doesn't." Her brief smile lit up her face with its brightness, just for a moment. It reached her eyes, their beautiful darkness gleaming, like moonlight over rippling night waters.

He hefted her pack and her bedroll, then led her toward his tent, nodding greetings to the faces that turned to them. What he'd wanted was to keep looking into those eyes, so different than the ones he was accustomed to, all in shades of amber and gold. But the surface of those night waters had rippled, and there was something lurking there that she hadn't revealed. Until she did, the risk of drowning, no matter how small, wasn't worth the consequence.

He'd already trusted a liar once. Watched Ata leave their family. Only to be crippled by the news of the truth.

Never again.

And Gavri—if she'd lied—

No, there was no excuse.

He settled Alessandra into his tent, and then went back to the heap of a *yurta* they'd left behind and packed it up. Unlike human royalty, he didn't travel with a legion of servants; dark-elves were expected to do nearly everything for themselves. Of course she wouldn't have known that.

Humans had such different values, but Alessandra... She

was to spend her life in Nozva Rozkveta. It wasn't easy being a newcomer to a strange place; if he had been tasked with living in Bellanzole, no doubt Alessandra would have helped him find his way among the humans. And he could do no less—*would* do no less—for her.

Once he'd finally put the bundled tent back in the cart, he dug through his pack for his pipe and glanced back to check on Alessandra.

Outside the tent, Gavri stood, arms crossed, her brow creased. Her fire-bright eyes smoldered, every inch of her battle hard. What did any of this matter to her?

It clearly did, though.

She'd done it. She'd lied.

When she finally looked away, he caught her gaze. That battle hardness softened, her gaze cooled, and her mouth dropped open a moment before she closed it anew.

He jerked his head to come hither, and biting her lip, she approached.

"Your Highness, I only meant to—"

Scowling, he held up a hand. "You lied."

She met his eyes, wouldn't look away, that crease returning to her brow as she crossed her arms. "She put on that *show* in her ignorant human city and made you look like some barbarian, abducting her from—"

He leaned in. "*I. Don't. Care.*"

Gavri had known him for his entire life. She should've known better. She had known better.

And this was about some minor hiccup in his arranged marriage? It had been a few years, but maybe she was still sore over Zoran making the Offering to Queen Nendra.

"Everyone at home is just suffering so much, and she throws

these little fits over her whims. Rebellion. Disobedience." She ran a hand over her hair, down the length of her braid, and exhaled a sigh through her nose. "You deserve—"

"I am not Zoran," he hissed, "and Alessandra is not Nendra. She has done nothing to you."

Gavri's eyes widened a moment before a scowl creased her face. "This has nothing to do with Zoran! This is about some *human* disrespecting—"

"You're dismissed."

She scoffed and shook her head, then turned away.

"From my guard."

She whirled back around, eyes wide. "What? I was defending you!"

"By lying to me?" he bit out, stepping to her. "You are sworn to truth. But more than that, I trusted you. And you try to sabotage the peace your queen worked so hard to build? To sabotage my marriage before Alessandra and I have even gotten to know each other?"

Her lower lip trembled as she breathed hard. "I know, I know it, but I was just—"

"Don't let me see your face again for the rest of this trip. And once we're back in Nozva Rozkveta, you'll be transferred from my guard."

With a sharp breath, she grabbed his wrist. "Veron—"

He shook her off and strode to his tent, fists clenched. Gavri was like a sister to him, but if she was going to betray his friendship, endanger what they were doing here, disobey Mati's orders, then she had no place among his inner circle. The cost of her recklessness could be catastrophic.

Outside the flap, he took several deep breaths. Relaxed his hands. Finally, he drew the flap aside.

Alessandra was already scrubbing her hands in a small basin of water she'd gotten from... he didn't know where. And two plates of Bellanzole bread, cheese, and figs sat between two neatly laid-out bedrolls.

"You don't waste time." When her dark eyes met his, he added, "Will you be—"

She moved the basin aside and, sitting stiffly, nodded him inside. "Please, this can't wait. We need to talk."

Talk? That was cryptic. Drawing his eyebrows together, he ducked into the tent, pulled off his too-tight boots, and lowered onto the bedroll across from hers, trying to roll the tension out of his shoulders.

On their wedding night, she'd mentioned wanting to speak to him about something, perhaps the same matter lurking beneath those night waters in her gaze. Was this it?

Rubbing her palms on her skirts, she faced him. "Veron, there's this group called the Brotherhood, and they're—"

"A rogue human army devoted to ousting all Immortals. I've... come across them before."

Alessandra nodded gravely. "I don't suspect Luciano is involved—"

He took a slow breath. Thank the Deep, the Darkness, and Holy Ulsinael. Calling one of those bigots *family* wasn't one of his life's goals. Besides, King Macario had sworn to Mati that he'd finesse the Brotherhood as part of the agreement.

"—but his brother, Tarquin, has given me reason to believe *he* is," she said, wriggling closer. "Veron, I think he might be... watching us."

"Tarquin," he said, testing the name as his claws bit into his palms. There had been a man in the abbazia who'd stared lances through him, the same man who'd cut into Alessandra's dance with her brother Lorenzo.

"His sister Arabella disappeared, and he blames the Immortali. Before we left, there was an attack on a light-elf settlement in the night, not far from Bellanzole," she said, wringing the gray fabric in her hand. "I don't know whether it's isolated or part of a greater plan, but I needed you to know in case…"

In case the Brotherhood came after the *monsters*. In case they *rescued* their human princess. In case they chose to *make an example* of him and his entourage, staking them out in the sun and starting the all-out war the Brotherhood so desperately seemed to want.

Her bearing tight, she watched him, those small, clawless fingers fidgeting. She blinked dark lashes over dark eyes, beneath a furrowed brow. "In case…"

"In case they come for my blood, and that of every dark-elf here."

CHAPTER 9

The early morning rays hit the distant red clay roof shingles of Stroppiata as Aless rode alongside Veron. She adjusted her right leg in the sidesaddle, spreading out her rosy-pink brocade skirts. The pink softened her look, a subtle contradiction to her infamous intemperance... or so her sister Giuliana had once said.

In less than an hour, they'd be inside the city walls. Normally, she was accustomed to riding inside a *carriage*, but today wasn't about comfort—it was about being seen. If it went well, it would set a good tone for the rest of the Royal Progress.

If it went poorly... the best case would make this entire maneuver a failure, and the worst would see her, Veron, and countless others dead.

She exhaled. Too bad those thoughts couldn't leave with her breath.

No pressure. None whatsoever.

She'd been on a Royal Progress once, when Lorenzo had

come of age. Just outside each city's gates, Papà, Mamma, and Lorenzo had mounted horses, while she, Giuliana, and Bianca had stayed in the carriage. Smiling faces had lined the streets, eyes wide and shining, as cheers had drowned out all but the clink of coins and clop of hooves.

The people need to see Lorenzo, who'll be their next king, Giuliana had whispered, leaning in. *They need to see us, their monarchs, up close. It makes us real, creates connection, gives us the chance to show them who we truly are... or who we want to be.*

Giuliana had gone on a Royal Progress in Emaurria with her husband, Crown Prince Robert, several years ago after their wedding. No doubt she'd been the perfect princess, claiming space in every Emaurrian's heart as she'd shown them who she'd truly been. Talented and strong, beautiful and charming, a singular person capable of taming conflicts with a well-placed compliment or just the right laugh. If only Giuliana were here. If only she'd survived. If only—

No. There would be no useful thoughts in that direction. Not today. She sighed.

Golden eyes narrowed, Veron peered into the distance at the city, his face masked in black but for his eyes. His head hooded, hiding most of his ghostly white hair.

The first time she'd seen him, back in the palazzo's court-yard, he'd been masked, hooded, cloaked—a black rider on a black horse, mysterious and intimidating, like some phantom hunter fallen to earth from the Wild Hunt.

The people need to see us.

"Veron?" she asked, and those golden eyes found her before he turned her way.

"Hmm?" A gruff sound, but soft.

Behind them, the cavalcade stretched so far back she

couldn't tell where it ended, but she and Veron needed to speak. Even if he chose to ignore her, as Papà always did, she needed to try.

This first visit was crucial—it would set the tone for the rest of the Royal Progress, and if it went well, maybe Veron would agree that they could maintain the peace as friends... and she could see her public library built. "Could we stop for a moment?"

He nodded and held up a hand.

The sharp-eyed guard bellowed, the first of a series of shouts down the line as it drew to a halt.

Veron dismounted that enormous beast of a horse, his motion practiced and fluid, and three guards followed suit as he extended a gloved hand to her. She removed her foot from the stirrup, then lifted her right leg over while turning in the saddle to the left.

It wasn't her first time dismounting a sidesaddle, but she took his hand anyway and hopped down. Ever since her... fashion statement at the wedding, it was more important than ever that she and Veron appear at peace. Especially with Tarquin's *pride* out there somewhere, watching.

Veron offered her his arm, and when she looped hers around it, he walked her to the blue-green maritime pine forest. A few feet into its concealment, he paused among some myrtle shrubs, his guards several feet behind and scanning the area.

When she'd told Veron about the Brotherhood and Tarquin, he'd taken the news calmly and said the Brotherhood wouldn't launch an attack in a human city, that she'd be safe in Stroppiata.

That had made sense, as all the previous attacks had taken place in Immortali settlements, and yet the entire dark-elf cavalcade seemed on edge, every guard more responsive, more watchful.

"I'll wait for you here," he said, his deep voice muffled through his mask as he nodded toward a farther patch of shrubs.

Wait for—?

"No." She smiled, shaking a ladybug off her rosy-pink skirts. "Not that."

With a glance at his nearby guards, she took his hand and led him behind a thicker orange-red trunk, where he looked down at her with glimmering half-moon eyes.

She reached up and brushed a finger along the edge of his black hood. "Do your people always wear masks and hoods?"

He looked away. "In the sky realm, yes." A matter-of-fact answer.

"Why?"

A pale eyebrow quirked. "People fear us."

People did fear them. Their imposing size. Those golden eyes, like those of predators in the night, with sharp canine teeth to match. Hair pale as a ghost's, come to drag them to the Lone. Blue-gray skin, so different from their own, its hue cold and stony. And claws... she well knew those.

Biting her lip, she slowly raised a hand toward his face, and when he didn't move, simply kept those golden eyes fixed on her, she tugged down the mask, revealing his sculpted jaw, the slate-blue of his face.

So close, his scent of earth and fresh water soothed its way to her nose, like a meadow after a summer storm, maybe, and she breathed in deeply, rising on her tiptoes to draw back his hood. Her finger brushed against smooth, pale hair, and for the briefest of moments, he closed his eyes, exhaled through parted lips.

For a second, everything paused. The breeze rustling through pine needles and myrtle leaves, the nearby whisper of a guard, the distant calls among those in the cavalcade, and everything waited as that slow, quivering exhalation rolled through him.

His eyebrows drew together as his eyes found hers once more, searching, questioning, but only a muscle twitched in his jaw.

No part of her would move while those eyes held her in place, not her hands, not her lips, not even her tongue.

Her pulse raced her breathing, and which was faster, she couldn't tell.

Dark-elves kissed, didn't they? That's what this felt like, almost a kiss...

Only... he dropped his gaze between them, and both her pulse and her breathing—thank the Mother—slowed.

He, too, had been frozen, but had it been in repugnance or discomfort? Unsettled that she might have been trying to kiss him? It had only been a few days since their wedding night, when he'd made it very clear he hadn't found her attractive in the least.

Had that changed, even a little? Or were his reactions a courtesy, so his human wife wouldn't feel like a fool? Or maybe a show.

Or duty.

There was no order of his mother's that he'd refuse. Even on his wedding night, utterly repulsed by his human bride, he would have done his duty if she'd demanded it. He'd been ordered to marry her, and any warmth, if that's what it was, would be in service of that order.

When he looked at her, he'd only ever see a human. Someone unappealing he'd been forced to wed. That's all she'd ever be.

Obedient as he was, he'd been kind to her. Sympathetic. Understanding. Patient.

And to her, now, the thought—of kissing him—

She sucked in a breath.

It didn't fill her with repugnance or discomfort.

It didn't unsettle her.

It—

She shook her head. This wasn't why she'd led him here. "People fear the unknown."

He blinked, those eyebrows still drawn together.

"The people need to see us up close," she said, repeating Giuliana's wisdom. "It makes us real, creates connection, gives us the chance to... show them who we truly are... or who we want to be."

The breeze picked up, and a lock of hair wisped across her face, but supple leather grazed her cheek as he tucked it behind her ear with a gloved hand.

"Alessandra," he said softly, his brow creased, "it's not the same. The people don't want us to be real. It's why we cover ourselves."

She took his hand. "But you are real. And the nightmares we imagine behind the masks and the hoods are more terrifying than the reality."

He grinned, but then suppressed it. "*More* terrifying?"

"That is..."

That pale eyebrow quirked again, and she laughed.

"You know what I'm trying to say!" She averted her gaze as her cheeks warmed. "Our people are more alike than they are different, and once the reality is known, there won't be as much to fear. Nor anything to fear, I hope."

He tilted his head, working his jaw. "What do you suggest?"

"No masks. No hoods. You're distributing food and coin, so let the people associate that with your looks. Smile—"

He did, exposing those longer, sharp fangs.

"—but maybe not too broadly," she said, wincing, receiving a huff in reply. "And if people give us flowers, bouquets, take them. It's hard to fear anything covered in flowers."

"Sound logic," he said, a smile still on his lips as he squeezed her hand. "But the gloves stay on."

She hadn't realized she'd still been holding his hand. "Why—"

He let her go, and the smile faded. "Because I hurt you," he whispered, and swallowed. "I—we—might not yet possess the awareness required not to hurt anyone else... anyone human, and avoiding any—"

"Accidents," she provided.

"—would be for the best."

"Veron," she said gently, "you didn't mean it."

"Not everyone will be so understanding."

As much as she wanted to, there was no arguing that. Not when people like Tarquin were looking for excuses to dehumanize Immortali like the dark-elves. "We'll need to show a united front. Hold hands, smile at each other, stay in close proximity—that kind of thing."

"Like this?" A deep, low murmur. He glanced from himself to her and back again. "Pretend a deeper intimacy?"

Her cheeks warming, she nodded. *Pretend.* That's what this was, after all.

The world knew so little of dark-elf culture that maybe the pretense wouldn't be held to Sileni standards. She hoped. But for a few moments in the public's eye, they could be like players on a stage and pretend affection for each other, couldn't they?

"Very well." Excusing himself, he spoke to the sharp-eyed guard, who acknowledged him and then headed toward the cavalcade. The other two remained behind while Veron offered her his arm.

She took it, keenly aware of his thick forearm and thicker bicep, of his broad shoulders and towering figure, of his summer-storm scent and the shiver it stroked up her back.

It *excited* her.

He excited her. A dark-elf. What on earth...?

No, the last thing she needed would be to fall for her dark-elf husband—and end up a trophy his mother would lock deep inside a cave somewhere. It would be the life Papà had always wanted for her, the life she could never stand to live. She'd never see Mamma's library realized, nor live her dream.

And worse, Veron didn't find her attractive. This was all still pretense for him, wasn't it? Developing genuine feelings for him would be...

She bit her lip.

No, they both had roles to play today, and that was all. They'd have to garner a positive response from the paesani during the entry, as well as the promise of friendship from the duchessa and the support of the nobiltà tonight at the banquet. She'd see Paladin Grand Cordon Nunzio there and discuss her plans for the library.

It would all go perfectly.

It had to.

Veron went utterly still next to her.

She froze, too. *Holy Mother's mercy*, not dragons again. This time, they would—

"Alessandra," he whispered, and leaned in, tipping his head slowly toward the heart of the forest.

She followed his line of sight, where something so impossibly immaculate hid among the pines. With a coat of pure white, it was a large, four-legged creature not unlike the enormous horse Veron rode, but with a long, flowing snow-white mane and tail, and with a pointed, spiraling horn peaking from its forehead. It bobbed its head, eyeing them with gentle, sable eyes.

Mamma used to read a book of myths to her when she'd been little, and this was—this was a *unicorn*. Gentle creatures devoted to peace and serenity. "We didn't scare it away," she whispered.

"He wants to be seen," Veron answered softly. "We've entered his domain, and he is greeting us. They normally stay hidden, keep to themselves, but something compelled him to emerge."

Greeting them? "How do you know?"

"Noc," he said, keeping his eyes on the unicorn. "He's a fey horse, a being not too different from *him*"—he nodded toward the unicorn—"and Noc has told me many things."

"Told?" she asked, and the unicorn tossed its head and swished its tail.

Veron's horse *told* him things?

He eyed her peripherally, a glimmer in his eyes. "I suppose you haven't been properly introduced. We'll have to remedy that," he said, a corner of his mouth turned up. "But like fey horses, unicorns are descended from the shapeshifting dragons. They once were dragons. Dragon Lords have guided other beings, often with a heavy hand, bending them to obedience, controlling them so they wouldn't err.

"But there was a group of pacifists among the dragons who dreamed of a world where every being would be treated like every other, and when at last they voiced their protests to the Dragon King, he cast them out of his kingdom. He took all memory of dragon society, and how to Change into a dragon, and gave them the shape you see. They wished to live peacefully and not to wage war, not to control others, and he made them so."

The Dragon King cast out his people, punished them, simply for disagreeing with him?

"What about their dream?" she whispered.

His gaze fixed on the unicorn, he drew his eyebrows together. "One day, you might ask them. Young unicorns must Change with the fullness of the moon and take the form of other lesser beings, but older, stronger ones—if they choose— can Change as they will, even turn other lesser beings, but only the purest of heart. Just like any shapeshifter, if they survive the fever, they become an Immortal." When she gasped, he smiled at her. "But what do you think?"

She watched as the unicorn blinked long lashes at her before snorting quietly and turning to disappear into the forest. He'd trusted them, enough to face away, and that meant a lot.

Thank you. I pray we meet again.

"I think... I think when terrible things happen, it's easier to do nothing. I'm sure they knew the likely costs, but they did a hard thing, a brave thing."

A gentle breeze blew, swept Veron's pale hair as he looked at her, eyelids drawn, a subtle smile playing about his lips.

If this was pretense, then he was the world's best player.

At the city's gates, Veron sat taller astride his horse as Riza presented their documents, provided by King Macario himself. Beyond the gate, distant crowds were already gathering, and massive tapestries hung from buildings lining the main thoroughfare.

He'd already briefed Riza on Alessandra's idea; he had only to give a sign, and everyone in the cavalcade would remove their hoods and masks. For the wedding, he'd gone unmasked... but only in the presence of some of the human nobles. Not out among the general human public. It wasn't the dark-elf way.

He shifted his feet in the stirrups, his boots too tight over the bridge of his foot.

Calm, Noc teased.

The calmest, he mocked in reply.

Noc's tail smacked his back. *Swatting flies.*

Of course, he thought with a grimace.

But for this peace to work, the humans couldn't fear them. Alessandra's idea was smart, and he never would have thought of it himself; had she been a dark-elf, any queen would have been fortunate to have her among her Quorum. He'd trust her in this.

Next to him, she had her shoulders back, her chin raised, a pleasant smile on her lips. Confidence, composure, joy. That was what she projected.

And he—he had to be nonthreatening. *Peace, sincerity, altruism.* An open, relaxed bearing. Making brief but genuine eye contact. Subtle—not fanged—smiles. He and the rest of his entourage would distribute food and coins.

As harmless as that was, every dark-elf would be watchful for Tarquin Belmonte and the Brotherhood. They wouldn't mount an assault in a human city—of that he was certain. The city was surrounded by open plains but for cliffs to the west. No sane commander would lead his troops down those steep cliffs to be picked off by the city's archers.

But there were other options besides full-scale assault.

The city guards opened the gates. Riza's gaze met his, and with a nod, he slowly removed his mask, and then his hood. It was time.

Riza signaled to Danika, and then did the same, and there was a rustling of leathers and wool behind them.

None of the city guards started—one gawked, but only for a moment—so Deep, Darkness, and Holy Ulsinael willing, this would work.

Danika and her unit preceded him and Alessandra, distributing boules and confections to the first families crowding the route. Eyes wide, they looked over him and his people, mouths gaping—but only for a moment before Alessandra waved.

"Terra's blessings upon you!" she called, her voice sweet but carrying far. She'd mentioned the piety of Stroppiata; the Terran shrine here was famous.

"And upon you!" came the shouted replies.

A woman raised a little boy bearing a bouquet of white flowers, and at Gavri's nod, Alessandra accepted them with a smile, handing out gold coins to beaming people.

As she brought the white blooms to her face and inhaled,

cheers rose up from the crowd, more densely packed the farther in they rode. Behind the front lines, heads popped up over shoulders, gazes locking on Alessandra's face, her gown, him, his fellow dark-elves. The wide-eyed shock was ephemeral, quickly chased away by grins, laughter, and cheers as he distributed gold coins.

Danika and her unit stayed in formation, gently guiding the crowd back. Tossed flowers graced the path before them, a welcoming carpet leading them toward the castle in the city's northern district.

"Veron," she said, like the softest moss feathering down the back of his neck, like warm breath on his skin, and he faced her.

Her eyes were the dark embrace of home, the bloom of night and beauty of shadow, and when she smiled, his breath caught.

She held out the bouquet, and when he took it, her touch lingered on his hand. "Nothing to fear," she whispered, for him and him alone.

With a nod, he smiled back, but restrained it before his teeth would show. *No teeth. Nonthreatening.*

A little girl with dark curls like Alessandra's squealed her delight, and Alessandra unclasped her pearl bracelet and handed it to Kinga, another of his kuvari, to give away. With a happy little laugh.

No, she wasn't spoiled. Her father had adorned her with luxury, but she didn't seem to hoard these things.

She called out to Gabriella, who removed several books from her horse's pack, and distributed them to older children.

Alessandra's fondness of books—he'd have to note it in *A Modern History of Silen.*

She didn't look like the fiercest dark-elf women, the ones young men dreamed of—equals in battle, ambitious subjects, the strongest among their people. Fiery lovers. But...

Honest, generous, wise, brave, kind... That anyone should find such traits in a partner was a blessing. One he'd never expected. All he'd been allowed to expect had been a marriage Mati deemed beneficial to Nozva Rozkveta. As was proper.

In the forest, Alessandra had been close, her perfume of some sky-realm flower so near he could've almost tasted it. Her fingers had stroked against his hair, a whisper of a touch, and he'd had to fight the desire to lean into it. As his heart had pounded then, there had been something in that dark embrace of her gaze. A curiosity. A question. An invitation...

One he'd been tempted to accept. Very tempted.

But did she feel the same? After her utter terror on their wedding night, he wouldn't push. If he misread her, it would only frighten her more, and trouble her. If the gap between them was closing, however, someone would have to broach the subject, admit the shift in perception. And it would be him. He'd have to confess his budding attraction to her first. And he would. No hiding. No dishonesty.

The final time he'd seen Ata, he'd only been a boy, not even old enough to go hunting alone with his father. *Can't I come, Ata?* he'd asked.

Ata had crouched to eye level, smiled, and patted him on the shoulder. *Not this time, son. But I'll be back before you know it.*

With a beaming grin and a nod, he'd watched Ata walk to his death. To end the war between Nozva Rozkveta and Lumia, Ata had willingly turned himself over, and had saved many dark-elf lives with his sacrifice, but he'd betrayed the love of his own children, of Mati. The stillness Mati had gone through, like living death... all because Ata had betrayed their love when he could have—

Dangerdangerdanger. Noc's fey-horse mind invaded his own.

Shadows cloaked them as they neared an arch, and he could still hear the flap of funeral shrouds, vast and heavy, the beat of each shake—

And gasps, horrified screams—

He blinked, and the flapping came from above, the beat of great, black wings that blotted out the sun.

CHAPTER 10

*E*normous wings spanned fifteen feet wide above them, two dozen harpies with too-wide mouths and razor-sharp talons.

A few swarmed the top of the arch, while the rest dove for the crowds. The humans would be slaughtered. Alessandra would—

"My bow!" Veron leaped off Noc's back and pulled Alessandra from the saddle, wrapping his cloak about her as the crowd dispersed in screams.

"Veron, why are they—"

A harpy swooped low, talons out, and Alessandra screamed. He shielded her. Nothing would harm her. *Nothing.*

Gavri rushed in, drew her bow, and the first harpy wailed as it hit the cobblestones before them.

"Hide anything that shines!" Riza bellowed in Sileni. Someone handed her his bow and a quiver full of arrows, which she tossed to him.

"Shines?" Alessandra shouted, ducking along with Gabriella.

Gavri's unit ringed them while Danika's covered the crowd ahead of them, and he shuffled Alessandra and Gabriella behind him to the narrowest point of the alley as he took aim.

One through the neck. Down on the cobbles.

Another in the eye, and arrows pierced its wings as it fell.

Riza's kuvari cut heads with vjernost blades—the only way to ensure the final death—and the arcanir caught the sunlight. Sharp, screeching cries pierced the air.

He took aim, burying arrows in wings and bodies, but—

Noc bucked, then kicked at a harpy—coins jingling in his saddlebags.

No.

"The coins!" Alessandra called. "If we could just—"

Get them on the street.

"Gavri," he snapped, taking his glove between his teeth and yanking it off. "Cover me!"

As soon as he sprang forward, arrows hissed through the air above him.

"Your Highness!" Riza growled, her vjernost blade meeting talons.

Hold still. He caught Noc's reins, then cut the girth free. The saddle and its bags tumbled to the street as he clapped Noc on the rump, sending him to Gavri and Alessandra.

Blood rained onto his head and neck—a harpy thudded to the cobbles, an arrow in its gaping maw.

He grabbed the bag of coins, opened it, then tossed it to the empty street ahead of them. Gold exploded on the stone in a chaos of clanging and clinks, bright sunlight glinting off hundreds of shining facets.

A dozen harpies descended over the glittering metallic sea.

Over fifty bows angled as one, myriad arrows burying in shrieking targets. Riza gave the kill order, and vjernost blades cut heads from bodies.

Booted footsteps hurried in. Two squads of city guards, whose commander Riza met with a blood-spattered scowl and recounting of the attack.

He wiped the blood off his own face... with a blood-soaked sleeve.

Hooves clopped behind him—Noc neighed his location as Alessandra led him.

She was all right. Thank the Deep, Darkness, and Holy Ulsinael—she was *all right*. At the first sign of the harpies, he thought she'd...

A sigh left him and, with it, the rigidity claiming his body. He took a step forward before she held out a handkerchief.

He paused. What had he been thinking? To throw his arms around her, feel her safe against him, to kiss her? No, he had to tell her how he felt first.

With a murmur of thanks, he took it and swabbed his face, then patted Noc's neck. *Thank you for the warning, old friend.*

Noc only nickered. He always had been a fey horse of few words.

City guards combed the streets, although there seemed to be no human casualties. A couple kuvari nursed wounds, but Riza already had their mystic, Xira, tending them.

The commander of the city guards, wearing a mermaid emblem, approached. A middle-aged man with graying black hair, he bowed low to Alessandra. "Your Highnesses, have you been harmed?"

Still wearing his cloak, Alessandra seemed uninjured. "I'm all right. Veron?"

"The only injuries are two of my kuvari, but you'll have to check with Captain Riza."

The commander's throat bobbed. "Please accept my deepest apologies for the bad luck. Her Grace had us take every precaution."

Every precaution would have included clearing the nearby harpy nest before the Royal Progress, or at least issuing a warning about reflections. But unlike the humans he remembered, these had a lot to learn about Immortals.

And *bad luck* would have meaning that would ripple throughout the human kingdom. That their human gods disfavored the peace, the marriage, *them*.

Alessandra took his hand, then with a deep breath, turned to the commander. "It wasn't bad luck, Captain...?"

"Scianna," the commander supplied. "But I don't understand, Your Highness—"

Alessandra handed Noc's reins to Gabriella, then walked with him back toward the alley he'd led her to, with Captain Scianna following. Gavri waited there attentively, but when he passed her, she lowered her gaze.

She'd fought bravely, capably...

But she couldn't be trusted. The first betrayal had been small, almost harmless, but the next could mean a life, or more. She couldn't be trusted. He turned away.

"Harpies are drawn to shining objects," Aless said, catching his eye for a moment, "like coins. Jewelry. Blades. Anything that might catch the sun, and their eye."

True enough. And she'd clearly been listening. Her idea with the coins had been brilliant. What was she planning now?

She reached the spot where he'd left her during the attack, the narrowest point of the alley, then turned toward the arch. Her finger pointed upward, to the top, where as the clouds cleared, a shine reflected, blinding white and large, toward the cliffs. As they'd approached from the south, they wouldn't have been able to see it. But from her vantage point in the alley, she had.

"I believe that's a mirror, Captain," Alessandra said. "What seems like bad luck was actually sabotage."

ALESS EYED VERON surreptitiously as a squad of city guards escorted them, Gabriella, and his guards into Duchessa Claudia La Via's castle. The duchessa waited in the great hall, where she and Veron would have to earn the duchessa's support and that of her nobiltà. If by the time they left, the nobiltà was all smiles and the duchessa extended a promise of friendship, their objective here would be a success.

But the duchessa had instructed Captain Scianna and her household to lead them inside discreetly to freshen up first.

Which was good... because next to her, Veron's ghostly white hair was a deep, dark crimson, stained with blood, which was smeared all over his pale, slate-blue face and neck, and soaking his leathers. Utterly chilling. Combined with his coiled rigidity and the grim set of his jaw, he looked like a demon warrior, made of wrath and malice, a thirst for blood in his narrowed golden eyes and not a shred of mercy to be found.

Phantom hunter from the Wild Hunt indeed.

The conspirators responsible for the attack weren't worthy of his mercy, and to her mind, deserved every ounce of wrath and malice he had. Even aside from the repugnance of trying to spark a war—that mirror had been left behind—there had been *children* in that crowd. She'd even given a little girl jewelry —which could have drawn the harpies. Thank the Mother none of the children had been harmed.

The attack needed a response.

Out the window, the garden was serene, a colorful geometric knot, but the window reflected her and Veron over its greenery.

Someone had planted the mirror on that arch—likely the Brotherhood. They hadn't openly attacked a human city in their war on the Immortali, but they'd been willing to let one breed of Immortali kill the other, even if humans would have been caught in the middle. Even if *she* had been caught in the middle. So much for Tarquin's promises.

This union had been about securing peace, but safety had gone. She was no longer the palazzo's Beast Princess, deflating oversized egos and raising eyebrows at court. She and Veron were now a symbol—a symbol some would try to use, and others would try to destroy.

Not without a fight.

"Veron," she whispered as they ascended the carpeted stairs behind a chamberlain, and Veron's hold on her hand tightened, ever so slightly, as his narrowed eyes eased, settled on her. Warmth, comfort, the callused roughness of a grip that had wielded bows and blades. That could protect her.

Somehow, from the streets of Stroppiata to the stairwell of this castle, she'd held his hand the entire time.

And he'd let her.

"Are you all right?" he rumbled, his voice low and his brow furrowed as he looked her over.

"I am. That is, I'd... like to start learning the bow." To start protecting herself, and him, and anyone who'd need it. It was past time. Papà had always forbidden it, but Papà wasn't here now.

Veron's mouth curved for just a moment, then he inclined his head. "We'll start tomorrow morning."

Those quiet words, offered freely, with the hint of a smile, warmed her, but that furrowed brow returned. Although he walked alongside her, held her hand, he was still out on the blood-drenched streets, still eye to eye with the harpies, among the screams and fighting.

It's all right, she wanted to say, but... no. It wasn't all right. Not in the least. But she'd find a way to make it so.

Thank the Holy Mother that the dark-elves had had their blades—made of arcanir—which seemed to disrupt certain abilities of the Immortali, and had ended the harpies.

The chamberlain led them to quarters, and the sharp-eyed guard, along with two others, swept the rooms before giving the all-clear. While she and Veron entered, Gabriella excused herself to oversee the delivery of their luggage.

The rooms were opulent—the ducal apartment, no doubt— with fine white silk upholstery, blackwood furnishings, and high ceilings. Veron approached the windows, peering out with a discerning eye. A wary eye.

After what had happened, what could she say to him?

The Brotherhood had risked much, and this wouldn't stop.

Revealing the setup could turn the public against the Brotherhood, but it would also shift national attention from the peace to the rebellion. And with the Immortali openly fighting in human cities, there was too big a risk that the Brotherhood would enjoy vocal support, whether it would deny planting the bait or not.

Publicizing the unrest could be exactly what the Brotherhood wanted. The entire purpose of the Royal Progress—spreading the message of peace—would be frustrated. Hushed. The focus would once more return to the *threat* of the Immortali.

But did it *have* to?

"Not without a fight," she murmured.

Veron, his arms crossed, turned to her with a raised brow. She'd start protecting him, herself, and everyone else—for now, with the only methods she knew.

"You think we failed." She moved toward him as servants entered with pails of steaming water for the bath, poured into a tub behind her.

He grunted. "We did fail, whether I think it or not."

"Everything was going well until—"

"The attack. And that's all anyone will remember." His low voice became practically inaudible. He lowered his chin, and his gaze dropped to the floor. His eyes shut, he stood in the window's sunlit radiance, covered in blood and gleaming, terrifying and bright.

As the winged shadows had sailed in overhead, she'd been frozen to her saddle, unable to move, unable to think, staring at gaping mouths with sharp teeth, at frenzied eyes, at razor-like talons. Seeing a vision of flesh torn and blood rain, an unholy feast in the sky above an anguished city. And then she'd been pulled from the saddle, wrapped in sheltering black, and moved to a tight alleyway.

Veron. The low rumble of his voice, the rainwater and fresh earth of his scent. His shielding arms, his dauntless form, his implacable mettle. He hadn't hesitated. Hadn't frozen. Hadn't panicked.

He'd saved her life.

She reached up to him, to where his long hair swept over his shoulder, and she pulled the tie binding his braid, slowly, gently. His eyes opened just a sliver, pale lashes catching the sunshine's luminance, and his breathing slowed.

The coppery tang of blood was overpowering, and with his arms crossed, those sharp claws rested on his biceps.

But she pulled that tie down and off. Looped her finger through the weave of his braid, undoing it, unbinding it, freeing it.

He didn't move, simply watched her through those slitted eyes, let her do as she willed.

I'm open to your wishes, he'd told her the night of their wedding. *You shouldn't fear rejection should you express them to me.*

He'd saved her life—and she could kiss him just for that. But when she did, she'd want him to kiss her back. And not just because of his mother's orders, nor because of duty, but because he wanted to. Which at worst was an impossibility, and at best, a challenge.

But challenges were made to be answered.

"Alessandra," he breathed, and she wanted to hear him say her name again, a hundred times, a thousand times. To call her the name she only allowed her loved ones to call her.

"Aless." She smoothed her hand from his hair to his leather-armored chest. "Call me Aless."

"Aless."

The smooth sound was a bare stroke, an intimacy, but she wouldn't close her eyes, wouldn't let herself descend deeper into the moment, read her hopes into his words, that he might see her as something more...

She wasn't more.

She was—how had Papà put it?—*willful, short tempered, sharp mouthed, and presumptuous.* Disobedient.

Everything a man didn't want in a wife...

On their wedding night, Veron had led her to understand that if she wanted more, he'd give it to her. Was that what he was doing? Giving her what she wanted, no matter how *he* felt?

But her fingers pressed against the leather.

He caught her hand, his hold careful, his claws well away from her flesh. Brushing his thumb over her fingertip, he smudged the bloodstain already on her skin, from the armor. "The blood."

Something thudded behind her, and she glanced over her shoulder. The last of her luggage, including the trunk Lorenzo had given her.

She turned back to Veron.

There was the blood, yes, but even more pressing, the duchessa awaited them. "There's a bath ready," she whispered.

With a deep breath and a nod, he looked past her and back again. "Will it offend you if I...?"

"Not in the least," she replied too quickly. "But if you wish me to leave, I'll—"

"No." He straightened. "Stay."

Before she could reply, he released her and passed her on his way to the tub.

"Lorenzo had me take a few things for you, since we would find ourselves among the nobiltà," she said, among the rustling of leathers and fabric.

"That was generous of him. It was a help at the capital."

Holy Mother's mercy, he was removing his clothes, right behind her, and her heart was in her throat, as if she'd never been around an undressing man before.

So instead she opened the trunk from Lorenzo and removed an assortment of men's couture. "I think the clothes will help bridge our people's differences. Sort of like the flowers."

A soft splash of water, and she was wringing a shirt in her hand. She cleared her throat. "Speaking of the flowers, I don't think we failed today."

"Aless—"

"No one died. None of the attendees were even injured. If anything, we proved that your people can deliver exactly what you promised—help against the other Immortali." She chose black velvet for him, a well-tailored jacket and trousers, without the color and ornamentation that would seem as though they were trying too hard.

He sighed. "It was inauspicious."

"If we leave things as they are, that will be the story." She laid out the clothing on the sprawling bed, to the soft slosh of water behind her. The Beast Princess would have strode before him, undressed, and slipped into the tub before he could remember to close his mouth. The Beast Princess would be bold, daring—

The *Beast Princess* was nowhere to be found.

Instead, here was this quivering, awkward mess, barely able to function in the mere *presence* of this one man. Some smelling salts would do her good.

This attraction—it would go nowhere. All he felt for her was duty, and she wouldn't be the pathetic wretch longing for a man who didn't long for her.

She'd meet with Nunzio today, discuss her plan for the

library, and no matter how it was done, she needed to live her dream, to help in any way she could. She'd explain it all to Veron. He didn't deserve this mess—he deserved the truth, to know her plans, even if it would upset or anger him. A decision had to be made, and soon.

Soon... That is, not right this instant. Tonight they had to sway the Stroppiata nobiltà to support the peace—with both human and dark-elf lives at stake, that had to take priority. But after that...

She heaved a sigh. After that, she'd tell him, and he... he'd understand her desire to cure the ignorance driving this rebellion, and if she helped solidify the peace during this Royal Progress, there would be no need for the second ceremony, for the marriage. With his mother's goal fulfilled, he wouldn't want to marry a human anyway, so he'd be free. He'd understand. He'd—

"That was our one chance," he said quietly. "The schedule has us spending the rest of our visit here with the nobiltà."

"Then the Brotherhood wins. They choose the impression we leave the paesani with, and we make no effort to change it, and appear resigned or, worse, afraid."

A loud splash and rustle of fabric. "What do you propose?"

"That we set the narrative. Let's keep Silen focused on the positive. On us." As footsteps approached the bed, she turned away. "We'll ask the duchessa to have her people spread word of your heroism, and your people's, during the *rescue* today. And tomorrow, let's plan an impromptu visit to the Terran shrine. I'll make an offering before the Mother of Stroppiata for a blessed union, and we'll do our best to seem affectionate and unified." It wouldn't be too big of a challenge, at least on her end.

"Will that work?" Velvet swished behind her, Veron changing, casting an interplay of sunlight and shadow stretching before her.

"Stroppiata is Silen's most pious city. It will be seen as an act of respect." They had the advantage of the public eye; while the Brotherhood hid and slinked in the shadows, she and Veron could use their visibility to win the public's favor, if they proceeded wisely. If they won that, the Brotherhood's cause would fail.

A brief silence.

She glanced over her shoulder as he buttoned a shirt beneath the open black jacket, over a sculpted, hard body, blue-gray like Carrerra marble from the North. Dreaming Sileni artists had built gods and heroes, powerful ideals of myth and legend, with such form. And he stood before her now, real and breathing and beautiful and strong, the godly and the heroic driving him in his earthly deeds. Layers of rumor and presumption and mystery that had hidden him before now swept away like dust, and he'd been here, beneath it all, this entire time.

"I'm glad it was you, Aless."

Her heart skipped a beat. Blinking, she fixed her gaze upon the parquet floor.

"Glad it was me?" she whispered, daring to meet his eyes as he now fastened the jacket's golden toggles. Holy Mother's mercy. Seeing him only confirmed her misplaced attraction.

But he'd said he was glad. Maybe it wasn't misplaced?

Holding her gaze, he abandoned the toggles midway and took a step closer.

Her heart pounded. Had he noticed her awkwardness? Was he teasing her? She swallowed.

He carefully took her hand, her shaking hand, and raised it

to his chest, pressed it there, over his heart. "When I arrived in Bellanzole, I'm glad it was you."

Her eyes widened, but he didn't waver, just held her hand there against the pulse beating in his chest. His golden eyes, soft and warm, held her speechless, breathless, and his hair, clean and damp, begged for her touch. The toggles on his jacket, halfway done—she couldn't decide whether she wanted to finish fastening them, or—

"Am I alone in this, Aless?"

He blinked, and for a moment, she couldn't breathe. She shook her head slowly. No, he hadn't misread her. He wasn't alone in... "I think there may be something here that—"

A soft rapping on wood came from the hall.

Veron's mouth curved as he searched her eyes. "It's time to meet the duchess."

It was time, and their discussion had been cut short, but it didn't matter—he *knew*.

He knew, and he felt the same.

CHAPTER 11

A corner of Veron's mouth turned up as he escorted Aless to the great hall, following a footman. By Deep and Darkness, he could scarcely stop himself from smiling.

Aless spoke not a word of Elvish. Didn't worship Holy Ulsinael. No combat prowess whatsoever. Couldn't hunt, nor even pitch a tent reliably.

But she was devoted to peace, generous with her things, loved her sister fiercely. She was determined, a strategic thinker, passionate about knowledge, and eager to learn new things. Charismatic and inspiring. Above all, honest. The more he learned about her, the more he liked her—something he hadn't expected in this arrangement.

Next to him, she practically glowed, darkly gleaming ringlets cascading over her shoulders, drawing his gaze down to the neckline of her silver-trimmed purple gown, plunging just past the curve of her breasts.

He shouldn't look, but—

Human fashion had certainly changed in two thousand years. Drastically, *gloriously* changed. Just like the sheer red thing she'd worn on their wedding night. A sheer red thing that now lingered in his thoughts.

With a sharp breath, he looked away.

The softest of giggles came from her, quickly stifled. "Something the matter?"

Quite the opposite. "Just an uncommon sight."

"Breasts?" she teased.

He cleared his throat. "The dress."

Her dark eyes gleamed as she blinked, long black lashes fluttering. How had he not noticed her strange beauty? She had dark hair, dark eyes, olive skin—outlandish among his people. No fangs, no claws, a soft—*too* soft—body. She was *human*. So different from dark-elf women, from the most beautiful of them, but...

It didn't make her ugly. No... Among a sea of stars, she was the moon. It was as though he hadn't looked up until now.

Those dark eyes weren't the amber of his people, but how they gleamed as her mind worked, sparked when she had an idea, softened when she looked at him, held mystery like the holy Darkness. And her hair wasn't white, but its shade was like the Deep, mystical and mesmerizing, and contrasting with the olive tone of her skin.

Her skin—sometimes when he looked at her, it pinked, turned such a delicate shade of rose on her cheeks, and she didn't have to speak her thoughts when they were so clear on her face. No shades of blue and purple and gray, but pinks. Like the Bloom protecting Nozva Rozkveta. The more he looked at her, the more she reminded him of home.

Her arm, looped around his, curled closer as she stroked his bicep softly. He carefully covered her hand with his as two men opened the tall double doors, and a third announced them.

"His Highness, Prince Veron of Nightbloom, and Her Highness, Princess Alessandra of Nightbloom."

The low din of conversation in the great hall quieted as he led in Aless, the crowd parting and every face turning to them. Wide eyes blinking, manicured eyebrows rising, painted lips parting. A spectrum of colors swathed the hall, where on the other end, a woman sat in a throne-like chair behind a massive head table. Dressed in a golden gown, she had a little emerald adhered high on her cheek, and blond hair pinned elaborately with a peacock feather adorning it.

This woman would have clad herself in all the wealth of Nozva Rozkveta's mines, and yet her smile seemed entirely genuine. The duchess. It was the promise of *her* friendship that they'd have to earn here tonight.

Beaming brightly, she stood and began a slow but confident clap, which the rest of the assembled guests joined.

"Prince Veron and Princess Alessandra," the duchess said with a ringing pleasantness. "You are most welcome. I thank you both for your bravery in defending my people." She curtseyed gracefully, and a ripple of bows and curtseys followed.

"We are honored, Your Grace," he replied, inclining his head with Aless as befitted their station.

"To the happy couple." The duchess raised a goblet of wine, as did everyone, except for a tall, large man near the duchess, who raised a glass of water and nodded to Aless, tattoos peeking out from under his sleeve.

Aless smiled warmly, inclined her head, and then tightened her hold on his arm. Someone she knew, then.

The duchess motioned to the musicians, who struck up a

winding tune, and the hall's conversations resumed as she approached them.

It was already a far warmer reception than he'd expected.

A troupe of vividly dressed dancers filed in, claiming the hall's center in an elaborate routine of swinging hips and fluttering silk.

At any dark-elf queendom, now would be when the traditional games would begin, light sparring testing one another's prowess. There was honor in challenging formidable opponents, in accepting, in winning, and even in losing, but above all, it was *fun*, and sometimes—as in the case of the humans' dances—a courtship.

"Some entertainment to celebrate your visit and your union." The duchess's green eyes twinkled. "There will be dinner, dancing, fireworks in the garden, and then a private party in my salon until the sun rises."

"The promise of the famous Duchessa Stroppiata's parties does not disappoint," Aless said as a young man brought them two goblets of wine. She must have spent a lot of time reveling in the royal court. Vibrant, energetic, curious, witty—she had no doubt shone brightly.

"I am an admirer of all things beautiful," the duchess said, looking him over with a slow smile. "It is not every day that I have the unique privilege of hosting dark-elf royalty. Hopefully not the last."

He could have laughed. Such attention wasn't unusual among dark-elf women, but he hadn't expected it here. "The privilege is all ours."

The duchess held his gaze, a smile on her lips. What would it take to win her promise of friendship?

Flames shot high above them—a pair of fire-breathers weaving through the crowd.

Aless started, her eyes wide. Perhaps she hadn't quite recovered from the harpies.

The duchess laughed heartily. "Do you like them? I invited them from Zehar. They're quite talented."

"They are," he said to the duchess as he stroked Aless's hand gently. "Your gardens, too, were beautiful from the window."

The duchess swept a jewel-encrusted hand toward the doors to the courtyard. "Allow me to show them to you properly."

He followed her, and Aless swallowed next to him and flashed a fleeting smile, holding his arm close. Did the harpy attack still affect her? Some air might do her good.

The silence was not like her at all. He'd become accustomed to battle, but that had been a lifetime of training with the kuvari and fighting alongside them, many of whom had made it into Mati's Quorum. Aless, however, had been kept from all training and fighting, and today's events had to have shaken her.

Footmen opened the glass-paned doors out to a colonnade. Beyond its arches, a scrolling pattern of hedges and flowers stretched far, lined by a border of trees, their dark-green foliage silvered by the stars. At its end lay a shimmering pool, steps cascading into its placid waters.

"My mother loved all things green," the duchess said, leading them on the paths among perfect hedges, and she nodded to the abundant purple flowers. "Lavender was her favorite. When I married the duke, he was twenty-six years my senior, and we had nothing in common. I spent my time here, with the gardeners, planning this—my sanctuary. Even now that he's gone, this garden is still where I find solace."

By her face, she was still young, in her early thirties perhaps. The way her eyebrows creased together spoke volumes of her late husband, none of it good.

"It's beautiful," Aless whispered, releasing him as she curled over the lavender and inhaled, closing her eyes. She held still for a moment—one he wished to commit to memory.

The duchess watched her, that crease fading, and joined her. Her hands clasped, she cleared her throat. "I won't mince words. Someone had the audacity to plan an attack in my city. That alone would have spurred me to side with the enemy of my enemy. But your heroism today, when you could have fled, makes me proud to offer you my friendship."

She placed her right hand over her heart and bowed to them both gracefully. "Should you ever require assistance, you have but to ask."

"Thank you, Your Grace," Aless whispered, as he inclined his head.

The duchess searched Aless's eyes, then glanced at him. "Enjoy the garden. Join me at your leisure for the feast."

With that, she nodded to them, gold dress trailing past them as she strolled back to the hall.

As soon as the door shut, quiet settled in once more, only the muffled tune and voices from the hall, along with the trilling of insects and the occasional bird call playing the music of the night.

"My mother had a library. That was where she found solace," Aless said softly, her eyes still closed. "I spent so much of my childhood there, with the scent of leather, paper, candle wax. Sometimes just opening a book will take me right back there."

A special place to her.

"I'd like to see it someday," he said.

Aless's eyes fluttered open, and she gave him a watery, sad smile as she straightened. "Papà had it destroyed."

"Destroyed?" He shook his head.

Aless stroked gentle fingers over the hedges, meandering the path for a few steps.

"Tell me," he said to her, and she looked over her shoulder with a half-smile, her gaze dropping, then shrugged half-heartedly. A fragrant night breeze swept through the trees' canopy, curling the flowers to its direction, and she shivered as her dark ringlets swayed.

Undoing the toggles on his jacket, he approached her, then took it off and settled it about her shoulders. She covered his hand with hers, holding it there a long moment, and he pulled her to him, slowly walking the path.

"My mother adored books," she said with an ephemeral smile. "They lined the hall to her heart, you see. My father built her a library and proposed to her there. She filled it with stories and ideas from around the world, from all time periods and cultures.

"She wanted to share that joy and knowledge with the world," she said, her voice breaking as her eyes teared up, shining in the lambent starlight. "Every week, she and her ladies-in-waiting would read to the local children in Bellanzole, and then teach anyone who wanted to learn. Many women learned, and they took new jobs and traveled, bettered their lives. A few years ago, a man came, saying he wanted to learn, but while she was teaching him, he blamed her for his wife leaving him... He had a knife... She died before anyone could do anything."

He held her closer, and she stopped, rested her head against his chest. Humankind had changed, in every way but the ones that mattered.

"Papà banned her ladies from returning to read or teach," she whispered, muffled against his shirt. "He destroyed every book in her library, and the place itself, blaming it for her death. I cried and begged him not to, but he had the Royal Guard restrain me while it was done. My copy of *A Modern History of Silen* was the last book she gave me."

Tucked into his embrace, she went utterly quiet, leaning into him, brushing his chest with her cheek, so small and slight. Not the woman who'd ridden at his side with her head held high, regal and formidable, indomitable.

Those were walls she'd taken down for this, for him, allowing him to see the little child inside whose father had destroyed not just a library but the precious memory of her mother. That loss still had to hurt, and so did her own father's coldness to her in doing what he'd done.

He shielded her from the breeze, his shoulders taut. He wanted to meet that coldness with warmth, that loss with comfort, destruction with creation. Nothing would harm her like that again, not while he drew breath.

Against a field of lavender, she gazed up at him, her face tear streaked, and he brushed the wetness from her cheek with a thumb, and leaned in. She raised her chin, and his lips met hers, so soft, her skin the smell of salt and summer flowers as she relaxed in his arms. Her palms glided up his back, her fingers pressing, no prick of claws, just her touch, her wanting.

She leaned into him, opening her mouth to his, the sweet

bloom of a dark red wine on her exploring tongue, slow, sensual. Her breaths warmed his mouth as they fell into rhythm, longing, urging, and by Deep and Darkness, it was all he could do to cup her face, deepen his kiss, meet her tongue's sensual taking with his own.

The muffled music from the hall stopped, and he pulled away just enough to watch her open her eyes and lick her lip, then smile as her cheeks flushed. He took her hand in his.

"Do you know of any other marriages between humans and dark-elves, Veron?" she whispered, searching his eyes. "I... I wonder how they work. And what would be expected of me as your wife?"

"I know there have been marriages between humans and Immortals, but I don't personally know of any," he answered, gently stroking her knuckles. "Our society expects dark-elf women to be fierce fighters and protect their families ruthlessly. But I didn't marry a human only to expect her to be a dark-elf," he said with a half-laugh. "Just be yourself, Aless. My only expectation is that you're honest with me."

She beamed, the smile reaching her eyes, but it began to fade. "Veron, I..."

He shook his head. "Really. Don't change a thing."

Her eyes brightened, and she nodded. "I won't. But, Veron..."

Little lights blinked into existence around them, glowing all around them. Pixies.

She gasped. "There are... There..."

"Pixies," he said softly, savoring the wonder illuminating her face. "Little winged people, no taller than your thumb. They love gardens, and live in the healthiest of them, thriving on nectar and pollen."

Her lips parted, she very slowly reached up toward a tiny glow, and the pixie flitted closer to her hand, just out of reach, casting a gentle light on her skin.

"They feel a kinship toward those who love gardens as they do, will even fight to save them."

"So little," she whispered, her eyes wide.

"No one is ever too little to fight for what they believe in."

She turned back to him then in his embrace, beaming a smile, her eyes shining, reflecting the ethereal glow in the starlit night.

His breath caught. Alessandra Ermacora was his wife, and he would do anything for her sake. And he knew it as clearly as the stars shone above them.

She lowered her gaze, her smile fading. "Veron, about the ceremony in Nightbloom..."

He raised her hand to his lips and pressed a soft kiss to it. "We'll discuss it after the party." Whatever she feared about the ceremony, he'd allay. It was different from human celebrations, but he'd prepare her. "Will that be all right? I think we're due for the feast."

"If you keep the duchessa entertained, I think it'll go very well." A brief glimmer in her amused eyes, and she nodded, turning to the hall with him.

So she hadn't missed the duchess's look. Of course she hadn't. And she wanted to use it to their advantage. He wouldn't expect any less.

And it would go perfectly.

His bride was human, and she felt the same way about him as he did about her. Nothing could ruin this night.

CHAPTER 12

*a*less tried to slow her racing heartbeat to no avail as they entered the great hall, each step echoing in the vastness. It was as though she could feel every hair on her head, and every swish of fabric against her skin, every individual thread. Where Veron's hand held hers, the barest touch, the merest stroke of his skin against hers tingled, warmed.

Holy Mother's mercy, she wanted to marry him. She wanted to marry him, and she was about to meet with Paladin Grand Cordon Nunzio.

She wanted to hide, go back to that moment outside and tuck her face against Veron's chest, shut out the world, shut out everything but him, and live there, in that moment, forever.

Nunzio probably wouldn't even agree to her proposal about the library and teaching there. The Order of Terra didn't want women so involved anyway, did they? It had been everything she'd wanted, and she'd been willing to try convincing Veron that they didn't need that second ceremony in Nightbloom, that they'd be better as friends, but...

But she wanted him. Veron *and* her dream.

Say a prayer for me this time, Bianca.

Holy Mother's mercy, if her dream had already been higher than she could probably reach, trying to take both would mean she'd need a taller ladder. A *much* taller ladder.

She'd just have to make one.

Maybe she could talk to Veron, and they could stay together *and* find a way to make the library happen together near Nightbloom? Maybe he'd be passionate about this, too.

And Veron... when she'd tell him tonight what her plan had been, he'd forgive her, wouldn't he? She'd planned all this before she'd truly known him.

There had to be a way for their marriage and her dream to coexist. She would just have to find it.

Against a backdrop of myriad mirrors, the duchessa sat at the head of a long configuration of elaborate place settings, with two empty seats at her side. For them.

Her reflection caught in one mirror—a betrayer, a *liar*—and it reflected in the next angled against it, and the next, and the next, and the next, a crowd of betrayers, of—

"Are you all right?" Veron whispered to her as they approached.

Can we please just leave? Can we disappear into our quarters, into each other, and never emerge?

But even as the thought surfaced, it was impossible. They had the duchessa's friendship, but they couldn't abandon her party and her nobiltà without consequence. It was a victory lap, but a necessary one. She glared at her reflection.

As long as Nunzio didn't approach her about the library

while she was here with Veron, she could keep the situation from spiraling out of control.

She cleared her throat and forced a placid expression. "I'll be fine."

With a warm smile, he led her to the table, seated her, and then himself between her and the duchessa, who had taken an obvious interest in him earlier. That would work to their advantage. He could describe Nightbloom to her, his culture, his people, and as long as the duchessa's curiosity held, the nobiltà would take her cue and support them as well.

A servant between them poured some bubbly white wine, and she tasted it.

"Princess Alessandra," a man's deep, gravelly voice greeted from her other side. "I received the plans you sent for your library."

She froze. *Holy Mother's mercy.*

No, not him. Please, not him. Not now.

As she caught the man with a peripheral glance, his eagle-sharp blue eyes met hers. That aquiline nose, full head of graying hair, cleft chin, and a build like Forza's, wrapped in sigil tattoos.

Nunzio.

She swallowed the wine already in her mouth. "Paladin Grand Cordon," she greeted, cordially but softly.

Slitting those eagle eyes, he leaned back in his chair, his gaze raking over her as if she were some ruffian he'd taken in for questioning. "Your proposal was quite... passionate."

For a moment, she paused, listening to Veron telling the duchessa about his brother in Nightbloom. As long as Nunzio kept his voice down, this night wouldn't turn into a disaster.

"Maybe we could discuss this another time," she said softly.

They could find a way to move forward on the project. Somehow. Maybe the Order would agree to help build the library elsewhere, closer to Nightbloom?

"Are you no longer passionate about literacy and cultural exchange?" Nunzio tilted his head. "Of building peace through shared knowledge and education? Those were your words."

Keep your voice down.

"Of course I am," she whispered, then sipped her wine. The rest of the nobiltà were deep in their own conversations. Thank the Mother for small favors.

Nunzio leaned in. "Then give me a name, any name, of a person who can manage the implementation of your plan," he said, "because I cannot in good faith meddle in this country's political agreements. How did you mean to both oversee the construction and management of a library while marrying and residing in Nightbloom?"

Each word elicited a shiver, even as she struggled to stay still. There was a lull in the conversation next to her, and she dared to look at Veron.

His eyes were wide beneath furrowed brows. He gave a slow, disbelieving head shake.

He'd heard it.

He'd heard it all.

No, no, no, no... She opened her mouth, but he raised his chin, went still—unnaturally still, the wideness of his eyes narrowing to icy, metallic gold.

Coldness.

With a deep breath, he was smiling again as he turned to the duchessa and said something about stone-singing.

What was—?

He—

Her chest tightened as Veron chatted with the duchessa, his steely velvet voice smooth with charm, his quiet laugh lofty.

She'd disappointed him, completely and utterly, and he had bottled it, continued trying to keep the duchessa and her nobiltà entertained. Inside, he had to feel...

"Princess?" Nunzio asked, and he continued speaking, but the sound of his voice faded as a high-pitched ringing found its way to her ear, grew louder and louder until she could hear nothing else.

Her gaze dropped to her lap, to her hands on the violet tulle of her gown, hands that had held Veron's not even an hour ago.

ALESS STOOD WHEN VERON DID, and although he guided her from the hall with a gentle hand at the small of her back, there was nothing gentle about his expression.

He bid the duchessa goodnight with an elegant smile and inclination of his head, called good-natured goodbyes to certain members of the nobiltà he'd chatted with. But beneath that charm was that cold gaze, the chilled gold of his eyes, and the look he'd given her at the table.

The night had been a blur. It still was. She'd eaten tonight and drunk, she supposed, and maybe even danced. Probably with him. But it was just a mess of colors and murmurs and laughs, and then a walk to an empty corridor.

She'd betrayed him. Before they'd ever met, she'd already been resolved to go back on her word.

No matter how badly she wanted to see Mamma's dreams realized, she'd sacrificed Veron's trust to pursue them. Now he knew. And hated her.

"I'm sorry," she said, as he walked her up the stairs, past the windows to the gardens where her life had changed. "I wanted to tell you tonight, but then the Paladin Grand Cordon was there first, and he had questions, and..."

And Veron didn't even look at her. Didn't waver from ascending the steps. Didn't seem to have heard her at all.

"Veron, please," she pleaded, gripping his arm tightly, but he didn't react.

She squeezed her eyes shut as they reached their quarters, where the sharp-eyed guard stood sentinel, along with another. Veron greeted them, and even those brief words were like balm to her wounds.

Inside, he closed the door and released her, then took off his jacket as he headed to the starlit window, where earlier today she'd seen the beauty of him, terrifying and enchanting. In his favor, he could be gentle, shimmering in the sunshine of quiet moments. In his malice, he could be terrible, drenched in the blood of their enemies. And she wanted him. All of him.

He'd brought her into a new world, his world, full of beauty and magic, and had shared it with her. She wanted to live in that world of beauty and magic *with* him. As his wife, his partner.

She had to try to fix this. She *had* to. "Veron—"

"I only had one expectation." His voice was low, cold, lifeless.

She took a step forward. "Please, I—"

"Do you remember, Alessandra?"

Trust is the one expectation I have, he had told her, on their wedding night.

She wrapped her arms around herself. "Trust."

"And all this time, you had this... plan." He clasped his

hands behind his back. "All this... nearness. Affection. Was it all just so I wouldn't suspect?"

"Of course not," she replied quickly, rushing up to him. She reached out to touch his arm, but he didn't budge an inch.

Swallowing, she stared out the window at the darkness, letting the silence settle.

A sprawling courtyard of tangled rose vines lay below, bathed in starlight, shimmering—

Ripped away.

She shook her head.

No, a dream.

Below lay the knot of hedges in the night, rows of lavender, the rectangular pool. She took a deep breath. "I didn't expect we'd like each other this much, Veron. I thought we'd always have an aversion to each other, but that we could become friends. Inspire peace through friendship. That you could be free to do as you wished, and I could see to the library, teach our people, keep fostering this peace—"

"This *peace* is built on the concept that a human and a dark-elf could bind themselves to one another even in marriage," he replied. "Even if only in semblance."

"I know that."

He turned on her. "And you thought separating would be conducive to that? I expected better from you, Alessandra."

"No, it would only mean that we still want to be friends but are on different paths—"

"That the symbol the peace is built on, our marriage, can't work. We'd be setting an example that would take root in every heart across the nation. We'd be doing the Brotherhood's work for them."

She reached out for him, but he avoided her grasp. "But our parents *forced*—"

"The two of us were sacrificed for an entire realm of peace," he said, his voice low. With a hand to his forehead, he sighed. "The worst part of it all is that I would have understood. If you'd just told me in Bellanzole that you wanted to be released, I would have understood."

"I don't *want* to be released."

He stared at her coldly. "I have orders. Even if you wanted me to, I couldn't. Even if I do understand."

He's the one who wishes he could release me. She exhaled sharply. "So that's it? One misstep, and you hate me forever?"

"I don't hate you, Alessandra, but I can't trust someone who has a hidden agenda."

"I made that decision before I ever knew you, Veron. You didn't deserve to be betrayed, but did I deserve to be married off against my will? Traded like some pawn? Was that to be the sum of my worth?"

He squeezed his eyes shut, then ran a hand up over his face and back over his hair. "I can't blame you for that. But the lying? Trust means everything to me. We could have come to an arrangement. But if this had come out some other way, had..." With a shake of his head, he strode to the bedchamber, and she followed. "You don't even see it, do you?"

What was he talking about? "See what?"

He plucked a pillow off the bed and a folded blanket off the chest at the foot of the bed. "Alessandra, tell me where Gabriella comes from."

What was he getting at? "She's my lady-in-waiting. She's from... the royal court."

He marched right back to the parlor, tossed the pillow and

blanket on the sofa, then began removing his boots with a grimace. "Her *home*." The sofa cushion dipped under his weight. "Where is she from?"

She shook her head.

"Gabriella takes care of your entire life. Where is she from? Does she have any siblings? What's important to her?"

"I—I don't know."

He rested his elbows on his knees and leaned forward, his cold gaze boring into her. "You've never asked, have you?"

No... she hadn't. She should've, but... but...

She lowered her chin, scrutinizing the crimson and sable rug, its fringe, broken in places.

"You don't even really know her. And she lives for you, Alessandra. But this—your plan to refuse the second ceremony —would have rippled and caused destruction for so many, those who live outside the tunnel of what you choose to see. Your father might have seen this as reneging, might have pulled the aid he'd given us, and do you have any idea what a baby's starving cry sounds like?"

A chill wove through her. She... She hadn't considered that.

Without the marriage, would Papà have trusted the dark-elves enough and keep sending them aid? Or would he have looked for an ally elsewhere?

And while Veron had mentioned how much people were looking forward to the aid from Bellanzole, she hadn't realized that people were... really starving. That babies were...

Those golden eyes speared her own a moment longer. "I don't blame you for fearing what this marriage would be. Nor even for not wanting it. But did it ever occur to you that, for the good of both our peoples, we might discuss alternate arrangements? That maybe I didn't feel too differently than you did?

Was planning to betray me, to run away without a care for the treaty, really the best course of action? Or just the easiest?"

He looked away with a sigh and stretched out on the sofa, his arm tucked behind his head.

Wringing her tulle skirts, she waited, but he wouldn't look at her. He'd said he didn't blame her, but that wasn't what this felt like. Their people expected so little from one another, and maybe he'd expected little from her, too. And despite a couple brief, glowing moments, she'd fulfilled those low expectations... instead of defying them.

They'd spent every night since Bellanzole together.

Not tonight.

She left for the bedchamber, where she shed all of her clothes, hairpins, and washed her face, donned her nightgown, found her old copy of *A Modern History of Silen*, and nestled into the bed, cocooned herself in the bedding. Such a wonderful night had been destroyed, and it was all her fault.

Veron was angry about the lie, but even more so about the betrayal.

Cradling the book close, she opened to the first page, traced her finger across Mamma's script. *Be brave, my rose, and fill the remaining pages with your deeds.*

As a child, she'd written in minor things. Things most people would deem trivial. Saving a cat from cruel children. Making a statement. Winning an argument.

Over the years, she'd set her sights higher. So high, the view blurred the sight of individual people, the ones she wanted to save, and even the ones around her. She'd focused so intensely on healing her spine, and earning Papà's love by doing so, and shut out nearly everything else until she'd succeeded—at least in recovering from her *curvatura*, if not in impressing Papà.

And then she'd worked so hard for peace, for realizing Mamma's vision, that she'd lost the instinct to see those around her.

She saw Veron now, or was beginning to. She'd see Gabriella. The dark-elf guards with them. And the people she intended to save. She wouldn't be anyone's pawn, but in her pursuit of Mamma's vision, she wouldn't sacrifice the lives of others by destroying the peace. Not the Sileni, not the dark-elves, not even the Brotherhood if it could be avoided. Enough lives had been lost.

And Veron might have given up on her, but she... she wouldn't give up on him. He was right about her not thinking through the consequences for his people, and even her own. He was right that she shouldn't have lied.

But not being able to trust her after this? When it came to that, he was dead wrong. And she would prove it to him.

Tomorrow he'd begin to see just how stubborn she could be.

CHAPTER 13

*B*efore Veron could properly open his eyes, there were already sounds coming from the bedchamber. Quick footsteps, the slosh of water, rustling fabric, and creaking hinges.

The sun hadn't even risen yet, and she was already up. He shook his head. The sun had to be mistaken.

He was on his feet and stretching when Aless walked in, wearing a form-fitting but utilitarian purple dress and holding the Offering bow. With a raise of her eyebrows, she met his gaze.

"I'm ready for an archery lesson, if you're going to the range." She sat in an armchair while he began his morning routine.

He nodded an acknowledgment, then washed up. All this time, from the moment he'd met her in Bellanzole until last night, she'd been lying to him. There had been moments when she'd wanted to confess—on their wedding night, and in the garden, at the very least. But she hadn't, in all this time.

He wanted to trust her, but if she was prone to hiding things, could she be expected to change now, for the rest of her life?

They were still married. He still cared for her. But in the garden, had there been a lie in her kiss, in her embrace? Had the touch of her hand borne deception in its warmth? Had the tears in her eyes welled with betrayal?

Would she have told him the truth eventually?

Even so, that wasn't trustworthiness. Where did that leave them?

He dressed, staring at his bow in the corner. Even if he and Aless didn't see eye to eye right now, he *had* promised to train her, and he wouldn't go back on his word. But he couldn't forget last night either.

He grabbed his bow and headed through the parlor and out in the hall. Her light footsteps fell in behind him, along with Riza's and Danika's.

Some of the kuvari were already in the training yard, practicing with their vjernost blades, and the duchess's men were somewhere between sparring and gawking. Seeing the kuvari in combat—honed for decades or centuries—was a thing of wonder, mesmerizing and deadly. One of them in Mati's Quorum, his sister Vadiha included, would someday take Mati's place. Their skills had to be impeccable.

At the range, Gavri was already shooting and moved to retrieve her arrows—clustered in the center, per usual—before her gaze snapped to his direction. She bowed, removed her arrows, and quit the yard.

Staying out of his sight, as he'd ordered.

He swallowed over a pain at the back of his throat.

With a tilted head, Aless eyed him, but he only took her bow and strung it for her. He didn't need to talk, not about this.

In the sword ring, one of the kuvari disarmed another, and whoops rose up from the Sileni guards clustered around them. He nodded to the victrix—Lira, who smiled knowingly. Only Mati and Riza could take her when it came to swords, and she well knew it.

After he gathered some supplies, he met Aless fifteen yards from a target, where she crouched, plucking clover. He pointed his chin downrange. "You said you've done this before."

She grimaced. "Poorly."

"Show me." He took a step back and crossed his arms.

She held out a partially braided clover chain until he reluctantly took it. Then, with a heavy sigh, she faced the target, nocked an arrow with her shoulders high, aimed, then closed her eyes as she released. The arrow landed on the ground five feet away.

She winced at him.

Poorly had been right. "Give it another try."

She puffed. "Veron, I..."

He only fixed her with a stare. No one was perfect without practice.

With an even heavier sigh, she turned back to the target again, but this time, he grabbed her shoulders—eliciting a gasp, but no objection—and turned her to stand at a right angle to the target. Using his foot, he tapped her feet shoulder-width apart.

Her shoulders were tight as a bowstring.

"Relax," he told her, patting her shoulders gently, and she smelled like... like—he frowned—like the lavender last night, and it soothed, made him want to close his eyes, breathe slow and deep.

With a nod to herself, she nocked another arrow, and he readjusted it under the nocking point on the string. As she extended her bow arm, he pressed her shoulders down.

"You're at full draw. Transfer the weight of the bow from your arms to your back. Now aim." As she did, he added, "See the string line up on the top bow limb a little to the right of the sight ring. Now pull your shoulder blades closer to each other as you relax your right hand's fingers, and keep aiming. Your relaxed left hand will let your bow drop a bit. Let it. And don't move until the arrow hits the target."

She released, eyes open, and the arrow missed just shy of the target.

Her eyebrows drew together, but then she glanced up at him, lips parted, purple dress battered by the wind. Like the lavender last night, when they'd...

Just a blink, a flutter of dark lashes, and he was in the garden again, his shoulders tensing as he wanted to wrap her in his arms, shield her from the wind, feel those soft lips against his once more...

He cleared his throat. "Not bad. Keep practicing."

Before she could reply, he headed for a target of his own, far from hers.

BEFORE A MIRROR, Aless rubbed her shoulder as Gabriella put the finishing touches on her hairstyle. She shifted in the chair, rubbing against smooth mahogany armrests, and flinching. Both of her shoulders hurt, and her arms, and her fingers... but she and Veron still had to make an offering at Stroppiata's shrine before they left the city. Although she felt like a mess of soreness and fatigue, she'd have to be perfect. Ideal.

Or at least *look* it.

Veron had kept his word and given her an archery lesson today. If she'd been a better person, she would have released him from the promise. Let him keep his distance. Let him forget all about her. Not worn the lavender dress. Not used the lavender perfume. Not seized the opportunity to get close, as she'd once seen another courtier do.

But she *wasn't* better. His touch, even through his mask of coolness, had been like a comforting whisper, telling her all hope wasn't lost. Maybe it wasn't. But whatever his feelings for her became, she'd heard him clearly last night: she hadn't examined too closely the things and people she hadn't wanted to see.

She would today.

And for their sakes, she wouldn't disrupt the peace in any way, even if Veron hated her for the length of their marriage. There had to be another way to realize her dream, one that didn't involve abandoning the marriage—and she'd find it.

"Well, what do you think?" Gabriella asked, smiling in the mirror as she evaluated the elaborate hairstyle, with warm hazel eyes.

The princess in the mirror didn't look like a cold-hearted liar or betrayer. She had shining hair, half of it up in soft twists with pearl pins, with the rest flowing voluminously in gentle brown waves. A delicate pink stained her lips, and the daintiest blush enlivened her cheeks.

Gabriella had suggested a yellow taffeta dress with gold-threaded embroidery, and it was bright and happy, with long, flowing sleeves that softened the look even more. The color of the sun, of the Goddess's bounty each harvest. Fitting.

"You've outdone yourself," Aless whispered as Gabriella laughed and fastened a strand of pearls.

"Today is important, so you have to look the part." Gabriella adjusted the pearls, keeping the closure at the nape of Aless's neck.

So much effort. "I thought you didn't like the dark-elves?"

Gabriella's hand rose to her chest. "I don't think anything of them—I—"

"Just with the talk of the Brotherhood, it seemed—"

"I only thought you wanted out of the marriage. That day we left the palazzo, you looked so... so..." Gabriella's round face sank in the mirror. "I just want you to be happy."

In the years she'd known Gabriella, there hadn't been a hateful bone in her body. Maybe there still wasn't. "Well, today I look it, thanks to you."

With an uneasy smile, Gabriella took a step back, clasped her hands, and gave a pleased nod in the mirror. Gabriella's dress was a plain but well-tailored mauve satin overgown with a white cambric kirtle beneath, feminine and cut fashionably. Always taking great care in her appearance.

"Have I ever asked you where you're from?" Aless whispered, meeting Gabriella's eyes in the mirror.

Those beautifully shaped eyebrows shot up. "Vistadelfino. Our fathers grew up together, and His Majesty made him the conte there. My mother was one of Her Majesty's ladies before..." Gabriella lowered her gaze and breathed deeply.

One of Mamma's ladies... before she was murdered.

"I became your lady shortly after..." Gabriella swallowed. "And you never asked me, but... you hardly spoke then."

After Mamma's death, all she'd done was read. About ancient wars, myths, and world-spanning romances. About women who fought, women who ruled, women who married for love. About mothers and daughters being strong together, and idealistic heroes bettering people's lives. About anything and everything that could take her from the misery of her own life then. Gabriella had been there with her, side by side, and had never pried or pushed. Just accompanied her when she'd most needed someone.

"Thank you," she whispered, and Gabriella raised a hand, shaking her head. "No, really. Mamma's been gone a long time, and I should have gotten to know you better—"

Arms closed around her, and she gasped, blinking, wrapping her own arm around Gabriella.

"Your Highness, it is *my* duty to take care of you, not the other way around."

"I'd like for us to take care of each other. You've been my friend for as long as I can remember, and I... I want to be your friend, too." She breathed in the gentle lilac of Gabriella's long, sable hair. "I want to know what's important to you."

Gabriella pulled back, beaming. "We're more alike in that than you think, Your Highness." She half-laughed under her breath. "My mother loved books and teaching with Her Majesty, helping the poor in Bellanzole. And when His Majesty forbade it... it broke her heart. She wants to see us doing that again. And so do I."

All this time, Gabriella had quietly supported her. As she'd helped distribute books and discuss plans, it hadn't merely been as a lady-in-waiting, but as a dreamer herself.

"I promise you that I will realize it. Even if it's with my dying breath."

"I know you will. And I'll be there to help," Gabriella whispered, just as the hall door creaked open.

"His Highness awaits you downstairs," a low, feminine voice called.

"We'll be right out," she replied. When the door shut, she stood and stepped into her matching yellow taffeta shoes.

She bit her lip. "Gabriella, do you know who that was?"

"Her name is Gavri, I think. She had a falling out with His Highness a few days ago."

AFTER SAYING their goodbyes to the duchessa, Aless let Veron help her into the carriage, where he sat across from her and Gabriella, who held the offerings of lilies, peacock feathers, honey, and pomegranates in a myrtle-wood basket.

He wore another of Lorenzo's gifts, a gold-embroidered black brocade overcoat, fitted from the shoulders to the waist, and then split and flowing from the hips to the ankles. It had an elegance to it, a drama that Lorenzo no doubt had loved, and a cut suited to strong shoulders and a fit physique.

Veron, and the other dark-elves, remained unmasked, unhooded. None of the duchessa's household seemed fazed, and hopefully their luck would continue with the paesani.

The carriage set out, and the castle's verdant, manicured grounds moved past the window, the standard of the Sileni nobiltà. Everything ordered and uniform, nothing like the sprawling wild roses in her daydreams. Not the variegated, messy, beautiful chaos of vines and blooms and ruins.

Leaning back against the seat, Veron rested an ankle on his opposite knee. He looked her over, and when his eyes met hers, he nodded toward the offerings. "What do they symbolize?"

She cleared her throat, trying not to seem too excited by the notion of him merely speaking to her. But it was progress. "They are Terra's offerings. The lilies are for loyalty. The peacock feathers for longevity. The honey is for abundance, and the pomegranates for fertility."

He raised a pale eyebrow and tilted his head.

Swallowing, she lowered her gaze to her yellow-taffeta skirts and clasped her hands. This was their one chance to leave a peaceful and positive impression in Stroppiata, instead of the harpy bloodbath of their arrival. But it was also her sincere prayer, for blessings she very much wished the Holy Mother would someday bestow upon her.

By the time they stopped at the shrine, a crowd of paesani had already gathered, watching as Veron helped her and Gabriella out of the carriage with an escort of dark-elf royal guards—kuvari—and cheering as dark-elves distributed food. More and more people moved closer, and the crowd grew and grew, voices shouting, hands reaching, bodies pressing closer, tighter.

"We have to move. Now," the dark-elf guard with the braid —Gavri—hissed to her. "On foot, we can't control this crowd. The situation could deteriorate quickly."

She'd trust Gavri's expertise—they would only stay long enough to fulfill their purpose. With a nod, she headed toward the shrine with Veron and his kuvari.

Along the way to the monumental bronze doors, Gabriella handed her the basket of offerings, and holding it with one arm, she clasped hands with an old woman, then two young women, and little girls. They'd all come to give their thanks at Terra's shrine, and in this, they were the same.

"Terra's blessings upon you!" an elderly woman offered.

"And upon you," she responded, the same response every Terran always gave to the blessing.

For his part, Veron smiled kindly at her side, offering cordial greetings and thanking the people for their blessings. His nearness was warm, comforting, and without even looking, she could feel his big form beside her, his watchful eyes glancing at her every so often.

As a pair of guards opened the bronze doors, Veron's gloved hand took hers, and they entered.

Some of the crowd filtered inside—as expected, to view this moment, to spread the word. Gavri and the other guards kept the crowd at a distance, while she and Veron faced the marble altar and the enormous golden statue of Terra beneath the saucer dome. She'd seen it before, hand in hand with Mamma, craning her neck to see to the very top and following Mamma through the prayer and ritual.

Maiden, Mother, Crone; She of the Heights; Protector of All. The Goddess towered before them in shining gold, a crown upon her head, a peplos draped about her, bearing a spear in one hand and a phiale in the other.

With one hand offering, and with the other fighting.

Her hand in Veron's, Aless approached the altar, knelt, then placed her offerings upon it. "O blessed Mother, worshipped and adored, called by women in tearful need and in rites at ancient shrines, please accept these humble offerings. Revered among the Eternan pantheon for the realms you protect, for the bounty you offer, for the life you bloom, we ask You to watch over us as we journey this path together toward Your guiding light."

A hush had settled over the shrine.

Holy Mother, please let us succeed in sowing this peace, in stop-

ping a war no one needs to fight. She kept her head bowed, as did Veron at her side. *Please guide me and let me be stronger, braver, more compassionate. Grant me the strength to follow your teachings.*

At long last, she made to rise, and Veron helped her to her feet. He'd been by her side, supporting her as she'd prayed.

"What do you pray for?" he asked, looking her over, his eyebrows drawn.

"Peace. Strength," she whispered back. And when it came to the peace, they could use all the help they could get. Especially the Holy Mother's. "But mostly just giving thanks."

When she grinned out at the crowd, some faces beamed back, but others faced away, murmurs spreading.

They hadn't been here long, but clearly long enough to allow doubt to enter, and questions.

"Monsters," someone whispered.

"Dangerous," said another.

No. She had to save this—*now*. The only way she knew.

She cleared her throat. "People of Stroppiata," she called out, "we thank you for opening your city and your hearts to us, and allowing us to share in our worship of the Holy Mother." She looked out over the people gathered as they quieted. "I have offered prayers for as long as I can remember, and today, I stand here blessed—with a husband both kind and strong enough to defend our people, and a new family, as both Sileni and dark-elves join together against the Immortali that would threaten us, and for the righteous cause of a lasting peace." *Both for survival, and our own betterment.* "We follow the Holy Mother's guidance—sharing our bounty with one hand, but with the other, defending one another against any dangers that would seek to destroy us, or to divide us. And together, we are strong. Terra's blessings upon you all, my brothers and sisters."

"And upon you," came the harmony of replies, the response every Terran instinctively gave, ingrained from early childhood.

She inclined her head, as did Veron next to her, but his golden gaze rested on her, intense, but softening as his mouth curved. That look remained as they exited the shrine, boarded the carriage, and headed for the city's western gates toward the dark-elf queendom of Dunmarrow.

Arms crossed, Veron leaned against the carriage's window, a smile on his face and a gleam in his eyes. "You were amazing in there, Aless."

So she was back to being *Aless* and not *Alessandra*. A step toward earning back his trust, maybe?

Don't put the cart before the horse.

Next to her, Gabriella grinned, but covered it and looked away. Nice of her.

"It was just some words," she answered, tapping his boot with her shoe. "Nothing like battling harpies."

"No," he said, with a slow shake of his head. "You know your people. You see them."

It was nice of him to say, but their argument had inspired her to look closer. And she would continue doing so. But... "I won't argue with that."

And so she didn't.

CHAPTER 14

Sitting on a blanket, Aless steeped passionflower tea before the campfire while watching the chestnuts roast. The late-afternoon sun peeked through the canopy of turkey oaks, sparse but a vivid green. Some of the dark-elves picked through the undergrowth and climbed a massive sweet chestnut tree, gathering more that Gabriella helped collect.

"Are they any good?" Gavri asked, nodding toward the tree.

Over the past couple of days, they'd spoken from time to time, as Gavri seemed to guard her when Veron wasn't around. She wanted to befriend Gavri if she could, but hadn't caught her for more than a few minutes at a time.

"I've had chestnut creme in desserts before. Very sweet. Tasty." *Crème de marrons*, as the Emaurrians called it. "I've read about soldiers in ancient Silen eating chestnut porridge the morning of battle."

Gavri grunted. "I'll take that creme thing over the porridge.

But considering we're going to Dun Mozg, maybe preparing for war isn't such a bad idea."

She frowned. "Why is that?"

Gavri leaned in, her braid falling over her shoulder. "Veron didn't tell you?"

She wiggled aside on the blanket until there was enough room to sit, and then she motioned to Gavri, who looked about warily before lowering.

"He told me about Queen Nendra, who's the most famous warrior among the dark-elves," she said, preparing another cup of passionflower tea.

"She is," Gavri replied, but with an exhaustion that could be a decade old. "And her queendom sits on the largest arcanir mine we've ever known. A really important one, worth almost any sacrifice to gain access. Dun Mozg prides itself on its weapons, and its soldiery."

Arcanir? That certainly was useful against the Immortali beasts. She handed the ready cup to Gavri, who accepted it with a raised eyebrow. "He also said his brother Zoran was chosen as her consort because of his prowess among your people in Nightbloom."

Gavri inhaled deeply, turned the cup in her hands, and nodded slowly. "Oh, yes," she said. "Zoran's... *prowess*... is well known to me."

It didn't seem like Gavri meant *battle* prowess.

She swallowed, pouring the boiling water.

It overflowed, and Gavri caught the kettle's handle.

"Y-you and—" she stammered.

Gavri set the kettle down. "Once upon a time." She sighed. "I was a very ambitious kuvari recruit. And he was one of Nozva Rozkveta's most accomplished warriors. The math told me I needed to best him to prove myself. I did, and..." She shrugged a shoulder.

Frozen, Aless stared and stared. Never had a sentence needed finishing more than Gavri's. "And *what*?"

"And for eight years, we tired each other out in the training yard and in the bedchamber," Gavri said with a grin, then took a sip of tea.

"*Eight years*?" How had they been together for eight years, eight *long* years, and yet he'd ended up Queen Nendra's consort?

Gavri nodded and took another sip. "What's in this?"

"Passionflower," Aless blurted, then motioned for her to continue.

"Passionflower? Like the aphrodisiac?" A skewed stare. "Are you—"

"No! Holy Mother, no!" Aless cleared her throat, gathering her composure as some glances turned her way. She was not drinking it for *that*. "While it *is* a mild aphrodisiac, it also soothes the nerves."

Grinning broadly, Gavri shrugged again. "Whatever you say."

"So what happened?"

"Nendra bested the previous queen of Dun Mozg, and she needed a consort. Queen Zara offered her the best." She sipped her tea. "You know, this stuff is really starting to grow on me."

"Just like that, and he was gone?"

Gavri nodded. "He was. As a prince, he would never be able to make the Offering to anyone but royalty." She sighed. "But then Prince Veron found me in the training cavern and asked me to spar. And then the next day, and the next. We became friends, and then Queen Zara assigned me to his guard."

So Veron had seen Gavri after losing someone she loved, and he'd befriended her. That sounded like him. She smiled warmly.

A gentle shiver stroked up her back, and when she looked across the camp, Veron was looking at her while he brushed Noc. She'd been earning Noc's trust lately, at least, with a couple apples here and there, and fables Mamma had read to her about unicorns and fey horses. If only Veron's trust could be recovered so easily.

Gavri followed her line of sight and started. "I... I should go."

She rested a hand on Gavri's knee. "No, stay, please."

Across the camp, a long, silky black tail smacked Veron in the face. He eyed Noc sheepishly and mumbled something to him.

As she smiled, a soft laugh bubbled next to her. Gavri's. But it soon faded.

"What happened between you and Veron? You don't speak to each other anymore."

Gavri set the cup down, tucked the braid over her shoulder, and fidgeted with its tip, her gaze downcast. "I... violated his trust." She took a deep breath. "I lost Zoran in an instant. And when Veron was betrothed to you, I expected... a lot. After the wedding, after your... dress... the reaction from your people wasn't invisible."

She lowered her own gaze. "I know. I regret that."

"It was between the two of you. I know that. But... I just wanted him to rebel against the marriage, too. I didn't want him to be understanding and reasonable and diplomatic as he always is. I wanted him to fight back," she said, clapping a hand on her thigh. "He wouldn't, so I... intervened. I badmouthed you and told him I'd given you a tent when I hadn't, just so you could seem spoiled. Well, *more* spoiled."

A half-laugh escaped her before she could stop herself, but Gavri met it with a fleeting grin.

"I probably deserved it, Gavri."

"Oh, you did. But *he* didn't. He didn't deserve me betraying him. He's not Zoran, and you're not Nendra. And you're—you're not what I expected." She chewed her lip a moment. "A bit spoiled, yes, but you actually care about nurturing peace between us and the humans. You tried to get them to accept us in Stroppiata, first with the mask thing, then at the shrine. I judged you too soon, and I was wrong."

Speechless, Aless could only give a nod.

"Veron doesn't let people into his heart easily." Gavri drained the tea and placed the empty cup before her. "Nozva Rozkveta was once at war with the light-elf queendom of Lumia. Veron's father, King-consort Mirza, killed the light-elf consort in battle, but we lost, and Lumia took many of our people as prisoners. Lumia threatened to kill them all unless Queen Zara delivered Mirza in exchange. Before the message got to her, Mirza had already decided to deliver himself. Regardless of the queen's wishes. Veron caught him leaving, and Mirza smiled. Told Veron he was going hunting and would return soon, so there would be no commotion, no fight. And then he left for Lumia, where he was executed before the light-elf queen released our prisoners."

The words, though spoken aloud, felt like air. Thick, dense, suffocating air, pushing in closer and closer until she could barely breathe.

Veron's father had gone against his wife and queen, had sacrificed himself for her, for their queendom, for Veron... But in doing so, he'd hurt his son, to the core, leaving a wound that had lasted for years, and maybe a lifetime.

"Veron was destroyed. Utterly destroyed. To his mind, Mirza had betrayed him, his entire family, because they'd loved Mirza and he'd ignored that to turn himself over. I don't think Veron ever forgave his father, and his trust, once broken, is unrecoverable."

Unrecoverable. The word hit her like an arrow, and she shuddered.

Gavri moved closer. "But he sees something different in you," she whispered. "Something special. And I... I see it, too."

Aless eyed her. "Too much passionflower tea, Gavri?"

A hearty laugh. "Not that. Although I'm certain it would help." She waggled an eyebrow.

Holy Mother's mercy.

"I mean... You think in an unusual way. At first, in your capital, you were using it selfishly. But then... on the way to Stroppiata, and when we were leaving, you handled matters in ways we usually don't. And Veron is a warrior, too, but he wants to see more peaceful means, diplomatic means, all he ever seems to dream about. And then here you are, as if you'd stepped right out of one of those dreams." Gavri pulled away, biting her lip. "If you'd been a dark-elf, you would've been perfect." A wink.

Smiling, Aless elbowed her. Every now and then, Veron looked at her for a while, contemplative, but kept his distance other than during their daily archery lessons. To his credit, she could now sometimes hit the target. *Sometimes.*

But what they'd had in the garden... That hadn't returned. And despite his contemplative looks, it might never return, no matter how much effort she put in.

But I won't give up. She'd earn back his trust no matter what it would take.

"I'm going to go see if I can help with that chestnut mush thing." Gavri rose.

"Porridge."

"That." Inclining her head, Gavri took her leave.

Well, if they were having chestnut porridge for breakfast, at least they'd be prepared for the queendom of arcanir and soldiery tomorrow.

VERON WATCHED Aless in the Dun Mozg tunnels, her staring, her gasping, her awe. She was impressed, and she would only be more impressed when she arrived in Nozva Rozkveta.

Perfectly circular, the rippled tunnels stretched through countless miles of solid rock, linking the dark-elf queendoms. No one but a Dun Mozg dark-elf knew about direct Gates between the queendom and the sky-realm, but the tunnels were used by every queendom, and he well knew how to get to Dun Mozg through them, even if it was taking them an hour so far on horseback.

"They're massive," Aless whispered, and her voice carried. "How can you be sure the—the *earthmover wyrms*—are gone?"

He laughed under his breath. She was right; the tunnels were massive, and they were but small ants in them. "Although the earthmovers created our tunnels and territories, we know they're here no longer because there haven't been earthquakes."

"Earthquakes?" Aless's dark eyebrows knitted together before they rose high. "Aha. *Earthmovers.*"

Soon, the tunnels began to twinkle in the light of their torches and lanterns, and she squinted. "What are...?"

"Gemstones," he supplied, and she gasped. "Arcanir isn't the only material found here, although it's one of the few *useful* ones."

Her mouth fell open. "But gemstones are—"

"Very valuable to humans." He smiled at her. "They barter timber, leather, food crops, livestock, and other valuable items to us, and in return, they want *shiny stones*."

She cocked her head. "When you put it like that, we all sound like idiots."

He shrugged happily. "Not all of you, but if the jewelry fits."

She stroked fingers over her pearls. "You know, it's not just the *shiny* aspect. Rarity means a lot, too. It means we've had to sacrifice to obtain something. An entire city crafting an icon of Terra out of gold means they sacrificed a great deal for the sake of the Holy Mother."

A little defensive. He bowed his head, hiding a smile. "Saffron is rare, isn't it?"

She pursed her lips. "A statue made out of saffron *might* not last very long, Veron." Despite her prickly tone, her eyes gleamed.

That gleam made his poking all worthwhile. There was something about her that just lightened his heart, made him feel almost weightless. The way she made him feel—that couldn't be possible if she were malicious, someone who'd betray affection freely given. Perhaps he'd misjudged her.

People had always been difficult for him to read, ever since Ata. How could he have gotten his own father so wrong? And other volodari, kuvari, and former lovers.

He cared for Aless. Perhaps even trusted *her*, but not

himself, not his ability to understand her well enough to predict when things could go wrong, and to stop them.

"So does Nightbloom get arcanir from here?" Aless asked.

He breathed deep. "Dun Mozg supplies us with arcanir weapons, yes. We, in turn, provide food and spices, since they're scarce here," he explained. "They've had to hunt a lot more than we have, and they've lost volodari to the Brotherhood. When we woke from the Sundering, all our farms had long since withered or been overgrown, so we couldn't supply ourselves yet, let alone Dun Mozg. While we re-establish our food crops and spice caravans, we need the trade Silen could provide."

Nozva Rozkveta had been starving, but Dun Mozg had suffered an even greater food scarcity; they'd deployed more volodari to address that, and had lost many to the Brotherhood. That would make them either happier about the treaty or more embittered toward the humans as a whole. Hopefully the former.

"You help against the other Immortali in exchange for our food," she whispered. "And then you provide food and spices to Dunmarrow for weapons..."

He nodded. Now she understood the basics of their trade with Queen Nendra.

Before long, they came upon the circular set of Dun Mozg's stone doors, where Riza dismounted, took one of the hammers provided, and pounded Nozva Rozkveta's knock. She replaced the hammer and stepped back.

"That sound was..." Aless whispered to him, her head tilted.

He urged Noc closer to her. "Each dark-elf queendom has its own. It's how we identify ourselves to one another."

She tapped her fingers against her thigh, the same rhythm

Riza had pounded. Nozva Rozkveta's rhythm. Again and again, as if she were practicing it.

He leaned forward, watching the movement of those elegant, tapered fingers as they sounded like home, his home, *their* home, and when the doors creaked open, minutes must have passed... or seconds. Clearing his throat, he straightened.

Zoran, Noc thought to him, with a swish of his tail and a rolling, blowing snort.

We'll see him soon. Veron patted him. Zoran had always visited the stables every day in Nozva Rozkveta, before becoming king-consort to Nendra, and had been fond of Noc in particular.

Once the doors were open, two kuvari stood in light arcanir armor, bearing halberds.

Riza stepped forward. "Hail, kin of Dun Mozg, blessed of the Deep, the Darkness, and Holy Ulsinael," she called out, and every dark-elf in the cavalcade saluted. "We of Nozva Rozkveta come as kindred, in the service of His Highness, Prince Veron u Zara u Avrora u Roza, Valaz u Nozva Rozkveta, Zpevan Kamena, Volodar T'my, and Her Highness, Princess Alessandra u Aldona u Noor u Elise, Valazi u Nozva Rozkveta, Valazi u Silen."

Aless leaned in. "Those are the names of my mother, my grandmother, and my great-grandmother," she whispered, her voice high.

Was she surprised? "My mother wanted to know everything about you," he whispered back. *And I wanted to know everything about you...*

"Dun Mozg bids you welcome," came the Dun Mozg kuvari's reply. "May the Deep, Darkness, and Holy Ulsinael guide you in our queendom." The two stepped aside, standing at attention as the cavalcade passed into the open doors. "Her Majesty, Queen Nendra, awaits you in the grand hall. Enjoy the games."

"Games?" Aless asked him. "Like you mentioned at our wedding?"

He nodded. "Our festivities include games, where anyone can challenge anyone in the ring to a light hand-to-hand match."

"Anyone?" Her voice broke.

Closing his eyes, he brought a hand to his face. It was so commonplace a tradition among his people, he hadn't even thought about it.

He should have.

He cleared his throat softly. "Yes. Anyone."

ALESS TIGHTENED her quivering fingers on the reins. There would be games tonight, and she—who'd never trained in combat a day in her life—could be challenged?

Gentle warmth rested on her hand, Veron's palm on her skin. Riding close, he dipped his head, meeting her gaze with his shimmering golden eyes.

"It's only light sparring, but there is no honor in challenging someone unskilled," he said delicately.

"Yelena," the sharp-eyed guard said with a cough, earning a glare and a hiss from Veron.

That couldn't be good. "What's Yelena?"

"Not *what*. Who," the sharp-eyed guard answered, while Veron waved her off.

"Don't listen to Riza. Yelena won't challenge you."

The sharp-eyed guard—Riza—scoffed, the sound echoing in the enormous dark tunnel.

Aless grasped Veron's fingers. "Who is she?" A rival? An old flame? An enemy?

He closed his eyes a moment and exhaled lengthily. "Yelena is spoiled—"

"Strong," Riza interjected.

"—and selfish—"

"Ambitious."

"—opportunistic—"

"And your former lover." Riza scowled at him. "She'll feel an instant rivalry."

Veron grunted. "Her people are starving and getting picked off by the Brotherhood. She knows better than to jeopardize this treaty."

Former lover...

What kind of woman was she, this Yelena? Strong, ambitious...

"She doesn't have to harm Her Highness," Riza said. "A challenge will be enough for everyone present to witness Her Highness decline. Dark-elves will never respect Her Highness after that."

So she couldn't fight, and she couldn't decline.

There had to be other moves to make. She just had to find them.

"I'll talk to her," Veron bit out to Riza.

"When has that ever worked?" Riza asked derisively. "Just ignore her. Completely."

"That might anger her enough to goad her," he replied as they neared the end of the tunnel.

"It's your best chance," Riza shot back, and they continued arguing, but it didn't matter.

She had no control over what this Yelena might do or not. All that remained was gathering what facts she could to determine a course of action. The *right* course of action, to both earn the dark-elves' respect while staying out of Yelena's way.

The tunnel opened to an unimaginably enormous cavern, so vast its end wasn't visible, washed in a soft green glow that illuminated buildings below. The cavern walls bloomed with green—

"Bioluminescence," Veron whispered in her ear, his steely velvet voice making her shiver. "Fourteen types of bioluminescent mushrooms grow in our queendoms."

Mushrooms? They looked like flowers, almost. Like petals. But beneath them was a city like black glass. Buildings with jagged edges, spikes, hard angles, but glossed and shining like mirrors. People wandered the black stone paths, chatting and laughing, while others disappeared into caves branching off from the main cavern. At the center of it all was the largest building, like a budding black crystal cluster, beautiful and majestic, surrounded by a glowing teal waterway that overflowed to the depths below.

Her heart froze, then pounded. "It's breathtaking."

Veron chuffed quietly, his eyes glittering. "Wait until you see Nozva Rozkveta."

It was like this, too?

But the cavalcade was already moving, and he cocked his head for her to follow. She urged her horse after him and Noc, a line leading up to a long building, where whinnies and nickers greeted them.

Veron helped her dismount and personally led Noc and her horse inside, through the bustle of people.

A man with long, unbound hair stood before one of the stalls, rubbing a horse's nose. Strapping, with long, flowing hair, a smile curling the corners of his mouth—it looked almost permanent. And the same shade of slate-blue skin Veron had, just a little darker than most.

"Zoran," Veron called. "I knew I'd find you in here."

Zoran? The same Zoran that Gavri had mentioned?

"Brother!" Zoran turned to him, those same golden eyes wide, and tackled Veron in a hug, patting him on the back. "It's been an age!"

Zoran had the same chiseled features Veron did—the high cheekbones, prominent chin, angular jaw—and yet they were louder somehow; Zoran's grin was broad and his laugh hearty, his movements sweeping and large. He himself was slightly taller than Veron's six and a half feet, and wider. Whereas Veron was quiet and intense, she could already hear Zoran's guffaws and booming voice.

"I knew that where horses were near, you couldn't be far." With a lopsided grin, Veron eyed his brother, clapping him on the shoulder. They stabled her horse and Noc, with a pair of stable hands coming to help.

Zoran gusted a heavy sigh. "Better here than the fortress. Nendra is occupied with her current favorite. A werewolf alpha."

Current favorite?

Veron's grin disappeared as he shook his head, earning a shrug from Zoran. "She'll tire of him soon enough. Too moody."

Wasn't the queen married to Zoran?

He looked past Veron to her. "And you must be Alessandra!"

Clearing her throat, she curtseyed, but he blazed right past Veron and hugged her.

"Glad to make your acquaintance, King-consort—"

"*Zoran*," he corrected, his arms tight around her. "We're family now!"

Despite his volume, his embrace was genuine, and he smelled familiar, of horse—she couldn't dislike him.

"Nice to meet you," she replied, meeting Veron's sparkling gaze as he stood, one arm crossed over his chest, and the other hand curled and covering his mouth.

He looked ready to burst out laughing himself, which would be a new sight for her.

Zoran released her and leaned against a stall, his face bright. "So how do you like my brother? Is he too quiet? Too severe? With his obedience and duty and peace and all that?"

Something like a bark of laughter came from Veron before he bowed his head and coughed.

"He's..." *Wonderful.* "I..." *Adore him.* "We..."

"Say no more." Zoran held up a hand. "Or it'll all go to his head."

She grimaced.

"Ah, so she does have a humorous bone in her body."

Veron elbowed his brother.

"What about the boot thing?" Zoran continued. "Does he still do the boot thing?"

A wry look from Veron. "I do *not* have a 'boot thing.' It's not my fault most boots are just not in the least—"

"You *so* have a boot thing." Zoran fixed him with a stare.

"Boot... thing?" she asked. If there was one man who could

make a perfect pair of boots, it was Lorenzo's cobbler. She'd have to write home.

Footsteps padded behind her, and the mirth faded from Zoran's gaze as he looked past her.

She glanced back, where Gavri had entered with a horse. Gavri quickly tried to back up, but there was nowhere to go.

Zoran bridged the distance between them, leaning in close. "Gavri." The word sounded like a greeting, a whisper, an apology, and an admiration all in one.

"I need to leave. Could you—" Gavri pushed through a trio of kuvari and their horses, but Zoran caught her hand.

"Meet me here later, during dinner," Zoran whispered to Gavri. "There's so much I need to tell you."

Gavri twisted in his grip, her hand going to her braid. "I—I can't. I have guard duty." She turned and picked through the crowded stable, but his glittering eyes followed her as she left.

Gavri really wasn't going to hear what Zoran—the man she'd loved, to whom she'd given *eight* years—had to say?

She moved to follow Gavri out of the stable, and Veron caught up with her.

"See you at the games," Veron called back to his brother, then helped her clear a path.

The games... the ones where—unless she got an idea in the next few hours—she would let down all of her new subjects with a single word.

CHAPTER 15

*A*s Veron entered the training cavern, Yelena was already there in her kuvari robes, practicing the sword. Her hair was up in the braided circlet as it always had been, and her movements were lithe and agile as ever.

"Did you miss me?" she asked with a sweep of her blade, smiling impishly.

"Two thousand years passed in the blink of an eye," he murmured, leaning against a blackstone pillar. Two thousand more could pass before he'd miss her—no, not even *then*.

Dark-amber eyes darted to him as she stepped into a lunge. "Look at you, all decked out."

He was already dressed in his combat leathers, ready for dinner.

"So your mother finally married you off. And to a human."

He crossed his arms. He cared for Aless, but rubbing it in Yelena's face wasn't going to win him any favors here. "I do as my queen commands."

She forced out a laugh. "I certainly would have used that to my advantage."

"It was never going to be yours to use."

Setting her jaw, she practiced a block. "You just couldn't see my vision."

Oh, he had seen her vision, all too clearly. An ambitious, royal-blooded kuvari who had known she could never have defeated her own mother in single combat... and so had used a love affair with him in Nozva Rozkveta to try to learn *Mati's* weaknesses, in a bid to seize the throne of Nozva Rozkveta. Her plan had relied on making the Offering to him, then dueling to join Mati's Quorum—but he'd learned about Yelena's lies first and had told Mati.

Instead, Mati had betrothed Zoran to Yelena's mother. And that had been the end of that.

"Your... 'vision' was a pack of lies," he said casually. "And I wasn't about to let you try to overthrow my mother."

"Try?" A deep laugh. "I would have succeeded."

Yelena was a skilled warrior, but not Mati's match, whom even Nendra would have struggled to best. But for a person desperate to step out from her mother's shadow, Yelena truly seemed to believe in what she was saying.

"You don't have anything to prove," he said. "Everyone knows you're one of the strongest kuvari. And not just in Dun Mozg."

She rolled her eyes, slashed low, and then high. "I don't need to be told that."

"Because you already know. Everyone already knows."

She blew a sharp breath from her nose. "Your point?"

He stepped in front of her, and she stopped a blow just

short of his arm. Her eyes wide, she looked him over, and he rested a palm on her sword-hand.

"My point is that Alessandra is a human," he said, keeping his voice low. "There's nothing to be gained from challenging her."

With a sneer, Yelena straightened, pulled away, and sheathed her sword, her pale kuvari robes dark with sweat. "Is that what you predict I'll do? Challenge your little human?"

"I know better than to try predicting what you'll do, Yelena." He peered down at her, at the wheels turning in her gaze, in her expression. "But our peace with the humans, our trade—even the food this queendom is getting—rely on my marriage with Alessandra."

"They're weak. Helpless. At the slightest challenge, they scurry like salamanders. No strength at all."

"Not in the ring. Not combat strength. But Alessandra has a different kind of strength," he shot back. Aless *wasn't* weak. *Wasn't* helpless. In a test of wits, Yelena would find herself vastly outclassed.

"There is only one kind of strength that matters, Veron," she hissed.

This was going nowhere. "I'm asking you this as a favor, Yelena."

"A favor? For old times' sake?" Raising her eyebrows, she looked away with a shake of her head, then crossed her arms. When her eyes met his once more, they were narrowed and dancing mischievously. A look he'd seen from her countless times. "Maybe one last roll in the moss, then, for old times' sake?"

He groaned under his breath. There was no sense in trying to reason with her when she would only toy with him for her own amusement. Yelena was determined to issue the challenge and embarrass Aless in front of everyone present, send a ripple through the queendoms about the new Nozva Rozkvetan *human* princess refusing to fight and thus having no honor.

No more toying. He'd simply beat Yelena to the ring and challenge her *first*. Once he defeated her, as victor he'd be able to choose his next opponent, and that would be that. Yelena would never even get the *chance* to embarrass his wife.

It was the right move.

He turned away and strolled to the exit. "Nice talking to you, Yelena," he deadpanned.

"See you at dinner," came the jesting reply.

ALESS ROSE from the stone bench in the chamber she shared with Veron. Decorated in smooth stone and metal, its surfaces were hard, sharp, softened only by what appeared to be undyed silk, a soft, cottony white. Silk bedding, cushions, curtains. Even a silk rug, woven in shades of white and tan. The room was a marriage of soft and hard.

In the mirror, she wore her dark-blue satin dress—one of her best—fitted through the richly embroidered bodice, with boots beneath, and the strand of Mamma's pearls around her neck.

She couldn't fight—true—but she was still a princess of Silen. And everyone who looked her way tonight would know that, and know that with her station came the aid they all enjoyed. And that if any harm came to her, they'd be without it.

Gabriella tightened the braid she'd coiled at the nape of her neck. "There. Perfect."

"I approve," Gavri commented from her post at the doorway, swirling the tip of her own braid around her fingers. "There's something I love about that hairstyle, but I can't quite put my finger on it."

As casual as Gavri seemed now, her meeting with Zoran had shaken her. She'd practically run from the stable after all.

"Very funny."

Both Gavri and Zoran had things they needed to say to each other, it seemed, questions that needed answers, wounds that needed healing. Maybe it would be better if they said them instead of keeping them bottled up inside. Easier for them to move on.

She strode up to Gavri and jabbed a finger at her. "You are going to meet him in the stables later."

"I am?" Gavri stared down at her finger. "I can't. What about guarding—"

Aless shook her head. "You need to hear whatever he has to say to you. You two have loose ends."

Sighing, Gavri leaned her head back against the door. "If Queen Nendra hears of it, even if nothing hap—"

"You can't help it if I need to get some air and require my guard to accompany me, can you?" With a grin, she breezed out the door.

"Good plan," Gavri said in a high-pitched voice, sidling up to her. "I like it."

In the hall, Veron strode toward them, over six feet of black-leather-clad muscle, the hard angles of his terrifyingly beautiful face tight, eyebrows drawn, golden eyes hard. Riza followed him with a scowl.

Had he spoken with Yelena, then?

But when he looked up, met her gaze, those hard angles gave way to a soft smile. One she'd put there.

He gave her a once-over, and the curve of that smile was unmistakable as he took her hands. "You look beautiful."

"All Gabriella's work," she said, rubbing her thumb over his hand.

He gave a friendly nod to Gabriella, who curtseyed. When his gaze wandered to Gavri, she bowed her head and looked away.

This disagreement between them would have to end. Maybe they could discuss it later tonight.

"How did your talk go?" she asked as he wrapped her hand around his arm and led her down the hall.

"Swimmingly," Riza snapped, shaking her head.

Veron hissed at Riza, then turned back to her, rubbing warmth into her hand. "She's eager to rule—"

"That's *one* way of putting it," Riza mumbled under her breath.

"—but is frustrated in her mother's shadow."

"She's frustrated, but she's not stupid," Gavri said, despite Veron's glare. "If she embarrasses Her Highness, when Queen Zara hears about it, that could affect relations with Dun Mozg. She won't endanger the alliance."

"You don't know her as well as I do," he snapped.

"*No one* knows her as well as you do," Gavri shot back, then her eyes went wide as she swallowed.

Veron went rigid, but Aless stepped in.

"How do the games work?" she asked as they crossed a corridor in the black crystal palace, their booted footsteps echoing.

"The first warrior may challenge until she or he loses,"

Veron said. "When the first warrior finally loses, the victor issues challenges until she or he loses."

"How do you win?"

"Get your opponent out of the ring, or until your opponent taps twice," Gavri supplied, and Veron nodded, but a frown slowly furrowed his face. "No blood drawn—it's bad form."

"What about the ring? What's in it?"

Veron jerked his head back. "*No*," he hissed, stopping near a stone bench.

"Sand." Gavri raised an eyebrow at him.

Sand... That wouldn't hurt too much. "It's light sparring, right?" she asked. "What if I accept the challenge?"

"*Absolutely not*," Veron said through clenched teeth.

"Not a terrible idea," Gavri replied while Veron scowled at her. "Hurting Her Highness would destroy the peace. She wouldn't use the games to truly injure Her Highness."

"If she endangers the peace, that could mean her people don't eat." She took Veron's arm with both of her hands until he looked at her. "If she wants to rule and she's intelligent—which I expect her to be, if *you* were fond of her—then she won't starve her people just to make a stranger look bad."

"She's passionate about leadership," he said with a sigh, "just extremely impatient, and sometimes myopic."

That sounded all too familiar. With a fleeting smile, she lowered her gaze as they walked endless stretches of gleaming black floors reflecting the light of mushrooms, glowworms, and torches.

Yelena—as a woman among the dark-elves—had a real chance, no matter how small, of ending up a true leader. When a dream became tangible, the temptation to reach for it became nearly irresistible. What had Yelena done?

Nothing too repugnant, if she was still free, still an heir to the throne here. She might have been impatient, but not deranged.

Soon, the din of myriad voices muffled through two heavy stone doors.

"If she challenges you," Veron whispered, "just decline. There's no good reason for you to take such a risk."

Two kuvari, armored in sage-tinted arcanir plate, opened the doors, revealing a sea of people crowding long stone tables and benches. Some of whom had arrived with her and Veron— her people.

Every reason for her to take such a risk.

"His Highness, Prince Veron u Zara u Avrora u Roza, Valaz u Nozva Rozkveta, Zpevan Kamena, Volodar T'my, and Her Highness, Princess Alessandra u Aldona u Noor u Elise, Valazi u Nozva Rozkveta, Valazi u Silen," a herald shouted, and every voice in the room hushed as Veron escorted her and Gabriella in, along with Riza, Gavri, and ten other kuvari. Every dark-elf stood, tall and straight, arms at their sides.

Floor candelabra and massive crystalline girandoles lit up the grand hall, reflecting firelight off surfaces like black glass, with an empty ring of sand at the center, outlined in white etchings. Their steps were the only sound, and as they passed several empty spaces on the stone benches, most of their entourage stopped but for her, Veron, Gabriella, Riza, and Gavri.

The air was thick with the savory spice of roasted sausage, and the lemon, olive oil, polenta, and rice-flour pasta. The aroma of Bellanzole's viands—human foods.

Veron led them to the farthest table, where a well-built, statuesque woman waited in a gleaming black throne, her long hair secured high, surrounded by four men, Zoran among them. No one else here seemed to have more than one partner, but this queen did. She wore impeccable plated black leather, and armor over her fingers.

"I am Queen Nendra. Welcome to Dun Mozg, Prince Veron, Princess Alessandra." With a measured smile, Nendra inclined her head, and she and Veron responded in kind. Nendra gestured to the men surrounding her. "This is my king-consort, Zoran"—who grinned and nodded—"and my concubines—"

Concubines?

"—Kral, Ivo, and Cipriano." A grim-faced muscular dark-elf in armor, a pale and slender well-coiffed man in a black coat, and a black-bearded, green-eyed man, olive-skinned just like her. Sileni?

Human? No, Zoran had mentioned a werewolf lover, hadn't he? What about Ivo?

But she greeted each in turn with Veron until Nendra gestured to the spitting image of herself, with her white hair braided in a circlet about her head.

"And this is my firstborn daughter, Yelena."

"A pleasure, Your Highness." She inclined her head to Yelena.

Yelena smiled, but it didn't reach her tawny eyes, and every shred of her brown leathers was pulled tight. A muscle twitched in Yelena's clenched jaw. "The pleasure's all mine."

Queen Nendra glowered at her, then glanced at a young girl seated next to Yelena. "And my youngest, Karla."

Karla, her voluminous hair tied in a high ponytail, met her gaze squarely, even while partially hiding behind Yelena's hip. A bold little girl, she could be no older than five or six, if dark-elf children aged as human children did. But even for a child, she was thin. When Veron had told her about the starvation, she hadn't wanted to believe him, but he'd been right.

Nendra turned to her people, arms raised. "Our honored guests have arrived," she bellowed. "After Kral saved two of our volodari yesterday, he has the honor of first match. Let the games begin!"

Cheers rose up from the crowds, who then seated themselves at the stone benches once more. A musician in the corner began a beat on a large, resonant drum.

Scowling, Veron gestured her to a nearby space, where she sat between him and Gavri on the cold, hard surface, with Gabriella beyond, and Riza at the end.

"What's wrong?" she whispered to him.

He shook his head. "I didn't realize anyone would have the honor of first match."

At least it wasn't Yelena.

The spread before them was colorful, with dishes of steaming pasta and sausage placed among Sileni boules, greens, fruits, and cakes. The entire table was laden with human food.

"Please tell me there's *butter*," Gavri murmured under her breath, patting Gabriella's arm. "Gabriella put some in my chestnut mush earlier today, and Holy Ulsinael, *she changed my life.*"

She laughed, and across from her, Cipriano was hiding a smile as he buttered a roll.

"Some things are worth the two-thousand-year wait," he remarked, his voice deep and gravelly.

"I'm going to need that. Really, really *need* that," Gavri said, her eyes fixed on the block of butter.

Nendra tipped her head up to Cipriano. "With this new

alliance, you can have all the butter you want. Just don't get fat, eh?"

"If I don't, it won't be for lack of trying, my queen." They shared a grin that would have been sweet if Zoran hadn't been sitting between them, blinking lazily.

"Would you pass the, er, gigantic human bread loaf?" he asked Veron, waving a fork around, and Veron obliged with narrowed eyes, sliding the boule over to him across the table.

Yelena observed the exchange with an aloof glare, her gaze raking over the spread of Sileni food. Karla sat next to her, her little pale eyebrows drawn together as she looked out at the dishes. Yelena gathered some pasta and bread onto her plate, whispering words in an encouraging tone.

As she offered her little sister human food, Yelena had to know what the peace meant. She *had* to.

While Zoran tore off a chunk of bread and buttered it under Gavri's avaricious gaze, Kral stood and took to the empty ring. At its center, he clasped his hands behind his back and faced toward Yelena, who still sat with Karla.

A series of whoops rose up and rhythmic thuds of hands pounding on the stone, until Yelena looked over her shoulder at him, thumped her chest twice with a fist, and stood to raucous cheering.

"And so it begins," Veron said on an exhale.

"Why fight during a celebration?" she asked quietly. "Why not just dance?"

"It can be like a sort of dance," Gavri said, her mouth full of buttered bread. "When two warriors are attracted and then equally matched, it's... probably what you humans would call a seduction."

Swallowing, she nodded. Dark-elves chose their mates by their strength, choosing equals.

And never in her life would she ever be equally matched to Veron in combat.

Kral and Yelena circled one another, exchanging jests and feints, before Kral threw a punch, his massive physique the charge of a bull. Yelena misdirected his arm and evaded, dodging an elbow before landing a knee to the gut, then the face.

She backed away, grinning at Kral, who rubbed his jaw. As they circled, he moved her closer and closer to the white ring, until she tried to dart left.

He blocked, enclosing her in his enormous arms, but she slammed the top of her forehead against his face. His grip loosened, and she grabbed his arm, twisted it, and with her foot to his back, shoved him out of the ring.

Cheers rose up from the crowd while Yelena held up a fist, grinning.

No blood—Yelena had to have pulled her punches?

"Is he going to be all right?" she whispered to Veron.

"Nothing the hot springs won't cure," he whispered back.

Prodding at his face, Kral headed back to the table, where a dark-elf in gray robes and bone necklace rushed to tend him. All the while, Ivo and Cipriano and even Nendra herself patted him on the back while others shouted calls of support.

When they quieted, whoops staggered across the sea of tables, and that rhythmic thumping on the stone began again, and in the middle of the ring, Yelena stood, her hands clasped behind her back—

And staring right here.

CHAPTER 16

*A*less shivered.

Holy Mother's mercy. It was happening. It was actually happening.

She just had to decline and—

Next to her, Veron stood, staring down Yelena with an unwavering ferocity, and thumped his fist twice against his chest.

Yelena shook her head and looked over at her.

Gavri stood, thumping her chest.

Another shake of the head.

Across the table, Kral sat, having lost but nonetheless earned the respect of his family, friends, and subjects. There was no dishonor in losing. Only in failing to rise to the challenge. And then not only would she disappoint the dark-elves of Nightbloom, her own people, but she'd also humiliate them in front of an allied queendom.

"Your Majesty," Veron declared, turning to Queen Nendra, "I ask your permission to take my wife's place in the ring."

Queen Nendra leaned back in her throne and scowled at Yelena, who still stared right here. The crowd had gone utterly silent, as if three hundred people had stopped breathing.

"The games are tradition, Prince Veron," the queen replied in an even tone. "They must be fought by those who are issued a challenge, or not at all." The queen's gaze shifted to her, widened just slightly.

Even Queen Nendra invited her to decline.

"Princess?" Queen Nendra asked. "You must accept or decline," she said slowly, "unless you are blessed by Holy Ulsinael."

Blessed?

The queen's gaze lowered to her belly.

Oh.

A way out? It would be easy to lie, the easiest thing in the world, but in a few months, the odds were that everyone would know it. She could lose their respect anyway.

But as the dark-elves sat around tables of human food, as their queen celebrated a human and dark-elf marriage, Yelena would have to be insane to harm her. And an insane person wouldn't so lovingly have tried to feed her little sister.

As Veron stood, fists clenched, his eyes met hers, intense, pained, and as committed as he'd been to the truth before, that intensity suggested the opposite now.

What about the consequences? How would this reflect on Veron, on his mother, on the people of Nightbloom? And would his mother retaliate over the embarrassment, as Gavri had suggested?

Even if Yelena was willing to risk her people's wellbeing—

Karla's wellbeing—*she* wasn't. Wasn't willing to risk anyone's wellbeing just to keep her own backside unbruised, especially when Yelena had every reason not to hurt her.

With a swallow, she stood. "Your Majesty, I am not in a holy state."

A ripple of gasps spread through the hall.

Veron took her hand. "Aless, no," he whispered. "Please."

She curled her fingers into a fist and thumped it twice to her chest, but the silence didn't break.

"Your Majesty," Veron called out, turning back to Queen Nendra, "I won't—"

Queen Nendra raised a hand. "The challenge has been accepted."

Yelena bowed elaborately.

"*Yelena*," Veron snarled. "*So help me Ulsinael*, if you—"

Riza and Danika rose to grab Veron's arms and forced him to his seat while he bucked their hold. Even Zoran approached to help, and they finally wrangled Veron onto the bench as Zoran murmured reassurances.

Two taps. A step out of the ring. That was all it would take.

She took Veron's hand and offered him a look she hoped was reassuring. "Please. I have to do this."

His eyes locked on hers, blazing and furious as he heaved forceful breaths. "If she touches you, Aless, I—" A madness creased his features before he shook his head.

But she hadn't miscalculated.

Yelena wasn't insane, and if she did someday want to rule her people, destroying this peace and starving them was not conducive to that. What were weapons in the hands of emaciated soldiers?

She'd wanted to embarrass the human. Maybe even frustrate Veron. But her bluff had been called, and in two taps or just a couple steps, this would all be over.

She rested a palm on his cheek. "Trust me in this, Veron, won't you?"

As he stared at her, she stroked his cheek softly before she kissed him. Then, with a nod to him and another to Gavri, she stepped over the bench and made her way to the ring.

In the center, Yelena waited with a bitter smile, her eyebrows raised. "That was foolish of you, human."

Aless stepped into the ring but stayed on its fringe, close enough to step out quickly if she needed to. "I married a dark-elf, and this is part of his people's traditions. I want them to be *our* people, and that means stepping forward. Joining."

"Brave words, human." Yelena lowered into a fighting stance, narrowing her eyes. "But how brave are *you*?"

Inside of her, everything trembled, but she kept her fists clenched, stood her ground. She couldn't fight, not in the least, but this wasn't about winning a fight.

She would do her best to take it as Kral had, and then sit down and be welcomed. Avoid an incident that could affect so many people.

Yelena circled her, feinting occasionally, laughing, but Aless didn't move. Couldn't move. It was either fear or determination, but as long as it kept her standing, she didn't care.

A kick breezed by her face—just inches past her nose—

Her heart threatened to explode from her chest as the crowd heckled Yelena, shouting her name in disappointed tones.

Yelena's steps surrounded her, and growls, grunts, hissed words. The blow could come from anywhere—from behind, from the side, from above, from below. It could hit her anywhere, and for the life of her, she couldn't *move.*

Yelena circled to the front, her face contorted, and Aless chanced a look at Veron, who leaned forward at the table, both of his hands on it, with Gavri, Riza, and Zoran clamping down on his shoulders. The intensity of his gaze pierced her—

A lunge forward, then Yelena swept her legs out from under her.

Her back hit the sand.

Air whooshed out of her lungs.

"*Yelena!*" Veron shouted from across the hall, his voice echoing.

She wheezed, trying to catch her breath, while Yelena pinned her, took both of her wrists in the grasp of one hand, the clawed fingers of her other hand poised.

"No attempt to fight me?" Yelena snarled, tensing those fingers.

Holy Mother's mercy, she couldn't move even if she tried. But if Yelena had wanted her dead, then she already would have been. This was something else.

She held Yelena's gaze. "I didn't come here to fight you."

Yelena bared her teeth. "Then this could be your *end.*"

Searching Yelena's eyes, she gave a slight shake of her head. If that were so, her end would have come as soon as she'd entered the ring, but Yelena had pulled all her strikes, had tried to get a rise out of her. Refusing the challenge would have shown fear. And cowering in the ring would have, too. Maybe *that* was what Yelena had tried to elicit. Fear. And assert all humans were cowards by association.

"No," she said quietly. "I'm your ally, and I trust you."

But even as she said the words and closed her eyes, a coldness swept over her, claimed her, raising every hair on her body.

Maybe it hadn't been *bravery* but bravado. Maybe she'd miscalculated, fatally, and Yelena would kill her.

She won't.

A hiss cut through the air, and a crunch hit, rippling impact through the sand and floor beneath her head.

She sucked in a breath, shaking, willing her hands to move, but Yelena's hold on her wrists was too tight.

The shadow over her shifted—Yelena—freeing her up to move a little.

Aless tapped her foot twice on the sand.

When she opened her eyes, Yelena was still above her, eyes narrowed, her brow creased.

"You—you don't belong here," Yelena snapped, then with a sharp breath, pulled away.

Minutes passed by, or hours, as she looked up at the black stone ceiling, waiting for her pulse to slow, for her breath to even out. Firelight flickered reflections in the mirror-like surface, and voices began to filter in. Cheers.

She pushed up to her elbow, her tailbone and her back sore as she brushed off the sand, and there was a sea of smiling faces, calls of encouragement. As she stood properly, Veron became visible between other people, held down still, his eyes wild as they met hers.

Yelena already stood at the center, paying her no mind, so she headed back to her spot at the table, nodding acknowledgments as others patted her on the back and offered kind words, and a dark-elf woman offering her treatment that she turned down. She was just a little sore, that was all.

Gavri winked at her, then she, Riza, and Zoran released Veron, who shot up from his seat.

He gathered her up in his arms, holding her tight, inhaling a sharp breath over her head before lowering his mouth to hers. Her heart raced anew as his lips pressed hard against hers, his kiss passionate and deep, his body taut and leaning into hers.

He pulled away, far too soon, and held her face cupped in his hands, searching her eyes with his own, his chest rising and falling in short, fast breaths. "Aless, that was—"

"A success?" she offered.

"—dangerous," he said quietly, before pulling her in once more. "And a success," he added, and she could hear the smile in his voice.

His arms around her weren't just warm and safe, but they soothed a loving familiarity into her, a feeling she wanted to wrap herself in and never leave, to fall asleep in and wake up in, to feel every day and every night, for as long as she wanted, whenever she wanted. She closed her eyes and breathed him in, the smell of leather and that forest stream, and something deeper, primal, that she couldn't get enough of.

Soon the whooping and rhythmic thuds sounded again, and when she turned back to the ring, Yelena stood at its center, arms clasped behind her back, staring down Veron.

"She picked the wrong day," he growled under his breath, then stood aside and thumped his fist to his chest. With one last glance at her, he rounded the table, cracking his knuckles as he strode to the ring.

"They were always evenly matched, but today, mark my words, by the time he's through with her, she'll be no more than a glorified mop," Gavri remarked, her voice low among the din.

She sat down, and her bottom rebelled, but she'd give it a

hot bath later as a peace offering. Gavri patted at her hair, shaking out the sand, and she grinned in quiet thanks.

As Yelena and Veron circled one another in the ring, their gazes locked, their movements perfectly synchronized, it really *was* like a dance. Yelena met his ferocity with a quirked brow and a mischievous gaze, and he matched her every move with a countermove, their bodies turning to one another's whims without even touching.

It was as if they'd done this a hundred times before, a thousand times before, and knew everything about each other, a sort of natural intimacy that would take years to build, or more.

Yelena threw a punch, and he spun away with a kick that she ducked. She countered, and he caught her foot, then hooked her heel out from under her.

But her legs closed around him, and she arched her back, her palms hitting the ground as she tried to throw him. He spun sideways, but caught the floor with a palm and swept a leg low that she leaped to evade.

They knew each other's moves, every single one, and flowed around one another like winds in a cyclone.

Evenly matched.

She started, lowering her gaze to the table, and her half-eaten plate of food. No, Veron didn't care about that, not with Yelena, but every moment she watched them together only reinforced how perfect they looked, what an ideal couple they made, and how she could never be his equal like Yelena could. Never as strong or as skilled. Never a dark-elf warrior. And this dance, this seduction, would be something she could never do.

As for what he *did* see in her—could it be enough? Could it ever be enough?

Had he forgiven her for the lie?

Someone walked past—Zoran—and left the grand hall. In the ring beyond, Veron and Yelena battled blow for blow, with Yelena's face lit up in a broad grin.

Yelena looked confident, but Veron would handle her. He won small engagements, and bit by bit, he weakened her.

With Zoran at the stable, all that remained was getting Gavri there, *not* alone, so Queen Nendra wouldn't suspect anything. And nothing *would* happen—Gavri knew better—but they'd finally have a chance to talk.

She stood. "I think I'll take some air," she said over Gavri's head to Gabriella and Riza. "Will you tell Veron I'll be right back?"

"Your Highness," Riza said, rising. "I shall accompany you."

"No need," she said with a happy shrug. "I'll take Gavri. We'll be back shortly." She nodded to Gavri, who rose as well.

Riza eyed the two of them, then glanced back at the ring. "Very well. I will inform His Highness."

Riza inclined her head and waited. Veron and Yelena were still fighting when Gavri escorted her out of the grand hall, into the ample glowing green light of the bioluminescent mushrooms.

"Thank you for this," Gavri whispered to her as they headed for the stables, traversing the black causeways over waterfalls and dark depths.

"You haven't seen each other for two thousand years," she replied softly. "I think a private conversation is the very least you deserve."

Gavri nodded, slowly brushing a fingertip over her lip. "By the way, what you did in there..."

With a shrug, she shook her head. "Now there will be no misunderstanding that my fists are useless."

Gavri grasped her wrist. "Strength isn't just in your fists. Strength is relying on your knowledge in the face of danger. It's standing up to a challenge with courage and dignity. Not running away."

She'd wanted to do right by Veron's people—now *her* people, too. If Veron had possessed any remaining doubt of her commitment to him or their people, he could now cast it aside. She would do whatever it took to protect them, to keep them safe, and to maintain the peace. Whatever it took.

Gavri lowered her gaze. "Actually something I needed to be reminded of."

Aless cocked her head toward the stables. "Then let's go see Zoran."

With a smile, Gavri escorted her there, where a quiet whinny came through the open doors. At a nearby stall, strapping Zoran was feeding Noc an apple.

"We're all feasting on human foods," Zoran said softly, "so why should he be left out?" He looked over his shoulder with a pensive grin, fixing Gavri with a soft gaze.

Gavri stood still, chewing her lip for a long moment before she exhaled sharply and ran to him, threw her arms around him. He gathered her up in his embrace, held her close.

"I'm sorry I never said goodbye," he whispered, resting his cheek on Gavri's head. "There was so much I wanted to say, but—"

Clearing her throat, Aless meandered to Noc's stall and opened it. "I think I'll take Noc for a walk and give you two some time."

Gavri glanced over her shoulder with teary eyes and nodded. "I'll come find you in a bit. Stay close, Your Highness."

She smiled. "I will."

While Zoran and Gavri whispered to one another, she strapped a halter on Noc and attached a lead. "You could use a little walk, couldn't you?" she whispered, rubbing his nose. "Let's go."

He snorted softly and nuzzled her before heading with her to the open doors. Outside, a few horses were corralled in dirt-laden paddocks, clustered around water and feed troughs, but Noc led her past them... despite *her* holding *his* lead.

Maybe a not-so-subtle message that he didn't need one.

A tunnel abutted the paddock area, not as large as the one they'd entered Dunmarrow through—no, *Dun Mozg*. Why did the Sileni call it *Dunmarrow* when the dark-elves called it *Dun Mozg*?

Or *Nightbloom*, for that matter? *Nozva Rozkveta*.

Sparse floor candelabra lit the tunnel as they entered, casting firelight on a million shining colors.

She gasped.

Every surface was embedded with veins of gems, glittering in a kaleidoscope of colors, reflecting their vibrancy on one another, and on her and Noc.

"You're a romantic at heart, aren't you?" she joked softly, and he swatted her with his tail.

She petted his neck, gazing at the beauty around her, unable to decide where she should look. The jewel-studded tunnel continued on an upward incline, and she neared the edge to smooth her fingers over the many treasures.

It was strange. Dark-elves claimed not to value things like this, and yet, if that were true, surely they would have bartered all these jewels away by now? But here they were, preserved in their natural beauty, a joy for all to look upon.

Noc tossed his head. She grabbed his halter as he pulled

her backward. "What's wrong?"

The ground beneath their feet quaked. Dust rained from above, and bits of rubble thudded to the ground as something heavy crashed down behind them. Distant shouts rose up.

Noc dragged her up the incline—

Veron—

"Where are you going?" She tugged on Noc's halter to no avail. "Do you know a way out? We need to go back. Veron—"

Safe.

The word appeared in her mind, more like a feeling than a voice, and the world slowed around her as she looked at Noc, really *looked*. He eyed her as he led her, and those dark eyes—there was something reassuring there, in that deliberate gaze, in that slow blink.

He really wasn't just some horse.

With a resolute nod, she kept up with him, and the scent of fresh forest air filtered in while the crack and collapse of stone rumbled behind them.

Holy Mother's mercy, this tunnel was coming *down*.

Noc pulled to a halt, and she reached forward, her palms finding a bar. A barred set of doors!

Grunting with effort, she pulled at the bar, trying to lift it, and it rose—

A little more, a little more—

Finally over the hooks, it crashed to the floor. She pushed at the solid stone before her while the ground bucked, and Noc leaned against it until it finally started to grind open.

They pushed through leafy overgrowth into a dark grove of tall turkey oaks, with the waxing moon casting its glow overhead. The rumbling echoed from the tunnel, no louder than before, as Noc led them to a grassy clearing.

Veron—would he be all right? Would Gavri, Zoran, Gabriella, and Riza? Everyone? Veron was still back in the palace, still in the city, where she couldn't go.

She clutched at the satin over her chest, trying to catch her breath. The dark-elves had lived underground long before, and they had to have shelters of some kind.

"What was that?" she asked, and Noc rested his head against her.

An earthquake? Veron had said since there were no earth-quakes, the earthmovers had gone. If there had been an earth-quake just now, did that mean—?

"Holy Mother's mercy," she whispered, clutching Noc's mane.

He squealed, an unsettled sound, and began to back up.

"We have to go back." She headed for the doors again, and whatever it took, she would—

Dark figures waded in from among the trees. Three of them, in long coats, with swords at their hips and crossbows in their hands.

Her pulse quickening, she stepped back, pressed herself against Noc.

As the three walked into the clearing, beneath the moon's light, they were men. Sileni men.

"Well, well. Look what our geomancer chased out." A crooked grin from one of them, a man with a mass of black curls.

"Your Highness," the second one mocked with an elaborate bow. "The general will be glad to see you unharmed."

The general. Tarquin Belmonte.

They closed in as Noc kicked out with his hind legs.

CHAPTER 17

*V*eron caught Yelena's kick and shoved her out of the ring when a great rumble trembled through the hall.

People leaped from the benches, and Yelena moved to his side.

"Earthmovers?" he asked, frowning as he tried to isolate the sound.

Yelena shook her head and looked toward Nendra. "Mati?" she called out.

"Witches," Nendra answered, standing at the head of the table, her voice echoing. "Dun Mozg's heart is arcanir. They will not get through to us."

No magic could penetrate arcanir, so they would be safe here. He looked to the section where he and Aless had been sitting, but only Riza looked back at him, her face grim. Where Aless and Gavri had been, only two empty spaces remained.

While the floor shook, he ran toward Riza, and she strode to meet him.

He grabbed her armored shoulder. "Where's Aless?"

"She went to take some air and took Gavri with her," she replied, grasping his forearm.

Behind her, Gabriella caught up to them. "Your Highness, I think she might be at the stables."

"The stables?" Why would she go there? But as he looked toward Nendra and her concubines, her consort was nowhere in sight. *Zoran.*

He marched up to Nendra and bowed his head. "Your Majesty, I must take my leave—"

"Find your wife, Veron." With a raise of her hand, she dismissed him, and he raced across the grand hall with Riza and Gabriella, and all of his kuvari followed in his wake.

Outside the grand hall, dust misted from the ceiling, and everywhere people scrambled for purchase as tremors wove through the rock. Gavri and Zoran wouldn't let anything happen to Aless. They'd keep her safe. No doubt everything was just fine.

Even knowing all this, he ran for the stables and didn't stop until he dashed through the open doors. Horses squealed in their stalls, but Aless was nowhere in sight. Neither was Noc.

Some horses circled restlessly in the paddock, but—

"Your Highness," Riza called.

He followed the sound of her voice to a pile of rubble at a tunnel opening, where Riza, Gavri, and Zoran pried debris off the pile frantically. Deep, Darkness, and Holy Ulsinael, if Aless was—if she was under the rubble—

His heart hammering in his chest, he was already running

before he could think to. He tore chunks of rock away from the rubble, clawing through it wildly.

"Your Highness," Gavri said shakily, "she left with Noc, only for a few minutes, and—"

He threw a slab of rubble aside. No words mattered right now. "Just find her," he snapped, and they all dug through the debris.

Holy Ulsinael, keep her safe. Deep and Darkness, cloak her in your sanctuary.

His hands bled, but he didn't care. Let them. Let them break, if it meant finding Aless safe, but there was nothing. Nothing.

Finally two of the kuvari cleared away a large piece of rubble. Behind it, two slabs formed a passage, and he darted into it.

"Brother!" Zoran called after him. "It's too dangerous! They could collapse if that—"

Rubble crashed behind him and voices shouted, but he squeezed through and picked a path until finally a night breeze blew in.

A doorway. A Gate.

He ran for it, and through, where the undergrowth gave way to sparse forest in the dark.

A loud neigh—Noc—and a scream followed.

Aless.

His heart caught in his throat, he bolted toward the sound, cutting through the foliage. In the clearing ahead, two men dragged Aless, kicking and screaming, south. Noc clamped his teeth down on the lanky one's shoulder, eliciting a cry.

Just ahead, a bearded man lay in the grass, groaning, with a crossbow nearby. Veron seized it as he passed—

Aless struck and kicked at Lanky, locked down by Noc.

"Just kill the horse!" Lanky shouted to a grim-faced third, who drew his sword.

Veron took aim with the crossbow and shot the bolt twenty yards directly into Grim's chest, making him stagger backward.

"Veron!" Aless shouted, repeatedly hitting Lanky, who struck Noc on the nose and dragged her away.

He closed in, grabbed Lanky by the coat, and threw him backward. Aless tumbled to the ground as Grim ripped the bolt from his own chest and slashed at him with the sword.

Lanky shot up to his feet, and Veron pulled the man to himself, catching Grim's sword with Lanky's gut.

"Behind you!" Aless shouted, laboring to her feet.

He snap-kicked Lanky's back, sending both him and Grim to the ground as footsteps crunched from behind.

A blade slashed across his arm before he could dodge as Beard pressed his advantage. A cut—he ducked—a lunge, and he evaded, caught Beard's sword-arm, and yanked him forward before burying his claws in Beard's neck.

Blood sprayed his face when Aless screamed, and a set of arms constricted his neck. He clawed at the gauntleted hands, grabbed for the man's head—

A sharp cry, and blood gushed over the side of his face.

The arms released, and he leaped away, spinning to face the man.

A body thudded to the ground.

Aless stood over Grim with wide, bulging eyes, gulping in breaths. The crossbow bolt was buried in Grim's temple, his face stained with blood, his eyes frozen in death.

"I... I—" she stammered.

She'd killed a man.

She'd killed a man to help *him*.

"Are you hurt?" He grasped her upper arms, but her haunted gaze remained fixed on the dead man. "Aless," he said, giving her a little shake. "Please, are you hurt?"

With a shiver, she looked up at him, wide eyes shining, lips parted, and covered her mouth with a hand before exhaling a huge breath. She began to fall, but he caught her, held her tight, rocked her gently.

"They were going to take me away," she blurted, her voice breaking. "Veron, I was so—I thought that—"

"I know," he whispered, stroking her back softly. This was where she belonged, safe in his arms. And never in his life, in centuries, in millennia, would he allow her to be taken. Ever. If she was in danger, he'd follow her to the end of the world, to the end of life itself. Because this was where he belonged, too. With her.

She'd looked so soft, so fragile, his human bride, but tonight she'd killed a man to save his life. The woman he'd married was tough—tougher than he'd ever imagined.

Her plan to leave him didn't matter. The lie didn't matter. Nothing else mattered but this, her, here. And she *had* to know how much he cared for her.

"Your Highness!" Riza bellowed from a distance, quieter voices and footsteps accompanying her.

Still holding Aless, he looked over his shoulder. Riza, Gavri, Zoran, and the rest of his kuvari paused in the clearing, splitting to check the perimeter.

"Dispose of these three," he said to Riza.

She approached, glowering at the bodies. "Brotherhood?"

He nodded. "Scouts. They must be using a witch to try to

force us out, then using scouts to pick over the area and find a way in."

"When these don't report in—" Riza began.

"Let's make sure Nendra is prepared."

Riza gestured to Danika and two other kuvari, who moved in on the bodies.

"Is Her Highness all right?" Gavri asked, taking a step forward with Zoran.

He glared at her.

"Veron," Aless whispered, "it wasn't her fault. I was just outside the stable and—"

"She should have been *with* you," he shot back.

"But the collapse separated us. If not for Noc leading me outside, I'd be..." She lowered her gaze as Noc trotted up to them.

I'm never done thanking you, my friend.

Noc bobbed his head.

But now it fell to him to tell Nendra battle was at her doorstep, and Yelena's harsh stance on the human and dark-elf alliance would only grow in popularity. "Come. Let's help Queen Nendra prepare as much as we can. We're together in this."

He ushered Aless past Gavri and toward the tunnel while Zoran took Noc; he'd have to lead him by way of another entrance.

"Veron," Aless whispered with a wince.

He slowed. "Are you all right? Are you hurt somewhere?" he asked, looking her over.

"It's my..." She blushed.

He suppressed a grin. He'd seen Yelena throw her onto her bottom. "I know just the thing for that."

A long soak in Dun Mozg's hot springs would soothe that ache... although he wanted—*really* wanted—to see to that himself.

Low, deep Stone Singing came from the Gate, singers asking the stone to remain stable.

Two kuvari rushed ahead of them into the tunnel, then called the all-clear. He and Aless crept through, squeezing through the tightness, back into the heart of Dun Mozg. Nendra's kuvari were already there, along with the Stone Singers, *stavbali* who built, and an *inzenyra* who designed.

"Veron," Aless began again, "I think we should send a message to my father."

He stopped, watching the rest of his kuvari exiting the tunnel.

"He won't want to risk this peace, not after all it cost him publicly to achieve it. And if a threat to my life isn't compelling enough, he can always be counted on to defend his pride," she added quietly.

"But your father isn't a direct ally of Dun Mozg," he replied. Would King Macario risk his soldiers and his reputation without a formal alliance between Silen and Dun Mozg?

Aless nodded. "You said dark-elves travel between queen-doms by way of the tunnels."

"I did."

"What if we send a message to your mother, too, and most of our cargo to Nozva Rozkveta by way of the tunnels," she said, "and then we travel light, by land, with our forces and lead the Brotherhood away from Dun Mozg?"

He crossed his arms, pacing before the paddock. If they stayed here and the Brotherhood laid siege, it could sour the people's view on the human and dark-elf alliance, but it might also risk terms between Dun Mozg and Nozva Rozkveta.

But if they did what Aless suggested, if they could stay ahead of the Brotherhood, it would mean leading the enemy to a prepared Nozva Rozkveta with—ideally—King Macario's army flanking. Strategically advantageous. And it would mean preserving favorable views of both the alliance with the humans and between Dun Mozg and Nozva Rozkveta.

And Mati would never want him to bring their problems to an ally's doorstep if it could be avoided. She'd back this plan.

"I like it," he said to her at last, and she rubbed her hands together—blood-stained hands. "I'll brief Riza and have her work out the details with Nendra. We'll set out before the rising call." He approached Riza at the tunnel entrance to do just that.

"What about you?" Aless called after him, following in his wake. "Us?"

He turned back to her, took her shoulders gently. Her large, dark eyes gazed up at his. She was brilliant, clever, brave. But tonight, she was completely and utterly his to care for, in every way she needed for as long as she needed, until she felt safe again.

"You were attacked tonight. I won't leave your side."

"I... I need to know..." She took a deep breath. "Have you forgiven me?"

Yes, he wanted to say instantly. He'd felt it as clear as a life-spring, only moments earlier.

She'd gone into this marriage under duress and had hidden that from him from the moment he'd met her in Bellanzole, and that... had been aggravating. Thinking they'd been allies, friends even—perhaps something more, when she'd been forced into this and planning to leave all the while. Would she have even said goodbye? Or would it have been easier to just leave with a smile on her face?

But it *had* been aggravating. *Had.* They'd spoken about it, and she'd made an effort time and again to prove her commitment. Sometimes to the point of recklessness, like tonight in the ring.

And although she'd hidden the circumstances from him, when he thought of it now, he had no resentment in his heart toward her. None whatsoever. It hadn't been a betrayal, malicious and sharpened to hurt. She'd been a scared human, sacrificing herself in marriage to a person she'd never met, from a culture she'd known nothing about—or worse, had been misinformed about. If she'd been weak, despite all that, she would have resigned herself to it.

But that wasn't the woman he'd married. His Aless was strong. When someone told her there was no way out, she made her own. She hadn't resolved to be with him because her father had told her to; she'd made up her own mind, and for that, he adored her even more. There was no betrayal in her affection now.

"Yes, I forgive you," he answered.

CHAPTER 18

*a*s Aless watched Veron speaking to Riza, everything else seemed to fade, to disappear. Colors blurred around her, sounds muffled to unintelligible vibrations, and her gaze wouldn't be lured away from her husband, who passed on instructions—her instructions—in an important matter.

He'd *listened* to her, heard her out, considered her input, and it wasn't the first time. He'd listened to her in Stroppiata, too, about the entry, when they'd fought the harpies, about the shrine...

It would have been easy for him to wave her off, walk away, ignore her "meddling" and tell her not to worry her pretty little head over such complicated matters, as Papà had always told her.

But to Veron...

To Veron, she wasn't just a *pretty little head*. She was *someone*. A person with ideas, with a voice, with a need to help and contribute, valid opinions, and he'd listened.

And then, tonight, he'd *forgiven* her.

Finally, that hasty plan from before the wedding didn't stand between them.

She would still follow her dream, but she couldn't imagine it any other way but with Veron at her side. Together, they'd see the library realized someday. She'd propose it to him, to his mother, to anyone who'd listen until it existed.

As Riza saluted and strode away, Veron glanced back over his shoulder, met her eyes with his own warm, golden gaze, and she had to remember to blink.

He returned to her, over six feet of warrior, strong, deadly, *hers*. Blood stained his jaw, his neck, his leather armor, and some of his hair, but she wanted nothing more than to wrap herself around him and kiss him until she forgot where she ended and he began.

With a smile, he offered her a hand, and she took it. He rubbed a thumb gently over the drying blood on her skin. "Let's get cleaned up."

He walked her toward their quarters across swaths of shining black pathways, past babbling streams and cascading waterfalls, shimmering with the soft sage glow of the biolumi-nescence.

A faint tremor shook the surface of the water, and she tightened her grip on Veron's hand.

"Magic can't penetrate Dun Mozg." He cupped her cheek. "It's encased in arcanir. You're safe."

She drew a slow, deep breath through her nose. Thank the Mother.

Veron pressed a gentle kiss to her forehead, and then to her lips.

Her fingers ached for him, and she moved closer, rested

them on the broad expanse of his chest, let them slip slowly to the sculpted hardness of his abdomen.

The rhythm of his breath changed, deepened, slowed.

Another tremor, and she blinked, meeting heavy-lidded, darkening eyes. He skimmed her jawline with his fingers, raised her chin, held her gaze. Her lips parted, and a shaky breath escaped them.

A couple of passersby smiled at them, and she became very aware of just how this looked. And how it *felt*.

Veron tipped his head in the direction of their quarters, and she nodded. The sooner they cleaned off all this blood, the better.

Once inside, she pulled off her boots as he did his, then began unfastening her bloodied dress. Veron lit a candle and then headed to the basin, where he dipped his hands and began to scrub them and wash his face.

Beneath her dress, she wore a short challis chemise tucked into trousers—her *stained* trousers, so she pulled those off, too. She moved to the basin next to Veron, washed her face and then her own hands together with his, using the olive-oil-and-rosemary soap she'd brought from Bellanzole.

She soaped up his hands, too, careful of his claws, as he smiled.

"It smells like you," he said, raising a palm to his nose. "What is it? This flower?"

"It's an herb. Rosemary."

Closing his eyes, he made a low, rolling sound in his throat, and warmth rippled into her, made her tingle all over. It was a sound she'd never tire of hearing, that would grace the best of her dreams—the ones she hoped not to wake from.

He set down the soap, rinsed his hands, then set about

unstrapping his leather armor. She reached for the straps, too, stroked her palms over smooth leather, helped him until he was down to his clothes, just a shirt and braies. There was a cut on his arm, and she took hold of his hand, examined the wound.

"Veron, you're hurt."

With a shake of his head and a smile, he pulled off his shirt and presented his bicep. The slash was already partially healed.

"We recover quickly," he said, although she dabbed at it with a clean washcloth. He took her hand. "I'm fine, Aless. Really."

He gazed down at her, his mouth curving, and there was a playfulness there. A teasing.

So he thought she was overreacting. Maybe she was. But the notion of him being hurt—at all—made her worry so much that she didn't know what to do with herself.

Apparently fussing wasn't the answer. She smiled to herself and glanced away, to his bare chest, strong and smooth, and the black sun tattooed there.

"It's beautiful," she whispered, stroking it with her fingertips.

"You'll have one, too, Aless," he said, his voice deep and flowing as he covered her hand with his, "if you choose to go through with the second ceremony in Nozva Rozkveta."

"I *do* choose to. Veron, I made that desperate plan before I ever knew you. Now that I've gotten to know you, I want to pursue my dream *with* you. And I want to marry you. As many times and in as many ways as you want."

Slowly, he leaned in, unbearably slow, then tipped her chin up to his and kissed her, taking her in his arms. His hair brushed her cheek as she opened her mouth to him, pressed herself against his hard body. Holy Mother's mercy, he *had* to know, *had* to understand that she'd never leave him, *ever*. That she'd chosen him, with everything she was and everything she had to give, no matter what she'd thought before knowing him.

With every breath, she inhaled the forest-stream scent of him, and that something deeper, something primal, that she couldn't get enough of. *Veron*.

His tongue claimed her mouth in slow, sensual strokes— strokes that made her whimper, made her heart pound. She wanted him. More than anything or anyone she'd ever wanted before, she wanted *him*.

I want you to know that I'm open to your wishes, and that you shouldn't fear rejection should you express them to me, he'd said to her once, on their wedding night.

She swallowed. As she leaned into him, against the hard, solid length of him—she gasped. His thoughts couldn't be too far from her own.

"Veron," she breathed between kisses, "I want to... I wish to..."

She'd been bold her entire life, had said things to lovers that would make a courtesan blush, but here, now, with *him*, she couldn't even bring herself to form a coherent sentence, and Holy Mother help her, if he *laughed* at her right now, she would just die, instantaneously, of embarrassment.

He pulled away, just enough for his soft golden gaze to lock with hers, and then intertwined his fingers with hers. Candle-light flickered, its warm glow cast against his skin. Her heart skipped a beat as he searched her eyes.

"I want to make love with you, Aless," he whispered, making her shiver. "I want to know you, as closely as one heart can know another, and I want you to know me."

Every inch of her tensed and trembled in equal parts, and

there was a good chance she was about to tackle him no matter what he said next.

"Do you want me to, Aless?" A teasing smile tugged at the corner of his mouth as he peered down at her with gleaming eyes.

She nodded—more than once—and threw her arms around him, rose on her tiptoes to kiss him, and he took her mouth, grabbed her bottom, and scooped her up. The spot was tender, but she didn't care, not right now, not until the need coursing in her veins got its due.

Her mouth never leaving his, she locked her legs around his hips, let him take her to bed, where she threw off her chemise as he pulled off his braies.

In his nakedness, he was the most beautiful sight she'd ever laid eyes on—as if his god or hers had sculpted him from marble, chiseled his fit physique to the perfection standing before her now. Her *husband*. He was big, strong, *hers*, and he would know it to the core of his existence by the time she was through with him tonight.

He gave her a slow once-over, devouring her with his eyes, his chest rising and falling with every powerful breath, and she would have given anything—*anything*—to know what he was thinking right now, looking upon a human woman, *his* human woman.

He took her in his arms, claimed her with his lips, his kisses roving down her neck as she buried her hands in his long, soft hair.

"Teach my hands how to touch you, Aless," he whispered, and his touch was gentle curiosity, unbinding her hair, raking through her curls; he brushed lightly over her breasts, and when she gasped, he firmed his touch, rubbed them, kissed them. He stroked along her ribcage and over her waist, down her thigh and all the way to her ankle, which he grasped and pressed to his lips.

"Teach my lips how to kiss you," he whispered, his kisses fluttering along her skin, so light she squirmed as they graced her quivering inner thigh.

"Endlessly," she answered softly, and he smiled before pulling her to the edge of the bed and descending to her. He kissed her belly, her hip, and lower, lower, until his lips met her core, making her gasp. Slowly, he pleasured her, his passionate, deliberate strokes coaxing her breaths out in erratic puffs while her hands clutched the bedding in tight fistfuls. Pressure rose in her, and built and built until she writhed beneath him, close, so close, tension rising, rising until it crested, peaked, bursting from her in cries as she reached for him.

"Please," she said, wiggling farther up the bed as he braced over it, teasing with feather-light strokes over her thighs, across her belly, over her breasts. The tips of his long hair tickled her stomach before he kissed her chest, lavished her sensitive spots with a playfulness that made her back arch off the bed.

She buried her fingers in his hair, urged him up to her face, and his mouth met hers anew, reclaimed her needy lips. As she angled to him, whimpering for union, heavenly, wonderful, *glorious* union, he was ready against her. *So* ready, but when she rocked against him, a sharpness skimmed her bottom where his hand gripped her.

Just a graze—no matter—she didn't react, kept kissing him, her own hands roving the corded musculature of his back.

"Aless," he whispered between kisses, "teach me to love you the way you wish to be loved."

She moved against his hardness, gasping, pushing, and

Holy Mother's mercy, if he didn't take her now, right now, she would die of want.

"Show me," he said to her, his usually deep voice an octave lower.

He didn't want to hurt her, maybe didn't want to presume, to lose control—he wanted to please her, to be who she needed, to provide what she needed. As she wanted to do for him.

"On your back," she whispered.

His mischievous gaze locked with hers, he did as bidden, and she sat astride him, held him at her core, watched his mouth fall open and his entire body go taut as he hissed an oath to his god.

With a gasp, she took him slowly, so carefully, until at last they were completely, utterly one, and despite his tense muscles rippling, he stroked her softly, her thighs, her hips, with perfect self-control. His eyes followed everywhere he touched, heavy lidded and intense, taking her in with a boundless hunger. There were a thousand things she wanted to tell him, a thousand memories she wanted to share, and millions more she wanted to live with him, to learn with him, to create together.

He wasn't afraid to hold her gaze, to watch the truth on her face, just as she watched his, the fondness there, the desire, and not just for this moment, but for countless more, and for her.

She knew in that moment, in those eyes, that he would never betray her. That he would always be there for her. And that he would always hear her voice, and listen.

As she moved, she held his gaze, too, looked into his eyes, adoring and awed, his eyebrows drawn tight. A frisson rippled through her lower belly; the hard fullness of him inside her was pleasure, unbearable pleasure, and with every movement, she trembled, breathed shakily, the heat of his every touch pooling at her core, where it only wanted, and wanted.

His slow, rough breaths, rhythmic and primal, began to quicken, and her own surrender was just there, within reach, and she took him harder, faster, chasing it, chasing it, until at last she caught it, cried out, again and again, waves of hot sensation cascading through her, throbbing through her veins, pulsing at her core. As he groaned, low and deep, she didn't stop, kept going until his eyes pressed shut and his mouth fell open, need claiming his face with creased determination that— with a hiss—pleasure freed and freed and freed with every panted breath. Warmth filled her up, heat spreading through every part of her, kindled by his touch, his care, and the love they made together.

Veron, *her* Veron, lay beneath her, gazing up at her with stars in his eyes, and she reached for his face, gently stroking along his jaw, over his lips, and down over the chiseled beauty of his black-sun chest and his abdomen.

With a grin, he urged her down to him, tucked her curls behind her ear, and kissed her. She took his lip between hers, explored his mouth with her tongue, teased it with playful strokes as he rubbed her bare back with firm, sensual pressure.

"Was it worth the wait?" she breathed.

He smiled. "*You* were worth the wait, Aless."

Completely serene, he watched her, and she leaned in to kiss him again.

"So is that how the dark-elves do things?" she asked with a grin. "Because I approve."

He laughed in his throat and shook his head. "In essence, yes," he drawled, "but with us, everything is a test of strength. Even lovemaking."

She tried to picture pinning him, gasping as he rolled her over, dueling between the sheets. If that was how things usually went, then with her, he'd been exceedingly cautious, had submitted himself completely to her whim, to her ways, and let her do as she'd pleased while he'd resisted his instincts, restrained his body. He'd been so taut, muscles rippling, quaking, and it had been *restraint*.

The day she'd first met him, he'd clasped his hands behind his back, but when she'd taken a step away, he'd revealed them, held them at his sides, shown her he'd meant her no harm.

"Veron," she said, and his embrace around her tightened. She lay down at his side, nestled into the crook of his shoulder, into the warmth of him, as he caressed her arm. "What's your home like?"

"Nozva Rozkveta?" he asked softly. "It's beautiful, brimming with life. It's a fortress, but you could spend hours watching the sparkling water, the gleaming surfaces..."

"Stone, right?" she asked, receiving a nod in reply. "Will we live in a stone dwelling?"

"In palace quarters. Not too different from this, actually," he added with a laugh. "Don't worry—we'll make sure to have some of your fluffy human things around."

She poked him, and he laughed again, then nuzzled her head with his nose before kissing her lightly there.

"Believe me, I have nothing but the utmost respect for human things," he said softly, slowly, and urged her onto her back.

There was no laughter in his eyes now, only rapt attention, and he reached out to brush her lips with his thumb before taking them with his own again.

His hands explored her gently, slowly, roving over her bottom, and then he went rigid. Froze. Pulled away.

He stared down at his palm, glanced at her, and left the bed.

Wriggling to the edge, she eyed him. "Veron?"

He rubbed his face with his hand, pacing the room, then held up the other.

Blood.

CHAPTER 19

*B*y Deep and Darkness, he'd *hurt* her. Again.

As desire had claimed him, he'd remembered to be gentle, to keep his touch light, to avoid injuring her—and it had happened anyway.

"Veron?" she asked again, rising from the bed. She tried to embrace him, but he pulled away.

He shook his head. No, he couldn't touch her like this, not again. Not with his claws.

"It's all right," she whispered, rubbing his back. "It was only a little scratch." She kissed his shoulder. "Come back to bed."

Every dark-elf of worth had claws—sharp, strong, battle-ready claws. Claws he had defended her with just earlier tonight. If they were broken, taken in battle, or maimed, it was dishonor. Weakness.

Aless locked her arms around him from behind, her delicate, slender arms, with her supple, fragile skin. His lover, his partner, his wife. His *human* wife.

He wouldn't risk hurting her again, not for all the honor and strength in the Deep. Never again.

He could never give her lavish human celebrations, with new dances every season and theatre and opera and fashion and excess. He could never give her a legion of servants in her household to pamper her as she'd been in the palace. Nor could he give her a place in the sun, in the sky realm, among her kind and sunshine and light. He could never impress her or court her the way a human man would.

But the very *least* he could do was never hurt her. Keep her safe. The very *least*.

As he approached the table of toiletries, she let him go, and he searched through them until he found her nail file.

"Veron, what are you doing?" Her voice quavered.

"What I should have done before our wedding," he murmured, then began filing down his claws.

She grasped his hand, her eyebrows knitted together. "But won't your reputation—"

He raised her hand to his lips, kissed it. All his life, he'd guarded his reputation fiercely, never wanting to be anything but a credit to Mati and Nozva Rozkveta. But Deep, Darkness, and Holy Ulsinael, what did his *reputation* matter in comparison to her wellbeing?

"I don't want to hurt you, Aless, ever," he whispered, lowering her hand. "And if anyone questions my battle prowess, I won't need claws to trounce them in the ring."

He had been trained by Mati and Zoran—the best—and he didn't need claws to fight.

He started filing them again, as short as her human nails, shorter even. They'd grow back in a month, but he'd just file them down again, and the month after, and the one after that, for the rest of their lives.

Backing up toward the bed, she tossed her long, dark hair over her shoulder and raised an eyebrow. "Are you certain you need to do this now?"

He'd already taken several steps in her direction before he realized it. With a shake of his head, he continued filing while she giggled. Their first night together, and she already knew the power she held over him—and she wasn't afraid to use it. If she ever brought out that sheer red thing from their wedding night, he wasn't certain there was anything he wouldn't do.

"Not sure I've ever seen anyone file their nails so fast in my life," she teased, hopping onto the bed and kicking her legs playfully. She leaned back, propped a foot upon the bed, and eyed him over her round, bare breasts.

She parted her thighs, only a little, and Holy Ulsinael, the nail file clattered to the floor.

VERON HELD ALESS'S HAND, leading her down the passage to the hot springs.

"Where are we going?" she asked with a tilt of her head, tightening the sash of her robe and looking around. "I can barely move."

He huffed a laugh under his breath. So far, they had spent the entire night in bed, and he would happily spend the rest of it there, but Aless couldn't leave Dun Mozg without visiting the hot springs—especially considering they had a couple of days on horseback ahead of them.

"After that landing in the ring earlier, I think you'll like where we're going." He smiled at her over his shoulder.

The air turned balmy right before the entrance, the soft splash of water babbling nearby. He led her inside, and she gasped.

Silvery moonlight peeked in high overhead, refracting off jeweled veins in the stone, flowing down to the steam rising off the vivid teal water. Streams cascaded from the rock into the spring with a pleasant, continuous sound. It was, thankfully, empty.

"I thought you could use some hot—"

She threw her arms around his neck and kissed him, then kissed him again... deeper, slowly; untying her sash, he moved toward the water, unwrapped the towel from around his waist before wading into the soothing heat. She let the robe fall to her feet—and Holy Ulsinael, he'd never tire of seeing her naked—and then she followed, entering with a lengthy, quiet moan.

Broad steps descended into the sultry water, and he sat on one, submerged to his chest, and she sank in next to him.

"Can we stay here forever?" she murmured, her eyes closed as she settled into his arms.

He sighed. "We can stay here... a little less than an hour."

With a quiet whine, she rubbed her cheek on his chest before resting against him.

To make their plan work, they'd be leaving Dun Mozg before dawn. As it was, they'd be traveling on little to no sleep, but he'd already planned on letting her sleep in the saddle while they rode.

"Veron," she said, lightly stroking his abdomen, "can we talk about Gavri?"

Clearing his throat, he straightened. No, they absolutely could *not* talk about Gavri while she touched him like that.

She giggled and settled her arm around him. "Sorry."

He rolled his eyes and sighed. "What about Gavri?"

As much as he cared for Gavri, her decisions hadn't exactly been brilliant lately—from betraying him, to carrying on with Zoran, to *derelicting her duty* to guard Aless.

She was quiet a moment, nuzzling his chest with her cheek. "Gavri told me that once lost, your trust is unrecoverable."

Gavri *would* say that, because up until recently, it had been the truth. After he'd lost Ata, he'd never wanted to go through it again. "One betrayal has the power to destroy everything. And I'm tired of losing things."

"But you forgave me."

He had. And it had happened through none of his own making—clearly his heart knew better than he did, and he wasn't about to complain.

Aless sat up and looked at him, her palm pressed over his heart. "People might sometimes betray your trust, Veron, and you might lose them. But if you choose not to forgive, you don't have to worry about losing them... because you've already pushed them away. It's still loss, but of your own making."

He blinked.

"Do you really want to lose Gavri?"

Even though Aless had lied, he hadn't wanted to lose her... had forgiven her.

He lowered his gaze to the water, watching its steam rise. But wasn't it better to lose someone knowingly, by his own choice, than to wait for a worse betrayal? Watching them walk away in deception, while he, without knowing the truth, was helpless to do anything about it? Wasn't it worth the years of wondering *what if*?

What if he hadn't let Ata leave that day? *What if* he'd followed him? *What if* he'd learned of Ata's plans?

Would he have been able to stop him? To save him? Would his father be alive right *now*?

"She told me about what happened with your father," Aless whispered. "You were just a child, Veron. It wasn't fair, but there was nothing you could have done."

He shook his head. "You're wrong. He was my *father*. I loved him, and I should have known him better than anyone. But I didn't." That day, he'd accepted Ata's smile without a second thought. "I have forgiven you, but there's a reason I don't forgive. I see people, Aless, but I don't understand them. I can know someone my entire life and not realize they're going to betray me. I can be in *love* with a person, and not know she's plotting to kill my mother. When it comes to understanding other people, I... I can't even trust myself."

If he trusted those who betrayed him, if he forgave them, would the next betrayal leave Aless dead? Or Mati? Or Riza? Or any of his sisters and brothers? His people?

He knew Aless would never betray him again, that she'd never hurt him or anyone he loved, and so he'd been able to forgive her. That had to be why.

But anyone else? He'd trusted Gavri after her lie, at least enough to let her continue performing guard duties, and what had happened? Aless and Noc could have been *buried under rubble*.

There was a reason he couldn't forgive betrayers. And it wasn't because they were terrible, or selfish, or evil. It was because he couldn't trust himself to understand them. And that could mean losing someone he loved... again.

Aless turned to face him, slowly brought her knees down

around his hips, and settled into his lap. She wrapped her arms around his neck, and as hot as the water was, the warmth inside of him wasn't from the spring, but the soft look in her eyes as she leaned in and lightly brushed his lips with hers.

"People you love will let you down, Veron," she said softly. "I've been let down and I've let down others more times than I can count. But no one is perfect. Everyone makes mistakes. If you don't forgive, the only difference is that they'll make their mistakes without you. Is that really what you want?"

Those mistakes hurt. But never laughing with Gavri again? Or losing her, Aless, or any of his loved ones?

"And may I remind you," Aless said, kissing him lightly again as she leaned into him, "that if not for your forgiveness, we probably wouldn't be right here, like this, right now?"

A solid point. A very solid point.

"You might not be pushing away just the bad, but the good, too." Her mouth fell open as she rocked against him, water lapping about them.

Just the thought of her caring enough about his friends— and *him*—to broach this was enough to make it worth considering. "I'll think about it, I promise," he replied.

"Good," she said with a smile, and he held her close as he lifted her from the water. "Because we have a long ride ahead of us."

And a few days' worth of traveling, too.

CHAPTER 20

*A*s the rain started to fall midafternoon, Veron tucked Aless's copy of *A Modern History of Silen* inside her cloak, into her belt. Riding double with him on Noc, she'd been reading it aloud all morning since they'd left Dun Mozg, and the trip had been far less dull with her animated voice spinning tales.

She was fast asleep now, her head resting against his arm, and Noc's gait had become all the smoother.

You're fond of her, he told Noc.

So are you, Noc answered.

He laughed under his breath. It couldn't have anything to do with the apples she'd brought in their pack, which had mysteriously disappeared after their rest stop. Even for that short reprieve, she'd been eager to learn the bow, and could even hit a target now... sometimes.

"You spoil her," Yelena murmured, riding up to him, hooded and cloaked.

He sighed. Queen Nendra had insisted that Yelena and some of her kuvari accompany them to Nozva Rozkveta, saying she wouldn't risk Queen Zara's son and a Sileni princess being killed on the way home from her queendom.

"She was attacked last night, in case you forgot," he shot back. "By fanatics and, earlier, by *you*."

She scoffed. "You know my mother would have me given into the Darkness if I destroyed the peace." She rolled her eyes. "Besides, let's not pretend this is about her little tumble in the ring, or the human scouts you killed." She gave him and Aless a stern once-over. "You were seen all over each other on the main thoroughfare. It was the talk of the cavern this morning. And then you"—she curled her upper lip—"*disfigured* yourself like that." She cocked her head toward his hands. "No dark-elf woman would have you now."

Aless nuzzled his arm sleepily, and he held her closer. He didn't want a dark-elf woman, or any other. The only one he needed was right here, would always be right here. "All that matters is she does."

Yelena shook her head.

"Let me guess—you disapprove."

A huff. "Well, she's no dark-elf." Yelena's eyes fixed on Aless. "But I heard she killed one of those scouts last night. A crossbow bolt through the head, *by hand*." She whistled softly. "She may not be a warrior, but she's not the typical scurrying salamander, either. I still don't like her, though."

From Yelena, that was a glowing endorsement.

"And I don't believe a word about those human deeds in her tales," she added with a grunt, "except the parts about all the dying and fleeing."

He suppressed a smile. So she'd been listening to Aless reading.

With the rain coming down, the day dragged traveling in the sky realm, but at least in the tunnels their cargo caravan wouldn't be slowed by it. No doubt the food and supplies from Bellanzole and Stroppiata would arrive in Nozva Rozkveta well before he did. He and Aless had also sent Gabriella with Danika to deliver the message to King Macario; with any luck, they'd take the tunnels as far as they could and stay out of the Brotherhood's reach.

Without carriages and cargo, his group made good time, even in the mud, moving fast enough to keep ahead of the Brotherhood's army while leading them away from Dun Mozg. He and Yelena had made sure to leave behind easily found tracks, so if the Brotherhood wanted him or Aless, they would follow.

Despite being faster, he and the rest of the group still took precautions—short rests only and sleeping in shifts. Scouts to make sure they weren't cut off by a forward team—Riza was out now with Kinga. With any luck, they'd be in Nozva Rozkveta tomorrow night.

Unlike Dun Mozg, however, Nozva Rozkveta wasn't encased in arcanir. While nestled on an enormous anima Vein, its only protection was that any magic used on it would mean the witch risking convergence—or what today's witches referred to as "fureur," according to Aless. Tapping into the earth's life force, its innate magic, would mean certain death for a witch. That and potentially upsetting the earth's anima.

It would be enough. Deep, Darkness, and Holy Ulsinael, it *had* to be enough.

Gavri rode nearby, and he'd promised he'd think about forgiving her.

One betrayal did have the power to destroy everything, but pushing someone away was destroying everything with his own hands. He couldn't predict others' actions with perfect accuracy, couldn't account for mistakes or betrayals, but when it came to people he loved, he wanted to be there for them through the bad *and* the good. When they made mistakes, he wanted to be there to help them, to support them, to save them if he could, instead of isolated, away, alone.

Malice didn't hide in every untruth. He was tired of losing things, but that meant he needed to stop pushing everyone away.

"Gavri," he called, and she looked over her shoulder, her wet braid swinging, and slowed. "I... I wanted to say I'm sorry. I overreacted."

Her eyes widened, and she glanced down at Aless before meeting his eyes anew. "You don't need to apologize to me, Veron. I understand."

He took a deep breath and brushed his fingers through Noc's mane. "No, I do. I want to."

She shook her head.

"I nearly let one argument destroy our friendship. Can you forgive me?"

With a subtle smile, she bowed her head. "Already forgiven. And I'm sorry I let things with Zoran interfere with my duties. It won't happen again."

The thought of Aless being under the rubble threaded rigidity through him, but she was right here in his arms. Everything was all right.

"How did things go with you and Zoran?" he asked.

Gavri rolled her eyes and heaved a sigh. "I'd resolved to lock up my heart, to keep him out. And then in Dun Mozg, he told me I was the love of his life, that it had been so hard to leave that he couldn't bear to say goodbye, and that we could never be together."

That much was true. Zoran's Offering to Nendra had sealed the alliance between Nozva Rozkveta and Dun Mozg. For as long as Nendra remained in power, Zoran had to stay by her side as king-consort if he wanted to protect that alliance. Zoran and Gavri had loved each other—did love each other—and could never be together.

And I get to be with Aless. In his arms was everything he'd never known he'd wanted, but if he'd been a little more skilled, a little more talented with a blade, he might have been the strongest of his brothers and been bargained away to Nendra instead of Zoran. That was an unjust twist of fate he felt keenly, that he should have Aless in his life when Zoran couldn't be with Gavri. "I have no wisdom for it. Would that the Darkness had shadowed your lives differently."

Her gaze downcast, Gavri lifted a dispirited shoulder. "We serve at Her Majesty's pleasure."

As she looked back at him over her shoulder, she raised a fist.

The entire group came to a halt. She gestured behind them, where two riders tore up the muddy ground at a steady clip. Riza and Kinga.

They rode up, and Riza slowed her horse to a trot, approaching him.

"Your Highness," she said, heaving tired breaths, "a forward team. Less than half a day behind us."

They'd relied on the likelihood that the Brotherhood would

follow, but a forward team made the situation vastly more dangerous.

"At this rate, they'll catch us tomorrow afternoon," Kinga added, panting.

"Send Gavri and Valka to keep an eye on them. And as for us, no more long stops," he bit out. They couldn't risk them. If they were pinned down, and the Brotherhood army caught up to them—he shook his head. "We pick up the pace."

Riza gave a curt nod. "You heard His Highness," she called out to the group. "Move out. Now!"

ALESS WOKE from dreams of vining roses and Veron's touch. As she blinked her eyes open, the sun was setting, and she was still in the saddle with Veron. She glanced around for Gabriella— but no, she'd sent Gabriella with Danika through the earth-mover tunnels to Bellanzole, with letters for Papà, Bianca, and Lorenzo, and even Duchessa Claudia along the way. *Holy Mother, keep her in your light.*

"Are you hungry?" Veron whispered in her ear, his voice a low rasp. He handed her some bread and cheese they'd gotten in Stroppiata.

"Thank you," she said softly, and nibbled on the food.

When had he last slept? Their pace had only picked up since news of the forward team, and it was taking a toll on everyone. They had to stay ahead, but they couldn't take much more of this. *Veron* couldn't take much more of this.

She'd woken a few times during their travel as they'd paused briefly to feed and water the horses, to rest them and switch to fresh mounts, but Veron had told her each time to go back to sleep. She was saddle sore and tired, but if they hadn't stopped for long since yesterday, he had to be exhausted. "Is there a way I could stay awake and you could sleep?"

He kissed her cheek. "We're almost there. Only a little more, and then we'll both get some rest. Promise."

His optimism was heartwarming, but she could hear the exhaustion rasping in his deep voice. He was tired. Beyond tired.

Next to them, Riza pulled up on her horse. "Your Highness..." Her voice drifted.

Riza wasn't one to mince words, at least not in the short time she'd know her. This had to be bad news.

Veron stiffened. "What is it?"

"Gavri and Valka should have returned from scouting by now, Your Highness." The words were quiet. Uneasy.

Maybe they'd gotten lost. Maybe one of their horses had lost a shoe. Or maybe...

"Could they have gotten lost?"

Veron took a deep breath. "Not out here. We know these wilds well—sometimes our hunting or scouting takes us out this far."

Which meant...

We have to look for them, she wanted to say.

But it was the wrong thing, and she knew it, deep in her bones. If the Brotherhood had captured them, then they *wanted* Veron to come looking. *Wanted* to capture him, and maybe even her, and do who-knew-what to everyone else here.

She and Veron needed to negotiate for their release—only... they had nothing but themselves to offer. And Gavri and Valka would only be leverage until Tarquin got what he wanted— vengeance for his sister, Arabella.

But Queen Zara would be in a better position. And yet...
"There has to be *something* we can do, Veron," she whispered.
"It's Gavri."

"Gavri and Valka know what it means to be kuvari," Riza
said, sternly but not bitterly. "They are prepared to give their
lives for our prince, and for Nozva Rozkveta."

"It doesn't need to come to that," Aless replied, twisting in
Veron's hold.

"There are no other options," Yelena said from next to them.
"We're in no position to negotiate, and the humans would be
waiting for a rescue mission if we tried that."

As much as she wanted to argue for Gavri, none of what
Yelena had said was incorrect.

Veron's grip on the reins tightened, and next to them, Noc,
unburdened and resting, blew out a breath and tossed his head.

Veron nodded. "No more scouts. We make for Nozva
Rozkveta, then I'm certain my mother will send a messenger for
terms."

"It's the right call," Yelena said.

It didn't feel that way, but getting themselves caught or
trading themselves in wouldn't help Gavri or Valka. They had to
handle this carefully, with Queen Zara.

Riza passed on Veron's orders, and the cavalcade picked up
the pace, pushing their horses to the limit. Noc ran alongside
the others, spurring them on, and she couldn't help but glance
around Veron's arms from time to time, searching the darkening distance for Gavri and Valka.

After hours of more riding, night had fallen, and she could
barely see her hand in front of her face, let alone the path
ahead, but Veron and the rest of the kuvari picked their way
confidently. She wanted to ask him about it, but her backside

and thighs were so sore, her entire body so achy, she couldn't even muster the words anymore. Her thoughts lingered on Gavri, and praying for her safety and swift return, along with Valka.

Her eyelids were drooping when something glowed faintly ahead. Like fireflies, lights winked in the darkness, flowing in lazy curls and scrolls. Pixies.

A fresh, alluring scent filled the air—roses—its density surrounding her, so powerful she could close her eyes, reach, and touch the velvety petals. A dream—no, a hallucination?

The glow of the pixies gently illuminated vines twining old ruins, climbing the stone, claiming it in sprawling, verdant green—an ancient courtyard—and bright crimson blooms unfurled amid a thicket of green, roses so large, so vivid, as if they'd grown from her dreams and fantasies. In full bloom, mysterious and lovely, exhaling that most spellbinding perfume in the pure air. So tangled, wild, and yet they shimmered in the glow, dazzled with an otherworldly beauty.

The only roses she'd seen even *approximating* their brilliance had been at the palazzo, during the wedding, but they hadn't glittered as these.

"Veron," she breathed, and her voice was no more than a thin, tired whimper. "These roses..."

Warmth met the top of her head in a kiss, and his tightening embrace pulled her closer. "We brought many for the wedding in Bellanzole, but once cut, they begin to lose their luster. They shimmer here, wild and free, because this is where they belong, where they can thrive."

As they approached, she gasped. For a lifetime, she could take in their beauty and never get her fill. These roses weren't like the trimmed, manicured gardens of the nobiltà, but an unfettered, chaotic beauty that nothing tried to contain.

Ahead, a thicket of them knotted in a massive bramble, thorny and breathtaking.

"Nozva Rozkveta is seated over the largest Vein of anima in the land, the force from which all life and magic springs. And for as long as we have existed here, so has the Bloom, cocooning our home from all who would do us harm, allowing in only friends to our kind."

It was as if the land itself protected Veron's people—now *her* people—enshrining them from danger.

Soon, Veron halted the cavalcade and everyone dismounted. He helped her down onto her sore legs, and it took some waddling while braced against him before she could even move properly.

They approached a Bloom thicket, knotted and twisted chaotically in vines and roses, but Veron didn't stop. The tangle parted for him, reshaping into an arched colonnade that he entered without hesitation. All around them—on the sides, above them, even below—vines writhed in living form, held that shape, as she accompanied him, as the others followed behind with Noc and the horses.

At the end of the Bloom's colonnade, the path lowered to a large stone door, ancient and massive, etched with runic script. Still holding her hand, Veron approached it and tapped a rhythm on its face, the Nozva Rozkvetan knock.

The massive door opened, ground against its stone frame, revealing a tunnel inside and two kuvari in leathers.

"Your Highness," they greeted in unison. "Nozva Rozkveta bids you welcome."

He thanked them as he entered, stroking her hand softly, and the rest of the cavalcade followed.

The tunnel was dark, but at its end was a lavender glow. As they approached, Veron raised her hand to his lips and pressed a gentle kiss to her skin.

"Welcome home, Aless," he whispered, and they stepped into a vast space.

Bioluminescent mushrooms climbed the cavern walls, bathing the realm below in that lavender light, along with radiant white glowworms and glittering vines of the Bloom sprawling as far as the eye could see.

She gasped, looking everywhere at once, at gleaming dwellings of mirror-like black stone and glistening streams weaving among shining paths. On the outskirts, fields of green shoots peeked up from ebony soil.

"H-how can they grow here, when—"

Veron grinned at her, his golden eyes soft. "The Vein. It seeps life into everything here. Into everyone."

Groups of singers ringed unfinished structures, their tones impossibly deep, their songs unlike anything she'd ever heard. Passersby stopped to bow and offer cheery greetings.

Veron nodded toward the tall, black towers peaking above a building like a cluster of crystals. "I wish we had time to stop at the lifespring first, but we need to tell my mother what's happened."

"Let's get Gavri and Valka back first," she said with a nod, and then she could ask what a *lifespring* was.

Riza joined them as they strode toward the palace, and every muscle in Aless's body rebelled. The long ride had been difficult, painful, but they'd made it here before the Brother-hood could catch up to them.

Nozva Rozkveta would have time to prepare for the attack, and by the grace of the Holy Mother, hopefully the food had arrived by way of the tunnels.

Four kuvari guarded the palace entrance, and they stood aside as Veron entered and proceeded straight down the main hallway to a set of massive doors.

Two kuvari opened them, and inside, the grand hall yawned, massive, the Bloom vines climbing its walls, ceiling, and stalactites and adorning them in glittering green and crimson roses that radiated a vivid glow.

This place *breathed* life, teemed with it.

At the end, a regal woman sat atop a translucent crystal throne, its peaks fanning out behind her. She had a diamond-shaped face, elegant and smooth, slightly lighter than Veron's, and voluminous platinum hair, cascading in curls sectioned with beads, a futile attempt to contain the wild tresses. Her clothes were a robe and peplos of the finest silk she'd ever seen, and Papà's imports had not been inexpensive. Her feet were bare and clawed, their points shorter than the sharp ones on her hands, where she wore a pair of arcanir bracers.

Every part of her was lithe, sleek, and even as her crossed leg bounced lightly, it did so with a catlike grace, and yet her arms and shoulders were muscled, toned. The queen sat upon a throne now, but her physique said she could have anyone pinned to the gleaming black stone within seconds.

Her eyes were a warm amber, gentle and placid, and yet they glittered with innumerable facets of jeweled wisdom so deep those eyes could be infinite.

Veron's mother. The queen. Queen Zara.

This was her husband's *mother*, and meanwhile, she'd arrived with Veron in wrinkled, dirty, rain-and-sweat-soaked clothes, looking like something feral and smelling... well, "worse" was putting it mildly. Clearing her throat, she swept some stray horsehair from her rain-damp riding habit, her other hand in Veron's warm hold.

The queen smiled as her gaze landed on Veron, genuine, sweet, in a way that lit her face radiantly. She stood from her throne, pushing off with a limber little leap, and strode the length of the distance between them.

Veron bowed before the queen, and Aless followed suit.

"Welcome home, Veron," the queen said evenly, her low voice mellifluous, pleasant. "And you, daughter"—a gentle hand touched her shoulder, and Aless slowly straightened to face a smiling queen—"I welcome with a glad heart."

The queen was so beautiful that it was difficult not to stare.

"Thank you, Your Majesty," Aless breathed. "I'm honored to finally meet you."

The queen glanced down to where Veron's hand still held hers, and somehow, the queen's radiant smile widened. "I hope in time you'll come to call me Mati." Turning to Veron, she added, "I am overjoyed for you, Veron."

A corner of his mouth turned up as his gaze turned to her briefly, soft and loving, shining and pleased, before he looked back to his mother, that gentle smile fading. "Mati, I wish we came only bearing good news."

"The supply caravan arrived by way of the tunnels earlier today, and we've already begun distributing food," the queen replied. "And they brought news of the Brotherhood army and your plan."

If only that were the only bad news.

Veron took a deep breath and nodded. "They've taken Gavri and Valka captive."

CHAPTER 21

*V*eron walked with Aless to his quarters, her hand in his, and stared at the floor. He'd brought home his bride, and his mother and queen already approved of her. He'd be making the Offering to Aless at the second ceremony in three days.

In those three days, they might already be embroiled in a war.

One of his best friends and another of the kuvari could be held by a radical faction determined to annihilate his people.

Mati had said she would be sending one of her kuvari to the Brotherhood army to discuss terms. One had already volunteered, even knowing it was likely a suicide mission.

If only they could send in a small team to rescue them—but that would have no chance of success. If Tarquin was smart, he was holding Gavri and Valka in the heart of the camp, and a dark-elf team would have no chance of making it through the outskirts. Gavri or Valka or both would be killed, along with the team.

The convergence of such keen anguish and the most ardent joy he had with his wife weighed like the sky of stone upon his shoulders. He held her hand, and allowing himself to feel even a fraction of that joy came with the sting of Gavri held prisoner, possibly hurt, possibly suffering, and their people stepping into what could be an impending war.

"Papà will come to our aid, Veron," she said, rubbing his arm. "He wouldn't make this alliance unless he was prepared to defend it. And we've already demonstrated its validity. Dark-elves defended humans in Stroppiata. We earned the duchessa's friendship. People embraced us. The Brotherhood alone is left, an embittered old radical on the back foot. Papà will snap up the chance to rid his land of it."

The lives and wellbeing of Gavri, Valka, and all their people rested with a man who had traded Aless—his brilliant, brave, wonderful Aless—away with not a care to her unwillingness, in the coldest, most unfeeling way imaginable.

"I wrote to everyone. I wrote to Bianca, and to Lorenzo, too," Aless added, giving his bicep a squeeze. "Lorenzo won't give up on this—unlike Papà, he actually cares about us. And maybe Bianca could have a word with Luciano, convince him to talk his brother down." She gave him a nudge. "We have multiple plans in place. Something will work in our favor. You'll see."

Those hopes were remote, but she was right in her optimism, in her *morale*. They had to believe in something, or else the battle was already lost.

"Besides, your mother already said she had a plan."

In an hour, Mati expected them over for a midnight supper with Vadiha, Dhuro, and Yelena. Before he and Aless showed up, he'd have to muster the requisite morale. Mati had given her orders. It was time to support them.

"You're right. I know you're right," he said, pulling her in to kiss her temple. "We'll find out more when our messenger returns." Not *if*, but *when*.

She gave him an encouraging nod as he opened the door to his quarters. Not much had survived since the Sundering, but he'd never needed much.

Inside, the space was bare but for his blackstone tables, laden with bowstrings, fletching, arrowheads he'd been making, and a boot brush and leather balm. Aless flitted to it and lifted the brush, grinning. "You really *do* have a boot thing."

He cleared his throat. "Taking care of your boots is just being responsible."

She lifted a brow, her grin broadening.

"If you don't, the leather can be hard, too stiff, unforgiving, and—"

That brow lifted higher, and she leaned against the table. "I'd say 'go on,' but I have the worst case of saddle soreness known to humankind."

Shaking his head, he smiled and closed the distance between them, grazing her cheek with his fingers. It was a surreal pleasure to stroke her without worrying about his claws harming her, and he couldn't get enough of her smoothness, of touching her, everywhere she wanted, in the way she wanted.

"If you're sore"—and he was, too—"I have the perfect cure for that."

Shuttering her eyes playfully, she tilted her head. "I am all for curing, although I should warn you that after days of riding in the rain, I reek like a farm animal right now."

He suppressed a smile. There was a possibility that something more amusing than Aless existed in the world, but it had to be slim. "I meant the lifespring. It has restorative properties."

Those eyebrows shot up and her mouth fell open before she tried to turn her face away. But no, he would get full view of this. Blushing, she looked everywhere but in his eyes until at last she relented and bit her lip.

"I'd love to hear all about this 'cure' you *thought* I meant," he teased, holding her gaze.

Her long, elegant fingers toyed with the fastenings on his jacket as that blush was soon joined by a coy smile. "Well, it would involve you, me, and..." She glanced toward the bed, then gasped. "Veron!"

He followed her line of sight to the enormous human-style mattress sitting on the platform below his blackstone headboard. *Her* mattress. "Someone must have brought it in from the tunnels."

She darted to it, ran her hands over it, then pressed a palm into its springiness. "This really is... How did you..."

"I thought you might like it," he said, "so I had it brought over from Bellanzole with us when we left." Along with all its bedding and pillows and countless other things that had adorned the beds in King Macario's palace—somewhere, in one of the carts.

Her eyes were wide but, when they met his once more, took on a mischievous gleam. "Oh, Veron... This bedchamber will see a lot of 'curing.' *A lot*."

He burst out laughing before he could help himself, and she only grinned back at him. He offered her a hand. "But first, the lifespring?"

Taking it, she nodded. "And supper."

ALESS RUBBED her neck as Veron led her into the smaller, private dining chamber of the queen. The ache she'd felt there —and everywhere else—had disappeared, along with every trace of soreness ever. A short soak in the lifespring, and she was completely renewed.

They'd met two women there, Vlasta and Rút, who'd thanked Veron profusely for his help.

He'd explained that they were *lifebonded*, a dark-elf ritual that somehow joined two lives as one. They made each other stronger, shared life, but if one died... they'd share death, too. An oddly frightening and yet romantic concept.

The mystic at the lifespring, a healer named Xira, had given her robes that the other dark-elves seemed to wear outside of special occasions and traveling or combat. Soft and a neutral off-white, they wrapped her comfortably, with matching trousers that tucked into boots. It was strange not wearing her usual garments, not to mention wearing the same clothes as Veron, but she wanted to make an effort to fit in. These were her people now, too, and her family.

The queen wanted to have a private meal with her, Veron, his brother, and his sisters, but there was so much happening that it seemed impossible to just focus on getting to know her new family.

And there was the matter of the library. Paladin Grand Cordon Nunzio hadn't seemed averse to the plan, and she had to strike while the iron was hot, but with the Brotherhood threatening all-out war, it would have to wait.

She took a deep breath. Tonight was about making a good impression.

"They'll adore you," Veron whispered to her as they entered the queen's quarters, where glowing Bloom vines wrapped pillars and climbed across the ceiling, like something out of a daydream. Veron led her off to the side, through a large archway into a dining room with a round blackstone table ringed by benches.

A number of people were already there—a stern-faced woman with long, tousled hair, carrying a little baby, and a man with her, the sides of his head shaved and his hair tied back.

There was a tall man with shoulder-length hair, his face simmering under a taut brow, and three women with wild hair only barely tamed into thick braids—clearly they'd taken after the queen. The three of them wore face paint, one with black smudges over her eyes, another with a strip across them, and a third with a line across each cheek.

All eyes turned to her and Veron as they entered, with the stern-faced woman holding the baby and the man with her rising first.

"Everyone, this is Aless," Veron said with a smile. "Aless, this is my sister Vadiha; her husband, Arigo; and their daughter, Dita."

Dita had large, sunny-yellow eyes with long lashes, chubby little cheeks, and little pointed ears, with fine white hair wisping off to the side.

"She was hungry, so she's up a little late," Vadiha said as she approached with Dita in her arms, who reached out a tiny hand for Veron's hair. He gave her his finger to clutch instead and kissed her forehead lightly.

"Veron," Vadiha breathed, her eyes wide as she stared at his hand. Her husband's eyebrows shot up, too. "What's happened? Did you—did you do that to *yourself*?"

His claws. He'd said they were a point of respect, hadn't he? This was a shock to his family, because he'd changed for her.

But that change... had meant everything. It had meant they could *both* set aside fear, and be together without worrying about accidents. He'd done it for the sake of their marriage. Even faced with his family's shock, she wouldn't take that back. Even if that made her selfish.

Veron gave his sister a cavalier shrug. "I'm happy, Vadiha."

But Vadiha's gaze meandered to her, blinking long, pale lashes.

Veron leaned into his sister's line of sight, blocking her. "Vadiha. I mean it." His carefree voice had firmed.

But his sister's eyes only hardened as they met his.

"Love," Arigo whispered to Vadiha, "it's not self-harm. Some things need to change when two worlds collide." Arigo offered her an encouraging smile and a nod as he accepted Dita from his wife. "It's great to meet you, Aless. Welcome to the family."

"Thank you," she said, with a smile and a nod in return. "I still have a lot to learn, so I appreciate any help as I find my footing here."

Dita cooed, blinking wide amber eyes at her, and reaching for her hair with tiny, clutching hands.

Arigo laughed. "I'm sorry. She seems to be in a hair-loving phase."

"I kind of want to touch it, too, though. I've never touched a human's hair," one of the women said as the trio approached, a strip of black face paint across her eyes like a blindfold. She pursed her lips. "Is that weird?"

"Playing with each other's hair? Not weird at all," Aless answered. She wasn't all that different from them, but if they were curious, she wouldn't shut them down.

"I'm Amira," she said, offering her hand. "You humans take each other's hands, right?"

"We do," she said, taking Amira's hand.

"Gentle," Veron warned his sister.

"I know, I know. Their skin is silk thin. I know." Amira's fingers were stiff as she kept her claws away. "Veron, how do you keep from accidentally hurting her? Even without the claws, I mean, the skin, you know—"

Pressing his lips together tightly, he gave Amira a slight shake of the head.

"It's not *that* fragile," Aless cut in. "I mean, I can get thrown on my backside in a ring and not explode."

A bark of laughter burst from one of the other two women.

"This is Zaida and Renazi," Amira said, cocking her head toward them as they inclined their heads to her, the one with the lined cheeks laughing to herself. "We're volodari, and actually headed out on a hunt shortly, but we didn't want to go without meeting our new sister."

The one with the smudges over her eyes took a deliberate step forward, the rest of her body perfectly controlled. "Amira's mouth runs away with her, but we are glad to meet you, Aless. I'm Zaida."

Her voice was a night-quiet, misty whisper, grave, the kind that could silence an entire room. Well, except for her sister Renazi, who still seemed to be laughing to herself.

"A hunt, given the situation?" Veron asked.

Zaida looked toward him, the rest of her countenance unmoving. "Mati has us in territory farther out, by way of the tunnels."

Amira nudged Veron's shoulder. "We'll be safe, Veron. Don't worry!"

"Just because we have aid doesn't mean we should stop our way of life. You know that, Veron." The man with the simmering frown approached, nodding to her, every part of him taut and clenched. "Dhuro," he said, looking her over before meeting Veron's gaze for a moment, his own speaking a thousand words she didn't yet understand. Dhuro seemed ready to pop like a bubble himself.

"Nice to meet you," she said, inclining her head.

His eyes narrowed. "I wish I could say the same."

"*Dhuro.*" Veron stepped up to him, every part of him rigid as he leaned in. "Apologize. Now."

Dhuro leaned in, too. "The kuvari and Yelena *talk*, Veron. Did you know *her* sister has married into the Brotherhood general's family? How do we know this isn't all a human ploy to sack Nozva Rozkveta? She could be biding her time, waiting for a chance to open the Gates—"

"The ring. Now," Veron hissed, and cracked his knuckles.

Dhuro thought she was a traitor waiting to turn on them? And Veron wanted to *fight* him? She touched his shoulder, but he didn't budge.

Footsteps approached from behind, and everyone turned as the queen walked in, wrapped in her flowing white silk robe and peplos. "There will be no challenges tonight," she said firmly. "Veron, take a breath."

Forcing a harsh breath from his nose, Veron leaned away, fiery eyes still spearing Dhuro as he shielded her from his brother's line of sight.

"Dhuro, sit down and keep your mouth shut until I give you permission to speak." The queen looked down on Dhuro, her stance ready—would she attack him? Her son?—until he sighed and plopped onto the bench, slapping his palms onto the table and raising his eyebrows.

Amira, Zaida, and Renazi greeted their mother before saying their goodbyes and heading out on the hunt, and Arigo excused himself to put Dita to bed.

And just like that, she stood with Veron, facing Dhuro and Vadiha, neither of whom seemed fond of her right now. At least Vadiha didn't call her a traitor to her face, so that was a win.

"Get the food, Vadiha," the queen said, jerking her head toward the archway, and Vadiha obeyed, but as she passed Aless, scowled at her.

"Aless, overlook my family's poor manners," the queen said to her, brushing her upper arm with a light touch. "They seem to forget that they have food on the table thanks to you, and that you and Veron have been standing up to the Brotherhood from the moment the peace was signed."

Behind her, a muscle flexed in Dhuro's jaw.

"I understand," Aless replied, fidgeting. "I'm new here. No one knows me yet. Trusting a stranger is a lot to ask."

Veron took her hand and rubbed her fingers gently. "But they all know me. And trusting me isn't a lot to ask of my family."

Dhuro rolled his eyes as Vadiha brought in platters of food. The queen gestured them to the benches, and they all sat. Across from Dhuro, Veron glared at him, eyes wild and intense, narrowed. She held his hand, giving it a squeeze every so often, hoping to break that intensity. To no avail.

Dhuro glanced at her from time to time, over the dishes Vadiha laid out. When she finished and everybody was seated, the queen took a deep breath, sweeping her voluminous unkempt tresses back over her shoulder.

"I'm only going to say this once: Aless is our ally and part of our family." She looked from one face to another at the table, meeting Vadiha's stern face and Dhuro's simmering frown unequivocally. "Dhuro, repeat that to her and apologize."

His face hard, Dhuro looked away, ran a palm over his mass of shoulder-length hair, and turned back to her. "You're our ally and part of our family. I'm sorry for accusing you of betrayal," he gritted out.

The queen looked to her. "Do you accept? If not, it won't be Veron thrashing him in the ring, but me."

What, *really?* The queen would fight her own son—no, *thrash* him?

Well, Queen Zara certainly ruled her family with an iron fist. And... perhaps it was best to remain on her good side.

Aless cleared her throat. "I accept. Thank you, Dhuro. No hard feelings."

He raised an eyebrow but said nothing more as they ate the spread of human food with some stew made from small game the volodari had hunted. The queen asked about the ceremony in Bellanzole and their trip, while Vadiha asked about the attack in Stroppiata and their skirmish outside of Dun Mozg. While Veron cooled, she answered most of their questions, playing with his fingers.

After a brief lull, the queen's kuvari announced Riza, who entered and saluted.

Queen Zara gave her leave to speak, crossing her long, elegant legs as she perched on the bench.

"Your Majesty, Halina returned with the Brotherhood's answer," Riza said, breathing erratically. Had she run all the way here? "It's... They're being difficult."

Queen Zara waited.

"My queen—"

"What was the message?"

Riza bowed her head, her eyebrows drawn together, and for a moment, she shot a pained glance at Veron, and then at her, before looking back to Queen Zara. "It said, 'If you do not comply by dawn, our geomancer will collapse all tunnels leading from your queendom. We will lay siege until you wither and die. If you wish to live to see the dawn, return our princess to us and you may have your two beasts alive.'"

Return our princess? She started, but Veron took her hand in both of his. With a grave face, he shook his head slightly at her.

The queen didn't move, simply stared evenly into space. "It said 'live to see the dawn.' There is nothing there about suspending hostilities beyond that."

"You're not actually considering giving Aless to them?" Veron demanded, a low growl riding his question.

"Of course not," Queen Zara hissed. "But I have to determine whether this is a good-faith starting point to begin negotiations before I issue a counteroffer. It sounds, however, as though even if we were to comply, it wouldn't mean anything but a ceasefire until the dawn."

"What about Valka and Gavri?" Dhuro spat. "We're leaving them to die? I say we do the trade."

Queen Zara twisted so fast that she grabbed Dhuro's throat before he could evade. "You *have* no say." She tapped a claw to his neck. "And you forget yourself, *child*."

Livid eyes held the queen's.

"Your Majesty," Aless squeaked, even as Veron shook his head at her, "with all due respect, he's not wrong. My life isn't worth more than anyone else's. Especially not two. Their general is my sister's brother-in-law. He's wrong, but... they won't kill me. I'm certain of it."

Even the scouts outside Dun Mozg hadn't hurt her—they'd only tried to capture her and bring her to Tarquin.

Queen Zara still gripped Dhuro's throat. "I appreciate your valor, Aless, but like Dhuro, you have no say in this." Queen Zara's gaze slid to hers, and the queen smiled softly before shoving Dhuro away. "Supper is over. I will summon the rest of my Quorum and prepare for the dawn. Veron, Aless, you will stay in your quarters. The next few days will be difficult, but we are well supplied and we will persevere, as we always have." With that, she nodded toward the archway, and everyone but Vadiha rose and headed out.

No say. Every part of her rebelled.

His hand at the small of her back, Veron guided her out, leaving Queen Zara with Vadiha and Riza.

Queen Zara planned to wait out the dawn.

And if she stayed in her quarters as Queen Zara had ordered, the Brotherhood *would* kill Gavri and Valka, without hesitation. Two lives—one of which was her friend—would be lost.

Not without a fight.

CHAPTER 22

*A*less was already pacing the room as soon as Veron shut the door. Her stomach fluttered, but she rubbed it through her robes. This was no time to get nervous.

The Brotherhood would kill Gavri and Valka at dawn. Once they did, the war would begin. Hundreds or thousands would die, and not just here, but across the country, as like-minded people rose up to take sides. If nothing changed, that was inevitable.

But the Brotherhood wanted *her* in exchange. There had to be a move there. Something.

There was no question that the Brotherhood would kill any dark-elf without hesitation. There was no way any of them could mount a rescue mission. But *her*?

You don't need to wear a mask, princess, Tarquin had whispered to her the day of her wedding. *Not with me. The pride is watching. Only say the word, anytime, anywhere, that you protest, and our strength will... relieve your solitude.*

The Brotherhood *wanted* her, but they wouldn't harm her. Tarquin wouldn't harm her. No, that first night, and even at the wedding ceremony, Tarquin had *wanted* her for something, had even tipped his hand to offer her protection. This was a man waging a war of hatred, but also Luciano's brother, Bianca's brother-in-law. And if he killed a princess of Silen, that egregious move would never go unanswered, as it would create a dangerous precedent. Papà would not only annihilate him but his entire family into obscurity.

No, Tarquin Belmonte would not hurt *her*.

And although Papà might not get involved with two dark-elves on the line, if *she* were captured, it would force his hand. He'd have to intervene and help stop the Brotherhood.

There was only one person who had a shot at freeing Gavri and Valka, and it was *her*. The most unskilled, worst candidate to do it, but the only human among them. If she got caught— and odds were high that she would—no one would die. Tarquin had promised to release Gavri and Valka in exchange for her. So she'd either successfully free them both and escape with them, or she'd be caught and demand the exchange. Either way, Gavri and Valka would live.

And unskilled as she was, being a human gave her an advantage. There were no women among the Brotherhood soldiers, but every army had camp followers. Silen's military often had wives and children among them, but the only women who'd accompany the Brotherhood anywhere would be cooks, nurses, sutlers, laundresses, and prostitutes.

She could disguise herself as one and slip in among the camp's outskirts. From there, no one would give a Sileni woman —a human and camp follower—a second glance as a threat.

She could search for Gavri and Valka even at the heart of the camp without garnering much notice.

But if she were caught—

If she were caught, the Brotherhood—no, Tarquin—would never release her back to Veron. If she left tonight, she might never see him again.

If she told him, he'd never agree to her going. Not only because he'd worry, but because his mother had forbidden it, and disobedience was unthinkable to him. He'd be furious, hurt, but if no one did anything and Gavri and Valka were killed, there'd be a war. A war Nozva Rozkveta might not win. One he might have to fight in, maybe even *die* in, along with countless other innocent lives. No. If there was a bloodless solution, she had to try, even if he hated her, even if he never spoke to her again. This was to save his life, to save their people, and she'd vowed in Dun Mozg that she would do whatever it took to protect them, to keep them safe, and to maintain the peace.

Queen Zara had confined her to quarters, and nobody disobeyed her orders. Nobody. But as much as she wanted to fit in here, fitting in had never been more important than making a difference. And she wasn't about to sacrifice countless lives just to stay in her mother-in-law's good graces.

Come what may, she had to try.

Veron's arms closed around her from behind, and he tucked his nose into her hair and took a deep breath. "I'm sorry about Dhuro and Vadiha," he whispered.

She stroked his knuckles. "I wasn't expecting them all to like me right away. Even you took some convincing."

A soft laugh puffed against her ear. "You took more convincing to like me."

After arriving in Nozva Rozkveta, she knew better than that. Far better.

"I'm glad it was you that day in Bellanzole, Aless," he whispered, kissing her cheekbone, "because I've fallen in love with you."

Even now, her skin pebbled at the words, every fine hair standing on end, a shiver stroking her spine as warmth spread in her chest. Smiling, she shook her head, swaying in his hold. "What you don't realize is that I have loved you long before I ever laid eyes on you."

He turned her, his eyes heavy lidded as he raised her chin. "How's that, my love?"

"I have dreamed of these abundant, sprawling, vining roses, wild and beautiful, even their scent," she whispered. "And when I came here, saw the Bloom—it can't be possible, but I dreamed of this place long before you ever brought me here. You were my dream, Veron, and you came true."

He stroked her face, swept gentle fingers into her hair as he tucked it behind her ear. "We are on the land's biggest Vein of anima, a wellspring of the life that courses through everything and everyone. We walk toward the Bloom, and it parts for us. We sing to the stone, and it reshapes. Nothing is impossible, my love, and I believe your dreams, too, because you dreamt them and we are standing here, right now, together."

She trembled, all over, and it wasn't out of disbelief or fear or nervousness; it was everything inside of her willing her to him, to hold him, to kiss him, to stay with him forever and never let go, and she listened to it, listened to it all in this moment, and clung to him, pressed her mouth to his, undressed him with hands that couldn't move fast enough, never fast enough, frantic, desperate.

Holy Mother's mercy, there wasn't enough time to get her fill of his love, of his passion, of him. To live as his partner, to realize the library together, to raise a family. There weren't enough hours, enough lifetimes, and if the cruel hands of fate parted them at dawn, then she wanted to live a hundred hours, a thousand lifetimes, in his arms tonight. "Love me, Veron," she whispered. "Love me tonight, like a dark-elf bride."

"Aless..." he hissed against her lips.

"I want to know what it means," she said softly between kisses, "to be yours in every way." She clutched him close, and his brow furrowed, he nodded against her, claimed her lips hungrily.

He pulled at her robes, seams tearing and fabric ripping until it was all on the floor, and when his fang grazed her tongue, she bit his lip, and he snarled, taking her mouth with renewed zeal as she pushed him toward the bed, her urging stronger and stronger, but his steps were even and slow, playfully resisting against her while his eyes gleamed. The amused smile he'd worn when she'd teased him here earlier had returned, playing on his lips.

When he reached the edge, she hooked his ankle with her foot, just as she'd seen him do in the ring, and he let her, lowered to the bed. She brought her knees down around his hips, raised his mouth to hers, and he twisted, tossing her onto her back, and pinned her to the bed.

She fought, just enough to rile him, to stoke his ardor, and the determined intensity in his gaze was enough to make her gasp, to make her stare, to make her want to immortalize that look in her mind for the rest of her life, and as he took her, she did, memorizing the set of his jaw, the lines of his brow, the blaze of fire smoldering in the warm gold of his eyes, and the rapturous dance of wildness and passion that was being his in every way.

AS TIRED AS ALESS WAS, she didn't let herself sleep, not completely, instead waiting until Veron's breathing evened out, until he slept soundly. After days of traveling, he needed it, and he'd had no reason not to trust her.

She tugged a lone blanket they'd found in one of her trunks over him gently and resisted the urge to kiss him. Even so, he only stirred a moment before resuming those even breaths.

This would hurt him. Deeply. But if she told him, he'd never agree to her going. But there was no living with the thought of Gavri and Valka dying for her sake, of a war beginning, of countless lives being lost, maybe even Veron's... when she could've saved them simply by stepping outside. She had to try.

It was the right thing to do. The only thing. But as she slipped from the bed, all she could think of was of Veron waking to find her gone, to realize she'd abandoned him, just like his father had.

I'm sorry.

It would hurt, but with this, she'd save lives. Maybe even talk Tarquin out of this course of action altogether. Now that she knew the dark-elves, she could meet his hatred with knowledge.

She bent for her robes. They were slightly torn in places, but not too noticeably. And besides, Veron's were huge—not an option. But if she wanted to be inconspicuous in Nozva Rozkveta, she'd get far less attention wandering around in dark-elf robes than in her clothes.

She carefully creaked open one of her trunks and looked for

something suitable to disguise herself in. She had no commoners' clothes, but the best among the prostitutes might wear something approximating some of her plainer things.

With a wince, she hastily grabbed a bustier, white chemise, and as plain a blue overdress as she could find, low cut and laced in the front, but made of fine velvet. She stashed them in one of Veron's knapsacks, similar to ones she'd seen other dark-elves carry.

Her copy of *A Modern History of Silen* sat on Veron's table, and with a wary eye on him, she slowly dug out her quill and inkwell. She had to leave, but she couldn't leave without saying goodbye, without letting him know how much he meant to her in case she didn't make it back.

She opened to the first blank page. What could she say that would ease the sting of this? Was there anything?

She'd just be true.

I love you.

Maybe he'd hate her, maybe he'd curse the day he'd met her, maybe he'd never want to see her again. But she couldn't do this, not even to stop a war, without telling him that one last time.

She left the book open, set her quill on the page, then at the door, turned to gaze at his slumbering face one last time.

Veron, prince of Nozva Rozkveta, I, Alessandra Ermacora, princess of Silen, offer you love—she rested a hand on her heart—*peace, and a life here, quiet, safe from the Brotherhood, and every enemy I can protect you from... to harness for your ends or ours, as we... as we walk our lives together from this day forward for as long as the Deep allows.*

Wiping at her cheeks, she took three deep breaths and slipped out into the hall.

All was quiet, and there was no one about. Everyone had to be sleeping at this hour. She could find her way to the life-spring, and from there, the tunnels were not far. There were clothes at the lifespring, including kuvari leathers, masks, and hoods, which she could use if she managed to sneak them, but from there on, she still needed a way to make it past the kuvari guarding the Gate.

Gavri and Valka were kuvari themselves, so perhaps she could use that to talk her way past.

As she headed out of the palace, no one stopped her. In fact, the few passersby she met greeted her warmly, by the proper form of address. The main part of the city—Central Cavern, as everyone called it—was empty, and she crossed its gleaming blackness toward the lifespring. Through the dark entryway, the lifespring pools glowed a bright teal, and the clothes would be in a small cave off to the side of the pools.

Inside, one of the violet-clad mystics spoke with a woman in one of the pools with her hair braided in a crown about her head.

Yelena.

Backing up, she turned to leave, but Yelena twisted and met her gaze. "*You*. What are you doing here?"

She straightened. "I could ask you the same."

Yelena huffed. "I'm practicing the sword. What does it *look* like I'm doing?"

"Convalescing."

"Those human eyes work after all. And you had the same couple days in the saddle I did." Yelena looked her over with appraising eyes. "Your robes are all tattered. Rough night?"

She cleared her throat. "You could say that."

Yelena smirked and swept an arm wide. "Well, then. Come and *convalesce*, human princess."

She took a step forward, but... there was no time for this. Was there even any sense in trying to disguise herself in a mask and hood? She'd probably be caught anyway. "I..."

"What? Is my company not good enough for you?" Yelena quirked a brow.

"No, no, it's not that—"

"What exactly are you up to? What's in the bag?"

Shifting the knapsack, Aless looked over her shoulder, and the mystic had gone. *I need a mask, a hood, and leathers, and I want to save Gavri and Valka and stop a war,* she wanted to say, and then... blurted it all out.

Yelena's brow furrowed and stayed furrowed a long while. Her head bobbed before she drew in a deep breath. "Well, if you need help getting rid of yourself, you've come to the right person."

CHAPTER 23

*O*utside the Gate and beyond the Bloom, Aless dropped her knapsack, removed her hood, mask, and borrowed leathers, then began changing into her bustier, chemise, and blue velvet overdress.

"What are you doing?" Yelena hissed in the dark. Confident and gruff, Yelena had led her through the earthmover tunnels disguised as one of her kuvari, and since Yelena wasn't a citizen of Nozva Rozkveta, no one had even tried to stop her.

"In there"—smoothing her hands over her velvet skirts, Aless tipped her head toward the Gate—"I need a mask and a hood to blend in. Out here, I might be killed on sight. Better they see that I'm human."

Yelena eyed her from beneath a frown, then took a deep breath. "Are you sure about this?"

"I thought you were pretty keen on getting rid of me?"

Yelena shrugged a shoulder and looked away. "Do as you will. I'll keep Veron's bed warm when you die."

Veron.

Holy Mother's mercy, just thinking of him right now, about leaving him like that, made her hands tremble, but she fisted them. This was to save him, to save everyone from war and death, and even if she failed and got caught, at least it would force Papà to intervene and stop this.

To do what she needed to do, she'd have to shove down that trembling feeling, the memory of Veron's passionate face, the sight of him sleeping soundly as she'd left. *Shove it down.*

She shook out her hair into an unbound curly mess, cleared her throat, and nodded to Yelena. "I'm sure he'd rather a harpy kept his bed warm than you, but thanks."

Yelena crossed her arms and shot her a sheepish grimace. "I'll wait here until dawn. If you're not back by then, I'm going back in there to tell everyone you're probably dead."

Yelena's words were harsh, but her help had been invaluable.

"Thank you, Yelena. Really."

Yelena gave her a final nod.

This is it. She turned south and headed toward the Brotherhood encampment.

The forest was dark and quiet, with the rare animal call interrupting the silence. The only light came from the faint glow of the Bloom vines and flowers, and the little star-like twinkles of the pixies fluttering in the night air.

After walking for a while, the quiet and the dark hadn't abated—she should've found the Brotherhood encampment already, shouldn't she? The Gate she'd exited from wasn't the same one as the Gate she and Veron had arrived by.

A pixie flew alongside her, and she sighed. "I don't suppose you can help me find Gavri and Valka? Two dark-elves in a human camp?"

The pixie flitted about, darting erratically, then took off toward the side.

Is a pixie actually helping me? It was ridiculous, really, but if she was lost, then following a pixie wasn't any more ridiculous than milling about in the wrong direction.

Her skirts clenched in her hands, she followed the pixie's dimming glow, and soon, sparse firelight flickered between the trees and the undergrowth, and a sea of tents.

She suppressed a gasp, hiding behind an oak.

You really did help me? She eyed the pixie, who hovered next to her behind another trunk.

Thank you, she mouthed, keeping a wary eye on the camp.

It was quiet, with very few Brotherhood soldiers—or anyone—about, but considering the hundreds of tents, that could easily change with one alarm. Most on the outskirts were little tents, with the bigger ones toward the center of camp.

A few sentries walked a circuit, which would have been no problem if she'd been Yelena or Veron. But right now, even *one* was one too many. There was no possibility of walking in unnoticed here by blending in. They'd be waiting for someone to try a rescue from the trees here.

But toward the back of the camp, there was movement to and from a well-lit area, and she stalked through the undergrowth, keeping behind trees as best she could, to get a closer look.

Makeshift bars dotted the back end of the camp, along with some tents where soldiers entered and exited, smiling and laughing.

The camp followers.

If there was any chance of getting to the center of the camp, this was it. It would have to be from there.

As a chorus of crickets chirped, she crept as near as she dared in the forest's concealment, fluffing her hair and pinching her cheeks, rumpling her gown, even dirtying its hem a little.

The pixie flitted closer, landing on her shoulder.

"Your light's going to give us away," she whispered, and the pixie's light dimmed down to almost nothing, a barely audible little chime coming from it. Speech?

With the light, the pixie looked like a tiny winged person the size of a butterfly, a pink-haired woman wrapped in a leaf. An utterly *adorable* little pink-haired woman.

Her chest fluttered, and if this were any time and place other than sneaking outside a Brotherhood camp, she might have squealed with delight.

The pixie darted into her unbound hair, clinging on with the slightest tug. Unexpected, but somehow, this wouldn't be as terrifying when there was someone with her.

She watched the movements of the camp, with two tents close to the edge completely dark, with no movements in or out. A lone man strolled down a lane and then ducked into a nearby, lantern-lit tent.

Be brave.

With a deep breath, she strode out of the forest confidently, with only the clothes on her back and a pixie in her hair. No one was about, and she only needed a minute or so to cross the clearing between the trees and the camp.

Just a little more.

If she ran, that would draw attention. At least walking, she might seem like a prostitute returning from relieving herself.

Her heart pounded as she neared the first tent, and voices laughed from nearby.

Just a little more. A little more.

She peeked into the first tent—a woman was sleeping—and a belt buckle fastened and coins clinked nearly just as she peeked into the second.

Empty.

She darted inside and drew the tent flap closed as booted footsteps emerged from the one next to her.

Holy Mother's mercy.

She gulped in breaths, trying to slow her racing heart, and looked around the dark tent. The stench of the bedroll was enough to make her gag. Wine, queen's lace, the bitter herbs...

A moment to gather her composure. She'd go to the center of camp, and if anyone stopped her, she'd say General Belmonte had requested her services. At best, she'd be left to go where she pleased, and at worst, she'd be taken to him—and of everyone here, Tarquin was still her best chance at not getting hurt, at the very least for fear of Papà's wrath.

She grabbed a bottle of red wine—holding something would at least make her feel better and give her trembling hands something to do—and then counted to three before emerging.

No one was outside, but as she headed toward the center, a few soldiers walked past, paying her no mind aside from the rare whistle and kissing sounds.

Thank the Mother.

An otherworldly scream came from the outer ring of the center, unlike anything she'd ever heard. That couldn't be Tarquin or any of the Brotherhood. Were any other Immortali being kept prisoner?

It's our best chance.

She headed toward it, and the line of tents here was utterly quiet, and the stench—

Swallowing past the lump in her throat, she peeked past tent flaps, finding posts, ropes, chains, and bloodied rags.

Holy Mother's mercy, had they *killed*—

No. She shook her head. They wouldn't have killed their only leverage against Queen Zara; the Brotherhood was hateful and violent, but Tarquin was not stupid, and underestimating his intelligence instead of accounting for it would only lead to failure.

A grunt came from the large tent ahead.

Everything inside of her wanted to freeze to the spot, but if the person emerged, that would only look suspicious.

A man in a white tabard with a clasped red hands insignia left the tent, smirking, his flinty eyes settling on her as his smirk abdicated in favor of a frown. "What are you doing here, whore?"

The harsh tone was accusatory, but as he approached, he looked her over, and the furrows lining his face faded.

Her heart pounding, she plastered a seductive smile on her face, relaxing her posture as she put a hand on her hip and gave the bottle of wine a shake. "It must get very lonely out here. I thought maybe you could use some company."

The smirk returned as his palm landed on her waist and traveled upward. "I wouldn't think a face like yours would need to work so hard."

Holy Mother help me. "Just trying to do my part."

He reached for her chin—

The pixie dashed out of her hair and past him—

He whirled, and she swung the bottle of wine toward his

head. It connected, shattering glass and spilling wine as he tumbled to the grass.

Her heart in her throat, she grabbed him by the tabard and struggled to drag him into the tent he'd emerged from while he groaned.

It had been too quiet, the contact too loud, and someone would've—someone had to be coming—

"Aless," Gavri hissed, tied to a post across from another dark-elf woman—Valka? They were dirty, their leathers tattered, faces bruised and bloody. "What're you—?"

She ran to Gavri, scrabbling for the ropes binding her wrists, and frantically cut at them with the broken bottle. They weren't—it wasn't—not sharp enough, not fast en—

That otherworldly scream pierced the air again.

"Behind you," Gavri snarled.

She spun as the man grabbed for her, and both Gavri and Valka yanked at their bonds. The pixie darting at his face, he pulled her ankle and tumbled her to the ground, dragging her beneath him.

"You—" he snarled, but a foot crashed into his face, sending him flying off her.

Gavri snatched the broken bottle from her hands and buried it in the man's neck, spitting at him. She took his short sword and cut Valka free, who stomped on his head.

The otherworldly screaming resumed.

"What is that?" Aless breathed, laboring to her feet as Gavri stripped bits of the man's gear and his weapons.

"They have a unicorn here," Gavri said, tossing her a sheathed hunting knife.

She tried to catch it, but it fell to the ground. A unicorn? Was it the one from outside Stroppiata? They had it here? She picked up the knife and tucked it into her boot, and the pixie fluttered past her face and landed on her shoulder.

"Thank you, Tiny," she whispered.

"Come on," Gavri said, nodding toward the tent flap. "That commotion won't have gone unheard."

Valka nodded, holding up the broken and bloodied wine bottle, and swept aside the flap. "No one's here yet," she said. "We make for the trees."

Gavri followed.

"What about the unicorn?" Aless whispered as it continued its screaming. What would the Brotherhood do to it? Torture it? Sell it? Kill it?

"No time," Gavri said.

No time? Something tightened in her chest, her breaths coming in short, quivering gasps.

"I'll follow you soon," she told Gavri, and then headed toward the screaming.

"Aless," Gavri hissed after her.

"Go," she whispered in reply. "I'm human. I'll be fine."

Eyes wild, Gavri stood frozen, but Valka grabbed her wrist and dragged her away as Aless cut through the lines of tents.

They *had* to leave. As dark-elves, they'd be identified and attacked in a second. But she'd gotten across the camp without incident. Human, well disguised, she stood a chance.

There was a chaos of shouting and boots thumping behind her, but she ignored it. Brotherhood soldiers yelling about Gavri and Valka's escape, and bellowing orders to chase into the forest.

The unicorn's screams quieted and quieted, faded to exhausted squeals and shrieks, and the clop of hooves was near.

A large, open tent contained a mass of sage-tinted chains, all binding the unicorn so brutally it could scarcely move. Red welts, old and extensive, marred its once-immaculate coat beneath the chains, staining it bloody, and the whites of its eyes showed as it regarded her warily. It was smaller than the one she'd seen on the way to Stroppiata, with a shorter horn, and even in the dimness, dazzling green eyes.

Holy Mother's mercy, how could anyone *do* this to an innocent being? Bind it, torture it, and for what? Why even keep the Immortals? As trophies, as prizes? To study them? Just for malice's sake?

Checking the surrounding area, she found it empty, and darted to the unicorn shuddering in chains. Where to even begin?

"I'm going to help you," she whispered, and Tiny flew out of her hair again to a post behind the unicorn, where it disturbed a key ring on a hook.

Voices came from behind the tent.

She ducked inside, squeezing between the unicorn and the tent's canvas, but the voices continued—two soldiers discussing the hunt for Gavri and Valka, wondering whether they'd hidden among the tents.

No! They couldn't find her—they *couldn't*. Not when she was so close to actually succeeding in her plan. Tiny fluttered back to her, taking refuge in her curls.

She sidled in the narrow space toward the post. If they did find her, then at the very least she could free this unicorn. It quieted, too, standing utterly still as she slowly reached for the keys.

Once she had them in hand, she followed the chains until

she found the lock at her side, and opened it with a barely audible click.

The voices stopped for a moment. Had they gone?

The unicorn pulled against the chains, clinking them, and the noise only worsened as it yanked into the lane between the tents, dragging the chains out with it.

An ache formed in the back of her throat, and the trembling in her limbs spread to cold fingers twisting and wringing the velvet skirt, wet with wine.

Yelling and booted steps converged, and she huddled against the tent, hiding behind the canvas next to the entryway, shaking, reaching for the knife in her boot. But if the Brotherhood knew she was there, that knife wouldn't save her. Running wouldn't save her. Screaming wouldn't save her.

But she could save Gavri and Valka. Divert the Brotherhood's attention—

"Get them," came an order.

"Sir!"

With a swallow, she straightened, forced her arms to her sides, and raised her chin, taking deep breaths. There was only one thing that could save Gavri and Valka now. Raising her voice.

"My name is Princess Alessandra Ermacora of Silen," she called out, firming her voice with every ounce of royal arrogance she could muster. "And I demand to speak to General Tarquin Belmonte at once."

Everything outside the tent went silent.

Holy Mother's mercy, would they charge in here, tie her up, drag her to him? Nothing and no one moved, only the sound of several men breathing indicating their presence outside.

You are a princess of Silen. Be brave.

Pulling her shoulders back, she stepped out from behind the tent canvas, into the entryway.

No less than two dozen men ringed the tent, weapons drawn, all of them abandoning further searching, by the looks of it.

At the center, Tarquin Belmonte's amused eyes settled on her, his thumb tucked into the belt binding his long white officer's coat. He grinned. "The pride welcomes you home, Your Highness."

CHAPTER 24

A softness tickled against Veron's bare skin, and his eyes still closed, he reached down. They hadn't been able to find pillows, and Aless had fallen asleep with her head on his stomach, but—

The weight of her head wasn't there. Perhaps it was her hair tickling him.

But when he grasped a handful, it was fabric. A blanket.

He opened his eyes, reached next to him.

The bed was empty.

Aless was gone.

"Aless?" He sat up, looking around the bedchamber, blinking. His clothes were still on the floor, his boots in the corner, but hers—

Hers were gone.

He sprang from the bed, raked his hair back. She'd only gone to relieve herself, or perhaps for another bite to eat.

Supper had ended abruptly, after all. He sank back down, his head in his hands.

It was just all of these problems with the Brotherhood. When Nozva Rozkveta had last gone to war, Ata had left. And now that war circled them anew, it dredged up old insecurities. That was all.

But as the minutes ticked by, Aless didn't return.

He swept the room with frantic eyes, and there, on the table, lay one of her books, open. He darted to it, set aside her quill, and read...

I love you.

She... Was this a—

No, she wouldn't—

But as he brushed his fingertips across the ink, across one line written in her *mother's* book, there was no other reason Aless would have done this.

Except to say goodbye.

She'd—she'd left. Without a word, she'd *left* him.

To do what? The trade? Surrender herself to the Brotherhood, who would do who-knew-what to her? The Brotherhood despised the Immortals, and the dark-elves among them, so what would they do to a human married to one?

They won't kill me, she'd said. *I'm certain of it.*

She'd staked her life on it, on Tarquin, a man who'd unleashed harpies on her, ordered a witch to collapse tunnels in a queendom she'd been in. A man who might rather make an example of her than protect her.

He grabbed his clothes off the floor and hastily threw them

on, dragged on his leathers and his boots, strapped his vjernost blades onto his belt.

She'd *gone* to that man, turned herself over, *trusted* Tarquin Belmonte.

Tonight, she'd been all smiles, affectionate, seductive. They'd spent the past couple of hours loving each other, together, *one*, no more fears or restraints between them. He'd fallen asleep wrapped up with her, tangled with the woman he loved, and despite the war at the gates, despite everything, he'd never felt so whole. He would have trusted her with anything, with his life, with his family, with his homeland.

And she hadn't even trusted him with her plan. Had shoved aside the trust they'd built together, their bond, and had left without a word. She wanted to trade herself to the Brother-hood, which might not even release Gavri or Valka, if they were even still alive. And then Tarquin Belmonte would shackle her, take her away, use her to achieve his hateful ends.

Holy Ulsinael, *he'd* been the one to tell her she didn't truly *see* people, see the consequences of her actions. Ever since he'd mentioned it in Stroppiata, she'd made genuine efforts to look beyond herself and what she cared to see, and to look at how she affected those around her and the larger consequences. She'd worked time and again to change that, sometimes to the point of recklessness, like in the ring in Dun Mozg.

Had she thought of the impending war tonight and decided she couldn't bear the consequences of inaction?

Mati had told her she'd had no say, to remain in their quar-ters, but... when someone told Aless there was no way out, she made her own.

And she'd expected him to agree with Mati and obey

instead of helping her with her plan... And if that's what she'd thought, she hadn't been wrong.

Disobedient, reckless, rebellious, selfless, brave, heartrending Aless.

Please be safe. Please.

On his way out, he grabbed his bow and quiver, then burst into the hallway.

Mati would—

No, Mati would order him to stay here. As much as she liked Aless, she wouldn't allow him to interfere with negotiations or risk being captured for leverage.

But once the Brotherhood had Aless, there might not be any more negotiations. Tarquin could launch the assault, or—or take Aless and leave. Or Aless could be killed, sacrificed to spark the war irretrievably.

Mati had ordered him to stay in his quarters, but orders or no orders, the Brotherhood would not be taking Aless anywhere. Not while he drew breath. He'd let Ata leave once and he hadn't followed—as a child, wouldn't have been able to follow—but he would *not* let Aless go. Mati could rearrange his face later and he'd accept it, as long as he could bring back Aless.

He strode down the hall, headed for Heraza Gate. Already some of the palace's residents were emerging from their quarters, and there wouldn't be much time before all of Nozva Rozkveta awoke to the whitening glow of the Bloom.

Passersby greeted him as he traversed Central Cavern, and he offered pleasant replies—perhaps he'd seem less suspicious, even jogging down the walkways.

Near the entrance to Heraza's tunnel, a group of people huddled tightly, Yelena and—and—

"Gavri," he called out, and she raised her head, her face marred with bruises, blood, and a black eye.

"Veron!" She ran to him, with Yelena and Valka following. "Aless is still out there—"

He grabbed her shoulders. "Is she safe?"

She blinked, shaking her head. "I-I don't know. Last we saw, the Brotherhood was coming after us, and she went in the opposite direction—"

He released her and passed—

"Veron," she said from behind him, "when Valka and I were scouting, when we got caught... two other armies were en route. Human armies."

Looking over his shoulder, he stopped. Two human armies? "Whose? Brotherhood reinforcements?"

"We were apprehended before we could investigate further, Your Highness," Valka answered.

Had Aless's father arrived after all? But what about the second army?

A loud series of thuds echoed through Central Cavern from the earthmover tunnels—a hammer knock. Dun Mozg's.

Yelena grinned. "My mother has arrived."

"Your mother?"

That grin widened. "If it is a fight the humans want, then Dun Mozg stands with Nozva Rozkveta, to the Darkness and beyond."

Then Nendra had come with troops and weapons. And the entire queendom would soon be awake and bustling with battle preparations—all while the Brotherhood held Aless. Even *if* her assessment of Tarquin was correct, would his army refrain from harming her if their backs were pressed to the wall?

Armies had arrived, with some hungry for war. If nothing changed, there would be unthinkable loss of life.

"We have to stop this," he bit out. "Someone has to find out the identity of these two armies. Open negotiations with them." Someone like *him*. If it was indeed King Macario, then perhaps he could sway the Brotherhood to release Aless and to surrender, before any of this came to battle and deaths.

He strode through the tunnel to Heraza Gate.

"Veron," Yelena shouted, "you have orders. You can't just—"

But he did anyway.

CHAPTER 25

*I*n the lavish officer's tent, Aless sat still in the chair, following Tarquin's every movement as he poured tea service for two next to the massive map of the area sprawling over the table. A marker sat below Nozva Rozkveta— the Brotherhood, surely—and two others, one far to the south and one to the west. What did they represent?

A tall, lanky young man with long, straight black hair stood at attention at the tent entrance in a white officer's coat, watching her with a hard, hazel gaze.

"Don't mind Siriano, Your Highness. Neither he, nor anyone here, will hurt you." Tarquin put a spoonful of honey in one of the cups and stirred it without a sound. "He's a mage captain from the Belmonte Company and loyal to a fault."

Loyal to whom? To Tarquin? To the Brotherhood? Certainly not to the Crown, if he was allowing anyone to keep a princess of Silen captive.

Also, Tarquin had said *mage captain*. Was this the geomancer who'd attacked Dun Mozg?

Tarquin slid the cup toward her before bringing his own up to his nose and inhaling deeply.

"The best Kamerish black tea comes from just outside of Ren," he drawled. "Wouldn't you agree?"

The only quality of this tea that interested her right now was how badly it would scald Tarquin Belmonte if she threw it in his face.

Beneath Siriano's watchful eyes, her fingers curled around the cup, but—scalding the only person keeping her alive was ill advised, even for the Beast Princess. "You didn't bring me here to talk about tea."

Tarquin laughed under his breath. "I didn't bring you here."

Mincing words?

"*Fine.*" She grimaced. "You aren't *keeping* me here to talk about tea."

He took a sip and then sighed lengthily through his nose. "Your Highness, I am the *only* person in this kingdom who has cared enough to save you from this forced arrangement. His Majesty manipulated you into this against your will, and that is a wrong that must be righted."

Pretty words. But if he thought she'd believe he'd mobilized an army and come all the way here just out of *care* for her, then he was about to wake from his little daydream. "And how would you right it?"

"First, by exchanging those two beasts for you. Then, by pretending to threaten your life if His Majesty doesn't annul your marriage—"

Only an unconsummated marriage could be annulled in Silen, but she'd keep that tidbit to herself.

"—and once he does, encouraging you to wed the man of your choice."

Veron. Veron. Forever and always Veron.

"And I assume by that you mean yourself?"

His mouth curled in a seductive smile. "The notion didn't seem to displease you the evening of the masquerade."

"I assure you, I was contemplating a far cruder notion."

"And found me to be a pleasing option."

Until he'd opened his mouth. A single word of hatred spoken could turn even a handsome face ugly. And Tarquin had spoken many.

Despite the idiocy of his assertion, she didn't dare laugh at him. Not while he held her captive here, thinking he'd win his path to princedom if only he just persevered. Shredding his daydream to tatters could mean he'd be holding a captive he didn't need anymore.

And imagining the outcomes flowing from that was an exercise in terror.

"Well, here I am," she said, holding his dark-brown gaze steadily. "If this is between you and me, you don't need an army. Or maybe we should be marching on Bellanzole." If she could get him moving the Brotherhood away from Nozva Rozkveta toward the capital, Papà would be forced to intervene.

"The people adore you. I have both the Belmonte Company and the Brotherhood at my command. Together, we could turn this nation on the right path, eliminate the Immortali that prey on us." Across the table from her, he lazily crossed one leg over the other. "You are a large portion of this puzzle, Your Highness, but other pieces remain."

"What other pieces?"

"Restoring the kingdom to its former glory. Before the Immortali invaded and ruined it."

"The Immortali are not some monolithic entity. They vary from person to person just like we do." Stating a belief to the contrary was just smoke. "You're a smart man, Tarquin, so I know you understand this."

His brow furrowed. "And in their shadow, danger follows. Life has never been more violent, more dangerous, than now."

"We're working to change that. The dark-elves can help us keep the dangerous among the Immortali at bay. Those who attack us first, who do nothing but murder and harm. Those are only a small fraction, but by working together, we can stand against them."

That furrow deepened. "We don't need to work together. We have mages." He nodded toward Siriano, whose hard expression didn't waver.

"But the dark-elves are just like us, Tarquin. They have marriages and families and babies. They want peace. They want love. They just want to survive."

"Spoken like a tender-hearted woman." He scoffed. "Do they need to be stockpiling weapons to survive? Our intelligence tells us that is exactly what the queendom of Dunmarrow is doing."

"Can you blame them? Humans have been attacking their people since they awoke. Wouldn't you prepare to defend yourself? Yet they want peace. They haven't taken a single human life."

He knocked the table with his knuckles. "Oh, but they did. Three of my scouts went missing near Dunmarrow."

"They attacked me," she blurted. That wasn't the dark-elves' fault. "I had to defend myself and killed one of them, and the other two were killed to protect me."

He shook his head vehemently. "Those men were sent to *find* you, and rescue you if the opportunity arose."

"They tried to drag me away kicking and screaming!" Her hands trembled, so she folded them in her lap. "Would you call that a rescue?"

He tilted his head, scrutinizing her. "You didn't want to be saved?"

This conversation was taking a wrong turn. "My father wanted to build a peace. That peace falls apart without me."

He stood from the chair, pacing the tent. "He built that peace on *your* sacrifice. You were a victim, just like Arabella. It wasn't right to begin with."

He wanted to talk about *right*?

"Tarquin, I saw what's been done to that unicorn. That wasn't right either."

"Unicorn? You mean that Immortali horse-beast?"

"It's not a beast. They are peaceful beings—"

He turned on her, his face contorted. "My sister, Arabella, was fond of your so-called 'peaceful being.' She was an inno-cent—she loved singing and picking wildflowers and admiring beauty of all kinds. She saw one of those Immortali horses and couldn't stop looking at it, searching it out. One day, she disap-peared, and not three days later, that beast trespassed onto our lands and started attacking our doors, breaking windows, terri-fying everyone, destroying everything."

"So you *tortured* it?"

He leaned in. "It kept coming back, wreaking havoc, so my men caught it. Due to its size and strength, they've been trying to tame it, but it's been a waste of time. They're of half a mind to just kill it."

"So you'll just let them kill anything that won't obey?" That was what all the unicorn's injuries were from? "Tarquin, that is an intelligent being. It has thoughts and feelings and may be vastly older and wiser than you and me. You can't just lock it up and abuse it like that."

"It is the reason Arabella is gone. If not for that... thing, she would have been safe at home."

"It's not a *thing*! It's a—"

A shapeshifter.

She paused.

Tarquin's frown faded slightly. "It's a what?"

Veron had told her all about them. She sat up. "Tarquin, unicorns have a territory they stay in. They abhor all violence. They're pacifistic by nature."

"Not this one."

She nodded. That was the problem. Something didn't fit. "You said it showed up three days *after* Arabella disappeared?"

A line formed between his eyebrows as he lifted a shoulder. "What of it?"

Holy Mother's mercy, if she was wrong about this—

"You said Arabella loved unicorns, that she'd go off in search of them, just to look at them." When he nodded, she continued, "Unicorns are shapeshifters, like werewolves. They can turn people, Tarquin. And you said this unicorn showed up a couple days after Arabella disappeared? And unlike their peaceful reputation, it was destroying things? If she wanted to become a unicorn—"

"You're saying that *thing* is Arabella?" he shouted at her, his eyes wide and blazing.

She flinched. Perhaps not her greatest move ever.

"If that's true—and it's too ridiculous to be—then why hasn't she changed back? If she's a shapeshifter?"

She swallowed. "You kept her bound in arcanir chains. It can interfere with the Immortali."

He scrubbed a hand over his face. "If this is true... If that thing was Arabella..."

"Then you've been torturing the very person you set out to defend."

He froze, standing still in the dim lamplight of the tent. So many evil deeds he'd done in the name of his sister, and there was a chance she was not only alive but had been in his custody all this time, harmed by his very own men, desperate to show her brother in any way she could who she was... to no avail.

"General," someone called from outside the tent, and at Tarquin's permission, Siriano pulled the tent flap aside and let in a young officer, who eyed her, gawking at her clothes—her *disguise*.

With a glower, Tarquin motioned the officer to continue.

"Sir, scouts say King Macario's forces have made camp south of us, on the hills abutting the river to the east. The duchessa's army has taken up position to the west and is building makeshift fortifications."

Her heart pounded.

Papà had come for her.

And the duchessa had joined him.

Tarquin moved the two map markers accordingly, his face a veneer of calm. "Send a message to King Macario. Tell him he shall annul the princess's marriage to the beast—"

How *dare* he call Veron a beast?

"—and that he shall contact the duchessa and order her

forces to withdraw along with his own, before dusk tomorrow. If he does not comply, Her Highness will be executed the dawn after."

No, he couldn't—with her life on the line, Papà would comply. But if Papà and the duchessa did withdraw, then there would be no one to stop the Brotherhood from starving out Nozva Rozkveta—causing tens of thousands to suffer.

No, he couldn't even be allowed to extend this offer to Papà.

She'd come this far. Papà's forces couldn't be allowed to abandon Nozva Rozkveta. And Tarquin wouldn't hurt her, not unless he wanted his entire family reduced to a pool of blood.

Tarquin's purpose would have to be frustrated to stop this now.

She swallowed. "My father can't annul the marriage, Tarquin."

His head snapped to face her, and his eyebrows drew together.

"It's been consummated."

CHAPTER 26

"*I* am Prince Veron of Nightbloom!" Veron shouted, holding his arms out to his sides as he cleared the forest. He slowly headed toward the sea of purple-and-white-striped tents through the tall grass, finding his footing in stiff boots. "Don't shoot! I seek an audience with King Macario of Silen!"

Had someone told him a couple of months ago that he'd disobey orders, betray Mati's trust, leave Nozva Rozkveta on the eve of battle, and would now be turning himself over to the mercy of humans, he never would have believed it.

This wasn't about trust. This was about protecting the ones he loved.

He'd disobeyed Mati, betrayed her, but people were more than their mistakes, and not every hurtful action was *about* inflicting hurt. Sometimes hurt, as grave as it could be, had to be a secondary concern to trying to save many lives. Or even just one.

The sun was just beginning to rise in the sky of pinks, golds, and blues as archers shuffled along the top of a hill, yelling to one another and to him.

"Stop right there!" one bellowed, and he did as bidden.

Their bows drawn, the archers descended the hill and surrounded him, demanding he surrender his weapons before they escorted him up and to the center of camp.

Officers in dark-purple coats surveyed him, and the king's page, Alvaro, confirmed his identity before he was admitted to the yurta at the heart of the royal encampment.

As soon as he entered, long arms pulled him into an embrace—Lorenzo's. Wearing a dark-purple gambeson, Aless's brother met him with those dark eyes so like hers, and a broad grin, his shoulder-length dark hair tied back. A dozen knives were sheathed in a bandolier about his chest.

"It's good to see you." Lorenzo clapped him on the shoulder.

"I wish it were under better circumstances."

"We are about to crush the Brotherhood," King Macario said from behind Lorenzo, eyeing a map as he stroked his close-cropped salt-and-pepper beard. "The circumstances are favorable." He stepped away from the map and gestured to a nearby chair. "How is my daughter? You both did well in Stroppiata and Dunmarrow, as expected. You must have made quite the impression on Duchessa Claudia, as she is here with her forces as well."

So *that* was the second army. "Your Majesty, Aless is in the Brotherhood camp."

Both King Macario and Lorenzo paused, exchanging looks, and Lorenzo closed his eyes and heaved a sigh, rubbing his face as he turned away.

"You were supposed to keep her safe." The king stepped up

to him, but soon deflated. "Only... I know my Aless. Always making a scene of some sort. Relentless, reckless, wild, *foolish*—"

"Your Majesty," Veron interrupted, a growl lacing his voice. "We didn't know whether you were coming, or whether anyone was. Aless traded herself to save two lives, which if they had been taken, would have set us on a course of no return. She didn't have complete information, but she's trying to save countless more." He held the king's gaze.

Perhaps the king's words might have once been true, but *his* Aless was brave, stood up for what she believed was right, and always with forethought. If she was wild, she was like the Bloom in her protectiveness, her boldness, her power.

Alvaro came in with a message that he handed to King Macario, whose face darkened as he read. He crumpled the message and waved off Alvaro, carefully lowering into a chair.

"Is it Aless?" Veron asked, taking a step forward, but the king didn't react.

Lorenzo pried the message from his hand and read. "To His Majesty, King Macario: You shall annul the princess's marriage to the beast, and shall contact the duchessa and order her forces to withdraw along with your own, before dusk tomorrow. If you do not comply, Her Highness will be executed the following dawn. General Tarquin Belmonte."

"Executed?" he demanded, and Lorenzo handed him the message. He read and reread the words, but they were the same.

"That's it," the king murmured. "The end of our strategy. He has Aless and isn't afraid to kill her."

Lorenzo slapped his hands on the table. "You saw the way Tarquin looked at her, Papà. He's bluffing."

"I will *not* risk her life," the king shot back, rising. "We have to get her back safely, whatever the cost."

On that, they agreed.

The king would accept Tarquin's terms, quit the area along with the duchess, and Aless would be all right...

And the Brotherhood would continue its siege of Nozva Rozkveta. If Tarquin did order his witch to collapse the tunnels, it was only a matter of time before Mati and Nendra would lead their forces to the sky realm and attack, annihilating the Brotherhood—

And putting Aless in danger once again.

At a threat to his daughter's life, King Macario was ready to surrender completely. Not something any dark-elf queen would ever do for a son—not even Mati.

If it were him—

If it were—

He shook his head, trying to clear it. If it were him in Tarquin's custody, Aless would be freed, sent back with King Macario, who'd then have no incentive to retreat. Both the royal army and the duchess's could stay and help Nozva Rozkveta.

And Mati would never sacrifice her people for his sake.

Aless would be safe... Nozva Rozkveta would have its allies...

And Tarquin would have *him*.

"Tell him to take me instead."

ALESS STARED at the paper as Tarquin finished his last bit of writing, but the letters were too small, too blurry, for her to make out the words. Under Siriano's watchful eyes in the corner of the tent, Tarquin folded the paper, sealed it, and handed it to one of his men.

There had to be some way to talk him out of this. There *had* to be.

He leaned back in his chair, his hands folded together as he regarded her evenly, some epiphany playing out behind that deep-brown gaze.

"You really did fall in love with that beast," he said expressionlessly.

"He's not a beast!" she shot back, and Tiny chattered in her hair, but she ignored it. "Veron's loving, kind, gentle—"

"Sorcery," Tarquin bit out. "He's bewitched you somehow. Those beasts have fangs, claws—"

"Dark-elves don't have magic! All they have is sangremancy, which anyone with blood, knowledge, and skill can use. You'd know that if you tried learning about them instead of just hating them from a position of ignorance."

He scoffed. "If they had a way to control your mind, do you think they'd tell you?"

"You're impossible. If they could control minds, you wouldn't be able to be here, hating them and waging war." She crossed her arms, which renewed the scent of cheap wine soaked into her disguise. "You're an educated man, Tarquin, and a general. Surely you understand the value of facts. You're acting from an emotional place, and worse, it's unfounded. Your sister wasn't killed by the Immortali. She elected to become one."

"You don't know that!" he snapped, pounding the table with a palm. "And you have no proof, just some tales you heard from beasts."

"Well, *you* don't have any proof she died, or that the Immortali killed her, yet you believe it!" she shot back. "If there's even a *chance* Arabella is alive, even as a unicorn, don't you at least want to find out if it's true?"

"You made sure I couldn't verify your tale when you released the Immortali horse." His voice dropped to a low, bitter rasp.

"I released the unicorn," she said, meeting his low voice with her own, "but I didn't make it run away. Your men did that with their abuse. You did that." When he only bowed his head, she added, "If that really is Arabella, then out of fear for her life, she had to flee her brother."

A long quiet settled in. "That's. Not. Her." He looked up, eyes fiery. "You knew you'd get caught, so you released that Immortali horse and made up a story. One you hoped would distract me from my purpose."

She shook her head. "Tarquin, *you* told me, right here, about Arabella's love of unicorns. *You* told me she disappeared in search of one. *You* told me that unicorn showed up a couple days later. *You* told me it was destroying things, attacking. That is what I based my conclusion on—what *you* told me—and I knew none of that before you sat me down in this tent." She leaned forward and added gently, "Set aside your battle plans and your hatred and everything else you've believed, and just think about these facts for a second, rationally. You know I couldn't have made it up before releasing that unicorn. You know it."

He took a deep breath and then sighed, meeting her eyes with a soft look. "Your Highness, if any of that is true, then all I've done is make one terrible mistake after another, mistakes I can never take back. If any of that is true, how can I live with myself?"

"By not making any more terrible mistakes," she replied. "You have the chance to find Arabella and tell her that you love her and that you're sorry. You have the chance to stop all of this before it gets any worse, Tarquin."

He lowered his gaze a moment, then glanced at Siriano before turning back to her. "I don't, Your Highness. Even if Arabella is still alive, even as one of the Immortali, the only people here who would stop this are Siriano and me. But there is an army outside who won't back down until a river of blood flows. And the two of us can't stop them." Before she could reply, he cut in, "So you see, Your Highness, what you're saying can't be true, and I have to believe that it isn't."

Heaving a breath, he rose and headed for the tent flap.

"Not just you and Siriano, Tarquin," she said, twisting around toward him. "I would stop this, too, with both of you. With everything in me."

He looked over his shoulder. "It doesn't matter anymore. The Brotherhood wants blood. King Macario offered to trade Veron of Nightbloom for you, and I just accepted."

CHAPTER 27

*T*he glowing red sun was faltering through the cloudy titian sky, and as Aless stood at the front of a company of Brotherhood soldiers, that dusky sky looked to her like a fire amid clouds of ash, billowing and graying as far as the eye could see.

The forested horizon was darkening. When she'd told Veron that Tarquin wouldn't hurt her, he might have believed that, trusted it, but Papà? Papà had never listened to her before, and he wouldn't have started now. If he'd believed Tarquin would kill her, if he'd agreed to retreat in exchange for her, that would have left Nozva Rozkveta exposed to the Brotherhood. Vulnerable.

And that, Veron wouldn't allow. He wouldn't allow his people to be abandoned by their allies, to starve, to do battle out of desperation, not if he could stop it. He'd sacrificed himself in marriage for them before. And if he arrived tonight, he would be sacrificing his life for them now.

Tarquin wouldn't hurt her, and not even the Brotherhood army would. But there was no such certainty for Veron.

Don't show up. Don't show up, Veron. Please. Don't show up.

Maybe Tarquin was wrong. Maybe Papà wouldn't agree to trading Veron. Maybe this was all part of a maneuver and an attack was imminent instead, while Veron would be kept safe, and the shifting feeling in her chest would dissipate.

In the darkness, the full moon rose in the sky, golden, enormous.

Tiny peeked out of her hair over her shoulder.

"Stay hidden, Tiny," she whispered, just barely audible. If any of the Brotherhood caught one of the Immortali—albeit a minuscule one—things could go badly.

Tiny flitted back into her locks and climbed up by her ear, chiming softly in her little bell voice.

Tarquin stood stiff as a rod next to her, his eyes searching the horizon, Siriano next to him, and a company of rigid men behind them. They were hard men, with hard eyes and hard faces, a sort of darkness emanating from them, a coldness, and it made her shiver. These were not men looking to make peace, no matter what the offer would be. That was not what they had come for.

She might have been able to turn Tarquin from this course, but the hundreds here, the thousands with him? Some had their own Arabella, and a truth behind her, and others believed things that were completely false, and yet others were so afraid of sharing the world that they cloaked that fear with aggression. They hated from a place of bitter ignorance, one they preferred to take out on the Immortali instead of taking responsibility for.

This world needed a library like the one she and Veron

dreamed of building. This world needed a hundred libraries. A thousand.

She looked away from them to the dim horizon, where a small group of silhouetted figures approached.

No, Holy Mother, please...

Yet she'd know the shape of him anywhere, his gait, from a mile away, in the dark—she'd know him.

Her feet were moving before she could think, but Tarquin grabbed her forearm and pulled her back.

"Not yet," he said sternly, and yanked her into place. "One hundred yards."

Holy Mother's mercy, she'd wanted to stop a war, had wanted to *protect* Veron, had never dreamed he'd disobey Queen Zara and come after her. She loved him for it, but now what had seemed like her best course of action had become her gravest miscalculation.

Papà had to have a contingency plan. This couldn't be it. He couldn't just be turning over Veron. He couldn't.

Her heart thudded in her chest as she stared into the distance, at the broadness of his shoulders, his long hair tousled by the wind, and as he approached, the shape of his face cleared, his sculpted jaw, his straight nose, his pale eyebrows, his jutting chin... and those intense golden eyes she had looked into countless times, had seen in kindness, in anger, in frustration, in pleasure, in love...

"Veron," she whispered, and every part of her trembled, willed her to go to him, to wrap herself around him and never let go.

Next to him was Lorenzo, in a violet brigandine over a darker gambeson, with a bandolier of knives around his chest and a small squad of Royal Guard. His face was slack, eyes downcast. So Papà had sent him.

"Aless," Veron said, his voice breaking, and a pain formed in her throat.

"Veron," she whispered, leaning forward, pulling at her arm in Tarquin's hold.

Finally, Tarquin moved forward with her in his grasp, Siriano at his side, and a squad of soldiers with him. She struggled in his hold, trying to break free, until at last he released her, and she ran to Veron, into his waiting arms. His embrace closed around her, and held her close, kissed the top of her head, and when she looked up at him, brushed her lips with his.

Holy Mother's mercy, after hurting him as she had, she had no right to this, to him, and he should push her away, shun her, *hate* her, but even knowing all of that, in this one moment, she couldn't fathom not holding him with everything she had.

"Veron, I'm so sorry," she said softly, her eyes aching as they watered. "I thought if they took me instead, they wouldn't kill me, and Papà would have to intervene... and that he could stop the war. I'm so sorry—"

"Shhh," he whispered in her ear, stroking her hair softly. "No more of that. Not now. You meant well—I know that. It hurt, deeply, but I know you meant well." He raised her chin gently, rubbing it with the callused pad of his thumb, taking her in with a soft gaze.

"Are Gavri and Valka—"

"They're safe. Worried about you," he said with a soft huff, "but safe." He was so calm, so incredibly, impossibly calm.

"I'm sorry I didn't tell you," she blurted. "I knew about your father, and I—"

"I know why he did it now, Aless." His voice was even, serene, as he searched her eyes. "My father. He left without a word because he couldn't let anybody stop him. He was determined to give up his life... because he loved us. It hurt me then, but I understand now. What he did wasn't a betrayal. It was the ultimate act of love."

There was something different about him, something settled and peaceful, something so unbelievably calm, and yet it tore her up inside, raged, so much that she wanted to scream and beg and cry, do anything and everything to chase that resigned expression away, and everything and everyone but Veron.

A pair of hands closed around her upper arms—a royal guard's.

"No," she said, and swung her head from side to side as Tarquin's men apprehended Veron, pulled him away from her, dragged him. "Please. Wait—"

She twisted to keep her eyes on him over her shoulder, where his eyes were still on her, too. A hardness rose in them, a restraint that turned his whole body taut as they bound his wrists.

"Veron," she cried, as Lorenzo took hold of her and whispered words of comfort.

"Live, Aless," Veron called out, his voice hoarse. "I love you."

One of his captors kicked at the back of his knee, forcing him to the grass, while another grabbed a fistful of his hair and pulled his head back.

She cried out, a shrill sound she didn't recognize, as Veron kept his jaw clenched, stayed soundless, rigid, and as a blade hissed free of a scabbard, she begged, pleaded, a string of words whimpering from her lips—

"*Please*," she cried, her pulse hammering in her chest, wild, violent. "*Don't! Veron!*" Her shriek cut the air, following by the thudding staccato of clopping hooves.

A streak of pure white burst from the trees—the unicorn—racing toward Tarquin, directly for him.

Men shouted, drew swords and bows, and the soldiers keeping Veron gawked.

"*Hold fire!*" Tarquin yelled, the unicorn closing in on a hundred yards, over a ton of muscle and power tearing up the grass.

"Shoot it!" someone shouted.

"Hold!" Tarquin faced it head on. "Arabella!"

The unicorn charged him—fifty yards, thirty—

Holy Mother's mercy, maybe it *wasn't* her—

Fifteen yards—

Four legs Changed to two, a shock of sable hair blooming from her head, and beautiful and lithe, she ran, weeping, stumbling over her own legs to trip at Tarquin's feet.

Murmurs of "unnatural" and "kill it" rippled through the Brotherhood forces as Tarquin raced to her, throwing off his officer's coat to wrap her in it. He fell to his knees before her.

"Arabella," he said, his voice breaking, and took her in his arms, where she sobbed into his chest. "I'm so sorry, Arabella. I'm so sorry." He rocked her gently, patted her back.

"Stop this, Brother," she croaked, her green eyes big and dazzling as she looked up into his face. "No more violence on my account. *No more violence.* Please."

Veron's captors didn't move, and neither did he, frozen on his knees, his head pulled back—but the hand holding it had loosened its grip.

Veron—please, be safe... Veron... She moved, but Lorenzo held her back with a shake of his head. He patted one of the knives sheathed in his bandolier.

The company of Brotherhood soldiers stood, some with bows drawn, others staring. A couple neared with readied crossbows.

"Stand down," Tarquin ordered.

The crossbowmen didn't waver.

"I said *stand down!*" He glared at the crossbowmen.

"You heard the general," Siriano bellowed, stepping up with his right hand glowing a faint green.

A crossbow fired.

Tarquin lunged in front of Arabella.

The bolt lodged in his shoulder.

Veron headbutted the captor fisting his hair.

Another raised his sword.

Lorenzo threw a knife into the man's neck.

Complete chaos broke out among the Brotherhood ranks, infighting and arrows loosed as Siriano raised an earthen wall between the company of men and their forward party. Lorenzo ordered his Royal Guard to attack, and they sprang into action, swarming Veron's captors as he fought them.

One of them charged her and Lorenzo, but she ducked, covering her head as Tiny flew out and attacked the man's face. He swatted at her but missed, and Lorenzo threw a salvo of knives into the man's leather-clad chest. He spluttered and fell.

"Tiny!" she shouted, and the pixie flew back to land on her shoulder, chiming angrily.

A royal guard cut Veron's bonds, and he grabbed a blade from the ground, fighting until every last Brotherhood soldier on this side of the wall lay dead.

She ran to him, and he turned, catching her in his arms,

breathing her in, and already they were moving back toward Lorenzo along with his Royal Guard.

"Veron, for a second, I thought—" Her voice broke.

His eyes fixed on the earthen wall, he held the blade out at the ready, but his gaze darted toward hers a moment. "So did I." He shot her an uneasy grin.

Tarquin lumbered backward toward them with Arabella and Siriano and, facing the wall, drew his sword.

Lorenzo drew his own. "Stay back, Belmonte! Or I'll have your head!"

Tarquin's eyes darted to his just a moment while he pulled Arabella in protectively. "I surrender. Please, I mean none of you any harm. I just want to make sure Arabella's safe."

The loud din of battle rose beyond the wall, chaotic, deafening, and men began to break through at the end of its length.

Siriano raised another perpendicular to it. "General, we need to *move*."

"Just wait," Lorenzo said.

"For what?" Tarquin hissed, and Arabella sobbed, trembling against him like a leaf in a storm.

The ground shook as she whirled around.

Heavy Sileni cavalry charged toward them—hundreds—thousands—with a glowing veil above them, lighting the way —pixies.

Tiny shot out and raced to join them.

"Move in!" Siriano yelled, and with a gesture, raised a triangular wall between them and the charging cavalry.

His first spell collapsed, and the Brotherhood's fighting broke through. With a nod from Tarquin, Siriano dispelled the second wall, and they all stood within the triangle's protection, huddled, as an earthquake of thundering horseflesh pounded past them and into the infighting Brotherhood forces.

Screams and shrieks tore the air, and the sounds of horns and shouted orders.

The Brotherhood was utterly decimated, broken bodies and blood—

Veron pulled her in, tucked her face against his chest, and she shook, squeezing her eyes shut. The battle, the violence, was horrific, but Veron was here, safe, his warmth soothing into her, his breath soft on her head, his hands stroking her back, *alive.*

"Papà planned to strong-arm the Brotherhood into returning Veron once you were safe," Lorenzo said quietly. "You didn't think we'd just hand him over, did you?"

CHAPTER 28

*O*n his knees in Mati's antechamber, Veron watched as she paced before him, Yelena, and Aless. There was a violence in her stride, in the contortion of her face, and he knew better than to speak until she spoke. Especially after all he'd done.

"Your Majesty," Yelena blurted, "I just want to say this was all the human's idea, and I didn't have anything to do with it. In fact, I wasn't even part of it until she asked me to be, and as a guest here, I didn't feel I could turn down a princess of—"

Mati stalked to Yelena, eyes wild, met her face to face, and roared. Yelena squeezed her eyes shut at the deafening sound, as he and Aless leaned away.

"*You*," Mati said with a sneer. "After your weak-willed, cowardly scheming to depose me, you now lack the *honor* to take responsibility for your actions? Queen Nendra has given you to me as a gift. To do with as I see fit. And your days as kuvara are over." Mati stayed in Yelena's face, her stare relentless, but still Yelena didn't open her eyes. The moment lingered long past comfortable. "You will henceforth be a *sluha* and serve the kuvari and volodari in any way they desire."

A sluha. She'd have to serve as a page.

Yelena winced but did not speak.

Mati moved to Aless. "And you. I give you my son, my blood, and welcome you to my queendom, only for you to betray me at the first opportunity. What were you thinking?"

Aless shook, her fingers trembling at her sides. "I-I thought if I f-failed and was c-captured, my father would have to g-get involved and help. And if I succeeded, the B-brotherhood would have n-no leverage."

Mati narrowed her eyes, but there was a glimmer. "Be that as it may, that decision was not yours to make. Flout my orders again, I will have you harvesting cave lichen until you forget what civilization looks like."

Aless nodded hastily. "Y-yes, Your Majesty."

"It is your dark luck that King Macario and I have chosen to declare this as a joint operation, in which we both agreed to trade you for my two kuvari as part of a larger strategy. I don't have to tell you what it would look like if the world believed I sacrificed my human ally's daughter or, worse, couldn't contain a single human barely out of her childhood years."

Aless swallowed audibly.

Mati glared at each of them in turn. "Any of you speak of this to anyone, and I shall claw out your tongues with my bare hands. Do you understand?"

"Yes, Your Majesty," they said in unison.

At last, she strode to him and crouched. "And you, Veron, who have ever been a credit to this queendom and to me, have disappointed me gravely with your disobedience." Her eyes softened a moment as her eyebrows pulled together. "For that, you are dismissed from the volodari for the foreseeable future—"

Dismissed from the volodari? It was the one thing he had any considerable skill in doing. But even as his body rebelled, he knew he deserved any punishment Mati had to give, and this—by all rights—was lenient.

"—and you will be placed with the stavbali to build whatever Nozva Rozkveta requires."

The stavbali did backbreaking work assisting the inzenyri and the Stone Singers, but he'd do whatever was required to make amends.

"With that said," she added, a faint smile curving her lips, "you did everything in your power to protect the one you love." Her face went slack a moment. "I am proud that you did, that you loved fiercely and forgave, even if your actions were reckless."

She was... proud? He didn't regret what he'd done, not even a little bit, because although Mati was angry and he'd disobeyed, Aless was still here. He was still here. All of Nozva Rozkveta was still here. What they'd done hadn't been right, but it had led them to this moment, where they were all still alive and had a future ahead of them.

Mati was angry... but sometimes there were more important concerns than not angering loved ones. Like saving the love of his life and trying to stop a war. And for that, he'd take this punishment, a hundred punishments, a thousand—as long as Aless still lived and breathed.

He glanced at Aless, who was still trembling, but if Mati was fortifying the stavbali, that could only mean one thing: Aless's dream was about to come true. Their dream.

Sighing, Mati rose. "Despite all of your actions, we managed to avoid all-out war, reaffirm an alliance, and build a new one. Now get up and join me in the grand hall, where King Macario, Queen Nendra, Duchess Claudia, and all of Nozva Rozkveta await."

᪥

VERON STOOD in the grand hall's periphery, Aless on his arm, as Mati shook hands with King Macario and then with Duchess Claudia. Lorenzo was at Aless's side, along with Bianca and Luciano, who'd come to change Tarquin's mind—albeit too late. The kuvari already had him in their custody at Heraza Gate.

"What do you think was the final agreement?" Aless whispered, leaning in.

That much he'd overheard. "A reaffirmation of the Sileni–Nozva Rozkvetan alliance. A more concrete agreement between Stroppiata and the allied queendoms. Roccalano to compensate Queen Nendra for the loss of her murdered volodari, with vast quantities of food and other supplies. The Brotherhood to be rooted out and ended by the coalition. And Tarquin Belmonte to be exiled."

It had been a kindness to Bianca and Luciano, and to Arabella. But also, as an exile, Tarquin couldn't be used as a martyr to further stoke the malcontents; he'd simply disappear and be forgotten.

Aless lightly rested her head against his arm, and there was something about her in Nozva Rozkvetan robes that pleased him as he looked her over. Her human clothes had always suited her—and he'd say or do just about anything to see her in that sheer red thing from their wedding night—but in these plain robes, she was saying something to him, to his family, to all of Nozva Rozkveta, without even a single word. That message mattered to him, a lot, even if his Aless could never fade into the background, never blend in—and he didn't want her to. That wouldn't be the woman he'd married... and was marrying again today at the Offering.

"What about Arabella?" she asked.

Arabella moved about Nozva Rozkveta freely, even now, although she seemed to spend most of her time with Noc, who could answer most of her questions about her new nature.

"She wants to learn control of her Change," he answered. "And my mother has agreed to help her." Unicorns had always been a benevolent force in the world, and Arabella herself had saved him from imminent death and prevented a war.

Soon, Mati would send out a team of the volodari to track other unicorns—who generally didn't want to be found—in an effort to find Arabella's maker, who could help her control her Change by lifebonding with her.

"And in exchange, Tarquin goes quietly." Aless took a deep breath.

"Something like that."

She gave him a faint smile, although it soon faded. This entire situation had hit her hard—they'd nearly lost one another, a war had almost been instigated, people had *died*, and not all of them hateful Brotherhood members. And all of it born of ignorance.

It was by Holy Ulsinael's dark grace that a peace had survived.

Mati turned to the assembly of humans and dark-elves and raised her hands. "Today, we reaffirm a friendship between the kingdom of Silen and Nozva Rozkveta, between humans and dark-elves, built on a shared land, a shared purpose, and the marriage of our children." Smiling, Mati gestured to them both, and Aless curtseyed as he bowed. "That friendship was forged with a wedding, and today we renew it with a wedding once more. I invite you all to join us at Baraza Gate in one hour for the Offering between my son, Veron, and his wife, Alessandra."

Everyone turned to them and applauded, and he couldn't help a jittery hum coursing through his veins. If Aless would but have him, today would change their lives forever.

He was a dark-elf, Immortal, and the love of his life was a human.

Today, he had come so dangerously close to losing Aless, and he never wanted to feel that way again. Ever.

"We have also chosen to share our knowledge with the sky realm, to forge a partnership going forward that will help protect both our peoples against those who would mean to do us harm, while welcoming the people of the sky realm to know us," Mati said.

Next to him, Aless's breath caught.

"A *library*," Mati declared, with applause filling the silence she left.

Aless held his hand tightly, practically brimming.

"We will invite knowledge from around the world that we could use to learn about our new circumstances, all the while sharing with the world *our* culture, *our* knowledge, *our* language, teaching any who wish to learn. To that end, the Order of Terra, a monastic order devoted to serving the goddess Terra, has agreed to be our partner." Mati gestured to the Paladin Grand Cordon next to Duchess Claudia, who inclined his head to the applause.

"My daughter-in-law will oversee the project and ensure it

meets everyone's needs." Mati smiled at Aless, who gasped, scarcely able to catch her breath.

Despite everything—or maybe even because of it—it was safe to say Mati had a fondness for his wife.

After another round of applause, Mati held out her hands. "Now, let's all get ready for a wedding."

"The library," Aless whispered, her cheeks reddening. "*Our* library... and the second ceremony. All in one day. Veron, I..."

"I know." He grinned. "Come on, let's prepare."

He was ready. Today, with all his heart, he would offer her everything he had and everything he was. And pray she'd say yes.

§

ALESS GRIPPED the ancient stone balustrade in the ruins behind Baraza Gate, where the Bloom curled around crumbling stone pillars and every bit of stone in the courtyard, a lovely weave of verdant vines and glittering red roses that only glowed brighter as the world darkened.

It would soon be dusk, and she'd be making the Offering to Veron.

They'd stopped a war, still had each other, and he didn't hate her after she'd abandoned him. *And* Queen Zara had announced the library. Soon, there would be several libraries across Silen, open to all, unwinding this ignorant hatred book by book.

It was happening. It was all happening.

She took three deep breaths.

"Alessandra," Papà's voice came from the steps. "You should be happy. You finally got your wish."

Did he mean the library or Veron? "Papà, this is the best day of my life."

He stroked her cheek, his gaze soft. "Your mother's wish came true, and she is gone. I wish you'd see the danger in this."

She shook her head. "Mamma died doing what she loved. It was important to her, and she—and her purpose—are important to me, too. I want to keep that alive. Maybe I would've been useless in your world"—and when his mouth dropped open, she added, "Yes, I heard you say that to Mamma. But I've finally found it. My world. I helped sow a peace, and I will continue to do so. The library will be a beacon of knowledge, education, and hope."

Papà heaved a sigh. "Alessandra, I have tried all your life to protect you. This—getting involved in something so risky, putting yourself out there and accessible to any lowlife..." He shook his head sadly. "You are still here, and your mother is *gone*. Leave the past in the past. You should just live safely."

It was not in her to hide and live a *safe* life. Not while she still had two hands, and there were people who thirsted for knowledge but didn't have the tools to acquire it. Mamma had tried to shine a light on the world, to fight the ignorance that begat fear, and that was a worthy cause, one she'd continue the fight for.

"Mamma is gone," she whispered to him, "but she doesn't have to be forgotten. We did that, by disregarding her wishes, her life's work, everything that mattered to her. I understand that you mean well, but I choose a different path, Papà."

Another heavy sigh left him, but he kissed her cheek. "Congratulations, daughter. I may not agree with you, but I know your mother would be proud. Both of your library and you."

She couldn't help but smile, and with a final nod, he descended the steps and headed to the front of the ruins.

Bianca crept up next to her with a beaming Gabriella. "Well, that was unexpected."

She couldn't help a laugh as Bianca looked her over.

"Are you sure this is the right dress?" Bianca asked.

Aless brushed her fingers over the rose-red tulle netting of her wedding gown from Bellanzole. It fit her perfectly, and the skirts flared out gently, a ten-foot train behind her.

Veron had asked her to wear this gown, this same gown, and she hadn't brought another for the second ceremony, so she'd reluctantly agreed. Besides, when everyone in Bellanzole had seen it as shocking, he hadn't—at all. It meant something different to him.

"I'm sure."

"You look beautiful," Gabriella said, sweeping a stray lock of her hair off her face. She and Danika had returned with Papà and Lorenzo safely, thank the Mother.

She took Gabriella's hand. "Thank you. For taking the messages to Bellanzole. You did a very brave thing that saved lives."

Gabriella blushed, then inclined her head. "It was my honor."

Bianca's eyes widened, and Aless spun to see Veron approaching, in his best leathers, astride Noc. She blinked, and suddenly she was in L'Abbazia Reale again, watching a dark-elf prince on a massive black horse trotting down the hall, decked out for battle, regal and intimidating, well built and hale like the heroes of old, hewn from Carrerra marble.

She blinked again, and Veron was the same man, but so much more. The man she loved, who loved her. The man who listened to her. The man who wanted to live her dreams with her. The only one she could ever imagine wanting to spend the rest of her life with.

She wouldn't live even a fraction as long as he would, but she'd live the days they had left together to their fullest, knowing he loved her just as she loved him. It was more than she'd ever dared to hope.

A smile on his face, he drank her in with his exploring gaze, and her cheeks warmed.

"I think he *does* like the dress," Bianca whispered in her ear with a giggle.

She shushed Bianca and approached the balustrade. "Is it time?"

"It is." He extended a hand to her, here, in this blooming courtyard of daydreams. "Will you do me the honor?"

She took his hand, descended the steps, and let him help her into the saddle. He gave a nod to Bianca and Gabriella, thick as thieves, who watched them leave. Bianca even gave her a wink. The troublemaker.

Their teasing made her heart flutter, and here, enshrined in Veron's arms, she had all the reason in the world to be giddy.

Her eyes closed, she tucked her head under Veron's chin, settled into his embrace, breathed in his pure forest-stream scent. "You're sure you like the dress?"

A soft breath. "I am. It suits you, my love." A light, playful tone danced in his deep voice. "But I do have something to ask you," he added, and that playful tone faded.

"Hmm?" She opened her eyes, straightened a little.

He let the silence stay a while. "Are you sure you want to do this?"

She looked up at him, but there was no room to see his face. Now, minutes before their Offering, he doubted her?

"I once told you I couldn't release you," he said softly. "But now, Aless, if you tell me this isn't what you want, I will help you, whatever it takes."

That's what this was about? He'd told her in Stroppiata that he couldn't release her, but she didn't *want* to be released. She wanted this—*him*—with every fiber of her being.

But he... he wanted her to *choose* this, not just accept it. He supported her decision, whether it was to do what he wanted or not.

If they weren't in the saddle, and about to stand in front of hundreds of people, she'd tackle him right now. "Veron, I want a life with you. I choose this. I choose *you*."

He let out a heavy breath. "That's a relief." A few deep breaths. "But I wanted—I needed—to ask."

"And I love that you did." She nuzzled his chest as Noc took them to the front of Baraza Gate, where no less than three hundred guests surrounded the vine-wrapped ruins. The Bloom shimmered all around them, glittered, and the gentle glow like stars all around was the pixies in attendance.

One raced from the rest, a little glowing star, and landed on her shoulder with a happy chime in greeting. A little pink-haired and leaf-wrapped pixie.

"Tiny," she breathed, and smiled. "You came."

"Tiny?" Veron asked, bending to look. "Hello," he whispered brightly.

Tiny fluffed her hair and crossed her legs, fluttering her wings as if to demonstrate their shimmering beauty.

"Did you do something new to your hair?" Aless asked, receiving a lively wing-fluttering in reply.

Xira, the mystic from the lifespring, stood at the top of the ruins' steps in her violet robes, her white hair ruffled by the breeze. While Queen Zara—Mati—seemed to preside over nearly all events in Nozva Rozkveta, Offerings were the mystics' preserve.

Veron dismounted and helped her down from Noc's saddle. "Thank you, old friend," he said softly, patting his neck.

Noc swished his tail and sprightly headed off to the side, where Arabella took in the whole assembly with interest, turning her horned head this way and that. Dhuro and Gavri stood with her, occasionally whispering things.

Veron took her hand, and together, they ascended the steps to stand before Xira. When her eyes met his, he was smiling, and she couldn't help but smile, too. They were doing this. They were finally doing this.

"Nozva Rozkveta bids you welcome," Xira announced to all the guests. "Today we gather in support of Prince Veron of Nozva Rozkveta and Princess Alessandra Ermacora of Silen as they make the Offering to each other, before Deep, Darkness, and Holy Ulsinael, and pledge to walk their lives together. Let us take a moment to welcome Holy Ulsinael here, to bless their union with his dark grace."

Xira clasped her hands together, closed her eyes, and bowed her head, as did Veron, as did Mati, as did every dark-elf in attendance, and Aless did the same.

Holy Mother, bless our union. Holy Ulsinael, bless our union.

She prayed, willing with all her heart that her prayers be heard, and when she opened her eyes, both Veron and Xira were grinning at her. Her cheeks warmed, but she only held his gaze, even as that playful grin warmed her cheeks even more.

Xira took their hands and joined them. "Make your Offerings."

Holding her hand, Veron stroked her fingers, his grin fading to a pensiveness, intensifying those warm golden eyes as he shifted in his boots. In Bellanzole, he'd arrived with a full arsenal of weapons and made an Offering to her right there, in L'Abbazia Reale, in the hallway. It had been a stunning moment, one she'd never forget.

Today, he had no sword, no bow, no knives, no shield, nor scroll.

He stood before her, holding her hand, regarding her warmly. "Aless, when we first married in Bellanzole, I offered you power, survival, skill, defense, and wisdom. I didn't know you then," he said to her, searching her eyes as a subtle smile claimed his lips. "But I know you now, and you require none of those things from me. You're a force to be reckoned with in your own right, and it is my great fortune to be by your side."

Her breath caught in her throat, and shallow breaths were all she could muster.

"Alessandra Ermacora, princess of Silen, I, Veron of Nozva Rozkveta, offer you my love, my loyalty, and my life"—he held her hand to his chest—"to harness for your ends or ours, as we walk our lives together from this day forward for as long as the Deep allows."

His *life*?

His golden eyes stayed locked with hers, and her shallow breaths only became shallower.

His life—his *life*—

Did he mean... a lifebond?

She gasped. "Veron..."

He couldn't! Holy Mother's mercy, a *lifebond*? Offering to

share his life force with hers, to strengthen her, to weaken as she weakened, to die when she died?

He nodded to Xira, who held a bright, metallic little star, shaped like a crystal cluster.

"I'm a mortal," she whispered. "You can't—"

He kissed her hand. "It won't make you Immortal. But together, we'll have something more than a mortal life, and something less than an immortal one. That much I know."

This was... She shook her head. "Veron, are you sure—"

"I want to spend our lives together, Aless. Always together. Whether that's a hundred years or a thousand, whatever the Deep, Darkness, and Holy Ulsinael allow. Please make me the happiest man alive and say yes."

Say yes? Say yes to a lifetime shared with Veron, to years and decades and centuries in love, in joy, together? His sacrifice was enormous, and she wanted to argue, but as he held her gaze, pressed his lips to her hand, he gave her his answer.

"Yes," she whispered, and when his smile broadened, so did hers. "I accept your Offering."

A beaming Xira nodded to her.

It was time for her Offering. She'd planned to Offer him her knowledge, her boldness, and her ambition... but he had been right. Those weren't the things they truly needed to Offer each other. "Veron, prince of Nightbloom, I, Alessandra Ermacora of Silen, offer you my love, my loyalty, and my life, too," she said, threading her fingers through his, "to harness for your ends or ours, as we walk our lives together from this day forward for as long as the Deep allows."

He held both her hands, and grinned. "I accept your Offering."

Xira held out the small, bright metal cluster, and placed it between their palms. As they squeezed, there was a pinprick, and Xira held their hands between hers, chanted in Elvish, and when she finished—despite the pinprick, there was no mark, no blood.

"You are now lifebonded," Xira said, "joined in life and death, able to sense each other, draw each other, call to each other."

What that meant, she'd find out in the coming days, but as long as she got to be with Veron, the lifebond was perfect.

"What Offerings made and accepted today before the Deep, Darkness, and Holy Ulsinael, let no other pursue," Xira declared to the guests. "We swear this by the Darkness."

"By the Darkness," the crowd murmured, and Veron's lips met hers.

CHAPTER 29

*A*fter an evening of feasting, games, and dancing—for the humans in attendance—Veron opened the door to their quarters with a sigh of relief.

"So you'll take me hunting tomorrow?" Aless asked, breezing past him as he shut the door. "I need more practice."

"Perhaps not tomorrow," he said with a smile. When she pursed her lips, he added, "The Stone Singers and stavbali are breaking ground on the library tomorrow. I think you'll want to be there."

"*What?*" She jumped into his arms, squealing. "*Tomorrow?* Veron, really? Tomorrow!"

"Yes, really," he answered. "Tomorrow."

Aless kissed his cheek once, then again, then his lips, then slowly claimed his mouth, her fingers raking up into his hair as she leaned into him, a soft moan humming in her throat.

"Hold that thought," he murmured, although his body had different ideas. As she smiled mischievously, he cleared his throat and led her out of the antechamber and into the bedchamber, where on his table was his copy of *A Modern History of Silen*. "I know we already gave each other Offering gifts in Bellanzole, but I wanted to share this with you." He held it out to her.

Her eyebrows rose as she took it, paging through it to get to the blank pages—only, some weren't blank anymore. He'd filled in the details of their journey, sketched in drawings of, well, mostly her. Nearly all of them—well, if he were honest, *all* of them, her.

She traced a sketch of her in the duchess's garden, surrounded by lavender and pixies, and gasped. "Veron, this is... This is stunning."

He stepped in closer to her and brushed her voluminous dark tresses over her shoulder. "My father taught me, when we used to study sky realm flora and fauna together. I hadn't drawn anything since he died."

For a long time, he hadn't wanted to do anything that had reminded him of Ata, and yet he'd become one of the volodari, just like him. The knot of pain Ata had left behind had untangled, faded, and he understood now. Understood what it meant to be ready to do anything—*anything*—for those he loved.

"It's beautiful, Veron," she whispered, and brushed his lips with hers. Smiling, she pulled away. "I'm not sure mine will mean as much..."

"You got me something?"

Her face bright, she rushed to one of her trunks, opened it, and pulled out a box. "You see, when I wrote to Bellanzole from Dun Mozg, I *might* have included a certain request to Lorenzo." She handed him the ribbon-wrapped box.

Raising an eyebrow, he pulled the ribbon undone—some days, he *did* miss the ease of his claws—and opened the lid.

Inside lay a pair of boots—perfect, supple, well-oiled leather, buttery soft, and—

"Try them on!" she urged.

"You found time in a war to ask your brother for boots?" he asked with a laugh.

She nodded happily.

He did pull them on, and—*Holy Ulsinael.*

He walked a circuit in the bedchamber, shifted on his feet, crouched, jumped, all while Aless laughed.

"By Deep and Darkness, you *laugh*, my love, but these—these boots are the most comfortable I've ever—" He leaned back into the heel, but it was just... pillowy... and...

She covered her mouth as she giggled. "Lorenzo's cobbler is born of a long line of cobblers, only he was born an enforcer, too. He uses his skills *and* his magic to make what Lorenzo calls 'the shoes of the gods.'" She smirked.

"Holy Ulsinael, he's not *wrong*, Aless. These boots are—they're—" It was unthinkable, but he almost wanted to go on a hunt right now. *Almost.* But it would be some time yet before Mati would allow him back among the volodari.

"Oh! One more thing," she said, clapping her hands together.

After making the Offering with Aless and lifebonding with her, if there was a thing in this realm that could make this day any better, he didn't know it.

"Close your eyes." Her dark gaze practically sparkled. What was she planning?

He did as she asked and then sank into the bed.

There were flitting footsteps, and the creaking of a hinge, more quick steps, rustling, and—

"All right. Open them." Her voice brimmed, and he was laughing under his breath when he opened his eyes.

By Deep and Darkness, it was the *sheer red thing*. His laughter ceased instantly.

She leaned against the wall in that ethereal red nightdress from their wedding night in Bellanzole, and its folds of thin fabric teased shadows and planes beneath a crimson veil. It hung from her frame by thin, delicate straps, its sheer fabric pooling on the floor.

Her shoulders and her long, elegant arms were bare, so much of her soft, beautiful skin bared to him, and his fingers clutched the mattress as they longed to touch her. That night in Bellanzole, he'd been prepared to do his duty as ordered, and neither of them had been ready for it, not in the least, but this image of Aless in her sheer red nightgown had lingered in his memory, more and more in the past couple of weeks.

And here she was now, as if she'd stepped out of that night into this one, his brave, intelligent, beautiful wife, his love, his Aless.

By Deep and Darkness, he wanted to see her, every part of her, commit her to memory, and know her by the tip of a finger or the curve of a collarbone.

Biting her lip, she took slow steps to him, stood between his knees, stroked through his hair, over his shoulders, along his jaw, and he closed his arms around her, pulled her in and down to him as he moved deeper into bed. His hands found the smooth skin of her back as her lips met his, as her kiss deepened, as she breathed the same air, and he rolled her over, pinned her to the bed.

Gleaming dark eyes danced as she looked up at him, a smile playing on her lips. "What will you do to me, dark-elf prince?"

He huffed a soft breath. Oh, he had plenty of things in mind, but above all one. "Love you till the end of time, Aless. Till the end of time."

EPILOGUE

The autumn wind gently rustled through the trees as Veron headed to the site of the library construction. Leaves of gold, red, and russet descended from the sunlit canopy.

He rubbed his chin thoughtfully. Although it wasn't uncommon for him to visit Aless during the day, it was rare indeed when she went to the trouble of inviting him. By note, no less.

He nodded to his fellow stavbali—Mati still had him on building projects instead of back hunting with the volodari—and to the Stone Singers and inzenyri. It had been four months since the library announcement, and the exterior of the building was almost complete. The longest task had been hauling in the stone for the Stone Singers, and as strong as his people were, the stavbali weren't omnipotent. He rotated his shoulder, as if he'd helped haul the stone just yesterday.

A sea of large white pavilion tents surrounded the construction, and beneath one were two ladies surrounded by children with quills and paper. Her blessedly dark hair dancing in the breeze, Aless removed one of her hands from her lavender cloak and waved at him before hiding her coy smile with a finger.

She spoke to Gabriella, then bid the children goodbye and trotted over to him while he jogged to meet her. Encircling her in his arms, he kissed her, allowing his fingers to slip through that silken hair of hers. Holy Ulsinael, he was a lucky man.

Pulling away, she smiled softly, her gleaming dark eyes searching his. Her smooth fingertips grazed his jaw, and her little smile widened. "Aren't you going to ask me why I invited you here today?"

He huffed. "Surely you know by now I'd never question a blessing, my love?"

Her cheeks colored, and she nudged him with her shoulder before taking his hand. As they strolled toward the library, she rubbed the small of her back a little, and he replaced her hand with his.

"You work too hard," he said. Since the start of the project, there had been nothing she hadn't done, from trying to help haul the stone to attempting to build the furniture. She'd kept herself busy even before she'd organized school for the local children and anyone who wished to learn.

"I can't help it," she replied, but he already knew that. "When your dream comes true, you don't rest on your laurels. This is only the first of many libraries, Veron."

Her vision sprawled wide, and he'd move mountains to achieve it with her.

"Besides, after our lifebond, I've never felt stronger in my life," she said brightly as they entered the building.

He snorted. "I didn't expect it would be such a thrill to a mortal, but... again, I don't question blessings."

"With this one, neither will I." She leaned in, and they headed toward the east side of the library, where the first panels of stained glass had already been put in. They depicted a rose, a shared beauty between the humans and the dark-elves.

She looked up at it, sunlight pouring through reds and greens, then at him, and his breath caught. Her face glowed with the dazzling colors, and when she smiled, she was a goddess in the flesh. "Veron, I'm with child."

His eyebrows shot up, and he scrambled for breath... and words, any words. But alas, all he could muster was inhalation, exhalation, frown... inhalation... pause, a word—no, false alarm—

She stifled a laugh, but her eyes were half-moons. Her hand squeezed his.

He pulled her into his arms, kissed the top of her head. "I was already the luckiest man alive when you said you loved me, Aless. And somehow, by Deep and Darkness, you've given me a fortune more."

A quiet gasp, and she leaned into him, clinging to him as she sniffled softly. "I didn't know if it could happen—I wasn't sure. But then my moonbleed didn't come for the second month, and when I went to Xira, she said... She said we're going to have a baby."

What he wouldn't have done to be in the room and hear the news with Aless. "I can't wait to meet her, my love."

He dipped his head down and raised her mouth to his lips, stroking away the tears rolling down her cheeks, teasing her tongue with his, coaxing her passion. His heart had swelled with love, and he hadn't thought it possible, but with her words, it had expanded all the more.

Soft footsteps echoed closer—Gabriella's—and he broke away with a grin. Did Gabriella know? If she didn't, he couldn't wait to see her reaction—

"Your Highness," Gabriella said, holding out a missive to Aless. "It's from Archmage Sabeyon in Courdeval."

Aless's brow furrowed, but she accepted the sealed parchment from Gabriella. "I haven't seen her since... Why, it's almost been a year." She cracked open the seal and read. "She... She asks if we can help perform a lifebond—"

A lifebond? Courdeval was the capital of Emaurria. A human kingdom. Humans had long sought the secrets of—

Aless gasped, her face paling. He wrapped an arm around her shoulders, steadying her. "What is it? What's the matter?"

She blinked, gaped at him, the shock of her open mouth widening to a grin. Tears welled in her eyes and spilled. "Veron... She... She says a friend of hers freed Immortali locked in a sea prison, and among them was a dark-elf... He says his name is Mirza... He says he's... He's your father."

Swallowing, she took his hand.

Mirza... Ata...

He licked his lips, shook his head. No, Ata had died. He'd died. They all knew—they all—

He sucked in a sharp breath. They'd been told. They'd been told by the light-elves that Ata had been killed. They'd never seen or received his body.

It was...

His heart skipped a beat.

It was possible. He wouldn't question it, not when there was hope.

"Veron, are you...? Is everything all right? Your father..." She huffed a disbelieving sound.

He breathed deeply, steadily, gathering his composure, and met her teary, gleaming gaze.

His father was alive. Ata was *alive*.

The love of his life, a child, and his father back in his life... At this rate, his heart would burst. And he'd welcome it with open arms. "Will you go with me, my love? I know you have the library here, and it's your dream—"

"That you're part of, Veron. The construction will continue while we're gone. We—as in, of course I'm coming with you." She beamed, her palm on her belly, and nodded. "To the ends of the earth and to eternity."

THE END

Thanks for reading *No Man Can Tame*! If you enjoyed the adventure, please consider leaving a review. The review rating determines which series I prioritize, so if you want more books in this series soon, review this one!

Ready for the next installment in the Dark-Elves of Nightbloom series? The next book is called *Bright of the Moon*, Dhuro and Bella's story, available now! Turn the page for a short preview.

AUTHOR'S NOTE

Thank you for reading *No Man Can Tame*, the first fantasy romance in the Dark-Elves of Nightbloom series. If you've read my Blade and Rose romantic epic fantasy series, you'll notice that those books and these interweave. Aless and Veron will be showing up again in *The Dragon King*, coming soon. And the next book of The Dark-Elves of Nightbloom features his brother Dhuro and a certain noblewoman turned unicorn!

If you'd like to keep up with news about my books and other updates, you can sign up for my newsletter at www. mirandahonfleur.com. As a thank-you gift, you'll get the prequel story to the Blade and Rose series, "Winter Wren," featuring Rielle's first meeting with a certain paladin.

All my books are only possible with the help of many people. *No Man Can Tame* is no exception! I'd like to thank the ladies of Enclave Authors—Katherine Bennet, Emily Allen West, Emerald Dodge, and Ryan Muree—for their help in critiquing this book. I'd also like to thank editors Deborah

Nemeth and Laura Kingsley for their insight, and extend my condolences to Laura Kingsley's loved ones. I only knew her for a short time, but she was a sharp mind, an intelligent editor, and a kind person, and she'll be greatly missed.

I'd also like to thank my proofreaders, Patrycja Pakula and Charity Chimni, who caught the many, many, *many* typos in this manuscript. Any left over are mine. Lea Vickery, thank you for being an awesome assistant and helping me stay organized. I couldn't do this without you! And a special thanks to Erin Montgomery Miller for her help and her eagle eye.

And as always, my husband, Tony, and my mom. Your love and support have meant the world to me as I pursue this passion that impossibly is also my career.

Thanks go to my amazing street team, the Queen's Blade, as well for helping spread the word about my books and bringing a smile to my face! I am so happy we found each other, and I'm excited to keep having fun in 2019!!!

And you, my readers. Without your support, I wouldn't be releasing a fifth book. Thanks to your messages, reviews, and sharing the word about my work, I get to do my dream job and be an author. I love hearing from you, so please feel free to drop me a line on: www.mirandahonfleur.com, Facebook, Twitter, and miri@mirandahonfleur.com. Thank you for reading!

Sincerely,
Miri

**Wrath consumes him as the dark does the night...
Until she rises. But can she chase away his darkness?**

Most would say the "sweet" and "quiet" Bella has lived a
quiet life as a young noblewoman in her family's
castello. But little do they know she pens treatises
criticizing the realm's warmongers... and now there's a
price on her head. As she struggles to hide her seditious
activities, a chance encounter with a unicorn leaves her
with four hooves and a horn of her own—and a form
she can't control. The dark-elf queen has offered her a
chance to acquire that control... if Bella can find the
unicorn who turned her.

Prince Dhuro of Nightbloom has never met a problem he couldn't solve with his fists—that is, until he fought his sister for a place in the army's elite forces and lost. When the light-elves defeated them and his father was executed, Dhuro's inner demons laid claim to the whole of him. Now Immortal beasts are growing in power and threatening his people.

Dhuro has a chance to help his people when his mother, the queen, sends him on a mission—helping a human newly turned unicorn find her sire, and asking the impossible: whether the elder of the pacifistic unicorns will stand with them against the beasts ravaging his people. Making things worse, Bella challenges his every decision, argues with him, infuriates him... until beneath the full moon, she shifts to her human form... and enchants him. Neither wants love: he's been betrayed by a former lover, and she's lost the love of her life. But their hearts might have no say in the matter...

A war is raging, Dhuro must marry for political advantage, and only Bella's sire can help her... And when the bounty hunters hunting her find them, Dhuro and Bella's worldviews collide like life and death. But can he be the answer to helping her control her form, and can she chase away his darkness? Can they find a way to be together and fight the war threatening to devour the land... or will it swallow them too?

Readers are saying if you like the fantasy and romance of Grace Draven's Wraith Kings and a snarky Swan Princess

tale with unicorns, BRIGHT OF THE MOON is the
bedmates-to-lovers romance that will lure you into its world
and not let you go.

**Dive into *Bright of the Moon*, and journey into a
medieval world of magic and Immortals, trials and
trysts, blood and passion, and a love lasting far longer
than forever...**

PROLOGUE

Her breath sharp like knives, Bella raced through the stark
forest as fast as her booted feet could take her.

Flashes of immaculate white darted through the grove of
chestnut trees, glimpses just barely visible in the distance. Low-
hanging branches snatched at her dress like desperate hands,
but she dared not slow down. Not if she wanted to catch up to
the unicorn.

She weaved through the slender trunks, her steps
crunching on frozen twigs. Her cloak pulled at her neck, caught
on a snow-shrouded bough, and she unclasped it. No matter.
The late-winter chill wouldn't halt her flight.

All her life, she'd secretly searched for others like her, who
believed in the sharpness of ingenuity over that of the blade.
At first, they had been only humans. But when untold
numbers of immortal creatures had awoken about a year ago,
more hope had blinked its eyes open. A war raged between
humans and Immortali. And if unicorns were real, then
maybe their mythical powers of peace were, too; she'd meet
this one face to face. Here. Today. Maybe it could help spare
another Bella somewhere from losing the love of her life to

war. At the very least, she wouldn't disappoint Cosimo's memory.

She leaped over a fallen tree. Her boot slid in the slushy deadfall, but she caught herself with a gloved hand.

Precious time. She was losing precious time.

But the magnificent white coat shone just ahead, in stark relief to the withered foliage and ash-brown bark.

The unicorn had stopped. It was waiting.

She slowed, testing her approaching steps cautiously. Chasing it had been one thing, but running toward it now? She couldn't risk spooking what she'd admired for so long. Not now. Not when she was so close and her idol so real.

Tarquin, Luciano, and Mamma would never believe her, but it didn't matter. The only thing the Belmonte family believed in was war. But as "Renato"—her pseudonym and secret political alter ego—she could introduce the kingdom of Silen to an entire society that had renounced war eons before Silen had even crowned its first king. With the help of the unicorns, she could change the course of not only her family but the realm.

As long as she could avoid the assassins chasing the price on Renato's head. The price on *her* head.

Now that she'd slowed, her face burned. She struggled to remain upright as she sucked in breath after life-giving breath. With any luck, her wheezing, grunting, and panting like a constipated barbarian wouldn't frighten it. Writers, perhaps, were not always the best of runners. Or breathers.

But it just watched her, flicking its tail, long, wavy silken hair swaying in the breeze. Although horse-like, calling it—*him* —a horse wouldn't have been right. He had a loose, open bearing, and gave a curious tilt of his head. A slight toss as if to say hello. There was a surprisingly human quality to his body language. Had he intended to lead her here?

She straightened. What did unicorns know of human society, anyway? Everything she'd ever read of them had suggested they were reclusive, isolated, kept to themselves, some even preferring solitude entirely. Wouldn't their communication—verbal or otherwise—reflect that?

Other sources had guessed at telepathic abilities. Had he read her thoughts?

Perhaps the two of them would be able to communicate? All the better. "Hello," she said shakily, cautiously. "I'm Bella."

From thirty feet away, she met his eyes. Bright, alluring violet, magical, as if the most coveted, priceless jewels had been given flesh and intention. Then—

The world blurred around her, a sweep of greenery. Her chest tightened as though she were falling, but her feet found the dirt beneath her.

The unicorn stood before her, his face level with hers, his horn a mere inch from her forehead. Violet. Brilliant, breathtaking violet—

She gasped. An arcane shiver trembled through her shoulders and down her spine. Magic. It was magic.

The horn—long, twining, and sharp—would be daunting on any other creature but the father of peace. Still, she dared not move but to breathe, and slowly, his gaze drew her in.

Those eyes were limitless, the boundless skies of another world, where the wind flirted through the endless summer grasses studded with vibrant wildflowers, where a herd of unicorns swept past, manes swaying, horns gleaming, beneath a warm sun...

Warm... and she was like them, her heart filled with quiet, the kind of peace lost on other worlds, except this one... This one was the dream. Where no one fought, no one killed. Where her family's armies had never killed her only love, Cosimo. Where she'd never been too blind to see it coming. Where battles were waged with words, and victories were bloodless. Where unicorns ventured out of their isolation and met the world with warmth and quiet hearts.

Their dream. Her dream.

If only she could become—

A pinprick heated her forehead. She blinked at deep eyes shrouded with long, dense lashes.

The unicorn stepped back, bowing his head, his gaze never leaving hers.

The tip of his horn was red.

Frowning, she blinked again. Red flowed down the twining horn, a swirl of bright ribbon against pearlescent white.

She raised her fingers to her forehead, and they came away red, too. Blood red.

All her research had said they were peaceful. They were, weren't they? But then, what was this? An accident, maybe? It had to be...

And before her was no longer just the unicorn.

A *herd* of them. *The* herd stood in a meadow.

She swayed, and her weak knees buckled.

There had to be at least two dozen. How—?

The world blurred around her again. He had to be taking her somewhere. But where? She turned in place, spun, but everything only blurred more, more and more and more...

She misplaced a foot and fell, descending like a feather on summer air, gliding down to the forest floor, impossibly green and lively. She fell through piles of leaves and colorful flower petals, through visions of the sun soaring across the sky, and then the moon rising, violet eyes and green ones and blue, her gloves slipping off and flying away from her grasp, the satin petals against her skin and cool grass, the sun, the moon, the sun...

The blur sharpened, slowly, brushstrokes of color coming together into the shapes of chestnut trees and fresh spring leaves in the predawn light, and the magnificent unicorn peering down at her, all of it framed in the most beautiful palette of glowing prismatic hues.

How was it possible...? It was winter after all, wasn't it...?

In this world, it is only a dream. You must make it come true, Arabella, a firm, soothing baritone said to her.

She tilted her head, but something tickled her nose. As she reached up to scratch it, a hoof rose beneath her.

Her arm wouldn't cooperate—her arm—her arm...

Her heart racing, she looked down at herself. At her long, immaculate white legs. At her hooves.

At her *hooves*.

With a gasp, she backed up, shaking her head. It wasn't possible. A human couldn't turn into... There was no way. She couldn't be—

But you are, the voice said.

Violet eyes. The voice—it was *him*.

Her legs continued to back up without her volition.

There's nothing back there for you, the voice said gently.

Nothing back there? Her family was there: Mamma, Tarquin, Luciano... Were they all right? Had something happened to them? This wasn't real. This wasn't—

Arabella, come—

She ran.

Past the grove of chestnut trees and far into the range of the northern Sileni hills, Bella scrambled home, the cold air stinging her teary eyes. This wasn't happening. It was some spell of the unicorn, some illusion, or... or she was still in that dream. It had to be. Merciful gods and empyreal Veil threads, it *had* to.

Once she was with her brothers and Mamma, it would all break. She'd be reminded of the real world, and rooted in it, whatever spell or dream this was, it would end. Unicorns in myths had dazzling powers of the mind. If she believed those tales—and considering she'd just seen a unicorn in the flesh— maybe a trick of the mind was all it was.

Just over the hill, the olive orchards stretched before the Belmonte castello and its city of Roccalano. She bolted among the thin young trees for the open gates of the city. The staccato of hooves against the cobblestone invaded her ears, beat further and deeper. No, it was a dream. The sound was unreal, just as it all had been.

The few citizens outside in the hour before dawn gasped and gaped, jumping out of her way, unlike their usual smiles and warm greetings. Every gape tore at the dream, challenged its fiber. *Maybe it's not a dream.* She shook her head and ran faster toward the castello gates.

Shouts rang out among the guards, but she made it through and into the courtyard bearing Cosimo's sculpture. She charged straight for the nearest door, paying no heed to the chaos building in her wake.

She reached up to knock, but hooves hit the mahogany wood, sending splinters flying.

Mamma! Tarquin! Luciano!

Try as she might, no voice sounded when she called. *Please, someone! Anyone, hear me!*

She hit the door again and again, and if the gods could but spare her a mercy, Mamma or one of her brothers would hear.

A bellowed order—Captain Sondrio and a squad of guards closed in on her with polearms. A stormy scent dominated the air.

Captain, it's me! Please!

But the squad only advanced, and she leaped away from the sage-green *arcanir* blade tips and their magic-nullifying metal. Pottery shattered and flowers crunched beneath her as she scrambled past a window. The shutters hung open, and inside, Tarquin stared back at her, his reddish-brown eyes wide.

Tarquin, she breathed, her heart soaring. Her big brother, her hero, the one who'd always bandaged her skinned knees and wiped away her frustrated tears. He would see her, dispel whatever this was, set everything right. *Help me!*

His hand reached for a sword that wasn't at his hip, not this early in the morning at home.

She tapped the glass, but it shattered, sending jagged remnants flying like daggers.

"Is it Bella?" Mamma's frantic voice called from deeper within the house. Light footsteps pattered nearer, quiet but audible on the thick-pile heirloom rugs.

Darkness passed over Tarquin's face as he shook his head. "Mamma, stay back," he called over his shoulder. "It's one of the Immortali beasts."

Beast...? Mamma! Tarquin, it's me! Couldn't they see through this illusion, or whatever it was?

Mamma stood beside Tarquin, scowling as she clenched a fist. Her reddened eyes teared up nonetheless, a grim match for the dark circles shadowing Tarquin's gaze.

A stab of white-hot pain seared Bella's side.

She staggered backward, avoiding the points of stabbing polearms. One of the guards lunged toward her, but Captain Sondrio held out a hand to stop him.

Her stomach clenched. They would—they would kill her.

"Captain!" Tarquin's voice boomed. "To bows! Someone get me a blade and get that beast out of here!"

That beast. *That beast.* This wasn't an illusion or some trick of the mind? She was truly a unicorn after all?

How could this happen? Why?

But as her heart slowed, every hair of her mane stood on end. It was true. Gods above, it was true.

If this was a dream, shouldn't she have awoken by now?

Arcanir. If this had been some spell, the arcanir blade of the polearm would've broken it. Arcanir cut magic, but there had been no illusion to cut.

Below her were still hooves.

Shuddering, she retreated, eyeing the guards, the smashed pottery, the shattered window, and the shards of glass. Fragments of an equine reflection stared back at her. Broken. Everything was broken.

An arrow clanged onto the cobbles just before her. Reinforcements.

She spun, faced with blades at every turn except the exit, and with a wound stinging her side, she bolted for it, back down the streets of Roccalano, weeping.

Whatever the unicorn had done to her, it wasn't some dream or spell that could be easily reversed.

They had always been described as pacifistic beings, ambassadors of peace, so why had this happened? Why had he done this to her? And if everything that had happened was real, then he'd made it clear she'd have nothing to return to.

But he was wrong. As she ran among the olive trees she'd helped tend all her life, the chill air stole away her tears.

She didn't always see eye to eye with her family, but she loved them and they loved her. She'd find a way to get through to them, to make them see it was still her in this body. They would look past the physical and find her in dire need of their help. Together, they'd uncover the answer to all of this, and fix her. She'd find a way to reverse this Change, return to her true form and her normal life.

She'd just have to keep trying... and pray Tarquin wouldn't order the guards to attack with lethal force.

Again and again, Bella returned to the castello, at all hours of the day and night. Her family had to know she was missing, but nothing in the myths had suggested humans could change into unicorns. Still, trying to get through to them was the only option she had.

In the short gaps of time she had before the guards charged in, she made a habit of interacting with things they would associate with her—nosing the courtyard bench where she'd often done her reading, pawing the soil of her small vegetable garden, nudging the unicorn statue Cosimo had sculpted for her, even tapping the windows beneath her chambers. Sparkles among the plants of her garden witnessed her futile attempts—pixies who'd recently moved in—but she couldn't stop now.

Something would inspire the epiphany she needed them to have. It had to.

On her third visit, she stabbed the tip of her horn at a lock, wishing it open, astonished to find her wish came true. Success! It was the heartening sign she'd needed to keep her going. She willed doors open and windows, and arrows not to hit her. That much worked, if not any wish that she be heard or seen as her true self. But she'd go to her chambers, knock over her favorite things. If she just gave her family enough clues, they'd understand it was her.

Tonight, nearly two weeks after her first visit, she willed away a part of the stone fortifications surrounding the castello and walked right through. Once again, she headed for the windows beneath her chambers, hooves clopping softly on the courtyard's cobbles.

All she wanted was for someone to see the real Bella, just one person, and help her become herself again. One. Just one.

No footsteps or shouts sounded yet; maybe the guards hadn't heard her, and she had more time?

She ripped white lilies from the garden and arranged them on the flagstones to spell her name.

Unicorn, an unfamiliar male voice spoke into her mind, *it's a trap. Flee!*

A sparkling little pixie clad in acorn shells, wielding a needle, pushed against her nose. They usually kept to themselves. What was he trying to...?

A familiar scent clung to the air, like the fresh, earthy smell after a storm, but—spiced, somehow.

Go, now! he urged.

She began to back away when metal clinked, and she bucked. Chains wove around her legs, and a heavy net landed on her back. The sting of the metal was instant and painful, burning into her skin like a brand. She screamed. The metal—sage tinted. Arcanir. They meant it to bind any magical abilities she had.

Tarquin! Mamma! Luciano!

The pixie flitted at a guard, lunging at his face, but the guard swept his hand back and forth to hit him.

No, don't! she wanted to scream, but only a sharp braying emerged. *Don't fight! They'll kill you!*

"Capture it alive!" Captain Sondrio commanded.

The chains and the net tightened. Although she leaped and kicked, guards closed in around her, multiple squads pulling the chains taut. The pixie ignored her, harassing the guards' faces.

Stop—please! It's me, Bella! She tossed her head, her horn scraping against chainmail, and one of her kicks landed with a squelching crunch.

A hit struck her back, and another and another. Wooden clubs beat her to the ground. The burning chains closed around her legs and threw her off balance.

She crashed heavily on the cobblestone with a thud, pressing the searing metal deeper against her skin. It burned with agony.

A guard slashed at the air with his sword.

The pixie screamed, plummeting to the flagstones. She opened her mouth, but before she could shout, the guard stomped on him.

Witam! another unfamiliar voice chimed in her mind.

Crying out, she fought and struggled to rise, but the hits

didn't stop until she went still, and the burning didn't stop at all, not even for a second. Weights pressed her down, one after another, the guards sitting on her as she rebelled, cheering and laughing to one another.

A small, shimmering pair of figures darted in and stole away the pixie's body. Was he dead? Had he died trying to help her?

Her heart seized. How, how had this happened? Under Mamma's watch, under Tarquin's watch? War was the Belmonte trade, but she'd never known Tarquin or his men to relish violence.

She searched the courtyard and the windows for a sympathetic face, just one, any one. Her window glowed golden with candlelight, and in it stood Tarquin, his arms crossed, brow furrowed, peering down at her. The way he looked at her wasn't with the warm eyes of the brother who loved her, but cold, hard, like a lone bronze statue in an empty town square. He watched it all. Cold. Wordless. Malevolent.

Her heart beat throbbed in her throat. *He doesn't know. If he knew...*

Her entire body blazed with arcanir, pain so white hot it blinded. With the weight of the guards pressing down on her, she tried to breathe but every breath was a battle, each harder won than the last, until finally the evening sky and all around her turned to black.

CHAPTER ONE

Four Months Later

A screech came from the marsh. Darting beneath the scant light of the stars, Dhuro found the fallen harpy writhing in the murky water and sedges, its broken wings flapping in futility.

And now you die.

Pinning its remaining arm, he slit its throat with one deep cut before burying his *vjernost* blade in its heart. His weapon's sage tint glowed for a moment until the light left the monster's eyes.

As the night breeze swept away its death rattle, he searched for any remaining threat among the marshland's swaying vegetation. One of the dark-elf *kuvari* warriors rose from the greenery's concealment, wiping the blood off her blade in the quiet. Her innumerable braids, beaded with amber, brushed over her shoulder and down her back. Kinga. Cold, calculating, capable Kinga.

She met his eyes across the undulating spikes and, as she sheathed her blade, gave him a slow once-over, twirling a white braid around her finger. Mm-hmm. He knew that look.

"Is that all of them?" his oldest sister and living bucket of cold water, Vadiha, called out.

"Yes, Vadiha," he called back, standing up as he cleaned his blade. As the strongest warrior among Mati's Quorum, Vadiha had been given charge of their home's defense—a duty that required increasingly more attention these days.

"I was asking Kinga." Vadiha approached him and, hand on her hip, sized him up dubiously. "What are you even doing here? Shouldn't you be with the volodari?"

"I was," he gritted out. As if his hunt were more important than the battle? "I was in my hunting blind when I heard the fighting."

Her golden eyes narrowed. "You should've stayed there. As you can see, we didn't need your help."

"You're welcome," he deadpanned, walking past her and shrugging off her oh-so-kind attitude. It wasn't enough that she'd kept him out of their army's elite forces when they'd been at war with the light-elves of Lumia. *No*, she needed to keep him out of every battle and skirmish she could.

He raked a hand through his shoulder-length hair, shut his eyes, and heaved a sigh. Vadiha never missed a chance to shove his face into the sand.

"Dhuro," she shouted.

Darkness, what else? He looked back over his shoulder and grunted.

"Mati has summoned you."

Had she tattled to their mother? At least it gave him an exit out of this pleasant conversation. "Well then, I'd best not keep her waiting." He gave Vadiha a reluctant nod.

Next to her, Kinga raised her eyebrows at him again in that look he knew so well. Nothing stoked the blood of a dark-elf like a good fight. Oh yes, he'd see about that look later. Although he'd spent many years among the humans with his best friend, Dakkar, and his father, he hadn't forgotten Kinga. Not how she'd used him to climb the ranks, and... not how she used to climb him either. All told, life as a volodar hunter in his mother's queendom wasn't bad at all.

With an inward grin, he crept through the marshy rushes, sweeping aside their hollow stems to make his way to Heraza Gate and their home, Nozva Rozkveta.

All women wanted something, whether it was just a night's pleasure or a stepping stone to his mother and the queen's inner circle, the Quorum. Kinga wasn't the only one, and never had been. No matter what it was, as long as they kept the emotional mess out of it, he didn't care. Considering how brilliantly that emotional mess had worked for his star-crossed parents, as well as for his older brother's decade-long doomed love affair, *that* was just another entry on the long list of things he never wanted or needed.

At the Gate, he beat the entry rhythm on the door, and it creaked open.

"Your Highness," two kuvari—Gavri and Danika—said by way of greeting. They barred the stone door after him.

"Do you know where my mother is?"

"At the training grounds, I think," Gavri answered. She'd spent time as his brother Zoran's former lover.

With a nod, Dhuro headed down the tunnel toward Central Cavern. What had that near-decade of emotional aching been for? Zoran had left to become Queen Nendra's king-consort in Dun Mozg, and his so-called beloved Gavri had been left behind. If they'd been wiser, they would've kept it simple.

These days, he stayed out of it. No one took his advice anyway, so it was a waste of breath; everyone seemed determined to learn the hard way. Even Veron had fallen for his human bride, and although they genuinely seemed to love one another, it wouldn't end well. It never did. He inhaled deeply and shook his head as he entered Central Cavern.

Ah, home. He never tired of looking at it. On the stalactites above, bioluminescent mushrooms lit the realm beneath with a lavender glow, mingled with the radiance of the white glowworms. The shimmering tangle of *roza* vines had sprawled and thrived since the Rift, their glittering red blooms dotting the stalactites with crimson stars. Nothing in the sky realm could compare to it, although by now he'd explored every bit of it.

The Stone Singers still worked tirelessly to restore the gleaming, mirror-like blackstone outbuildings, where glistening streams fed fields of green sprouts fighting their way out of the fresh cave soil. Deeper into the heart of Nozva Rozkveta, most of the dwellings along Central Cavern's interwoven pathways had already been stone-sung, and its most precious jewel —the palace—blossomed in black crystal perfection, ringed by the shining teal waterway that tumbled down into the Darkness below.

The black stone paths were empty and quiet today, unlike a couple weeks ago when Veron had married his human princess, Alessandra. Although the violence from the human Brotherhood had dwindled to nearly nothing, the Immortal beasts had begun attacking with unusual fervor.

Was that why Mati wanted to see him, to give him a position with the queendom's defense? Maybe Vadiha, for once in her life, hadn't complained about him to their mother. Vadiha had defeated his challenge once, only *once*, and it had been thousands of years ago now. There had to be some limit to how long her victory could shackle him.

With renewed purpose, he headed for the palace's black crystal spires, passed the four kuvari at the entrance, and strode down the side corridors to the training grounds.

The *vykrikovati* shouts echoed—short, loud, and forceful— and he had to fight back a smile. It had been a long time since he'd been among them, alongside Dakkar, but not long enough that his body didn't remember this. His instructors had made a warrior out of him, out of all the dark-elf children; with every strike, he'd abruptly tensed his abdomen, forcing the shouted breath out to generate as much power as possible. What had been sheer joy as a child had been the terror of the battlefield, as dark-elf legions had struck fear into the hearts of their enemies.

Two glaive-bearing kuvari stood aside as he entered. "Your Highness."

With catlike grace, Mati sparred with the young novices in her white silken peplos, haloed by her voluminous, jewel-beaded cascades of platinum hair. She held back just enough to check the novices' skill, and as expected, they were fierce. After all, this motley troop of youngsters represented the future of Nozva Rozkveta.

Mati met a strike with her vjernost bracers, and a smile cracked her diamond-shaped face. The smile met her amber eyes, and then she turned to him. The sparring stopped, and as she stepped away, the novices resumed their training with one another.

He bowed his head to her. "They look strong."

"They'll get stronger." She brushed his arm and, with her bare clawed feet on the black stone, led him alongside the training rings, amid the novices' vykrikovati and the instructors' shouted encouragement and orders. "The kuvari have informed me you took part in the battle."

Tattling it was, after all. *Thanks, Vadiha.* Mati had said it matter-of-factly, but he knew better than to trust that.

"I did."

If Mati wanted to make a point, then trouncing him here amid the children would accomplish that, far harsher than he'd earned. As their people's best warrior, it would be child's play for her.

"Your ambition is relentless." She paused to watch another group of novices spar.

He joined her. "I take after my mother."

An amused flicker of her gleaming amber eyes, and then she returned her attention to the sparring. "We can handle the beasts. We always have. But while there will be humans above us building the library, we must take additional precautions."

His people had always been skilled fighters; they built their lives around martial prowess. But if more winged creatures like today's harpies attacked, they couldn't keep the land above their domain safe from invasion, not entirely. And all it'd take to reignite enmity from the humans would be one human fatality. Darkness forbid it would be Alessandra.

All he wanted was to live up to Mati's expectations. That meant protecting his—and his people's—way of life and earning his place as not a hunter but a warrior. If Mati wanted his help in the defense, she'd have it. And then he'd be free tonight to go find Kinga. "I await your orders."

Her even expression didn't waver as she continued watching the novices. A pair of girls sparred, then wrestled each other onto the sand while the instructor barked commands at them. "You're familiar with the unicorn among us."

How could he not be? He stifled an inward half-laugh. She stood out like a unicorn among dark-elves.

"When we exiled the leader of the Brotherhood, he agreed to go quietly." She clasped her clawed hands behind her back, her shoulders stiffening. After the battles the humans' Brotherhood had waged against all the Immortals, no doubt she'd wanted to rip Tarquin Belmonte's head off his body. Exile, however, had been more palatable to the humans and likelier to lead to a lasting peace, especially when the alliance had been sealed by an Offering and human marriage between his brother Veron and Alessandra. "Part of the terms involved aiding his sister, which we do willingly."

Belmonte's sister, a human turned unicorn, was safe here, learning more about her kind from Noc, a fey horse and friend to him and his brothers. The unicorn had saved his brother Veron and had helped stop the war with the Brotherhood, which despite her questionable familial ties, set her apart from the trash Belmonte had led.

"Although she's learned much in her time here, she needs to learn control of her Change. Our scouts have returned with information about a herd of unicorns near Dun Mozg—probably Gwydion's—and we must move swiftly. I'm sending a team to take her there to find the unicorn who sired her."

It wasn't a long journey through the tunnels; he and Dakkar had traveled it countless times. "Dun Mozg isn't far."

"The team will go by land."

Frowning, he tipped his head up. Roza blooms studded the bioluminescent vines sprawled above, consuming the stalactites and the ceiling. It hadn't been so long ago that his people had suffered a food shortage, but with the human alliance, they'd come back from it stronger than ever, and that bounty had been shared with Dun Mozg. The neighboring queendom had no compelling reason to cause them harm. And considering Zoran was king-consort, and Dakkar, not just his best friend but a prince of Dun Mozg, had been fostered here, their ties were nigh unbreakable.

He eyed Mati. She didn't suffer questioning, but if he was to avoid the tunnels, there had to be a reason. It would be better if he knew what he was getting into rather than proceed blindly. And ignorantly.

She sighed. "These beast attacks aren't random. There's a leader, assisted by a dark unicorn. These attacks are their strategy to keep us at bay. They've joined forces to conquer the humans."

A few months ago, he would've said *let them.* But as much as it galled him, when his people had been most in need, it had been the humans who'd lent a hand. And his sister-in-law, Alessandra, wasn't *so* bad. "Why aren't the humans handling it?"

Mati's mouth tightened to a grim line. "They don't know who's in charge. And they must not know."

Then information didn't flow so freely in this new alliance.

"The dark unicorn is Gwydion's responsibility, so he must be made aware. Arabella's sire will likely be among his herd. You will take her there."

He nodded. If that's what Nozva Rozkveta needed, then he'd see it done. With Gwydion's help, these malcontents would be disbanded. Unicorns possessed the rare ability to induce calm, even among a bloodthirsty army of beasts and rebels... *if* the unicorns could be persuaded to enter a conflict. Something Mati was tasking *him* with.

Once he finished this mission, he'd return home and take his rightful place as a kuvar. Things would finally be as they always should have been.

Mati cleared her throat. "Whatever Gwydion wants in order to forge the alliance, give it to him. He'll have heirs who take elven or human forms. Seal it with an Offering between you and one of his line."

"What! Why?" he blurted. Darkness, she would sacrifice him to a political marriage as she had Veron. Deep, Darkness, and Holy Ulsinael, of all the—

"Because the leader of this rebellion is *our* responsibility, and he must be stopped before the humans discover he's a dark-elf. And he will be stopped, with Gwydion's help."

His head spun. "The dark-elf rebel leader... Who—?"

Mati turned to him, facing him squarely. "Dakkar of Dun Mozg."

To read on, check out *Bright of the Moon*, available now!

ABOUT THE AUTHOR

Miranda Honfleur is a born-and-raised Chicagoan living in Indianapolis. She grew up on fantasy and science fiction novels, spending nearly as much time in Valdemar, Pern, Tortall, Narnia, and Middle Earth as in reality.

In another life, her J.D. and M.B.A. were meant to serve a career in law, but now she gets to live her dream job: writing speculative fiction starring fierce heroines and daring heroes who make difficult choices along their adventures and intrigues, all with a generous (over)dose of romance.

When she's not snarking, writing, or reading her Kindle, she hangs out and watches Netflix with her English-teacher husband and plays board games with her friends.

Reach her at:
www.mirandahonfleur.com
miri@mirandahonfleur.com
https://www.patreon.com/honfleur

facebook.com/MirandaHonfleur

twitter.com/MirandaHonfleur

amazon.com/author/mirandahonfleur

bookbub.com/authors/miranda-honfleur

goodreads.com/MirandaHonfleur

instagram.com/mirandahonfleur

pinterest.com/mirandahonfleur

Made in the USA
Las Vegas, NV
20 February 2021